NEMESIS

KAT ROSS

To Thing #1 and Thing #2, for letting me warm my feet on your bellies when I write

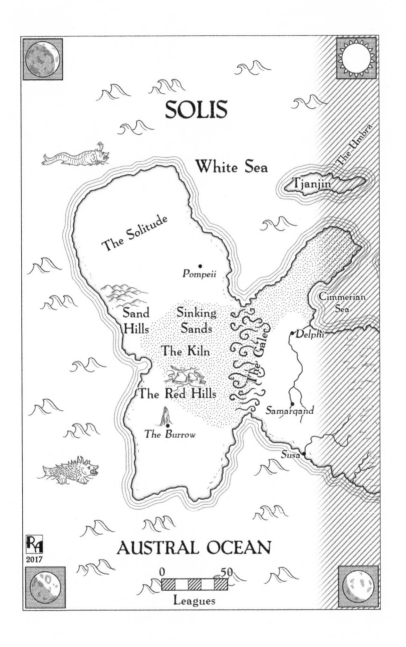

SOLIS

White Sea

The Umbra

Tjanjin

The Solitude

Pompeii

Cimmerian
Sea

Sand
Hills

Sinking
Sands

Delphi

The Kiln

The Gale

The Red Hills

Samarqand

The Burrow

Susa

AUSTRAL OCEAN

0   50

Leagues

R·A
2017

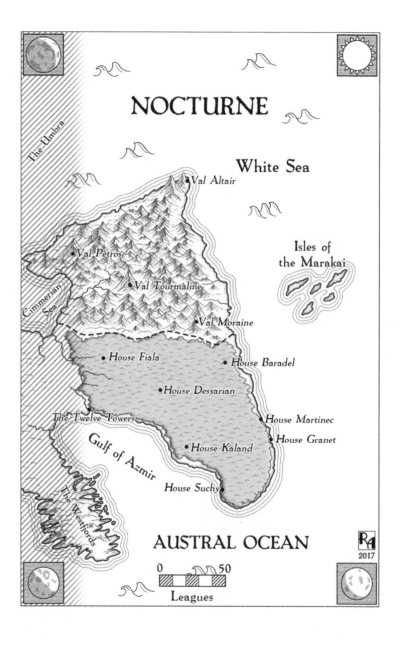

NOCTURNE

The Umbra

White Sea

Val Altair

Isles of
the Marakai

Val Petros

Cimmerian Sea

Val Tourmaline

Val Moraine

House Fiala

House Baradel

House Dessarian

The Twelve Towers

House Martinec

House Granet

Gulf of Azmir

House Kaland

House Suchy

The Westfords

AUSTRAL OCEAN

RA
2017

0   50

Leagues

CONTENTS

Fragment from the lost diaries of Nabu-bal-idinna, alchemist to the Persian King Teispes in the years 506-513 A.S.*

And so it came to pass that on the ninth day of my wanderings, I spied a tower in the wilderness, hexagonal and made of dark stone resembling obsidian. From a distance, it appeared to have no means of entry, but as I approached, an archway appeared in the gloaming. A woman stood just within the threshold. Her skin was pale as alabaster, her hair the black of a raven's wing. I would not call her beautiful, but she had a force of will that arrested the eye.

Never before had I encountered another living soul in the Dominion. I made her a courteous bow, though my heart beat with apprehension.

"What is thy name?" she asked sweetly.

I told her, and explained my purpose: To map the shadowlands for my king.

She listened with polite interest, never moving from her place just within the archway. I had the strong impression she could not pass beyond the confines of the tower.

"Have a cup of wine with me," she said with an enticing smile. "Few visitors come this way, and fewer still who are young and handsome."

I suspected she was flattering me and my instincts warned me that she was dangerous, but I have always been burdened with an insatiable curiosity.

I bowed again and entered the tower.

*AFTER SUNDERING

THE LOST PRINCE OF VAL
TOURMALINE

F*lying.*

The smell of the stables—dry dung and saddle oil and the pungent musk of the abbadax—triggered a physical ache, like an essential part of him had been ripped away. Mina spent half her time prowling the distant corners of the keep, searching for some sign of her son Galen, and during these periods of solitude, Culach had lain in bed and fantasized about long flights over the mountains and sea, each breath a communion with the elements. He remembered the way the moonlight burnished the waves to a cold gleam. The sweep of powerful wingbeats and stinging frost on his eyelashes. Sometimes he'd taken jaunts over the great forest, though he took care to keep out of arrow range in case the Danai sentries spotted him.

In his darker moments, Culach thought he'd forgotten the taste of freedom, but coming to this place always reminded him.

"Ragnhildur?" he whispered.

There was no cry of greeting this time. No scrape of claws on stone. He moved forward, fingers trailing the wall of ice.

"It's me," he said, his voice too loud in the claustrophobic hush. Once, the stables had been wide open to the sky, scoured by wind and with an inch of fresh snow underfoot. Now they were a tomb.

"Where are you, my darling?"

Silence stretched out and a bone-deep fear gripped him. Culach had grown accustomed to losing things.

His kin.

The ability to wield elemental power.

His sight.

Even his name. All that was gone and he'd finished mourning it. But the thought that Ragnhildur had died alone drove a spear of ice into his heart.

"I meant to come yesterday," he whispered brokenly. "I was just so tired."

Dreams of the Viper still hounded him. Fire and torment and virulent hatred for the other clans—and even the Viper's own. Seeing through the man's eyes exhausted him. Culach knew he'd been sleeping too much, but he couldn't help it. If not for Mina, he might have ended the dreams the coward's way with a cut to the wrists. He carried a knife, though he hadn't used it yet. It made him feel safer. Val Moraine was full of ghosts. He thought he heard them sometimes, creeping about....

Culach nearly jumped out of his skin at a soft, rasping sound.

"Ragnhildur?"

Another faint sound, like a sigh. Culach dropped to hands and knees, crawling forward. He reached out and touched a beak. She lay on her side against the ice wall. He pressed his cheek to her foreleg. And now she did chirp, though it was weak. The bonds around his chest loosened a notch.

"Don't worry, my love, I have something for you." Culach felt along her wing until he reached the razor-sharp feathers at the tip. He slashed his palm along the edge and pressed the wound to her beak. "Drink," he urged.

Her rough tongue lapped at the cut. Culach let her feed until his head spun. Then he took his hand away and stanched the bleeding with a corner of his coat. A bitter laugh spilled from his throat. His blood wouldn't go to waste after all.

"I'll give you some each day," he whispered. "You won't starve, my dear."

He heard other pathetically eager sounds as the rest of the mounts smelled his offering. Culach's jaw tightened. He could hardly feed them all. Victor had to free the poor creatures.

He wondered what his father had done about the mounts during the long siege of the Iron Wars. Eirik must have had access to fresh meat. Perhaps he'd kept animals in the food caverns. Whatever his other faults, Eirik understood strategy and planned ahead. Victor Dessarian was obviously flying by the seat of his trousers. But Culach wouldn't stand by and watch the abbadax waste away. He resolved to find Victor and tell him this in no uncertain terms.

His head turned as hisses erupted from the far pens, followed by a shriek from closer by. Katrin had returned to the keep with Halldóra, along with two others from Val Tourmaline. They'd struck an alliance—until the disaster with Gerda. But in their haste to flee, the abbadax had been behind and now a fight was breaking out.

He stood, dizzy from the blood loss. If they attacked each other, Ragnhildur would die for sure. She was stirring, but in no shape for a brawl. And he knew what the mounts could do to each other when they got their hackles up.

More hisses, followed by the sharp snapping of beaks.

"Hey!" he shouted to the opposite end, where a group of Danai watched the tunnel.

"What?" a distant voice responded.

"I could use some help over here."

Laughter.

"Are your birds pecking each other again?"

"It'll be worse than that if we don't stop it!"

"Victor said we're to stay here. Can't you handle it?"

Culach swore under his breath and inched forward. He cleared his throat. It seemed ages since he'd been a general, barking orders in a tone that demanded instant compliance. He drew himself up to his formidable height and glared in what he hoped was the right direction.

"Stand down," he growled. "You are *mine* now."

Air buffeted his face as one of the Val Tourmaline mounts flapped its wings and screeched a challenge.

No fear. That was the trick with abbadax.

He strode forward, closing the distance to the far pens. He sensed the coiled tension of their bodies, the burning intensity of six yellow eyes.

I must be mad.

"Stand down, or I'll pluck you naked—" His feet caught on something and Culach tumbled forward, palms slamming into the stone. He cursed again and groped behind him. His hand closed on a muscular thigh.

What in Nine Hells?

Whoever it was, they were still warm. His hand crept cautiously higher. Definitely male. And in Valkirin leathers, though that didn't mean much since all the Danai wore them now. He felt the hard planes of the face, the stubbled jaw, some sort of *iron collar*—and a strong hand clamped down on his wrist. One of the abbadax burbled angrily, hot breath blasting his cheek.

"Where am I?" The voice was hoarse and confused, but Culach knew it. Daníel of Val Tourmaline.

"At Val Moraine," Culach whispered. "Get your mounts under control. They're about to attack."

To his credit, Daníel obeyed without question. Culach assumed he'd gone with Katrin and the others, but he must have been left behind. He spoke soothing words and the mounts settled back on their nests.

"Fetch Mithre," Culach bellowed at the Danai. "Right now!"

There must have been some of the general in him yet, for this time they didn't argue. And so a short while later, Culach, Mithre and Mina gathered in Eirik's study with Halldóra's grandson, the heir to Val Tourmaline. Mina managed to find one of Gerda's bottles of foul but potent brew. She poured some into Daníel, who had apparently been sleeping in the pens for the last three days and smelled like it.

"Halldóra," he croaked. "I saw her.... Is she dead?"

"Yes," Mina replied gently. "We put her in the crypts."

"Did you see what happened?" Culach asked.

Daníel stayed silent for a long moment. The chair creaked as his weight shifted. When he spoke, his voice sounded stronger. "We were out in the hall. I heard yelling. It sounded like my grandmother. There was a powerful surge of air. Katrin kicked the door open." He swallowed. "I saw Victor Dessarian with a bloody sword. Are you sure Gerda did it?"

"I despise Victor, but he had no reason to harm your grandmother," Culach said. "Quite the opposite. No, I fear Gerda had her own motives."

"Victor told me she believed the Vatras were coming back," Mithre put in. "She wanted Halldóra to ally with them. Halldóra refused and Gerda lashed out."

"Where is Victor now?" Daníel demanded with some of his old spirit. "I would hear the story from him."

"He's around somewhere," Mithre replied with a touch of irritation. "But first you'll tell us why you were out there bedding down with the abbadax. We thought you'd left with Katrin and the others."

Daníel didn't answer this and Culach wished he could see the man's face.

"Where are the others I came with?"

"Run off," Mina said tightly. "With my son, Galen. Do you know anything about that?"

Daníel gave a heavy sigh. More creaking from the chair. "I'm afraid I might."

7

Skirts rustled as Mina leapt to her feet. "*What*? Speak it!"

"I am a traitor," Daníel said hollowly. "The mortals never helped me to escape from Delphi. Coming here was part of the Pythia'a plan."

"And you said nothing? What kind of cowardly—"

Culach's hand shot out, seizing Mina's arm before she could do violence.

"Let him finish," he said mildly. "If you wish to kill him after, I'll help you."

"No one's killing anyone," Mithre said, weariness in his voice. "Gods, I knew those women couldn't be trusted. Go ahead. Tell us all of it."

"I don't blame you for despising me," Daníel said once Mina had reluctantly sat down again. "I have no excuse, other than to say I was not myself. They did things to us...." He trailed off and Culach heard him drain the cup of wine.

"I know how the collars work," Mithre said with a note of pity. "I wore something similar myself once. Don't judge him, Mina."

"Where is my son?" she snapped. "That's all I wish to know."

"Was he weak in earth?" Daníel asked.

"Oh gods. She took him, didn't she? The one called Thena?"

"She may have, yes. It's what the Pythia sent her here for."

"And how did she get out of her locked chamber?" Mithre asked.

There was a long pause. Daníel sounded remorseful. "I let her go."

Mina's chair scraped back and Culach heard a resounding slap.

"You bastard," she hissed. "How could you? How could you do this?"

"I tried to kill her but I.... I couldn't do it."

"Well, you could have just left and locked the bloody door again!"

Daníel said nothing.

"How did they leave Val Moraine?" Culach asked.

"There was a Talisman of Folding. Thena hid it near the cistern."

"So you're telling me my son is in Delphi, a prisoner of the Pythia, and wearing one of those vile collars right now?" Mina drew a deep breath. "We have to get out of here. Immediately." She rose and began pacing the chamber. "You're Halldóra's heir, aren't you? Make a bargain with your kin! Tell them you saw Gerda kill Halldóra. They'll believe you."

"If I can help break this siege, I will," Daníel said. "And I'll go with you to Delphi." His voice hardened. "I would see the Pythia pay as well. It is her hand behind it."

"It won't work," Culach said. "He was with Katrin and the others from Val Tourmaline. They know Daníel stayed out in the hall. And they're convinced Victor did it."

"And what of Runar and Stefán?" Mithre asked. "They arrived yesterday and they want our heads on a sharpened stick. Eventually, they'll get tired of waiting. They'll try to storm the keep. We'll have to collapse the tunnel. And no one gets what they want."

"I'll go out there and talk to them," Daníel said.

Mithre laughed. "No, you won't. I'm not giving up our only leverage."

"So I'm a prisoner?"

"Hell yes, you are," Mina snapped.

"Where is Victor, anyway?" Culach asked. "Not that I miss him, but I'd expect him to be here."

"No idea." Mithre sounded annoyed. "I've barely seen him in days."

Culach felt a twinge of unease. Victor Dessarian had grown strange of late. He didn't smell right, for one thing. His scent was *cold*. Metallic. And Culach had heard him muttering to himself when they passed each other in the corridors. In another man, Culach wouldn't be surprised. Victor was under a tremendous amount of pressure. His wife and son were missing, the latter almost certainly dead. His own mother had left him to twist in the wind.

Except that Victor wasn't the sort to snap. He'd rage and bully and brood, but he lacked the imagination to lose his mind.

"So what we do?" Mina demanded. "I'm not sitting here while that woman tortures my son to death."

"She won't kill him," Daníel said. "He has value. She believes he is the talisman. That he has some extraordinary power."

"And what exactly does she intend to use him for?"

"I don't know." Daníel blew out a breath. "I don't know."

No one spoke. Culach rubbed his forehead and groped across the table.

"Any of that wine left?" he asked hopefully.

2

REUNIONS

Artemis climbed above the western peaks, a pale blue disc next to the warm yellow of Selene and the silver of Hecate. It was strange to see *three* moons, Nazafareen thought. When she'd first arrived in Nocturne, the Wanderer had been a tiny dot, hardly distinguishable from the surrounding stars.

But over the last months Artemis had drawn closer and now it dwarfed Selene, the second-biggest moon. When it reached its full glory in a few weeks' time, Artemis would summon tides to cover the land for leagues.

A portent of the war to come? Or simply a celestial coincidence?

Nazafareen gripped the next outcropping of icy rock and hauled herself up. Even in a fur-lined glove, her fingers had gone numb. The thin air of the high passes made the moons look close enough to touch, but it also left her fighting for each breath.

At least the night was clear and calm. Despite her exhaustion, Nazafareen felt at peace in the mountains. She liked the clean smell of snow and the way it crunched beneath her boots. The sky spread out above, inky black and dense with stars. The Valkirin range had its own unforgiving beauty that seemed to suit the daēvas who lived there. Nazafareen had come to know both the Danai and the Marakai fairly well, but the Valkirins remained a mystery. The other clans considered them aggressive and bigoted. They'd tried to kill her several times, so she couldn't really argue with this assessment. Still, she had to convince them to join forces against the Vatras—a task that Victor had made exceedingly difficult.

Behind her, the cloaked shapes of Herodotus, Megaera and Darius moved up the steep slope. After emerging from the gate, the four of them had roped themselves together for the climb over Langjökull glacier, with Nazafareen in the lead. Val Moraine should be close if Herodotus's calculations were correct. She imagined Victor's surprise when they turned up at the holdfast. She would be glad to see him, though Darius's father was not the one she braved the mountains for.

She reached an icy ledge and stepped aside to make way for Darius. Like the rest of them, he wore a heavy cloak with a scarf wrapped around his face, leaving only his blue eyes visible. They waited together, breath steaming, for Megaera and Herodotus to inch their way up.

"I think Val Moraine is just over the ridge," the scholar said through chattering teeth.

"I hope your father has sentries posted," Megaera muttered to Darius, leaning heavily on her staff. "Because I'm not climbing another cursed mountain after this one. You say there's tunnels?"

"Should be," Darius replied, his voice muffled through the scarf. "That's how Victor got inside."

Megaera looked up with a grim expression. "Then let's get this over with."

The pass across the glacier lay a hundred paces above. Nazafareen studied the slope, finding a line of crevices, and started up again. They ascended the eastern face, which was exposed to the wind from the White Sea. It had scoured away most of the snow, but ice coated the rock beneath and she placed each step with care. More than once, the rope suddenly grew taut as someone below slipped. Darius took most of the weight—he seemed to have no trouble with his footing—and each time, Megaera or Herodotus was saved from plummeting back down the mountain.

At last she gained the saddle to the next valley. Moments later, Darius clambered over the rim and hauled their companions to relative safety. More peaks marched into the distance, jagged white teeth against the sky. Nazafareen searched for Val Moraine but saw only ice and snow. Surely such a mighty holdfast would be visible in the bright moonlight. Her heart sank. They had relied on Herodotus and the secret maps he studied before their departure, courtesy of the Emperor of Tjanjin, that showed the location of Gates in both the Dominion and the Valkirin range.

"It must be here," Herodotus said faintly, scanning the mountains. "It *must* be."

Nazafareen and Darius exchanged a look.

"Perhaps you misread the runes," Megaera said. "Or chose the wrong gate."

Herodotus gave her a level look. "Of course, it didn't say *Val Moraine*, the markers of the Gates are far older than the holdfast, but I'm certain the one we came through corresponded to the maps. I have many faults, but my memory is not one of them!"

Megaera blinked. Herodotus was usually mild-mannered, but he looked nearly as angry as when Darius told him about the Oracle kidnapping daēvas.

"Then it must be close," Nazafareen said soothingly. "Perhaps we should rest here for a few minutes and get our bearings."

"Yes." Herodotus sagged a bit. "I'm sorry. Let me think. Hecate always rises in the west, so I know we've been going in the right direction. How many leagues would you say we've covered?"

"Not as many as you might expect," Darius answered wryly. "With the elevation gain—" He cut off, gaze lifting to the skies above the glacier. He held himself still for a long moment, like an animal sniffing the wind. Then his shoulders stiffened. "Get down," he hissed.

Nazafareen sensed nothing but dropped to a crouch immediately, pressing into the shadowed recesses of the rock wall. Herodotus and Megaera were a beat slower to react and Darius launched himself across the narrow shelf, dragging them both flat just as four winged shapes soared overhead.

Nazafareen watched them pass, the dark silhouettes of hooded riders clear against the moons.

"What *were* they?" she whispered once the party had passed out of sight.

"Abbadax," Darius replied in a sober voice.

"What in the name of Dionysus are abbadax?" Megaera demanded.

"It's said they originated in the Dominion," Herodotus replied, squirming a bit under Darius's bulk. "Some intrepid Valkirin must have brought some eggs back a very long time ago. The clan uses them for transport, military actions, hunting and simply for sport. They're an integral aspect of the culture—"

"That's all fascinating," Megaera grumbled, shoving Darius away and pushing up to sit. "But why are they here? Aren't the other holdfasts hundreds of leagues away?"

Darius and Nazafareen exchanged a look.

"I don't suppose they could be Victor's scouts?" she asked hopefully. "Maybe they managed to tame some."

He shook his head. "It's possible but unlikely. We have to assume Val Moraine is under siege."

Nazafareen blew out an unhappy breath. "I suppose it was inevitable. Your father really is a fool."

"That's a kind way of putting it," Darius replied. "I only hope he still lives. How long can he defend the keep against an army? They might already have taken it back."

She looked at her companions. Frost rimed Herodotus's beard. Megaera was blowing on her hands and shivering. Darius simply looked weary. They'd come all this way on her whim. She could hardly ask them to continue now, when there was no hope of getting inside Val Moraine. Nazafareen swallowed her disappointment.

"We'll turn back," she said firmly, rising to her feet. "If we're careful, we can make it to the gate undetected."

To her surprise, no one moved.

"What if Kallisto and Rhea are here?" Herodotus said.

Megaera nodded. "They were flying on those things...the abbadax, when we saw them in the globe."

"If so, they're either prisoners or they've made friends with the Valkirins," Herodotus said. "If it's the former, we cannot leave them. If it's the latter, then we still might have a chance of accomplishing our goal." He turned to Darius. "But I leave the final choice to you. Of all of us, you have the most to lose."

Darius thought for a moment. "They've never seen my face. Nor yours, Nazafareen."

"It's a terrible risk," she said quietly. "I would never ask you to take it."

"I know." He peered up at the glacier. "Here's what I propose. We gain a decent vantage point and assess the situation."

"And if we're caught?"

"My name is Daraya, a mortal from Delphi. You're my wife, Ashraf. We are loyal followers of Dionysus, aiding Herodotus and Megaera in their search for the talismans."

"Won't they know you're a daēva?"

"Blue eyes are exceedingly rare among the Danai. As long as I stay away from the Nexus, there's no reason they should suspect." He fingered his plain wool cloak. "The forest garb of the Danai is well known to the Valkirins. These clothes were bought in Susa."

Nazafareen pulled her glove off with her teeth and rubbed the smooth skin of her stump, thinking. "But they'd still never let us inside Val Moraine."

He smiled. "One thing at a time, North Star."

"We'll, if you're willing, I say let's go. We have to face the Valkirins eventually. And here they are, conveniently in one place."

They started ascending the glacier as fast as possible, but it was an arduous climb and utterly exposed. Nazafareen tried not to think about the long fall below, or what would transpire if scouts happened by. Pace by pace, they followed the winding crevice. Her legs and arm burned by the time they neared the top. When the slope leveled out, she dropped to her belly and peered over the edge, Darius at her side.

Dozens of abbadax wheeled and dove across the valley below, black dots against the snow. After watching them for a minute, Nazafareen noticed that the activity centered around a tall, sheer-sided peak. Unlike the surrounding mountains, it had no veins of darker rock. The summit was shrouded in a thick layer of ice.

"Val Moraine," Herodotus whispered raggedly, still fighting to catch his breath. "You can still see the circular shape of it, if you look closely. The Maiden Keep."

There seemed to be three distinct camps surrounding the mountain. Riders took off and landed at regular intervals in formations of four or five together. The main force was hidden, but Nazafareen noticed tiny figures moving in and out of tunnels dug into the opposite slopes.

"So that's how Victor's been holding out," Darius said in a soft voice. "They can't break through the ice."

"What do we do now?" Megaera asked. "I'm not sure I fancy going down there. Look at their numbers." She shifted, pointing with her staff. "Once we're in their frosty clutches, there's no going—"

Her weight must have unbalanced the delicate shell of ice and snow capping the glacier because a small chunk of it broke off. They watched as it bounced down the slope, gaining speed as it went and triggering small rivulets of loose snow. Megaera gave an apologetic cringe.

"Sorry," she whispered.

"Get back," Darius snapped.

They wiggled away from the edge. Nazafareen tried to steady her pulse. It was only a small bit of ice. She looked around, but the summit offered no cover.

"Dig down," Darius urged. "Camouflage yourselves."

They scrabbled like badgers, burrowing into the dry, crumbly snow. No sounds of alarm came from the other side. No shrill cries or rush of wingbeats. Nazafareen wished she could see what was happening.

She had just managed to nestle into her hole when something large exploded overhead. It swept past, followed by three more. Through a gap in her hood, she watched them soar over the valley behind.... And circle back around, silent as wraiths. Each carried a hooded rider.

"I think they've seen us," she hissed to the lump of snow next her, which she assumed was Darius.

"I do, too," his muffled voice replied.

"Don't you dare try to work earth," she muttered. "I'll do the talking."

"Somehow that's not reassuring."

Megaera seemed to have forgotten the plan completely. She sat up, her eyes wild. "Herodotus! Since you're the expert on these vile creatures, tell me one thing. How do I kill one?"

The riders drew closer, arrowing straight for the huddled group.

He brushed snow from his face. "Yes, well, it's not easy. They have razor-sharp wing feathers and hooked beaks capable of tearing—"

A ferocious gale howled across the glacier, drowning out the rest of his words. It snatched Nazafareen into the air, her roped companions trailing behind like a tail. Megaera shouted as they plunged over the edge. Serrated outcroppings sped past only inches away. Just before the bone-crunching impact at the bottom, the wind tightened, slowing their descent. Nazafareen landed hard in a drift of snow so deep it enveloped her completely. She was trying to free herself when the rope went taut again and yanked them into the air.

The world streaked past in a dizzying blur that ended abruptly in yet another deep snowbank. She lay there for a moment, disoriented and shivering with cold. Snow packed every crevice of her body—including her undergarments. Nazafareen gingerly tested her limbs and found nothing broken, though her head still spun. She clawed her way out and blinked snow from her eyes.

They were on a wide ledge opposite Val Moraine. The drift hugged the rock wall, but most of the rocky ground was clear, the inch or so of snow remaining trampled with boot and claw prints. The riders landed as her companions emerged, dazed and spluttering. A moment later, they unbuckled harnesses and leapt from their saddles. Air pinioned her arms as rough hands stripped off her sword and hurled it into the deep ravine that plunged down only a few paces away. The tip of a blade lifted her chin. She stared into a pair of light green eyes.

"Mortal spies," her captor declared, contempt in his voice. "Did you truly think to creep up on us?"

Nazafareen bit her tongue against a defiant retort. "Not spies," she said, making her voice waver in fear. "We are friends of Kallisto. She went to Val Altair to warn the holdfasts of a great danger. Do you know her?"

Something flickered across the Valkirin's face. "How did you get this far on foot?"

Nazafareen saw no way around the truth, but it fit the rest of their story. "We traveled by gate."

"That is forbidden," the Valkirin snarled. He had sharp cheekbones and a nose that had clearly been broken more than once.

"By who?" Megaera demanded. She squatted on the snow next to Herodotus and Darius.

One of the Valkirins yanked Megaera's staff away and snapped it like kindling, tossing the broken pieces to the side. The look she gave him would have curled shoe leather, but he simply gazed back with icy condescension.

"By the masters of these mountains, mortal," Broken Nose replied. "Which would be *us*."

"Well, we didn't know that," Nazafareen said reasonably. She looked around, but still saw no sign of the holdfast. "Who's in charge around here? I need to meet with her."

"You will see Runar of Val Petros at his pleasure," the Valkirin replied stiffly. "Until then, keep your mouth shut."

After prodding everyone to their feet, the scouts led them into a rough-hewn tunnel that looked like an abandoned mineshaft. Smaller passages branched off at regular intervals, carrying a dank breeze. Broken Nose went on ahead, returning to escort them into a low-ceilinged chamber lit by a single lumen crystal.

An enormous man with a short, gold-flecked beard perched on an invisible ledge of air. He had white hair, shaved over one ear where an old scar bisected his temple. He wore a belted leather coat with rubies and sapphires gleaming on the high, stiff collar. An iron sword hung from his hip. He regarded them for a long moment without speaking.

"You make an odd party," he said at last in a rich, rumbling voice.

"My name is Ashraf," Nazafareen said. She pointed to Darius. "This is Daraya. And Herodotus and Megaera of Delphi. We're friends of Kallisto of the Cult of the Maenads. Do you know her?"

"I might." There was no warmth in his expression. "Why are you here, mortal? If there are more of you in these mountains, we'll root you out."

"There are no others. We came to warn you."

Runar grinned. He was missing a few teeth, but the ones he had looked white and strong. "To warn us, eh? Of what?"

"The fire clan. The Avas Vatras. At least one has broken loose of the Kiln. He seeks the heirs to the power that destroyed the

Vatras a thousand years ago. It passes on, you see. He could be coming here next."

Runar's smile died. "Go on."

"His name is Nicodemus. He nearly found the Marakai heir, but she managed to escape him and return to her people. We just came from Tjanjin. Their talisman is a child of twelve from the Selk named Mebetimmunedjem. She's a direct descendant of Sakhet-ra-katme." Nazafareen paused. "Sakhet is dead. The Vatra burned her houseboat. Send an emissary to the Marakai and you will discover I speak truly."

"I will do better than that." He turned to Broken Nose. "Bring Stefán and Frida, as well as Stefán's guest."

Time crawled as they waited in silence. Then the door opened and Kallisto rushed in, followed by two Valkirins. The first had short silver hair that stood up like a brush. Her face looked young, but she gave off an aura of calm authority. Vivid emerald eyes assessed Nazafareen and the others with guarded curiosity. The other was male and clean-shaven, short for a Valkirin though solidly built. Where Runar's face was bluff and broad, Stefán of Val Altair had a fine-boned, foxlike quality.

Nazafareen grinned as Kallisto ran to Herodotus, pulling her husband into a long embrace. It had only been a fortnight since she last saw Kallisto, but Nazafareen realized how much she'd missed her wisdom and calm counsel. If anyone could make the Valkirins see reason, it would be Kallisto. She looked the same as ever, dark hair streaked with grey and worn in a coil of elaborate braids. She held her pinecone-topped staff in one hand. With the other, she briefly touched Herodotus's cheek, dark eyes shining with emotion. He smiled and bent to kiss her, then whispered something in her ear.

She gave no sign of having heard, but when she turned back to the assembled group, her face was composed. The Valkirins had been talking in low voices among themselves, discomfited by the display of affection, and Nazafareen didn't think they saw it.

"Herodotus is my husband," Kallisto said to Stefán. "He used to be the archivist at the Library of Delphi before the Pythia accused him of treason. Ashraf and Daraya helped me to free him. They are loyal followers of Dionysus." Kallisto told this lie with perfect sincerity, though Nazafareen noticed that she'd propped her staff against the wall and no longer held it in her hand.

"Megaera is one of my parthenoi, warrior maidens who serve the talismans and oppose the Vatras. Their arrival is unexpected, but I'm glad to see them alive." Her warm gaze took in Nazafareen and Darius. "I left them in the Isles of the Marakai to hunt for the heir."

Stefán's eyes narrowed. "That is all very well. But how did they know to find us here?"

"There was a globe of seeking in the emperor's collection," Herodotus said quickly. "He generously permitted us to use it."

"Indeed." His gaze took on a speculative light. "I don't suppose you still have it?"

Herodotus gave a weak smile. "I'm afraid not."

"Too bad. We could discover what those Dessarian dogs are up to. Ah well."

The tension in the room dissipated, though Nazafareen noticed that Darius's face had gone excessively smooth.

"Now," Kallisto said briskly. "What's happened? Where is the heir? You must tell us everything."

Nazafareen left this task to Herodotus, who did a masterful job of weaving the truth with bald-faced lies. He picked up the tale just after Kallisto's departure, relating the encounter at the Mer and how Nazafareen—Ashraf—realized the Vatra's knife had belonged to Sakhet. The pursuit to Tjanjin and Meb's abduction into the emperor's palace. When Herodotus reached the part about the wave, he made it sound it as if her power had spontaneously manifested itself.

"And where is Meb now?" Kallisto asked softly, a dangerous glint in her eye.

Herodotus tugged at his beard. "With the Marakai, my dear. They were rather insistent."

Kallisto did not seem appeased. "You were supposed to bring the girl to the Temple of the Moria Tree. She would have been safe there."

"Yes, well, Meb preferred to go with her own people. And she *is* the talisman."

"What about this Vatra?" Stefán interjected. "I'd say he's our main concern at the moment. Where did he go?"

"He fled into the shadowlands," Nazafareen replied. "But he will be searching for the other talismans. You must be ready."

"We're always ready," Frida replied, her green eyes disdainful. "But if he works fire...." She shared a look with Runar and Stefán. "We will have to join forces and kill him quickly, before he can touch his power."

Runar turned to Broken Nose. "Triple the sentries. Tell them to watch the gate." He scowled. "They should have been anyway."

The Valkirin nodded and hurried from the chamber.

"Where's Rhea?" Megaera asked.

"She's in Stefán's camp," Kallisto replied. "We arrived at Val Altair just as most of the holdfast was departing to meet Runar and the others at Val Moraine." She glanced at Stefán. "He doubted my tale at first, but when I swore on this"—Kallisto picked up her staff—"he knew I spoke the truth. We have been his guests since."

Stefán grimaced, though amusement laced his voice. "I tried it out myself first. I attempted to say I was heartbroken at the loss of Eirik Kafsnjór. The damned thing wouldn't let me. Gave me a quite a jolt when I persisted."

"And the Valkirin talisman?" Herodotus put in.

"Remains unknown," Runar said, exchanging a look with Stefán.

"Are there no records from that time?" Herodotus persisted.

"A secret library, perhaps?" His voice took on a wheedling tone. "I do read old Valkirin and I'd be more than happy to assist."

"I wish there were," Runar replied. "I can tell you who the original talisman was. A woman named Freydis Sigurdadottir. The power then passed down to her daughter Ranveig and to *her* daughter Torhild. The lineage was guarded closely. Only the heads of holdfasts knew about it. I imagine Erik Kafsnjór did."

"But there was no telling which of the descendants would inherit the gift," Stefán said, picking up Runar's thread. "It could be the firstborn or the last. And some of those old Valkirins were quite fruitful. My mother said they tested children to determine who was weakest in air, but after a few hundred years, the practice waned." He looked uncomfortable. "Being burned out was our greatest shame. No one wished to remember it anymore and it didn't seem like the Vatras were coming back."

"Can you narrow it down to one of the four holdfasts?" Nazafareen asked.

Runar shook his head. "There's always been intermarrying. The bloodlines are all mingled." He crossed his massive arms. "Stefán and I can both personally vouch for the riders we brought. They wouldn't be here if they weren't the strongest we had. There are a few back at the holdfasts, of course. It's also possible the talisman died at Val Moraine." He looked at Frida. "What about Val Tourmaline?"

Frida shook her head. "None of mine, I already told you." She hesitated. "There is one I don't know well. It's unlikely though. She's known for her ferocity and skill in battle."

"Unlikely or not, I would speak with her, if you'll permit it," Kallisto said.

Frida considered this. "I don't see the harm. I'll go find her."

When she was gone, Herodotus turned to Runar. "Does Frida lead Val Tourmaline? I thought Halldóra was mistress of that holdfast."

"You know a great deal about us, mortal," Runar replied suspiciously.

Herodotus spread his hands. "I'm a scholar, driven by simple curiosity about the world. I've studied the Danai and Marakai as well, of course, but I've always had a particular admiration for your people. You thrive in these harsh, inhospitable mountains, a feat no other clan could attempt. And you have tamed the abbadax, the fiercest creatures of any species." He tugged absently at his beard. "I don't mean to pry, but your customs and hierarchy are fascinating. I even wrote a little book about them, which was well-received among my peers." Now he coughed in an embarrassed manner. "I wish I had a copy to make a gift to you, Runar of Val Petros, truly that would be the highlight of my career."

Runar preened a bit at these words, no doubt as Herodotus intended. He had a way of buttering people up while seeming perfectly sincere, even a bit hapless, like a friendly dog you can't resist patting on the head. By the end of their sea journey with the Marakai, Nazafareen felt sure he'd extracted every bit of information worth knowing about them, all without them quite realizing what he'd done.

"Yes, I see," Runar grumbled. "Well, back to your original question." His expression darkened. "Victor Dessarian, that cowardly cur, murdered Halldóra in cold blood after they'd reached agreement to unite against the Pythia."

Nazafareen exchanged a quick, shocked look with Darius.

"He invoked a talisman that formed a shield of ice around Val Moraine," Stefán said angrily. "We're at a stalemate for the moment, but we're not going anywhere until Halldóra is avenged and her heir restored to us."

"Halldóra's grandson, Daníel, was a prisoner of the Oracle but managed to escape to Val Moraine," Kallisto explained. "He's still inside the keep. They fear Victor will kill him."

"That son of a pig," Runar muttered. "He not only killed

Halldóra, but also Eirik's great-grandmother, Gerda. One of the oldest among us and he struck her down like she was nothing. He will not have a swift death when we get inside, that I can promise you."

Nazafareen listened as they ranted on about Victor. She could strangle the man. At one point, Darius opened his mouth to say something and she stepped hard on his foot. He made a small noise and shot her a slit-eyed look, but remained silent.

As Darius had advised her, one thing at a time. It sounded as if Victor had been busy digging his own grave. Perhaps she could convince them to let her inside to talk to him....

The door swung wide and Frida entered, trailed by another woman. She was tall and broad-shouldered, with chiseled cheek-bones and eyes like green glass. She exuded arrogance and barely restrained violence.

"This is Katrin Aigirsdottir," Frida said to Kallisto. "The last survivor of Val Moraine, except for Culach. She found us over Mýrdalsjökull glacier and pledged herself to Val Tourmaline. She was in the hall when Halldóra and Gerda died."

Kallisto swept forward. "I'm pleased to meet you Katrin," she said warmly. "Thank you for coming."

The woman nodded brusquely.

"What is it you want? I was in the middle of a patrol."

She glanced over Kallisto's shoulder, surveying Darius, Herodotus and Megaera with thinly veiled dislike. Then her gaze landed on Nazafareen and the blood drained from her face. Nazafareen looked back at her uncertainly. She didn't know Katrin, she felt sure. But then she had those damn holes in her memory.

"You," Katrin breathed, every muscle rigid.

The temperature in the room seemed to drop another ten degrees.

"What's wrong?" Frida demanded, staring between Nazafareen and Katrin.

"You're supposed to be dead," Katrin snarled, incandescent with rage. "We set chimera on you."

Nazafareen reached for the hilt of her sword, but of course they'd taken it.

"You're wrong," she said with a calm she didn't remotely feel. "You must have me confused with someone else."

Katrin's livid gaze fixed on her stump. "It is no mistake. You killed my sister!"

❧ 3 ❧

KALLISTO'S STAFF

Darius tensed as the Valkirin reached for her sword.
The last survivor of Val Moraine.

She must have been there when Culach's soldiers poured through the gate. He didn't remember her face, but his attention had been focused on Nazafareen and how to stop her from dying in his arms.

Of all the bloody people....

A tide of earth magic pulsed against his skin, begging to be used. It was strong so deep within the mountain. He could crack bones with it. Open the ground beneath their feet.

Or he might bring the mountain down on *all* their heads. And then the Valkirins would know him for what he was.

Darius drew a sharp breath. He moved to stand in front of Nazafareen, ready to unleash hell and face the consequences, but the attack never came. Katrin's fingers gripped the hilt of her iron blade, her teeth gritted, as if she were trying to draw it but couldn't.

"Release me!" she yelled.

Power crackled in the chamber—air power. Frida's hair ruffled in a breeze that seemed to be focused exclusively on her and Katrin.

"Calm yourself," Frida snapped. "What are you talking about?"

"I don't know her name, but I know her face. I'll never forget it. She's the one who broke the wards on the gates. Then she turned on us!" Katrin could barely get the words out. "She's an abomination. We sent Petur to kill her, but he failed."

"And then Eirik sent the chimera." Stefán suddenly looked more wolf than fox. "Yet here she stands." He turned accusing eyes on Kallisto. "This girl is no mortal."

"Her magic doesn't work here," Katrin ground out. "Let me kill her before it's too late!"

Three sets of icy eyes fixed on Nazafareen.

"Well?" Stefán asked in a dangerously soft voice.

"I'd like to see you try," Darius snarled.

Nazafareen drew herself up, pale but composed. How he loved her at that moment.

"Katrin is right," she said. "I am a Breaker. My true name is Nazafareen. I lied because I feared exactly this reaction. But I acted in self-defense that day. There was a creature from the Dominion lurking just inside the gate. It latched onto Culach somehow. It would have killed him, and then me."

"Lies," Katrin growled.

Nazafareen stared back at her, unafraid. "Hate me if you will. But you need me. I'm the only one who can fight the Vatras. I can break flows of magic. And when you find your talisman, you'll need me to break the wards that suppress their power. I did it with the Marakai girl."

Kallisto raised an eyebrow. "You...?"

"We saw it," Herodotus put in. "Nazafareen meant to break the gate so the Vatra couldn't escape with Meb, but her power struck the girl instead. We thought she was dead. But when she resurfaced, she called the wave." His eyes grew distant. "I've never seen the like."

"What are they talking about?" Katrin demanded. "What is a Vatra?"

The three leaders of the holdfasts exchanged a long look.

"She doesn't know," Frida said. "I'm not surprised. Most of us don't."

Runar sighed. "A thousand years ago, there was a fourth clan of daēvas. The Avas Vatras. Children of fire. They waged war against us. As you can imagine, they were unstoppable. They burned the holdfasts and the forest. They would have hunted every one of us down, but then three daēvas appeared, one from each clan, gifted with extraordinary power. They made the Gale and banished the Vatras to the other side."

Katrin shook her head. "Fire daēvas?" she repeated hoarsely. "How can it be?"

"It's true," Frida said. "Halldóra told me the story. She said the power was passed down, but over the long years, we lost track of who had the gift. No one thought the Vatras would come back. They faded into legend."

"But how could such power go unnoticed?"

"The descendants couldn't wield it freely like the first talismans," Stefán said. "Kallisto says the sign of the heirs is a *weakness* in the power." He looked at Nazafareen. "But it seems this woman can shatter whatever magic holds it in check."

Herodotus cleared his throat. "There is an ancient scroll speaking of a Fourth Talisman. Without her.... We would be naked before the storm."

Katrin had stopped struggling, but she still looked furious.

"Fairy stories," she muttered.

"Believe it or not, I don't care," Runar said sternly. "But her fate is ours to decide, not yours." He managed to loom down at Katrin though they were nearly of a height. "Which brings us back to the reason you were brought here in the first place. The Marakai have their talisman. But we have yet to learn who ours is. So I ask you, Katrin Aigirsdottir, are you weak in air?"

Katrin stared at him. Broad shoulders hunched defensively.

"I am Valkirin," she finally managed. "What you ask is shameful and insulting—"

"There is no shame," Frida interrupted. "Everyone knows your skill with a blade. It's legendary. Your worth is not in question."

Katrin shuddered. Darius almost felt sorry for her. Her deepest, darkest secret was being dredged out, and in front of despised strangers no less.

"I.... I do have trouble sometimes...." Her face went blank.

Stefán's eyes narrowed. "It's how the Dessarians managed to take you alive, isn't it?"

Katrin didn't respond. She seemed beyond hearing. Red blotches burned her pale cheeks and she stared miserably at a spot on the far wall.

Frida laid a hand on her shoulder. "Don't be a fool, Katrin. This is cause for celebration, if you are indeed the heir." She turned to Nazafareen. "How do you free her power?"

"I have to be in Solis. The magic is tied to fire, although that is not my main talent," she added hastily. "I'm not like the Vatras."

"Then she must go with Katrin to the sunlands without delay," Runar exclaimed. "I'm happy to provide an escort."

Stefán frowned slightly. "I will send a delegation as well. We all have an interest in the outcome."

The two Valkirins eyed each other sideways, mutual distrust thickening the air.

"Of course," Nazafareen replied easily. "But since we're being honest, I will confess the real reason I came here. I wish to see Culach. And perhaps I can talk some sense into Victor while I'm at it."

"Culach?" Katrin snarled, embarrassment vanishing as her enmity returned in full force. "Are you mad? He'll spit in your face."

"That's what I told her," Darius muttered.

In the tension and revelations of the last few minutes, the Valkirins seemed to have forgotten him. But now Frida's gaze lingered on his dark hair and broad shoulders, his proud beak of a nose.

"What did you say your name was?"

"Daraya."

"*Daraya*." She turned to Kallisto. "Give him your staff."

Kallisto didn't move. "Is this really necessary?" she asked calmly.

"You already lied to us once. And I seem to recall this girl taking refuge in the Great Forest of the Danai." Frida's jaw set. "I say it again. Give him your staff. If he has nothing to hide, he should not fear it."

Stefán and Runar watched impassively. When she still failed to comply, Stefán made a brusque gesture.

"I've treated you as a guest. Don't make me regret it."

Left with no choice, Kallisto stepped forward and offered the staff to Darius. He examined it for a moment, pretending mild curiosity, then curled his fingers around the haft. A tingle ran though him as the wood touched his palm, like sliding into a bath of cool water.

"My trust for strangers is small," Frida said. "These are dark times. War brews in the mortal lands. The Danai think they are cuckoos, roosting in a nest built by others." She pointed to the staff. "There is no question that this talisman compels the truth. All of us sense its power. So I will ask you, *Daraya*, are you a mortal?"

Darius opened his mouth to confirm it, but no sound came out. He cleared his throat and tried again with the same result. The tingling grew stronger, nearing the edge of pain. Stefán stared at him intently, as if he knew exactly what happening.

Darius swallowed, his mind racing.

"No," he said at last, and the unpleasant sensation from the staff instantly receded.

Broken Nose gripped his sword, but Runar shook his head.

"Not yet," he said. "Let us hear the rest."

"Your true name," Frida demanded.

He licked his lips. "Darius."

"Of the Danai, I presume?"

"Yes."

"What House?"

Darius steeled himself.

"None."

The word spilled from his tongue clear as a bell. The staff seemed to accept this answer. He hadn't been certain it would, though in fact, it was literal truth.

"Really?" Stefán's shrewd eyes regarded Darius. "How so?"

"I was born in a different land. A world that lies through the Dominion." Darius met his gaze with perfect innocence. "The same that Culach Kafsnjór sought to invade."

Runar nodded slowly. "I have heard of it."

"I come from there as well," Nazafareen put in. She looked thrilled to divert the questioning along a different tack. "It is a mirror world to this one in many ways. Herodotus here can confirm it."

Runar cast her an annoyed glance at the interruption. His hard gaze returned to Darius.

"Daēvas are native to this place then?" he asked.

"Not exactly." The staff allowed him to speak the words, but it didn't like this answer and Darius couldn't suppress a quick grimace of pain. "No."

"So you have kin in *this* world?"

"Yes."

"Ah." Runar's mouth set. "And what House do your kin belong to?"

Darius felt the Nexus pulsing at the edge of his vision. He ignored it.

"Dessarian."

Katrin gave a low growl. Runar and Stefán exchanged a dark glance. Frida slouched against the wall, her gaze locked on Darius. The atmosphere in the small chamber vibrated with tension.

"Your mother's name?"

"Delilah."

"And your father?"

And so they had arrived at the heart of the matter. He squeezed the staff. Felt the grain of the wood, the currents of power running along them. He tried to think of a loophole he might wiggle through and came up blank.

Darius's voice was tight. "Victor."

As he spoke the name, before the second syllable even left his lips, Nazafareen spun with astonishing speed and kicked Broken Nose in the throat, knocking him backwards and wrenching his sword away as he fell. In one fluid movement, she had the blade against Runar's neck, to the juncture where his pulse beat. Everyone froze. The only sound was Broken Nose's soft wheezing.

"Use the power on me and I kill him," she spat, her eyes glowing with a feral light.

Runar simply gazed at her in a considering way. Broken Nose glared in impotent fury. Stefán and Frida looked shocked to the marrow. They hadn't known what she truly was, though they certainly did now.

The hair on Darius's neck stood up. At least one of them was in the Nexus.

He saw the scene play out before him in the blink of an eye. They would lash out with the power, but Nazafareen would kill Runar. She nearly had the reflexes of a daēva now.

Then it would be a free-for-all. And no matter how it ended, once blood was shed, there would be no going back. Ever.

"No," Darius said quietly. He leaned the staff against the wall, the movement slow and deliberate. "Not this way."

Nazafareen's eyes skewered Runar, waiting for a single twitch.

The other Valkirins watched in silence, tight as coiled springs. He had to get through to her before they snapped. Had to stop her somehow.

"There can be no bad blood. The clans must stop all that nonsense. Sound familiar?"

A muscle in Nazafareen's jaw feathered.

"Did you truly expect any different?" he persisted. "They would have found out eventually. Put the sword down."

She muttered something under her breath.

"If you harm him," she told Runar, "I'll hunt you to the ends of the earth."

Nazafareen lowered the sword. In an instant, bonds of air squeezed Darius from head to toe. Broken Nose backhanded him, his heavy rings giving the blow vicious power. The taste of blood filled his mouth. Nazafareen screamed in rage, but the sound cut off as though severed by a knife. They must have gagged her.

As if from a distance, Darius heard Kallisto arguing with Runar, but all he saw was Nazafareen as she toppled like a falling tree. Megaera tried to run to her, but Herodotus laid a restraining hand on her arm, whispering urgently. The old scholar looked stricken.

"Bring them outside," Runar snapped. "Not the Breaker. She can stay here and stew in her bonds for a while."

Fingers seized his hair and dragged him into the hall. Despite the hot throbbing in his jaw, despite the knowledge that there was worse coming, Darius felt dizzy with relief.

Outside.

If they'd put him in a small stone chamber and shackled him, he feared he might lose his mind.

Even so, he felt panic rising in his throat at the feeling of confinement. And he understood that even though he'd escaped his cell in Delphi, some part of him had never truly left.

What is your true name, Andros?

Dark eyes, alight with madness.

Do you know the story of Eros and Psyche?

Bright sunlight in his eyes. The sour, animal stink of his own body.

I treat my witches well.

Do you know how many I've broken, Andros?

And always, when he refused to speak:

I'm sorry. Truly, I am. But you brought this on yourself.

❧ 4 ❧

A BARGAIN

They left Nazafareen in darkness, arms and legs pinioned with air. She lay on her back, stiff as a plank, trying to ignore the itch on her nose. Not for the first time, she cursed the fickle nature of her power. It seemed that whenever she needed it most, she couldn't touch it.

Whoever devised huo mofa should be flogged, she thought, glaring into the blackness.

She tried not to dwell on what might be happening to Darius. Kallisto and Herodotus and the two Maenads wouldn't let the Valkirins kill him, that she knew for sure. And they couldn't stop Darius from working earth, if it came down to it. She couldn't see him submitting meekly to death.

Nazafareen thought of the hell he went through in Delphi, all on her account. And now here he was again, in the hands of their enemies, trussed up like a chicken waiting for the pot to boil. She tasted the bitter dregs of regret.

It'll serve them right if the Vatra does show up, she thought savagely.

An indeterminate amount of time passed. And then Nazafareen saw a faint light creeping under the door. It opened and Nazafareen squeezed her eyes shut, blinded by the sudden glare.

"Who's there?" she demanded.

"Keep your voice down," a familiar voice whispered. It was crisp and cultured like the scholars at the library, but with a distinctly feminine lilt.

"Rhea!"

The Maenad hurried over and knelt gracefully before Nazafareen. She set the lumen crystal on the ground, laying her staff across her knees. Her grey eyes were solemn.

"Are you hurt?"

"I'm fine. Can't move, but at least they took the gag off. How's Darius?"

"They've wrapped him in coils of air." She paused. "He's dangling over the ravine."

Nazafareen fell silent for a long moment. "I'll kill them. Painfully."

Rhea arched an eyebrow. "Not in this state, you won't. But they don't plan on harming him, not yet at least. Runar got the idea of trading him to Victor for the diamond. They put him out there so the Danai could get a good look."

"Diamond?"

"The talisman that shrouds the keep in ice." Rhea shivered. "It must be awful in there."

Nazafareen's eyes rolled toward the open doorway. "The Valkirins let you come visit me?"

Rhea smiled. "I snuck up on the guard and cracked him over the head. He'll be out cold for a while."

Nazafareen tested her invisible bonds. They were as solid as before.

"If it's not the guard, who's holding these flows?"

"I think they have a way of tying them in place. They do it at the holdfasts. The one we saw was open to the sky, but shields of air form the outer walls." She shook her head in wonder. "I never knew daēvas were so strong. It's marvelous the things they can do."

"Now you sound like Herodotus," Nazafareen grumbled. "Admiring the fine teeth of the wolf just before it rips your throat out. What about Kallisto and the others?"

"Runar made us swear our true names and purpose on Kallisto's staff. He's satisfied that we don't intend the Valkirins harm, but he won't hear a word about Darius. Kallisto's in a terrible temper." She studied Nazafareen with reproach. "Why did you come here? It was very foolish."

"I suppose it was. I wanted to see Culach. Thought I could set things right." She laughed mirthlessly.

"I've heard them talking about him. They hate him as much as Victor, maybe more. They think he betrayed them to the Danai and plan to make him suffer when they get their hands on him."

Nazafareen shifted. "Could you scratch my nose? It's driving me mad."

Rhea eyed her with distaste. "Not *in* your nose?"

"Just to the side. No, the left.... Ah, thank the gods. Listen, I have to get inside Val Moraine. Have they sent someone yet?"

Rhea discreetly rubbed her fingers on her cloak. "No, they're arguing over who would go. I think they don't trust each other either. This diamond is a powerful talisman. They each want possession of it."

Nazafareen thought for a moment. "Good. That might make things easier. Tell them I want to see them. That the Fourth Talisman demands an audience. If they don't, I won't break Katrin's ward. Everyone will have a talisman except for the Valkirins. Tell them that."

Rhea nodded. "So it *is* you. Kallisto said so, but.... The Fourth Talisman."

Nazafareen felt uncomfortable at the tinge of awe in her voice. "It's just a silly title. But it might impress them. They seem like the types to go in for that sort of thing. Honestly, I haven't changed a bit." She jerked her head toward the door. "Go on. Off with you, now."

Rhea glanced at her. "No, you have changed. You're bossier, for one thing." She rose with a sly smile. "I shall convey the message, O Mighty One."

Nazafareen made a rude noise. The door eased shut and the light faded.

They made her wait for a while, which was no less than she expected. Finally, Runar, Stefán and Frida showed up and loomed over her in a semicircle.

"First things first," Nazafareen said briskly. "I'm not craning my neck to talk to you, so you can loosen the bonds on my legs. Unless you're afraid I'll kick you in the shins."

Runar scowled, but Nazafareen felt the chains of air evaporate, though only on her lower half. She stood awkwardly, pushing her back against the wall for support, and stamped her feet a few times to get the blood going.

"Thank you. Now, I understand that you plan to trade Darius for Victor's diamond. It's not a bad idea, actually."

"What is it you want?" Frida demanded.

"I want to be your emissary."

Stefán laughed. "I don't think so."

"No? And what do you think will happen if one of *you* shows up, making demands? You've already dangled Victor's only son like a worm on a hook. Think! What do you know about Victor Dessarian?" Nazafareen shook her head sadly. "Yes, he's dumb as rocks sometimes. But his defining trait is pride. If you get his dander up, he'll have to refuse you." She turned to Frida. "Sure, he'll come around eventually. But how long to you want to draw this out? And he does have his own hostage. Halldóra's grandson. Who knows what Victor might do if you really make him angry?"

She could see this hit home with Frida, although the others didn't seem to care as much what happened to Daníel. He was from Val Tourmaline, after all.

"And why do you wish to go inside so badly?" Runar demanded.

"I told you before. I need to speak with Culach. I'll swear on Kallisto's staff, if you wish. That is my only motive. But Victor knows me. Trusts me. If you want to end this siege, you'll accept my offer."

When they hesitated, she felt her temper—so carefully held in check—begin to rise.

"I fought a Vatra and won," Nazafareen said coldly. "I have traveled in the Dominion. I have dissolved chimera. Having me for an ally is much better than the alternative."

"We'll think about it," Runar said.

She stiffened as the bonds around her legs tightened again.

"Wait!" Nazafareen cried as they strode to the door. "You should know one other thing."

They turned back, looking at her with stony faces.

"I love Darius." Her voice wavered with emotion. "I'd die before he came to harm. So I would never betray you. In fact, I'll make damn sure Victor gives up that diamond, whether he likes it or not."

Frida crossed her arms, facing the two older men. "I have to say, that sounded sincere. More than the boasting and threats. I saw the way she looked at Huda when he struck Victor's whelp across the face. She wanted to murder him. So I say let her go." She snorted. "I trust her more than either of you."

Runar seemed offended, Stefán merely contemplative.

"We can't send her in alone. We need a representative," Stefán said.

They all began speaking at once then, arguing for one of their own.

"Hey!" Nazafareen barked.

Three heads swiveled her way.

"You'll never agree. So I propose you send Katrin. She's not from any of your holdfasts."

Frida laughed. "And what makes you think she won't kill you?"

"Because she wants her power more than she wants revenge. And if she kills me, she'll never have it."

Nazafareen hoped this was true.

"I don't like it," Stefán said. "Katrin has a bad temper." He eyed Frida with sudden suspicion. "And she's sworn herself to Val Tourmaline."

"That's only because we found her first. She would have done the same for either of you."

"And what if she tries to kill Victor?"

"We'll make it clear that if she does that, she'll be an outcast. Katrin won't risk it. She's not stupid."

They turned back to Nazafareen.

"Agreed," Runar said sourly. "Katrin will accompany you into Val Moraine."

"Good. There's one more thing. You'll all swear on Kallisto's staff that the Danai will be free to go home. I have to be able to tell Victor the guarantees are ironclad."

"Free to go home?" Frida smirked. "Fine. But I will not vouch-safe his life after that."

Nazafareen knew this was the best she would get. Victor had done too much damage.

"Fair enough," she replied, grinning. "So who gets to give Katrin the good news?"

𝕊 5 𝕊

THE ONES WE'VE BEEN
WAITING FOR

Damp sheets clung to his skin as Nicodemus rolled to his back and stared blearily at the ceiling. His head pounded from last night's plundering of the Archon's wine cellars. He should have watered it. But he'd wanted to get drunk, if only to dull the unsettled thoughts rattling around in his brain.

The day before, he'd found himself alone in Domitia's chambers while she met with her generals. Stacks of old records from the Great Library covered the writing table, all with a fine layer of dust. Since the capture of Galen, she'd lost interest in tracing the family trees of the other clans. But Nico had learned to read several mortal languages during his time in Tjanjin and, out of boredom more than anything else, he'd started to peruse the scrolls and stacks of vellum.

What he found came as a shock.

The world outside the Kiln had not been what Nico expected, yet he'd clung to his hatred. Gaius ingrained it in the children as soon as they were old enough to come to his burrow for what he called history lessons—long, angry lectures that often went on for hours. They all knew the story of the exile. The other clans grew jealous of the Vatras and their mastery of fire. Somehow—Gaius was vague on this part—they gained extraordinary powers to sunder the heavens and conjure the Gale, leaving the Vatras on the wrong side. Condemning them to short, brutal lives.

But every account of the mortals claimed the Vatras started the war without provocation. The sources were too numerous and varied to be wholly inaccurate, and included firsthand witnesses to the horrors. Cities burning, the desperate flight of the Marakai. They spoke of Gaius and the atrocities he had committed.

Domitia must know, yet she didn't seem to care. Now his mind churned with doubts. Nicodemus rubbed his forehead. Was everything he knew a lie?

He'd left Domitia's chamber before she returned, saying nothing when they'd crossed paths later. But he'd drunk himself into a stupor and now he was paying for it.

At least he found himself alone in the enormous bed. It was plated with bronze and anchored at the corners by winged women with pendulous breasts. Nico vaguely recalled persuading one of the serving girls to have a cup or two with him, but she must have left when he passed out.

He sat up with a tender groan. The low sun slanted across the whitewashed rooftops of Delphi. In the middle distance he could see the Acropolis, with its sheer, fortified sides, and the Temple of Apollo, sixteen stone pillars capped by a flat roof. In his wretched state, the building had a sinister cast. The records weren't the only thing that disturbed him. He'd known about the daēva collars in theory, but seeing them with his own eyes was another matter.

Nicodemus padded over to a basin of water and splashed some on his face. Plush carpets from Samarqand covered the floor in overlapping layers. A mirror hung on the wall behind the wash-basin and he examined himself with detachment. He looked bad, though not as bad as expected. Dark red hair hung over one eye. He shook it back and examined his teeth. His mouth tasted like a tavern floor in Tjanjin's City of Bliss.

Besides the washbasin, the room contained a writing desk, several chairs, a wardrobe decorated with silver swans, a few cedar chests and that ridiculous bed. Nico could easily imagine the debauchery it had witnessed and would have taken another more modest chamber, but he had a point to make.

If you requisitioned the palace of an Archon, you ought to do things right.

He poured a cup of water and swished some around, spitting it into the chamber pot. Then he lifted the jug and drained it. He needed to get a handle on things—on Domitia, in particular.

The woman he'd known in the Kiln preferred to operate alone, disappearing for weeks on hunting trips into the waste. She had no friends except for Nicodemus and even he was more of a mascot than a friend. She claimed he brought her luck. Occasionally, she let him come along, which is how he'd learned most of his tricks.

After escaping the Kiln, Domitia went to Solis, Nico to the Isles of the Marakai, and later, Tjanjin. He'd wormed his way into the emperor's favor, but Domitia managed to get herself appointed the Oracle of Delphi, the most powerful position a woman could hold. It required a degree of finesse and subtlety he'd never even suspected she possessed.

Nicodemus found the whole situation more than a little surreal.

He'd refused to stay at the Temple with her demented teenaged initiates, but the crowded inns held no appeal either. Then an alternative presented itself.

Nico turned at a tap on the door. The Archon Basileus peered through the crack. His face went pale.

"A thousand apologies," he murmured, averting his gaze. "I'll return later—"

"Now is fine."

Nico took his time strolling over to the wardrobe. He flung the door open and selected a pair of trousers and soft linen tunic while the Archon fidgeted in the doorway. The Archon's seam-stresses were skilled and his new clothes fit well.

"My knives," he muttered with a frown, looking around the chamber. It was a bit of a mess. An empty wine cup lay on its side next to a stack of parchment, now stained a deep red. "Where....?"

The Archon cleared his throat and cast a meaningful glance at the tapestry adorning one wall. It depicted a satyr frolicking with a bevy of nude nymphs. A pair of knives jutted from the satyr's equine hindquarters.

Nico didn't remember throwing them, but he must have. He walked over and eased them out of the wall. A fanged eel coiled around the hilt of one. The other was long and sharp and beauti-fully balanced, chased with silver on the handle. It still reeked faintly of fish guts.

Nico slipped them into his belt and turned to face the Archon.

"Breakfast is laid out in the dining room," Basileus said, clutching a sheaf of parchment in his hands. "I must go to the Temple, but the servants will provide anything you require."

"Why?"

Basileus blinked. His dark hair was neatly combed back, his crimson cloak resplendent, but shadows hovered beneath his eyes and his nails had been chewed to the quick.

"Pardon?"

Nico pulled his hair into a topknot and bound it with a leather thong. "Why are you going to the Temple?"

"I have reports to make to the Oracle—"

"You'll give them to me."

The Archon swallowed.

Nico pointed to a chair. "Sit down."

Basileus sat.

"Let's be perfectly clear. You're mine now. You make all

reports to me, and I determine which you pass on to the Pythia. It will be a mutually beneficial arrangement, I'm sure."

A swift calculus ensued as Basileus weighed his options. His gaze flicked to the window and the outline of the Acropolis, then to the rumpled sheets. Nicodemus suppressed a smile. The man thought himself a master manipulator, but he was simple enough to read. He feared Domitia, but she wasn't here, sleeping in his bed. And he'd been standing there when the Polemarch's charred helmet rolled across the floor of the adyton.

"Certainly," Basileus said smoothly. "Where do you wish to begin?"

Nico gathered his muddy thoughts. He really should eat something.

"Is there any news of the Breaker?"

"None. She vanished from Tjanjin with the Danai and their companions. They must have traveled by gate, but they have yet to resurface."

So she could have gone anywhere. "What else?"

"The Marakai are gathering. It's difficult to obtain reliable information, but my sources say their ships sailed from Tjanjin, every one. They say a Marakai girl conjured an enormous wave. One of the talismans, I assume."

"I watched her do it."

Nico thought briefly of Meb and what a peculiar girl she was. Having seen Domitia's collars, part of him felt relieved she got away.

"Will they attack?" Basileus fingered his heavy gold chain of office. "Delphi is less than twenty leagues from the coast. Could she...?"

"Flood the city? Probably. But there's not much we can do about it. What else?"

"The Danai are coming in force to liberate their captive kin. My scouts say they'll be here in a matter of days."

"And what is the Oracle doing about it?" He felt faintly ridiculous calling her that, but he didn't think Domitia would like the Archon knowing her real name. And Nico wouldn't make an enemy of her unless he had no choice.

"The army is readying to march out and meet them." Basileus didn't meet Nico's eyes. They both knew a mortal force wouldn't stand a chance on its own.

"Do the soldiers know what she is?"

"Not yet."

"Who does?"

"Only myself and Thena." The Archon wiped his forehead with a scrap of silk. "The secret is perfectly safe with me, of course. But the girl…. I don't know. She strikes me as unstable. She was always a zealot. She despises the wi—" He cut off with a strangled noise. "Pardon, my lord, but that is what we were taught to call the daēvas."

"Witches, you mean?" Nico shrugged. He'd been called worse. "I'm surprised the Oracle hasn't silenced her."

"She brought the Danai talisman back from Val Moraine. She followed him through the shadowlands and collared him when he tried to free another Danai. So she has proven her worth. And more importantly, she has the talent to wear the bracelets."

This was news to Nico. "So not all mortals can control the collars?"

"No. Only a select few. And most of the other experienced acolytes are dead." Basileus ticked them off on his fingers. "Let's see, Maia was attacked by her captive Valkirin and died in her bed. Korinna never returned from the mission to Val Moraine. A brain fever, apparently. And Phoebe had her head bashed in by Nikias, a Danai."

Nico digested this in silence. "So Thena is the last one?"

"Not the last. There are a few girls with the talent, but none have ever broken a daēva. Thena has…a reputation."

"For what?"

"Utter ruthlessness."

Nico vaguely remembered a mortal in the adyton when he arrived. She had stood next to the Danai heir, a bracelet on her slender wrist.

"Long black hair, olive skin?"

"That's the one."

He sighed. "Keep an eye on her. We'll move on for now. What else do you have for me?"

Parchment shuffled. "The Archon Eponymos has fled, but we will find him, never fear—"

"I don't give a shit about that," Nico snapped. His temples throbbed. "What else? Something *interesting*."

Unruffled, Basileus sorted through the pile.

"Here's something. A shepherd boy claimed he saw a wind ship headed in the direction of the Gale."

Nico leaned forward. "A wind ship?"

"I'd dismiss it as fantasy, but it's corroborated by other reports, on other days. A barge captain, a merchant caravan on the river road. The ship had no insignia."

"Where exactly?"

"All between ten and twenty leagues north of Samarqand."

Nico thought for a moment. "Send some men to the area to ask questions and spread coin around. Not Shields of Apollo, they'll attract too much attention. Ones you trust to be discreet. I'm sure you have a few on the payroll. They should send on their reports, then stay and keep an eye out. Find me immediately if you get word of another sighting."

Basileus nodded. "It will be done, my lord."

"I'm not a lord," Nico replied absently. He found his boots under the bed and pulled them on. "Is there any legitimate reason a ship would fly west?"

"None that I can think of. There's a few farms, but they're along the river. The land beyond is barren, of course."

He cleared his throat, eyes shifting away. Mention of the Kiln obviously made him uncomfortable.

"Could a wind ship cross the Gale?" Nico persisted, more than a little intrigued.

The Archon frowned. "I don't think so, no. I've never seen the Gale myself, but I imagine the winds would tear the ship apart."

"Yet someone has tried. More than once."

Basileus looked skeptical. "It could be related to the current political situation in Samarqand. A new king has been crowned at the Rock. Prince Shahak succeeded his father, Cambyses. They say he is a fearsome alchemist." Basileus gave a dry cough. "No doubt stories planted to build his reputation."

"What are the stories?"

"That he slaughtered half the royal guard and turned his mother and brothers into grotesque animals."

Nico laughed. "How inventive."

"Indeed. Spell dust is common there, but it does seem far-fetched."

"What are his intentions?"

"No one knows, but I have sources within the palace. I will uncover them soon enough." Basileus droned on for a while about the various noble factions among the Persians, the strength of their army, and the effects of the trade embargo imposed by the Pythia. He appeared relieved to be back on safer ground. Nico tuned most of it out. He had no interest in mortal intrigues. He just wanted his brother back. And to have some breakfast.

"That's enough," he said finally. "You can tell the Oracle everything except for the part about the wind ships. We'll keep that our secret for now."

Basileus bowed and withdrew. Nicodemus moved to the window and watched the muscular litter bearers lift the Archon to their shoulders and whisk him off to the Temple. He supposed he could demand similar treatment, but he preferred his own feet. They'd worked well enough in the Kiln, where he might range thirty leagues to find supper and a skin of water.

He went down to breakfast in the airy, elegantly appointed

dining room. The servants were well-trained enough to pretend nothing was amiss, though one plumply pretty girl kept glancing at him through her lashes. Nico pretended not to notice. He forced down a meal of barley bread and olives, leaving the wine cup untouched, and made his way down the hill into the city. The stench of the place filled his nostrils—dung both human and animal, rotting fish, the cloying perfume the rich wore to cover the fact that they rarely bathed. It still amazed him the way marble palaces practically rubbed shoulders with mudbrick hovels.

He tossed some coins to a boy who sat in the street entreating passersby in a piteous voice. The child looked a little like Atticus, but with a large growth on the side of his neck. Nico expected he'd just hand the money over to the hard-faced man watching from a doorway across the street, but the poverty here was much worse than Tjanjin and his pockets were full of the Archon's gold.

A few wind ships floated over the rooftops. Even from a distance, he could sense the fires burning in their braziers. Nico eyed them speculatively. If a wind ship could cross the Kiln, he'd take one and find Atticus himself. He could walk away from Domitia, from the talismans, from all of it.

But Basileus was probably right. Crossing the Gale was impossible.

The long walk helped to clear his head. He found the weather pleasant, even a touch cool, though a pair of farmers who'd stopped their wagons to gossip were complaining about the heat. They should see the western reaches of the Kiln, he thought. Nothing grew there, not even scrubgrass or the thorny bushes that offered shade and camouflage elsewhere. The sands appeared devoid of life.

Appeared being the operative word.

He reached the steps of the Acropolis and jogged up two at a time. A few supplicants waited in the plaza outside the Temple, hoping for an audience with the Oracle. They eyed Nico without interest, faces set in lines of weary determination. He'd questioned Basileus when he first took possession of his palace and learned that since the massacre of the Ecclesia, Delphi's populist assembly, the number of visitors to the Temple had declined dramatically. The Sun God was still a beloved figure, but most people chose to leave their offerings at the smaller temples scattered throughout the city. They knew the Pythia was behind it even if the Polemarch gave the order.

From all that Nico had since heard about the Polemarch, he had no regrets for roasting him alive.

Nicodemus gave a wide berth to the fountain with its stooping eagle. The sparkling waters hid the shattered gate below, but it still made him uneasy. The Shields of Apollo guards knew him and let him pass. Scorch marks blackened the flagstones around the fountain. Basileus said one of the Maenads had done that with her staff.

He found Domitia in the adyton, sitting on her tripod like a spider at the center of its web. As always, she wore a white gown, the virgin bride of the god. The serpent brooch pinned at her shoulder was a talisman that created the illusion of dark hair worn in a braid that hung over one shoulder. Only her pale blue eyes looked the same. Distant, yet calculating.

Nicodemus slouched against the wall. Between the incense and the fumes wafting from cracks in the floor, his hangover was seriously contemplating a comeback.

"It's like a sewer down here," he said, wrinkling his nose. "How do you put up with it?"

"I find the holy miasma conducive to my visions," she replied serenely.

"Your visions." He studied her with a frown. Nico wondered if Domitia had finally lost it.

Then she laughed, a sudden, hard bark. Her old laugh.

"Just kidding. We can go to my chamber if you prefer."

She leapt gracefully from the tripod. For an instant, he saw her as she used to be, the cloak blending with the desert sands, bright red hair roughly hacked at chin length, thigh-bone spear propped over one shoulder. He wondered what the adoring masses of Delphi would think if they saw the Oracle as she truly was: A dirty scavenger who tore the legs off giant crabs and ate them raw. No doubt they'd run screaming in the other direction.

They walked to her quarters and Nico felt a sense of relief to leave the adyton. The smell was bad enough, but it was a lightless place, almost as bad as a burrow.

"I spoke to Basileus," she said. "There's no word of the Breaker."

Nico nodded thoughtfully, as if he didn't already know. "She'll turn up."

"If you hadn't lost your globe, we could find her easily."

"Where's yours?"

She jerked her chin at a rock shelf in the corner. Nico picked it up and turned it over in his hands. The runes at the base had been partly melted.

"I might be able to fix this," he said. "I spent a fair amount of time studying the talismans in the emperor's collection in Tjanjin."

"I already tried."

"Yes, but you've never had a light touch, Domitia."

For once, she didn't seem offended. "I made the collars."

He'd always wondered about that. They must be complex and frankly, way out of her league.

"How did you come up with the design?" Nico kept his voice casual. If she thought he really wanted to know, she'd refuse him out of spite.

Domitia stretched her slender white legs. "Before that woman broke my gate, I took a few trips into the Dominion. On one of them I met a mortal wandering lost in the forest. He wore leathers made of human skin." She said this in the same tone one might observe that a cloak had daisies embroidered on the sleeve.

"It wasn't difficult to extract his story. He claimed to be a necro-mancer who had served a woman named Neblis. He wore a ring around his wrist that connected with a chain to several iron collars. A talisman, but one that drew the life force from its victims. I took it from him and adapted the basic design."

"And what happened to this necromancer?"

Domitia gave a merry laugh. "I peeled him like a piece of fruit. I'd thought to make my own cloak from him, but it turned out to be messy and not worth the trouble."

Nicodemus eyed her. The tale made him uneasy. "Where did he come from? Are there others like him?"

"Not that I've seen." She shrugged, losing interest. "Fix my globe if you can. We need the Breaker. But if you cannot, I will her make come to us regardless."

"And how do you plan to manage her? If we caught her on the dark side, it might be possible. But if she's in Solis, she's untouchable."

Domitia grinned. "You're scared of her."

"Don't be ridiculous."

"Yes, you are. She bested you." Domitia sighed, her gaze soft-ening. "It's strange, but the woman reminds me of myself some-times. She has courage."

"She's vicious."

"Nothing wrong with that. She has her task and we have ours." She paced, humming with nervous energy. "We're so close, Nico. So close. A thousand years the Gale has stood, and we're the ones we've been waiting for. You and me."

"We haven't done it yet."

She gave a secret smile. "We will."

He shook his head. "And what about the Danai?"

"They're the key. I'll admit, I didn't plan it this way, but the escape of the captive has worked to our advantage. The clan is coming to us. Once they realize what we are, they'll have to surrender. We'll trade them to the Breaker."

"I don't know if she'll go for it."

"She has a temper, yes?"

Nico remembered those amber eyes, shining with malice.

"That's one way of putting it."

"All Breakers do. It's why they die young. They end up picking a fight they can't win." Domitia stopped in front of him. She looked pretty and full of brash enthusiasm, like she used to be. "I know her better than she knows herself. We're kindred spirits."

Nico said nothing. Perhaps they were.

"Do you remember the time we ranged all the way to the coast?" she asked.

"I remember."

The southern peninsula of the Kiln was a no-man's land. He'd hoped they would find something—anything. The ruins of fabled Pompeii maybe, though Nico would have settled for a single tree. But it was just like the rest. Empty and punishing.

It took them three days to reach the Austral Ocean, which was wild and stark with combers twenty paces high breaking in clean lines.

"You went out too far and almost drowned," she said.

"And you hauled me back to shore. Shook me until I puked."

She laughed. "I'll never forget the color of that water. Like the sun through a piece of green glass."

Atticus had begged to go, but he'd left his brother behind with another family. They were all dead now.

"We were crazy to try that," Nico muttered.

Domitia shrugged. "No crazier than seeking the gates."

"Maybe. And what will you do?" he asked with a smile. "After the Gale falls. Name yourself queen of the mortals?"

She didn't smile back. "I'll think I'll go home," she said quietly.

He looked at her in astonishment. "You don't mean the Kiln?"

"Is that so strange?" Her shoulders hunched defensively. "I miss it, Nico. I felt alive there."

"But you're the only one Gaius listens to. He's.... You know how he is."

She knew. He could see it in her face. She'd always known.

"He does what he must."

Sudden helpless anger seized him. "He rapes children. Murders those who try to stop him. He's a monster."

Cold blue eyes turned on him and for an instant, it was as though he were looking at Gaius. Nico felt a chill.

"He ensures that we continue. The only failure is to die. Yes, my father is a hard man, but you wouldn't be standing here if he wasn't."

Nico mastered himself with effort. Domitia was a true believer. Many were. The Kiln was a crucible, burning away everything but the primal instinct for survival. Compassion, empathy, love—these were luxuries that would get you killed in a hurry.

Yet he loved Atticus. And Nico had glimpsed a different way since he left the Kiln. The possibility that he had changed in some irrevocable way disturbed him.

"Do what you will," he said. "But the collars have to be destroyed once this is over. They're too dangerous." He looked at her slender neck. "Don't you ever worry about the mortals trying to put one on you? Now that they know you're a *witch?*"

Domitia gave a merry peal of laughter. "None of them are stupid enough to try."

"Yet they're trained in capturing daēvas."

"Alone and unsuspecting daēvas. The other clans are weak, and not just in the power. They wouldn't last a day in the Kiln." Her forehead creased slightly. "But perhaps I should have a talk with Thena. She's the one who brought me the Danai heir from Val Moraine. She wears his bracelet."

Nico vaguely remembered her from when he first arrived.

"Where do you keep him?"

"In the initiates' chambers."

"I wish to see him."

Her gaze narrowed. "For what reason?"

Nico himself wasn't entirely sure. He shrugged. "Curiosity. Are you denying my request?"

She gazed at him for a long moment. "No, go ahead. And tell Thena I wish to speak with her."

He strode over and picked up the damaged globe, slipping it into a pocket. "I'll work on this later."

Nico crossed the dusty plaza to the three-story stone building that sat next to a walled yard. Flies droned inside, but it was otherwise deserted. He climbed the stairs, pausing to check the rooms on each floor. Several had chains set into the mortar, although the occupants were absent. Others clearly belonged to the initiates.

When he reached the top, he heard a voice. Nico moved silently down the hall. When he reached the door at the end, he paused outside to listen. A girl was speaking. Her voice sounded cheerful and friendly, but something about it made Nicodemus uneasy. It was as if she were playing a part, like the dramas the Greeks staged at the amphitheater.

"...shall I call you? You need a new name. A proper name."

There was no response to this.

"I already know your old name. It's Galen Bacera. Your father is Victor Dessarian, but you don't carry his name." He heard the rustle of skirts. "You look like him though."

"May I have some water, Mistress?"

"In a minute. We have to decide on your name first. Calix, perhaps. What do you think of that?"

A hint of sullenness. "I don't care."

"Now, now, Calix. You mustn't pout. It's a fine name and you'll get used to it in time." A pause. "I must say, you're far nicer than your brother."

The chains clanked. "I don't understand, Mistress."

"Your brother, Darius." Her voice took on a slight edge. "I called him Andros. He didn't want to tell me his true name. You wouldn't believe the things I tried, but he still wouldn't tell me. Not to the very end."

"Is he...dead?"

"I'm afraid so." Her voice grew harder still. "He died badly, screaming in the brazen bull. Poor thing. But you wouldn't care, would you? You helped the mountain witches set chimera on him." She laughed. "I made Nikias tell me all about it. I know what you did. So you see, I don't feel sorry for you, not one bit."

Nicodemus doubted the girl had ever felt sorry for anyone in her life. Where did Domitia find these people?

"Ah, well. Witches are traitorous. It's in your blood."

Nicodemus heard a splash of water, like a ladle being dipped into a bucket.

"Here you are, Calix. Good behavior is rewarded, just as wicked behavior is punished." The benevolent tone returned. "I promise to be clear about which is which, and as long as you listen closely and follow the rules, we'll come to be good friends."

"Yes, Mistress."

"You see? Already you are proving to be much more pliable than your brother. I am pleased with you. But it's important that you renounce your evil ways. Magic is a sin. I would hear you say it."

Silence.

"Don't be obstinate. It won't end well, Calix, I promise you."

"The Pythia worked magic," he burst out.

"Shut your filthy mouth." The words came slowly, each one spat out like a mouthful of rotten meat. "Don't you ever, *ever* speak such a lie in my presence again." Heavy breathing. "I think a lesson is in order."

A sharp scream cut the air. Nicodemus kicked the door wide and strode inside. The smell hit him in a foul wave. Old blood and fear sweat. It reminded him of the burrow he'd found his mother in. A dark-haired youth slumped in chains fixed to the wall, his eyes glazed.

"What's going on here?" Nico asked quietly.

The acolyte's face, which had been ruddy with rage, instantly shifted to a dimpled smile that didn't touch her eyes.

"Nothing. I'm simply minding the wi...the talisman, as I was instructed to do."

"Ah. Were you instructed to torture him?"

The smile slipped a notch.

"I was only reprimanding—"

Nico stared at her, gratified to see a flash of fear. "The Pythia has summoned you to her chambers. I wouldn't delay."

Thena scurried off. Nico studied Galen. He was young and sturdy, with the dark good looks of the Danai. But his face bore the ravages of suffering and bitterness. Nico knew the look well.

"Does she always treat you like that?"

Galen finally raised his eyes.

"No. She's usually much worse."

The iron collar made Nico's bile rise, though he understood its necessity. Still, he wouldn't condone Thena's bullying.

"I'll talk to her."

"Who are you?"

"My name is Nicodemus."

"That's not what I meant. *What* are you?"

Nico was taken aback. Had no one explained matters? "A daēva, like you."

Galen licked his lips. "I don't understand."

"I am a Vatra."

Nothing. Not a flicker of recognition.

Nico felt a sudden surge of anger. The other clans had erased his people from the histories as if they'd never even existed. Left them to die. At least the mortals still remembered.

"You can't be a daēva," Galen whispered. "I saw you work fire."

Nicodemus tamped down his fury. It wasn't this boy's fault.

"It's our birthright," he said, quoting the words Gaius had

ingrained in all of them. "Fire purifies. It's the only element that can't be polluted."

Galen looked at him like he was mad.

"Have you never wondered about the Kiln?" Nico snapped. "Have you never wondered who made the Gale and why fire is forbidden in Nocturne?"

There was a long pause as Galen considered this. "Not really, no."

"Fucking hell," Nico muttered.

The chains clanked as Galen shifted. "Tell me one thing."

Nico waited.

"What will she do with me? The Oracle?"

The raw plea in his eyes was too much. Nico couldn't afford to feel sorry for the talismans. Meb had been a nice enough kid too, under the grubby, feral exterior.

"I have to go," he said brusquely, turning away.

"Wait!" Galen's voice chased him out the door, fading as he strode down the corridor. "Please!"

Nicodemus hurried past the Shields of Apollo and down the long, winding steps that descended from the Acropolis. He wanted to be alone. To get as far as possible from the mingled smells of burning laurel and blood and whatever it was that oozed from the cracks beneath the temple. He'd return to the Archon's palace and try to repair the globe. He also had the talismans he'd taken from the emperor's collection to look over.

But as he walked through the crowded streets, he kept thinking about that iron collar, about Thena, and Nico felt a cold stab in his belly. The collars would work on any daēva, Vatras too. Would work on *him*, if he stepped out of line.

What exactly had Gaius told Domitia to do?

❧ 6 ☙

APOLLO'S ARROW

Thena strode across the yard, her face perfectly composed. But her heart thudded in her chest, a sickening stew of rage and confusion.

She knew the witch spoke truth. She'd seen it with her own eyes, the one called Nicodemus burning the Polemarch and the Oracle of Delphi summoning flames to dance on her fingertips. Neither of them had used spell dust. They worked elemental magic.

They were witches.

Fire witches.

In the holy Temple of Apollo.

The Pythia claimed she spoke for the Sun God, but that was another lie.

Thena's mind and soul rebelled at the thought of how she'd been used, but it was useless to pretend otherwise. Worse than useless. It would be cowardly, and she was not a coward.

So the question was, what did it mean? For the last two years, she'd listened to the Pythia and the Archon Basileus talking about the Vatra War. If they were fire witches, why hadn't they burned everything like they did before? The answer was obvious. Because they wanted the talismans. But for what exactly, she wasn't sure.

She entered the Temple, its lintel bearing the words *Know Thyself*.

For the first time, Thena felt lost. She could simply run away. But where would she go? Back to her father's farm? She couldn't imagine that mundane life anymore. She had done things, seen things her sisters would never understand.

And she had grown to enjoy wearing the bracelets, to revel in the power they gave her.

She could try to steal away with the Danai talisman. But she'd never get him past the Shields of Apollo. They guarded the temple day and night now.

Thena knew she was supposed to go straight to the Pythia, but her feet took a different path through the corridors, until she reached a storeroom on the eastern side—one she had not visited in weeks.

It was the place of her nightmares. Of her greatest shame.

The brazen bull gleamed in the torchlight, it's wicked horns curling to sharp points. She knelt by the hatch and pressed a trembling hand against the cool metal.

Flashes of memory shivered through her. The Pythia, urging her to climb inside. Those cold, ageless eyes.

If you are truly innocent, he will spare you....

And then:

May you be purified, child.

The smell of burning flesh. Her dress catching fire. Screams echoing in her ears.

Thena's hand fell to her legs, rubbing the scar tissue through the thin material of her gown.

And she saw the truth. It was not the god who had judged her, but the witch.

A trick.

The Pythia made her think Apollo was punishing her, when she summoned the flames herself.

Tears ran down Thena's face. She angrily brushed them aside. She still had a higher purpose. The witches were scheming to do something terrible, and she would watch and wait, like she did before.

I am the god's instrument. His shining arrow.

She touched one of the sharp, curling horns with a fingertip, then hurried to the adyton.

The Pythia sat on the tripod with her eyes closed. Once, Thena would have wondered what mystical secrets Apollo was revealing to her. She would have felt awe and a touch of jealousy. Now she knew better. It was all a sham. Thena erased the loathing from her expression and knelt at the Pythia's feet.

"You called for me, Mother?" she asked.

A long moment passed before the Pythia deigned to respond. Finally, her pale eyes slid open.

"How do you fare with the talisman?"

"I gave him his new name today. Calix."

"Names mean nothing. I want him broken."

"Yes, Mother. It takes time—"

"We don't have time, you stupid girl."

Thena fixed her eyes on the stone. "I won't fail you, Mother."

The Pythia stood. Suddenly, the room felt stifling. Sweat trickled down Thena's back.

"I still speak for the Sun God. Do you believe me?"

"Yes, Mother," Thena said meekly.

But the Pythia seemed to hear a false note in her voice. She seized a hank of Thena's hair and jerked her head back.

"Do you believe me?"

"Yes, yes!" Thena cried, wincing in pain. "You speak for the Sun God! You are the true Oracle!"

The Pythia's fingers tightened in her hair. "Have you told anyone what you saw the day Nicodemus came to the temple?"

"No," Thena panted. "No one, I swear."

"Good. If I find that you do, I will strip you of the bracelets and you will be nothing. A scullery scrubbing the temple floors for the rest of your life. Do you understand?"

Thena had to admit a grudging admiration. The witch knew her well. She could have threatened Thena's family, but she seemed to grasp that Thena didn't particularly care what happened to them. But to have the bracelets taken away? That would be worse than death.

Thena kissed the hem of the Pythia's gown. The lie came easily.

"Yes, Mother. I will never betray your trust again, I swear it."

The Pythia's fingers relaxed and she stroked Thena's hair like a child. "That is good. I don't wish to treat you so roughly, sun daughter, but I had to be sure. Leave me now."

Thena kissed her hand and walked out with as much dignity as she could muster, her scalp still stinging. On her thin cot that night, she thought of the many ways she would like to see the Pythia die. She thought of Demetrios, her pale Valkirin prince, and she thought of Darius. The one who had nearly broken her. She'd hoped taking his brother might ease the loss, but the slight resemblance between them somehow made it worse.

I will find you.

Thena's cheeks flushed with anger and a peculiar kind of desire. She arranged her raven hair so it fanned out against the coarse blanket.

Yes, I will, someday.

It was only a matter of time.

❧ 7 ❧

VICTOR'S FOLLY

Nazafareen stomped to the lip of the rock shelf, squinting through thin flurries of snow. She wanted to punch someone. Any Valkirin would do.

Atop the facing peak, the icebound fastness of Val Moraine caught a shaft of moonlight as the ragged clouds parted. Between it and the place she stood stretched a chasm so deep it seemed to have no bottom. And floating over that chasm like a bit of dandelion fluff was Darius, though at least they'd hung him the right way up. Nazafareen scowled as Frida strode up next to her.

"Why are his eyes closed?" she demanded. "Is he unconscious? Did you hurt him?"

Frida shook her head. "The Danai sleeps. He has nerve, I'll give him that."

Nazafareen clenched her fist. Part of her almost laughed. The rest was quietly appalled. "He must be freezing."

"Even the Danai don't feel the cold as mortals do. He'll live."

The sight still made her skin crawl. What if the bonds accidentally loosened?

"Well, you have to take him down," she said briskly. "You've made your point. If you want me to soften Victor up, it won't make my task easier to have his son twisting in the wind."

Frida crooked a finger. Darius swept toward the ledge, blinking sleepily.

"Careful with him now," Nazafareen hissed.

A moment later, Darius was deposited on solid ground again. She went to his side, reaching for his poor bruised face, but it struck an invisible barrier. She let the hand fall with a sigh.

"How's your jaw? Broken?"

"Don't think so." He spoke tightly and she could see it pained him.

"You'll be free soon, I swear it. They're letting me go inside. Any message for your father?"

His blue eyes flickered. "Leave it to you. Megaera said she... taught you some choice obscenities."

Nazafareen smiled. Her heart ached with tenderness and fury both. Someday, she'd pay Broken Nose back for that blow. Oh yes, she'd break something else, something he valued more than that lump of flesh on his ugly face.

"It's time," Runar called gruffly.

Darius gave her a brief nod.

"I'll just wait here," he mumbled.

She gave him a twisted smile and walked over to Runar. He stood near the edge with Frida and Stefán—and Katrin, who stared daggers at her.

"We'll ride together, Breaker," Katrin said. "Be sure to tighten your buckles. The crosswinds can be strong."

If this was a veiled threat, Nazafareen paid it no mind. Her gaze was fixed on the dark spot across the chasm, where the tunnel led inside to Val Moraine.

"Do they know we're coming?"

Katrin didn't reply. She gave a piercing whistle and an abbadax slunk over, its yellow eyes staring at Nazafareen with baleful intensity. Katrin mounted with an acrobatic leap, reins in her hands and gaze fixed straight ahead.

Nazafareen took a step forward and then Frida was at her side, showing her how to climb up without getting slashed to bits. A second saddle had been placed behind Katrin, with a waist harness and straps to secure her legs. Frida started to attach them, but Nazafareen pushed her hand away.

"I can do it."

The buckles posed little challenge; she buckled her sword on every day. But the waist harness was another matter. She sensed Katrin's impatience as she fumbled with the straps. Finally, Nazafareen managed to get herself situated. She surveyed the assembled Valkirins coldly.

"If you touch one hair on Darius's head, the deal is off," she said. "I'll use the diamond to entomb you all in ice."

Runar waved a hand. "Bring it out and you'll have him back. As we agreed."

"I'll watch over him while you're gone!" Megaera called as Katrin whispered a command and the abbadax tested its wings.

It ran for the edge in an ungainly waddle that didn't inspire confidence. Darkness loomed ahead. She sucked in a breath as it dove over the edge of the ravine, tilting into the powerful currents. Nazafareen's harness went taut with strain. Her weight shifted hard to the left. The whole apparatus seemed to *slide* a bit. She wondered if perhaps it wouldn't have been prudent to let Frida attach everything correctly, and then the abbadax leveled out, flapping hard.

The wall of ice surrounding Val Moraine drew closer. It appeared smooth as glass except for a semicircular hole about ten paces across and jagged at the edges. Fifty paces away, they hovered on an updraft and Katrin raised her empty hands, kicking Nazafareen to do the same. A lone figure appeared in the recesses of the tunnel. It wore white leathers like a Valkirin, but Nazafareen caught a glimpse of waist-length black hair. There was only one daēva she knew who fit that description.

"Mithre!" she called, throwing back her hood.

The figure moved toward the tunnel entrance and a familiar face emerged from the blue-tinged shadows. Dark and vulpine, with a hooked nose and thin lips. He went rigid with surprise.

"Nazafareen?"

"I bear a message. Let us land!"

Mithre scanned the empty skies. He beckoned once, then disappeared back down the tunnel. The space looked very narrow. Nazafareen eyed it doubtfully, though she knew Katrin had done this once before. The abbadax wheeled around in a wide circle. They passed over Darius and the Valkirins waiting on the other side. Then the mount banked sharply and flew straight at the tunnel mouth, gathering speed as it went. At the last instant, Katrin leaned forward, pressing flat against its serpentine neck. With a curse, Nazafareen ducked down as the creature tucked its wings against its body and skidded into the tunnel, using its claws to arrest the slide.

A moment slower and she would have lost her head—something Katrin had clearly been hoping for. Nazafareen gritted her teeth but said nothing. After about twenty paces, the tunnel opened into a much larger space, thick with a pungent, musky smell. Pens stretched to either side and she saw more abbadax, though they hunched unmoving against the inner wall. Only the creatures' reptilian eyes showed they were alive.

Katrin guided her mount to the farthest of the pens. The three abbadax there made excited chirps as they caught the new scent. Nazafareen undid her buckles and slid to the ground. Katrin ignored her, muttering soft words to the creatures.

"We'd given you up for dead," Mithre said, striding forward. "When I saw Darius out there...."

"I know. So much has happened, Mithre. I'll explain it all, but the most important thing is that the Valkirins are willing to strike another deal. Where's Victor?"

Something indecipherable flickered across Mithre's face. "Inside."

Nazafareen turned to Katrin, who stood stiffly next to the abbadax, watching them.

"Wait here."

"I'm coming with you," she snapped.

"No, you're not. You'll muck it up."

Katrin's green eyes burned. "That's not what you agreed to."

Nazafareen sighed. "Swear you'll keep your mouth shut and your sword in the scabbard. Swear it on your honor. Or you stay right here."

The muscles in Katrin's neck tightened. Nazafareen planted her feet, ready to brawl. But then the Valkirin woman seemed to think better of it.

"I swear," she muttered scornfully. "On my honor."

Nazafareen brushed past her and followed Mithre into the keep, Katrin trailing behind. It was dark and almost as cold as outside. They passed through long corridors of naked stone and finally reached a heavy bronze door. Mithre stopped. Katrin lounged against the far wall, watching them closely.

"Victor's inside," he said in a low voice. One hand massaged the other in a nervous gesture, rubbing the webbing between thumb and forefinger. "You should know, the occupation has taken a toll."

"What do you mean?" Nazafareen asked. "Was he injured?"

"Not physically. But he keeps his own counsel. Barely speaks to me anymore. I get the feeling he's determined to still *win* somehow, whatever the hell that means." He paused. "When we told him Darius was being displayed like a trophy head, he laughed. Claimed it was a Valkirin trick."

Nazafareen frowned. "Don't worry, I'll set him straight. I always got on well with Victor."

In truth, she saw more than a little of herself in Darius's father. They were both headstrong and inclined to violence over diplomacy. Where Darius exuded chill calm, Victor was bluster and reckless charm. And he had a soft spot for her.

They used to spar together in a clearing in the forest. He would call her *Water Dog* to rile her up and break her concentration, but he always said it with a teasing grin. And the one time he'd accidentally nicked her with his blade—a scratch, really—Victor had been beside himself with remorse, fussing over her like a mother hen. He had a tender side, though she suspected it mainly came out with Delilah.

"It'll be fine," Nazafareen said. "Trust me."

Mithre looked dubious but pushed the door open. The chamber beyond seemed familiar. She realized she'd seen it through the globe. A long rectangular table occupied the center of the room. The shadows were so thick it took her a moment to make out the man who sat at its head.

"Victor?"

He looked up, his face catching the blue light of a single lumen crystal. Nazafareen recoiled at the sight. His strong jaw sagged beneath the weight of loose skin. Streaks of white winged his raven hair and his eyes were cavernous hollows, full of suspicion.

"Who's there?" he demanded.

"It's me. Nazafareen."

Victor's gaze narrowed as he studied her, but then his expression softened.

"Is it truly you?"

She walked over and took his hand. It was freezing.

"It's me."

"I thought the chimera...." He squeezed her fingers so hard it hurt. "Did Delilah find you?"

"She did. She was intending to return here, but she's with Tethys now."

He closed his eyes. "Thank the gods."

"She's gone to fight the Pythia, Victor. And you should be at her side."

"The Pythia?" He looked lost for a moment, his eyes unfocused.

"The Oracle of Delphi. She holds captive daēvas." Nazafareen paused. "She had Darius for a time, but he escaped."

Victor hunched forward. "I knew it was a trick," he muttered.

"Listen to me," Nazafareen said firmly. "It's not a trick. Your son is out there, in Valkirin custody." She pressed on before he could ask why they'd come. "I'm here to make you an offer. They're willing to trade Darius for Val Moraine and the diamond."

Victor pulled his hand free and slipped it inside his coat.

"No more deals," he snarled. "They can't be trusted."

Nazafareen wanted to throttle him, but she kept her voice even and soothing. "Runar swore it to me on a talisman that compels the truth. He said he would let you and your Danai go home. Stefán of Val Altair swore the same, and so did Frida of Val Tourmaline."

His mouth set, thin and crooked like an obstinate old man. "Damn Darius for putting me in this position."

At least Katrin had the sense to stay out of sight in the hall. Nazafareen could only imagine Victor's reaction if he saw her there. But Mithre, who'd been hovering in the doorway, strode forward at these words. His face was tight with suppressed fury.

"Damn Darius? You should be thanking your lucky stars they're willing to trade! We've been here far too long. Half of us are dead, and the other half are drunk all the time. No one's seen Arjan in days. He either stumbled over the edge taking a piss, or, far more likely, decided to jump. Tomorrow, it will be another." His voice dripped with contempt. "It's over, Victor. It was over a long time ago. You're the only one who can't see that."

Victor lip curled in a sneer. "Cowards. I won't cede the Maiden Keep, not for some—"

Nazafareen seized a fistful of Victor's coat and pulled him closer, until they were inches apart. She could smell his bitter breath.

"You listen to me, Victor Dessarian," she said softly. "There's a gate not far from here. Or you can walk home if you choose. I don't care. But I will *not* let you sign Darius's death warrant."

The muscles of his face jerked as he tried to form words. Nazafareen rode straight over him.

"Your son was chained by the Oracle of Delphi and I'll not see him suffer at the hands of the Valkirins. So you'll put your bloody pride aside, for Darius's sake if not your own."

Victor tried to pull away, but Nazafareen held him fast. Once he would have shaken her off like a mastiff with a flea. She peered into his flat, glittering eyes. He was so far from the man she remembered, they might be two different people.

"Things have happened while you holed up at Val Moraine. There is a fourth daēva clan, Victor. They work fire. The Danai and Valkirins must unite against them or we'll die."

"Lies!" he shrieked, spittle flying into her face. "You're with *them*, aren't you? They sent you here to rob me of my prize. You treacherous little—" He trailed off at the rasp of Mithre's sword leaving the scabbard. Nazafareen hadn't even heard the daēva move, but now he loomed next to them.

"Take it, Nazafareen," Mithre said in a dead voice. "It's on a chain around his neck."

Victor tried to push back from the table to draw his own blade but Nazafareen planted her boot on his hand, trapping it against his thigh. She saw a glint of gold and snatched at it, yanking hard. As the chain broke, Victor let out an unearthly howl that echoed through the silent keep.

"The fuck?" Katrin burst into the chamber. Her hand rested on her sword, but she hadn't drawn it, not yet. When Victor saw her, he scrabbled away, his face contorted in rage.

"Traitors," he spat. He ran for the door but Katrin blocked his way.

"Let him go," Nazafareen snapped. She held up the chain and showed her the huge white diamond dangling from its setting. "I have the talisman."

Katrin hesitated. A look of mutual loathing passed between her and Victor.

"Let him go!"

She glared at Nazafareen but stepped aside. Victor stumbled through the door, vanishing into the shadows beyond. Mithre eyed the diamond with revulsion.

"Get rid of it as fast as you can," he told Nazafareen. "It's a foul thing. I suspected, but I wasn't sure until now." He sheathed his sword, tension giving way to weariness. "I'll tell the others we're going home. And I'll find Victor. He'll come back to himself in time."

Nazafareen nodded. "I'll warn the Valkirins about it. Where did Victor come by the diamond?"

"It belonged to Eirik. The Kafsnjórs used it during the Iron Wars to defend the keep. Culach told him about it."

Nazafareen slipped the diamond into her pocket. It was an icy weight, but she felt nothing from it. No taint of evil. Perhaps it only worked on those who were already susceptible. Or maybe it required time and solitude to work its magic.

Either way, she was eager to be rid of it. But she had another task first.

"Where is Culach?" she asked. "I need to see him. It won't take long."

Katrin sneered. "Why? So you can taunt him?"

Nazafareen ignored her. "Mithre, where is he?"

The daēva looked at her oddly. "His room, most likely."

"Don't tell him in advance. Just take me there."

Mithre studied her for a moment. "Well, I suppose you can

handle yourself. And he's blind, else I wouldn't risk it. But don't expect a warm reception."

"I don't." She turned to Katrin. "Wait at the stables." When Katrin opened her mouth, Nazafareen held her gaze, giving her a glimpse of the beast that had been straining at its leash for the last day. "Just do it."

She hadn't raised her voice, but this time, Katrin didn't argue.

❦ 8 ❧

A VISITOR FROM BEYOND

"That's not the price you quoted me."

The Marakai sighed. He was sweating heavily in the desert heat, ebony skin glistening with moisture despite the dampened cloth wrapped around his forehead. "I gave you an *estimate*. The water is much deeper than I thought. It's not my fault if you drained your well so quickly."

The corners of his father's mouth turned down. Farrumohr knew the look well.

"It's always the same with you, isn't it? Think you can blackmail me into paying twice what we agreed."

The Marakai shrugged. "Take it or leave it. You won't find anyone to do the work for less." He glanced at the dark-haired Danai who waited patiently at his side. "You did warn me about this guy. I should have listened."

Farrumohr's father bristled. He was a powerfully built man with a sharp nose and sunken eyes that peered out at the world with perpetual suspicion. Once, his hair had been flame red like Farrumohr's, but the years had leached the color out, leaving it a faded rust. Stooped shoulders made him appear shorter than he was. Sometimes Farrumohr felt his father was being slowly erased and one day he might simply fade away altogether, like the shimmering heat mirages on the horizon.

His father could be hard, but he was smart—smarter than the other Vatras, who let themselves be fleeced without a word of protest.

"What do they say about me?" he demanded.

The Marakai laughed. "That you're tighter than a knot soaked in saltwater. That you'll spend hours under this cursed sun arguing down the value of a day's labor and still go off grumbling—even when whoever you hired finally accepts a pauper's wages just to see the back of you." He sniffed. "Dig for the water yourself. We won't do it for less than two talismans of summoning and three of shrinking."

Farrumohr saw his father's face darken and thought he might burn them on the spot. He'd never actually done such a thing, but he'd talked about it, especially after the well ran low. He blamed the Marakai. They'd delved too shallow on purpose so he'd have to hire them again to fix it.

His family's homestead was one of the smallest and meanest in the Western Barrens. Farrumohr often heard his parents fighting about it. His mother would rail at his father, every word audible through the thin walls. She cursed the day she laid eyes on him. Cursed his laziness and obstinacy. Sometimes his father yelled back. But mostly he just suffered in silence. Farrumohr knew her anger was displaced. She couldn't see that they were being punished for standing up to the outrageous demands of the other clans.

"Five talismans for a simple well?" his father demanded. "You're criminals." He clenched his fists. "I ought to teach you a lesson. One you'll never forget."

Farrumohr felt a sickening mix of fear and excitement. But then his mother's shrill voice came from the house, calling him in to supper, and his father backed down, as he always did.

"Liars and thieves," he muttered. "Just get out."

The Danai and Marakai glanced at each other, smirking in shared amusement.

"Get off my land!" his father shrieked. "Go!"

They sauntered away, shaking their heads.

Farrumohr watched his father trudge to the house, shoulders slumped, and wondered what he might have done if *she* hadn't interrupted. If she hadn't beaten him down. And for an instant, he felt such a white-hot rage it made him tremble.

After that, none of the other clans would set foot on their homestead. The well ran dry. Their little oasis withered and died. And the fights got worse.

Farrumohr knew his mother despised him. She'd always been affectionate with Julia, but she never so much as hugged him or spoke a kind word. His father saw what she was like and tried to make up for it. He told Farrumohr that he was a special boy. He encouraged him to experiment with talismans, praising his first clumsy efforts. His father taught him the most important things. Farrumohr could see that his mother was killing him slowly. Sucking the life from him like a lich.

Even at the tender age of eleven, he understood that something had to be done.

No one expressed surprise when she disappeared. They'd fallen into poverty and his father assumed she up and left. None of the other clans would trade with them now. Their talismans sat in the corner of the workroom, gathering dust. His father finally swallowed his pride and tried to hire the Marakai to fix the well. They refused. So he asked for help from the neighbors. *It's your own fault*, they said, and turned him away.

All except for one: Gaius's family.

For the sake of the two motherless children, they agreed to take his father on as a gardener and allow them to stay at the sprawling homestead. Farrumohr knew his father found the situation deeply humiliating. The Vatras were a hard-working, independent people. They'd tamed the desert and tending your own land was a point of pride.

But Farrumohr accepted the new situation without complaint. Unlike their peers, who often singled him out for ridicule, Gaius was friendly. He sensed the older boy's potential right away and worked hard to cultivate his interest. In time, Farrumohr became Gaius's playmate and confidante, flattering his ego and stoking the flames of his ambition.

Gaius's family treated them decently, but everyone knew the story. At school, the other children either ignored him or stared sidelong, whispering together, like he was some kind of freak. Without Gaius's protection, Farrumohr knew it would have been much worse. But they loved Gaius as much as they hated Farrumohr.

In private, his father nursed his hatred. He had grand plans to settle the score with the other clans, but they never seemed to come to fruition.

I'll help you, father, Farrumohr would say. *Please, tell me what to do!*

And his father would pat him on the shoulder. *You're a good boy. Never, ever trust them. They want what's ours. Always have.*

And then one day, Farrumohr went looking for his father to show him a new talisman he'd made, one that could summon water from great depths. His heart pounded with excitement. His teachers had been impressed, praising his ingenuity and aptitude. He knew they didn't like him, even though he was an eager pupil and top of his class. Some of them even seemed a bit scared of him, which Farrumohr didn't mind. But it wasn't their opinions he cared about. He would give the talisman to his father and they could go home.

As an added bonus, he thought he might be able to use the talisman to siphon away the water from the neighbors' wells. Let *their* lands wither and die, he thought with glee. Father will love that.

Farrumohr had found him curled up next to the broom he used to sweep the constantly encroaching sands from the elegant patio of Gaius's house. His mouth and eyes were open, but his skin was cold.

They said his heart gave out, but Farrumohr knew what had killed him.

Who had killed him.

A small, ignoble death for such a great man.

No one came to the funeral, not even Julia. She'd moved away by then, to her little house out in the desert. Farrumohr buried his father's body at their old homestead. Afterwards, he wandered through the empty rooms, filled with drifting sand. He lay down in the tiny room of his boyhood, too exhausted and bitter to weep.

He dreamt of fire.

A hand touched his shoulder, gently shaking.

Farrumohr? Wake up, it's Julia....

CULACH JERKED TO CONSCIOUSNESS WITH A STRANGLED CRY. Someone was in his chamber, he felt certain of it. He sat up, the furs falling away from his bare skin. Not Mina. He knew her scent. It was a woman, though, and she smelled familiar. But from where?

Then she spoke and he knew.

"Culach?"

A soft voice, and not menacing. But his heart thudded painfully in his chest. Lines of phantom flame traced his scars. For a terrible instant, he felt the roaring heat of the flames, the agony as something inside him tore loose from its moorings.

"Get away," he cried, his voice high and cracked with fear.

Ghosts. The keep was full of them. She was dead, torn to

pieces by the chimera, and now she'd come to haunt him. To take her revenge.

"Please. I only want to speak with you."

Culach groped for his sword. He always kept it leaning against the wall next to his bed, more out of habit than any expectation of needing it—or being able to stab anyone if he did. His hand struck the blade and it clattered to the floor. He dove after it, fingers questing across the stone.

"Return to the shadowlands," he growled, his hand closing around the hilt. He brandished it in the direction of the specter. "This blade is pure iron. Anathema to your sort. I shall smite—"

"Um." The voice moved closer. He shrank back. "I'm not dead, if that's what you think."

Culach froze. The voice sounded so *reasonable*. But she couldn't be here. It was impossible. He couldn't think of a single thing to say.

"May I sit?"

Bloody hell.

He waved the sword in a noncommittal fashion and heard light footsteps move to a chair and a body settle into it with a sigh.

"I know you wanted me dead and I don't blame you for it." She sounded nervous and determined. "Not too much, at any rate. But there's things you need to hear first, and then if you want me to leave, I will."

Culach lowered the sword. He was suddenly aware he had no shirt on and pulled the furs over his shoulders.

"First, I didn't mean to hurt you." She paused. "There was something waiting just inside the gate, Culach. Something dark and evil. I saw it latch onto you when you passed through."

His gut tightened. Part of him remembered that too, though he'd been unsure if it was just a fever dream.

"When you got to the other side, you weren't yourself. I don't know you well, but I don't think your intention was to slaughter everyone." Her voice quavered slightly. "You called them a pile of corpses. I saw flames in your eyes. And then that thing inside you.... It tried to take *me*."

He stared at the darkness, swept into the undertow of memory.

"I did what I had to. I fought back. I drove it out. And in the process...." She trailed off.

He swallowed hard. "I was blinded."

And severed from the Nexus. But he wouldn't—couldn't—tell her that.

"Yes. I nearly died myself, but Darius carried me back through the gate to Nocturne, where the fire magic burned itself out."

"This thing," he said at last, a horrible suspicion taking shape in his mind. "Do you know what it was?"

"Not for certain. But there was a creature your sister kept. Almost like a pet. A...demon, for want of a better word. Its name was Farrumohr."

The hair on Culach's arms rose up. "Farrumohr?"

"That's what Neblis called it. She asked if I wanted to meet it, and I didn't." A strangled laugh. "But I think I saw it once. A creature of—"

"Shadow and flame," Culach finished, the words a whisper.

"Yes. You *do* remember." She sounded deeply relieved.

"Some. I thought I'd imagined it." He scrubbed a hand through his hair. "I know who Farrumohr is. Or was. He's been dead for a thousand years."

"Dead, but not dead," she said grimly.

"So it seems." He fisted the fur blankets, a rancid taste in his mouth. "Since that day, I've dreamt of him. He was an advisor to King Gaius of the Vatras."

She drew a sharp breath. "He was a *Vatra*?"

"Not just any Vatra. Farrumohr schemed to start the war. He despised the other clans and manipulated Gaius into an attachment with a Danai girl who spurned him."

"They nearly destroyed the world over a woman?" She muttered an oath. "That's the stupidest thing I've ever heard."

Culach smiled at her vehemence. "I don't think Gaius would have gone along with it, except that the Viper—that's what the others called Farrumohr—did everything in his power to turn the king against the other clans." He frowned. "But it was more than that. Farrumohr forged a talismanic crown. It gave him a pathway to poison the king's mind, and perhaps the rest of them as well."

"Just like the diamond," she muttered.

Culach laid the sword across his knees, fingers absently stroking the blade. "Some talismans are forged not only using the elements but also the emotions of the adept. It gives them added power—like the chimera. Farrumohr murdered his own sister to make the crown. It needed grief and hatred. But that wasn't enough. He whipped himself raw...." Culach trailed off, repulsed by the memory.

"Sounds like a charming fellow. Do you know how he died?"

"I've dreamt it a hundred times," he said grimly. "He was fleeing into the Kiln when the sands swallowed him up. Some kind of sinkhole. The other Vatras saw it happen, but none stopped to help him. He was long in dying."

"That must have been awful for you," she said softly.

"By the end, once I knew what sort of man he was, I welcomed it."

"I can imagine. So you dreamed of him because he inhabited your body, however briefly," Nazafareen said musingly. "Some... residue of the man was left behind."

Culach suppressed a shudder. "Residue? Bloody hell, I hope not. Other than the dreams, there doesn't seem to be any connection. I'm not his puppet." He paused, flushing. "But if you hadn't driven him off, I would have been."

"It was self-preservation," she replied. "But you're welcome."

Despite her mild tone, Culach's shame deepened. "The

chimera.... That was Eirik's doing, though I didn't stop him. He asked my permission and I gave it. I take full responsibility."

"Forget it. I unmade them."

He blinked. Well, of course she did. "And Victor's son?"

She gave a mirthless laugh. "Oh, he outwitted the chimera, so your hands are clean. But now your cousins hold him prisoner."

"The other holdfasts?"

"Don't worry, they've agreed to trade him for that diamond you gave Victor. It's why I'm here."

Now Culach did detect an accusing note. "Victor asked for it." He paused. "So they're coming in?"

"Soon enough. But listen, Culach. The Vatras are trying to return. One has escaped the Kiln already."

"That's what Gerda said. So it's true."

"Gerda?"

"My late and great grandmother."

She was silent. "The one Victor killed, you mean."

"Oh, Victor killed her, but only after she killed Halldóra. Gerda had a notion that we ought to ally with the Vatras against the Danai. Halldóra disagreed."

"I'm relieved to hear it. I never would have thought Victor capable of cold-blooded murder, but I wondered." She sighed. "We're seeking the talismans that stopped the Vatras before. We already found the Marakai and she's safe. The Valkirin is a woman named Katrin Aigirsdottir."

Culach's eyebrows climbed a few inches. "Katrin?"

He heard Nazafareen rise. "She's waiting for me in the stables. Perhaps we can speak more later. I would hear about your dreams. But I must return to Darius—"

"Wait," Culach called as she moved to the door. "I know who the Danai talisman is."

Her footsteps halted. "Who?"

"Galen. But he was taken by a mortal woman from Delphi."

Her voice hardened. "What woman?"

"No one told you? A Danai and a Valkirin showed up here just before Victor deployed the ice defenses. They were with two mortals. Claimed to have stolen a Talisman of Folding to escape from the Oracle of Delphi."

"The Oracle? Darius was captured by her as well."

"I wonder if he knows them. It turned out to be a ploy to get inside the holdfast. They were hunting for the heirs to the power. Mina, Galen's mother, says he's weak in earth power—"

"Galen? Are you certain?" Nazafareen swore richly. "How did they escape?"

"I don't know. Likely the same talisman. But the woman, Thena—"

"*Thena* was here?"

He blinked at the murderous rage in her voice.

"You know her?"

"Darius does. She was the one who tortured him. How long ago did they leave?"

"A few days. I'm a bit fuzzy on how many exactly."

He heard a sound that might have been her teeth grinding.

"I learned about the plot from Daníel. He's the heir to Val Tourmaline. We found him in with the abbadax. He was in rough shape. This woman, Thena, had convinced him to play along. He eventually rebelled, but he let her leave." Culach couldn't keep the disgust from his voice. To his surprise, Nazafareen didn't erupt in fury.

"Thena's methods are beyond vile," she said. "Daníel can't be blamed. But don't worry, the Danai are going to Delphi as we speak to liberate the Oracle's prisoners." She swept toward him and a small, warm hand clasped his own. "They'll get Galen back. You should go with Victor and Mithre. I'll make sure you're given safe passage." She squeezed his hand once and let it drop. "Take good care, Culach Kafsnjór."

He felt a lump in his throat. "And you, Nazafareen."

She moved toward the door and paused.

"Something strange," she muttered.

"What is it?"

"Like we're being watched. Don't you feel it?"

Culach wordlessly shook his head.

He heard her pacing the room. She stopped before the chair Mina had thrown her dress over. Fabric rustled as she tossed the garment aside and sucked in a breath.

"Where did you get this?" she demanded.

Culach's frustration rose. "Get what?"

"Sorry. It looks like a globe."

"Oh, that. We found it in Gerda's chambers. Do you know what it does?"

There was a long pause. Then Nazafareen snarled, "You!"

❧ 9 ❧

THE MASK FALLS AWAY

I t happened almost by accident.

After returning to the Archon's palace, Nicodemus passed a few pleasant hours with the servant girl who'd flirted with him at him at breakfast. She had coarse black hair and a sweetly innocent mouth, though her eyes looked far more businesslike than the rest of her. She probably thought him a rich lord, perhaps a relation of Basileus. She clearly had no idea Nico was a Vatra because she wasn't afraid of him in the least.

In fact, *she* had pursued *him*, offering to draw a bath and then hanging about when he disrobed, blushing prettily as if she'd never seen a naked man before. Nico doubted this, but he desperately wanted to erase the memory of that stinking cell, and other than raiding the Archon's wine cellars again—which he'd sworn to himself he wouldn't do—she was the quickest path to oblivion he could think of.

They'd rolled around in Archon Basileus's bed and she'd finally fallen asleep, one arm flung wide like a child. Nico still wasn't tired so he decided to have a look at Domitia's globe. It was a complex talisman to say the least. Whoever had designed the globes found it amusing to have the glass orb show random weather scenes, but that aspect didn't seem connected to its true purpose of Seeking. No, the real power lay in the runes at the base.

He turned it over in his hands, probing with delicate weaves of fire and air. As sometimes happened when he spent time in the emperor's collection, a maudlin feeling came over him. How much knowledge had been lost, never to be found again? He could use talismans, but had no understanding of how to forge one from scratch. Yet Nico had learned a few things in his studies.

He was examining the melted runes at the base, wondering if they could be fixed, when the girl woke with a gasp and dashed off, saying she was late to lay the dining room for supper and the cook would have her hide. Nico barely heard. He could sense the places within the talisman where the currents were distorted. The runes were merely a focal point for the power. So he'd done something with fire and earth that felt right, and immediately they'd begun to glow blue.

He had idly thought of the Breaker and now....

Here she was. Glaring at him.

And holding her own globe.

His first thought was that he wished he wasn't lying on the Archon's ridiculous bed, though why that mattered, Nico wasn't sure. Yes, the décor was tacky, but it's not as if he held any moral high ground.

His second thought was that he was glad she wasn't in the room with him.

And his third was that he could use her somehow, if he was smart and careful.

"I see you found my talisman," he said mildly.

She scowled. "It's not yours. It belongs to the emperor of Tjanjin. You stole it."

"That's a bit harsh. I thought of it as borrowing."

"Well, it's been returned to its rightful owner."

He frowned, digesting this bit of information. "So you found another one."

She bit her lip. She realized she shouldn't have said that. Why? Because it offered a clue to where she was, that's why.

Now she squinted at the bed, obviously trying to figure out the same thing about him. "I see sunlight coming in the window," she murmured. "You're somewhere in Solis." She sounded surprised. Her gaze wandered over the naked, gilded statues. "A house of ill repute?"

"I'm staying with a friend." Nico smiled. "And you're in Nocturne. I see lumen crystals. But the Danai don't build with stone so you must be with the Valkirins." Added to the fact that she had a globe, it wasn't hard to piece together. "You're at Val Moraine, aren't you?"

Her face didn't change, but Nico knew he was right. Then another voice cut in, distinctly male, though too low for him to make out the words. Nico pulled the view back and saw she wasn't alone. A large Valkirin sat on the edge of a bed, a sword across his knees. His gaze was oddly vacant.

"Who are you with?"

"None of your business," she snapped.

"Where's Gerda? What have you done to her?"

"So you *did* know her."

"We spoke a few times. She was a sweet old lady."

The Valkirin made a choking sound.

"She's dead," Nazafareen said. "I didn't kill her, if that's what you think." She sounded a tad defensive. Her gaze hardened. "Listen, you won't win this fight. The clans are uniting against you. You lost Meb and you'll never get the others now."

Nico heaved a discouraged sigh. "Now that you put it like that, of course I can see you're right. It's hopeless. You hold all the cards." He scratched his head. "Except one. Almost forgot about him. What's his name again?" Nico snapped his fingers. "Galen! That's it."

She went blank again, but behind the mask of self-control he saw anger, and even a touch of fear.

"I know precisely where he is," Nico said. "About a ten-minute walk from here. But we also both know that he's useless until you break his ward. So perhaps we can come to an arrangement."

"What have you done to the boy?" the Valkirin demanded.

"I won't say he's well, but there's been no permanent damage. Yet." He leaned forward, his mind racing. "I don't wish Galen harm. And we don't have to be enemies. I want the Gale down, but it's for my own reasons. Personal reasons. If you just—"

Nico tensed as the door to the Archon's bedroom flew open. Domitia strode inside, Basileus at her heels, looking terrified. Livid spots of color burned her cheeks.

"Negotiating behind my back?" she said tightly.

His own temper rose up in a red tide. He cast a furious look at the Archon, who quavered. "How dare you come bursting in here?"

"That's *my* globe," she grated.

Nico felt the heat building and dove from the bed an instant before it erupted in flames. The silk sheets went up like parchment, curling and blackening. Basileus uttered an incoherent sound of distress. Domitia made a sharp slashing gesture and the flames subsided, leaving a heap of charred wood and the lingering smell of smoke.

In three strides, she was at his side, wrenching the globe away. She peered into its depths.

"Nazafareen?" she whispered, her face taut and pale.

Nico almost felt sorry for the Breaker. She'd clearly had no idea. Not a bleeding clue. But to her credit, she recovered quickly.

"So you know my name," she said. "What shall I call you? Not the Pythia. Not the Oracle of Delphi. Those are false titles. Masks of convenience."

Domitia devoured her image in the globe, her lips slightly parted, eyes soft, like a woman pining after an absent lover. There was something greedy and disturbing in it.

NEMESIS

"How I've wished to speak with you."

"Your name, Vatra."

"Is it important to you?"

"I like to know who it is I'm going to kill."

Domitia smiled indulgently. It was obvious she liked this girl despite everything. Perhaps *because* of everything.

"I'll tell you when I see you."

The Breaker didn't say anything. Nico could tell she was examining this new piece of the puzzle, turning it this way and that, to see how it fit with the rest. It didn't take her long to grasp the new picture. Her amber eyes widened, very slightly. She began to rub the stump of her right wrist in a distracted manner.

"You see now," Domitia said, with the bright tone of a teacher bestowing praise. "Very good. Yes, the Danai are coming. They expect to face a mortal army. Perhaps two or three captive daēvas." She studied Nazafareen. "And now you intend to save them. How could you do otherwise? They sheltered you when the Valkirins wanted your head. Well, you can certainly try, though I don't think you'll make it in time."

Nico expected threats or curses, but the Breaker surprised him.

"What is it you want?" she asked calmly.

"Meet me at the Gale. If you do, I'll spare the Danai. And once Galen has unraveled the line of storms, you may have him back. He's of no further use to me anyway."

Nazafareen nodded thoughtfully. "I'm not in Solis. You must give me three days to get there."

"One," Domitia countered with a chill smile. "You have one."

She released the flows on the globe and turned to Nicodemus. Her anger had vanished, replaced by wry amusement.

"If stupidity was a crime, you'd pass the rest of your days in the Polemarch's dungeons." She slipped the globe into a fold of her white gown. "Did it never occur to you that the girl you defiled this afternoon might be one of my spies? Oh, of course

89

not. I'm sure you thought she couldn't resist your masculine charms."

She reached out to pat his cheek and Nico jerked his head back. As often happened in his dealings with Domitia, he felt helplessly outmatched.

"Poor Basileus had nothing to do with it, so don't go and burn him up in a snit." She drew a deep breath and gazed at them both. "The army will march for the Umbra when Hecate rises. We'll intercept the Danai there and inform them of the situation. They will accompany us to the Gale as hostages. If needed, we'll make an example of one or two. That ought to settle them down." Her gaze grew distant. "I told you, Nico. I told you she would come to us."

He didn't respond as she strode to the door, where two Shields of Apollo waited to escort her back to the temple. Before it had closed, Basileus was on his knees, ashen and trembling.

"My lord, please, I swear I didn't know. It's as she said, the girl—"

"Hush." Nico stared at the charred bed. "I believe you."

"Thank the gods." He rose and staggered over to a half-empty decanter left over from the night before. Basileus drank straight from the jug and wiped his mouth with his sleeve.

"My lord, when the Gale comes down...." His Adam's apple worked convulsively for a moment. "You'll tell them, won't you? Tell them how I cooperated. I can still be of use."

Nico rubbed his forehead.

Nazafareen.

The name sounded exotic and foreign to Nico's ears, not Greek or Persian, definitely not Tjanjinese. When had Domitia learned it? And what else did she know that she wasn't sharing?

"You can be of use right now," he said. "Dismiss the servants. All of them, down to the last stable boy. If I am betrayed again, we'll both know who did it."

"Immediately, my lord."

Nico didn't bother correcting the man. The title seemed to reassure Basileus. It was something he understood.

"And open the shutters. Let's have some fresh air."

Basileus scurried to the windows and threw them wide. The last vestiges of smoke blew away on a fresh breeze.

"Shall I carry out your order now?" Basileus wondered. "The first one, I mean, about the servants." Each word was enunciated with weary precision, like a man on his deathbed dispensing his final wishes.

"Not just yet."

A quick check of the hall confirmed that no one was out there, ear pressed to the door. Nico closed it again. He sat down and propped his feet on the desk, carelessly easing a pile of parchment to the floor. He looked at Basileus for a long moment.

"Despite this lapse, I'm going to take you into my confidence," he said. "First, what did Domitia promise you to make you her creature?"

The Archon blinked. "Domitia, my lord?"

"The Oracle. That's her name. The one she didn't want to give up just now."

"Ah, I see."

"Well? What was the carrot she dangled before your nose?"

Basileus fingered his chain of office. "She said she would make me Tyrant of Delphi."

"Of course. That would be a tempting incentive. And do you still expect her to actually fulfill this promise?"

The Archon was corrupt and ambitious, but not, apparently, brainless. "No, my lord."

"I don't either. Which leaves you in a difficult position, don't you think?"

Basileus said nothing. He was waiting for the point.

"I've known Domitia a long time. She's not a person either of us would be wise to cross. I'm sure I don't need to tell you that." Nico paused. "But nor am I willing to hand her the keys to the kingdom, so to speak. You've never met her father. Just as you were Domitia's creature, she is his. He's not like me." Nico let these words sink in. "He's not even like Domitia. Gaius is...." He searched for a way to explain that Basileus could grasp. "A man beyond right or wrong entirely. These things have no meaning for him. Your own darkest deeds wouldn't even scratch the surface of what Gaius is capable of. So I'll ask plainly, which side will you choose?"

The Archon studied him for a moment. He seemed to gather the shreds of his courage. "The one that wins, my lord," he replied dryly.

Nico laughed. "Good for you. An honest answer. I think we understand each other now. But if Gaius escapes the Kiln, there will be no side to choose. You will die. That is simple fact. What I offer you is a chance, a slim chance, to live. I make no promises. But if we fail, I will likely die too. Do you accept?"

"Accept what?"

"You mean, what is my devious plan? How will I stop her from giving her father free rein over heaven and earth?"

"Yes." Belatedly, "My lord."

Nico leapt to his feet, causing the Archon to rear back in alarm. He kicked a piece of charred wood, sending it spinning across the floor. It might have been a head, or perhaps a breast, as they'd been approximately the same size.

"I don't know yet. But she must have a weakness we can exploit."

"There is none I have ever discovered," Basileus replied in funereal tones.

"No, she does have one. The collars. She cannot control them herself. She must rely on others to manage her captives." Nico thought for a moment. "Tell me more about this acolyte named Thena."

Basileus shrugged. "She's a fanatic."

"Yes, but what *sort* of fanatic?"

"She is a devotee of the sun god—"

"Precisely!" Nico exclaimed. "Of the sun god. And she gobbled up that nonsense about the witches. Now she knows what Domitia truly is. A *witch*. And not just any witch—a Vatra. Would the mind of a fanatic be turned to a new path so easily?"

"I suppose not. But she has remained loyal."

"Just as you have, Basileus?"

"I see your point. But what good can she do us?"

"That remains to be seen. But she must have a secret desire in her heart. Not to be Tyrant, of course, but something else. We all have secret desires, don't we?"

Basileus took the question as rhetorical and ignored it. Still, Nico could tell he was chewing over the possibilities. He was a man who relished a juicy intrigue.

"Find out what you can about her. Where she comes from, how long she's been at the temple. I wish to know everything."

"As you say. But the Pythia—"

"Domitia, Basileus. Let us call her what she is."

"Domitia said we're marching for the Umbra." He glanced out the window, where Selene was sinking below the rooftops. "Within the hour."

"Then you'll arrange to ride on the same wagon with Thena. Let her know your loyalty is to Apollo. Be sympathetic. Like a kind old uncle."

He nodded glumly. "I suppose I'll have to pack my own bags. If I'm dismissing the servants."

"A terrible burden, but you'll manage somehow." Nico paused. "When you speak to them, don't be hard on that poor girl. I'm sure Domitia threatened her." He glanced at the bed. "It's a shame. That was a nice mattress."

Basileus pursed thin lips in distaste.

❧ 10 ❧

TO THE UMBRA

Nazafareen watched as the globe returned to a scene of wispy fast-moving clouds driven by some ethereal wind. Her fingers relaxed their death grip on the glass, although she wanted nothing more than to slam it into something hard.

I'm a goat-brained fool, she thought, the fury she'd repressed nearly boiling over.

How they must be laughing at her right now.

Nazafareen drew a deep breath, exhaling it in a white mist. She should have guessed the truth—she'd always sensed something strange about the woman—but she'd blindly accepted the facade of a fanatic, just as the Pythia intended.

"All this time," she muttered. "The same enemy. They were always the same."

Culach rubbed his chin. "Let me get this straight. The Oracle of Delphi is a Vatra. The same Oracle who calls us witches and says magic is a sin."

A bitter laugh spilled from Nazafareen's lips. "Don't you see? It's perfect. Who would ever suspect her?"

He shook his head in wonder. "What a twisted creature."

"No, she's very clever. She has the mortals bowing and

scraping to her, and by the time they realize they've been used, it will be too late."

Nazafareen palmed the globe, mastering her emotions with a great effort. She could rant and rave later, once Darius was free and they were on their way. "May I keep this globe? I intend to find the Danai first, if I can. For some reason, I don't trust the Pythia's promises."

"Of course," he replied without hesitation. "But if you go to war, I would give you another gift before you leave."

"That's kind, but there's no time—"

"I expect Runar and Stefán took your sword."

Nazafareen grunted in assent. She pocketed the globe. "I'm pretty sure they threw it into the ravine."

"I would give you another."

He looked so earnest, she could hardly refuse. And she felt naked without a sword, even if iron had little effect on the foes she faced. "Thank you, Culach. I accept."

She expected him to offer his own, but he rose and pulled a coat on, then strode confidently to the door. Mithre waited outside. Victor's second pushed off the wall and walked over, a guarded expression on his face. He scrutinized Culach, then Nazafareen, as if searching for injuries.

"Prepare whoever's left to depart the keep the moment the ice defenses are lifted," Nazafareen said briskly, peering up at him. "I'll have the Valkirins fly you out by abbadax. And find Victor. The siege of Val Moraine is officially over. No plunder, they might search you on the way out and I don't need another headache." She paused. "Oh, by the way, the Pythia is a Vatra. I intend to meet her at the Gale. And crush her."

Mithre's eyebrows rose, but little seemed to faze him at this point.

"We're bloody well going with you then."

Nazafareen gave him a tight grin. "I imagined you would. Best get moving. I plan to be gone from these mountains within the hour."

Mithre gave her an ironic salute, but his steps quickened as he moved away, shouting for the other Danai.

"You handled him neatly," Culach observed, guiding her the opposite way.

"I think I'm getting better at diplomacy."

He laughed. "That's one way to put it."

Culach led her down a series of staircases deep into the mountain. He didn't seem hindered by his lack of sight and she found herself hurrying to keep up with his long strides. The vast bulk of Val Moraine lay buried within the mountain and she was only just realizing how enormous it was.

"Where are you taking me?" she asked finally, trying not to show her impatience.

"The catacombs. Don't worry, we're nearly there."

"You mean where you keep the dead?"

"Yes. Does that bother you?"

She thought about it. "No. Not really."

They passed into a series of twisty tunnels. The ceiling grew lower, the air even more chill. Culach pulled a lumen crystal from his pocket and thrust it at her.

"Can you use these?"

"I...yes." Nazafareen ignited the talisman with ease. She hadn't held a lumen crystal since that fateful night the Valkirin assassin came to her house. How she had struggled with the simplest flows then. It seemed a lifetime ago.

"I don't need it, but you'll want some light," Culach said. He seemed uncomfortable, though she had a feeling it wasn't because of his blindness.

"Thanks."

Culach rounded a corner and the first bodies appeared. They lay on rock shelves, a patina of frost glittering on hair and eyes. Nazafareen looked at them with frank interest. She knew so little about the Valkirins. They had proud, haughty faces, but they certainly liked shiny things. She saw rubies and sapphires, diamonds and emeralds, and other precious stones in unusual hues—violet, lilac and rose.

"It's just ahead."

Culach halted at a niche containing a woman with short silver hair and eyes precisely the same green as his own, like new grass. Her face was youthful, but marked with lines of pain.

"This is my mother, Ygraine Grimsdottir."

Nazafareen didn't speak. She felt indecent gawking at the body and averted her gaze. Culach reached out, tentatively, his fingertips brushing Ygraine's cheek. She sensed some powerful emotion churning within him.

"I never knew her. She died in childbirth. But Gerda told me stories about her. She was a fierce warrior, but she also had a sense of humor." His fingers wandered to his mother's breast and the sword that lay there. "This was forged in Delphi. Normally, we don't name our swords. They are not children or pets. If a blade is sharp, one is as good as another. But the smith who forged this sword decided to give it a name. It's called Nemesis, after the Greek goddess of revenge."

"Nemesis," Nazafareen repeated softly.

"My mother found it appropriate." He touched the hilt. "Pick it up."

Nazafareen reverently slid the iron blade from Ygraine's frozen hands. It was not a broadsword, but a shorter, more nimble weapon, double-edged and with a leaf-shaped design.

"It's called a xiphos. They're one-handed. You see the curve? That gives momentum to the point of impact. It's a nasty little weapon." Culach's mouth curved in a smile. "Of course, she added her own motto."

Nazafareen traced the silver lettering engraved on the blade.

"I can't read it," she admitted, the familiar flush of embarrassment and wistful longing creeping up her neck. "I never learned how."

He laughed. "Very few mortals could read these runes. It's in Old Valkirin."

"What does it say?"

"No battle is won in bed," Culach replied, amusement in his voice.

Nazafareen smiled. "I like that." She paused. "Are you sure—"

"Ygraine would want it to be wielded again. Not by anyone, mind you. But against the Vatras? She would *love* that." He paused. "And after this, our debt is cleared."

"There was never a debt, Culach."

He waved a hand, his face growing serious again. "You must stop them, Nazafareen. I've seen things...." Culach trailed off, his gaze haunted. He cleared his throat. "You must stop them. No other can."

"I will."

"Take the baldric, too."

Nazafareen picked up the leather sheath. In contrast to Ygraine's jeweled belt, it was unadorned, with nicks and scratches from long use.

"It's worn over the shoulder," Culach explained, demonstrating. "Like so."

She sheathed the blade and slid the baldric over her arm, feeling the weight against her right side. It fit perfectly. She looked at Culach, overcome by this gift he had given her and determined to be worthy of it.

"Come with us," she urged.

"I'm not fit for battle anymore." He said it with resignation. "I would only be a hindrance. Besides which, Galen's mother Mina is here and we're ... fond of each other. I must find her and tell her everything. The choice of where we go will be hers."

"Oh, I see." Galen's mother? Truly, there had been some strange goings on at Val Moraine. "Well, don't worry. I'll get assurances from the other Valkirins that you and Mina have safe passage from the keep." She laid a hand on his arm. "I must go now, Culach."

He nodded. "I'll escort you out."

She picked up the lumen crystal from the rock ledge and they made their way back toward the upper levels.

"Tell Mina I will do everything I can to free Galen. Tell her I forgive him for what he did." This wasn't entirely true, but Nazafareen resolved to set aside her grievances against Galen—for the moment, at least. Seeing Victor had been an object lesson about where clinging to grudges could lead a person.

"She'll be glad to know that." He paused. "Though I wonder if her people will be so forgiving of *me*."

Nazafareen detected a note of worry in his voice and felt sorry for Culach. He didn't belong to any clan now, in a world where blood ties meant everything. An idea formed in her mind.

"You could always go to Meb of the Marakai. She's young, but I know she would welcome you. You'd be safe with the sea clan."

"She's the heir to the power?"

"Yes. She's in the Isles, meeting with the Five. Can an abbadax fly that far?"

He considered it for a moment. "Perhaps. I'll keep it mind."

They reached the door to the stables. Nazafareen looked up at him, taking in the winding scar and crystalline eyes, still a bit mesmerizing even without sight.

"Goodbye, Culach. I hope you and Mina find happiness together. And I will carry Ygraine's memory with me."

He nodded stoically and Nazafareen rose to her tiptoes and hugged him around the waist. He patted the top of her head, awkward but with a foolish grin. Then his face grew solemn.

"Be careful, Nazafareen." Culach paused, as though searching for words. When he spoke, his voice was soft. "There are things worth dying for, but hatred isn't one of them. Try to remember that."

"Yes, of course. I will. Goodbye, Culach!" she cried again and ran through the door, past the silent abbadax, to where Katrin waited with their mount. She stared hard at Nazafareen's new sword, mouth tight, but said nothing. And then another Valkirin appeared out of the shadows of the pen. He looked thin, almost wasted, and had straight silver hair that brushed his shoulders. A heavy iron collar ringed his neck.

Her mind instantly conjured up the image of Darius, chained and screaming as a faceless woman stood over him. Nazafareen tore her eyes away, swallowing the bile that rose in her throat. An abbadax slunk along at the Valkirin's side.

"My name is Daníel," he said. He seemed wary. "Mithre says I'm free to leave."

"Of course you are." She smiled warmly, hoping he hadn't sensed her revulsion. "And I'm Nazafareen."

He laid a gentle hand on the abbadax's beak. "She is Valdis, but she calls herself Wind from the North."

The abbadax nuzzled his palm.

"Let's go," Katrin grumbled, throwing herself into the saddle. "The holdfasts have waited long enough." She cast a final dark glance at Nemesis and turned away with the offended posture of a stepped-on cat.

Nazafareen fastened her harness with less trouble this time around and a minute later the pair of abbadax soared across the chasm between the ice tunnel and the Valkirin encampment. Runar, Stefán and Frida waited on the other side, Darius kneeling at their feet. Kallisto, Herodotus, Megaera and Rhea stood in a tight group a few paces away.

And beyond them, on similar snowy ledges, hundreds of hooded figures watched in silence. Nazafareen felt the weight of their eyes as she slid from the saddle and took the diamond from her pocket, holding up the chain so they could see it. She pointed her stump at Darius.

"Release him this instant or I throw it into the crevasse."

Runar and Stefán stared hungrily at the talisman. Frida rushed to embrace Daníel, a radiant smile on her face. She pressed her cheek against his coat and murmured words too low to make out. Daníel held her for a moment, but his gaze remained on Nazafareen.

"Do it," he snapped at Runar and Stefán.

The invisible bonds restraining Darius vanished. He stood gracefully, as if he hadn't been on his knees for hours. The bruises on his face had already faded to a greenish yellow and the swelling was nearly gone. Daëva blood healed quickly. As he strode to her side, she saw a quick narrowing of his eyes. He'd noticed Daníel's collar.

Nazafareen wanted to squeeze him until his bones ached, but she had other business to attend to first.

Stefán held out a hand. "Give it over."

"In a minute." She tilted her head. "I have new terms. You must also grant safe passage to Culach Kafsnjór."

He frowned. "That's a Valkirin matter."

She walked up to him, the snow crunching beneath her boots. Stefán crossed his arms and peered down his long, patrician nose. A number of choice comments occurred to her, but Nazafareen bit them back.

She spoke loudly so her words would carry. "Gerda Kafsnjór had a Talisman of Seeking. I just used it to speak with the Pythia. She's a Vatra."

Stefán blinked. "What?"

"She has the Danai talisman and she'll burn him and his kin if I don't get there first. So my patience for petty grudges is running thin at the moment."

Daníel stared at her in disbelief. "The Oracle? How can this be? She despises us."

"Yes, but not for the reasons you think. She's using the mortals, poisoning them against the clans. Her intention is to bring down the Gale. *That* is the end she's been working towards.

But she no longer cares about subterfuge. She will come into the open soon enough."

Nazafareen turned to the others. Runar stroked his thick beard, brow creased in thought. Stefán's face gave little away, though she saw a flicker of worry in his eyes.

"I need abbadax," she said. "We fly for the Gale. The Danai in the keep are coming as well."

"And the Maenads," Kallisto added. "We have long stood against the Pythia. If she is a Vatra, then she is our enemy twice over." She shook her grey-streaked braids in disgust. "I cannot believe she was under our noses the entire time. If she has shown herself, it is because her goal is in sight. She thinks she has already won. But she shall not have the Danai talisman!"

Megaera nodded, clearly impatient to be gone. Herodotus scribbled furiously on a scrap of parchment. Rhea leaned on her staff, her gaze fixed on Katrin. Rhea had a quick intellect. She understood.

"Katrin Aigirsdottir," Nazafareen said.

The Valkirin woman turned slowly to face her.

"What will your choice be? If you come to Solis, I will break the ward that binds your power."

Katrin raised her chin. "I will go."

Nazafareen felt the knot of tension in her gut ease somewhat.

"But I do not promise to stay," Katrin added. "My place is here."

Runar nodded approvingly.

"How generous of you," Nazafareen muttered. "I'm sure your ancestor, the one who stood with the other clans to face the Vatras and turn them back, would be proud."

Katrin opened her mouth for an angry retort. Stefán laid a restraining hand on her arm.

"You claim the Oracle is a Vatra," he said. "Perhaps it is true. But we must sort out the disposition of Val Moraine before taking any action. You're free to go." His lips thinned. "But we can't spare any mounts—"

"They can ride with Val Tourmaline," Daníel interrupted. "Frida, you're in charge until I return."

"You would go to Delphi?" Runar demanded in astonishment. His gaze flicked to the collar. "After she chained you like a beast?"

"Of course," Daníel snapped. "As you should too." His lip curled. "Is it pride or cowardice that makes you abandon the forest clan to their fate?"

Runar turned beet red. Everyone started shouting at once.

Darius leaned over to whisper in her ear. "Who's the Danai talisman?"

She gave him a dark look.

"*Who?*"

"Galen."

"You're joking."

"Nope."

Nazafareen raised two fingers to her mouth and gave a shrill whistle. The hubbub died down. They all turned to glare at her.

"I don't care what you do, but we have no time for this." She held up the diamond. "Give me your word you won't harm Culach once Victor has ceded the keep." She eyed Stefán's cunning features and Runar's barely controlled fury. The fox and the bear. "Swear it on the staff."

Daníel did so on behalf of Val Tourmaline without hesitation. Runar and Stefán followed suit, though with ill humor.

"Good," she said. "Here you go."

She tossed the diamond into the air. Runar and Stefán scrambled for it, elbowing each other like children fighting over a piece of candy. In the end, Runar's meaty fist caught it. He grinned with broken teeth.

"When the ice spell is broken, you should get rid of that," Nazafareen said, knowing they wouldn't. "The talisman has an evil influence."

Runar held up the diamond. The facets caught the moonlight, reflecting it back in a dazzling prism of colors.

"Det som goms i sno, kommer fram vid to!" he cried.

Later, she would ask Herodotus what it meant. An old Valkirin proverb, he said.

What is hidden in snow is revealed at thaw.

The stone emitted a sudden burst of white light. Nazafareen threw a hand over her eyes, wincing at the afterimage, like a dark sun flaring against the Aurora. When the blinding brilliance began to fade, she peered through her fingers. A thin line fractured the girdle of ice surrounding the Maiden Keep, just to the left of the tunnel. Runar let his hand fall. A palpable current of anticipation rippled through the Valkirins.

For one long minute, nothing else happened. Then the silence was broken by a series of ear-splitting cracks as the entire carapace broke away and tumbled into the ravine. It seemed to fall in slow motion, shattering against the lower slopes with explosive force. The reverberations triggered avalanches across the glacier, but the Valkirins threw up shields of air to divert the thundering masses of snow.

For the first time, Nazafareen saw the mighty holdfast. To her astonishment, it had almost no exterior walls. She could see straight inside through a series of tall archways. The Danai were gathered in the stables, far fewer than she'd expected. She heard the distant cries of abbadax and two dozen riderless mounts soared out. They banked and alit on the snowy ledge, flanks heaving. The creatures looked exhausted from the short flight. They huddled together, their feathers dull and ragged.

Daníel eyed them with pity. "These mounts were Eirik's. They have no masters anymore," he said to Runar. "You can keep them, to replace those we'll take. But you must treat them well. No riders for at least a week, and they must be fed every few hours."

Even Runar seemed moved by the creatures' plight. He nodded gruffly and shouted for fresh meat. The skies came alive with Valkirin riders as the watchers on the ledges made for the holdfast.

Only one abbadax remained in the stables. It peered over the edge, then retreated back into the shadows.

"Ragnhildur," Katrin said softly. "Loyal to the last. She'll never leave without Culach."

Nazafareen stared at the stables, willing him to appear with Mina. She'd feel better knowing they were safely gone before she departed. But she saw only Danai, moving back to make way for the riders.

Then Darius took her hand, pulling her aside to the privacy of a rock outcropping, and Culach left her mind as she wrapped her arms into the hollow of his strong back, breathing in his smell, like clean wool and a moonlit forest glade and just *him*. She hadn't allowed herself to imagine what might have happened if things turned out differently. But now that Darius was safe, she fought to keep herself from trembling.

"You have a new blade," he murmured in her ear, hands moving over the baldric.

"Culach gave it to me. It was his mother's."

Darius lowered his mouth, a delicious heat in his gaze, and kissed her thoroughly. "So you entered his worst enemy and emerged with his dear mother's sword. Considering your usual style, I have to admit I'm surprised."

"It's called Nemesis. It's a..." She tried to pronounce the word as Culach had. "Zee-fon."

His eyes danced with amusement. "You can't lose this one, Nazafareen."

"I won't." She grew sober. "He told me things, Darius. Troubling things about the Vatras. I don't know what they mean."

"Try me."

So she did, relating Culach's dreams of Farrumohr.

"They called him the Viper. He's dead. Culach said so, and I'm sure of it because I saw him in the Dominion. He was Neblis's pet. Or perhaps it was the other way around." A trickle of ice ran up her spine. "He lived in a well. He had no flesh, more like thickened shadows. But there were two pinpoints of flame...."

"Do you think he's making mischief?"

She shook her head. "I don't know. I hurt him when I cast him out. But how he might be connected with Nicodemus and the Pythia, I've no idea."

"You spoke with her."

"She knew my name. She seemed unafraid." Nazafareen took his hand. "You were right. We should have gone straight to the Danai. I'm so sorry."

He shook his head impatiently. "So she'll hold them hostage and force you to break Galen's ward?"

"That's what she implied. But there must be more to it. She knows something we don't. The woman was serene. Confident. She gave me a day to get to the Gale. I feel a fool running into her trap, but what choice do we have?" She scowled. "If only Katrin wasn't such a you-know-what. It rhymes with hunt and I'm guessing it starts with a *k*."

Darius had fallen quiet. His thoughts seemed far away. "We have to reach the Danai first. At least they have Charis and Cyrene."

"Of course. I'd clean forgot." Nazafareen closed her eyes. They felt heavy as lead. She needed time to think. She needed sleep. But neither of those things were likely for the foreseeable future. Then her fingers brushed the lump in her pocket. "We have another globe. Culach let me keep it."

Darius reached for the talisman, but she'd already ignited the runes, seeking Delilah. He blinked in surprise, then leaned in to study the twilit scene.

"Where are they, Darius? It must be the Umbra, but where exactly?"

Delilah strode along next to Tethys and six other women, all with dark hair and ageless faces. Arrayed behind them was a host of daēvas armed with yew bows. Each of the Houses carried its own banner—a bat for Fiala, a firefly for Granet, a striped badger for Dessarian, a screech owl for Kaland, two muskrats for Martinec, a bushy-tailed fox for Suchy, and a sprig of lyreleaf for Baradel. Nazafareen couldn't see either of the Maenads, though they must be somewhere in the ranks.

"Pull back a bit."

Nazafareen widened the view. Her heart sank. The plain was barren and featureless.

"Look at the quality of the light," he said. "It's still dark, yet not completely. I'd put them somewhere in the middle. And do you see that glint? It's the Cimmerian Sea."

"So if we fly along the shoreline, we might be able to intercept them. How many leagues to the Umbra?"

"Less than two hundred. The wind currents blow east to west so they'll be with us. The abbadax should make good time, but it will be close—very close. And if the Danai start running, we're done for."

She let the flows vanish. "There's a chance then."

Daniel had left to supervise the evacuation and ensure no one decided to settle any blood feuds on the spot. They watched his riders ferry the Danai across the ravine from Val Moraine. All seven of them. Nazafareen didn't know how large Victor's original force was, but their numbers had clearly been winnowed.

Victor and Mithre were not among them. Nazafareen had hoped to spare Darius the full story, but she saw no way around it now. He scanned the stables with worried eyes.

"Your father," she began, choosing her words with care. "He isn't well."

Darius looked at her sharply. "What do you mean?"

"The diamond." Nazafareen rubbed her stump. "He didn't want to give it to me," she mumbled.

"He what?"

She cleared her throat. "He didn't want to give it up. I had to take it from him. At sword-point."

Hurt flashed across his face, there and gone in an instant.

"That sounds like Victor," Darius said coldly. "Death before defeat."

"You don't understand. He said it was a Valkirin trick. That we were traitors. He looked awful, Darius. All mean and pinched. Mithre told me he's been like that for a while. It must be the diamond. He wore it on a chain around his neck. Howled like a baby when I took it away." She glanced at Runar and Stefán. "Those idiots wouldn't listen, but the talisman is poison." She sighed. "He ran off afterwards. I don't know where he went. But Mithre will find him. There's only one way out."

The riders from Val Tourmaline alit with their Danai passengers. Nazafareen knew two of them by name, Aedan and Kelyn, and embraced them warmly.

"Thought I'd never bloody get out of there," Aedan said, shaking his head. He was as tall as Victor but barely half his bulk, with long arms and legs well-suited to the sword he wore belted around his waist.

"Wasn't so bad. Bit chilly," Kelyn replied, flashing her broken front tooth in a grin.

"Well, it'll be hot in Delphi." They laughed, though there was an edge to it.

The other holdfasts poured into Val Moraine, crossing in waves until the encampments were nearly empty. Runar and Stefán grudgingly provided three abbadax, which accepted the blood scents of their new masters with only a few subdued hisses. Frida demonstrated how to safely mount the creatures and fasten the waist harnesses, as well as a few basic commands.

Over time, the clans had adopted a common tongue, but tradition dictated that Old Valkirin be used to communicate with the abbadax. *Fluga* meant take off, *elda* meant land, and *aras* meant attack. There were many subtler commands to signal deep or shallow dives and other evasive maneuvers, but there was no time for Frida to teach them.

"The mounts know what they're about," she said briskly. "Give them free rein and they'll see you through safely."

Kallisto would ride with Herodotus, Rhea with Megaera, and Nazafareen with Darius. Daníel had offered him a broadsword, but Darius politely declined, instead arming himself with a variety of wicked-looking knives. Saddlebags were hastily packed with three days of supplies. At last all was ready.

Daníel called for volunteers. Only five stepped forward. Each would carry a Danai. Neither side looked thrilled, but their hatred of the Pythia seemed to trump their hatred of each other.

Selene and Artemis shone side by side, buttery yellow and pale blue, as Nazafareen mounted with Darius. She took the reins and her mount spread its wings, lumbering to the edge of the ravine and diving over the side.

Nazafareen burned with impatience to leave the darklands. She wanted her huo mofa back, wanted it badly. When the power surged inside her, she felt invincible, though she knew this was a dangerous belief. She would need to be careful. But she was tired of submitting to the whims of others. To being *weak*.

Nazafareen skidded to an abrupt halt in the stables, her gaze searching for Victor. Mithre waited alone.

"Where is he?" she demanded.

"I can't find him," Mithre growled. Nazafareen could see he was furious.

"We can't stay and search," she said. "If he knew what Delilah faced, he wouldn't want us to."

Mithre tore his gaze from the group that circled the ravine behind them. "I can't leave him, even if he deserves it. The man's here somewhere. We'll catch up with you."

She sighed. "I'm sorry."

"Don't be. It's *his* fault." Mithre spun on his heel without another word and stomped back inside, pushing through the Valkirins clustered around the door.

"I feel bad," Nazafareen said.

"For Victor or Mithre?"

"Both."

"Yeah," Darius said. "But I feel worse for Mithre."

Nazafareen leaned forward. "*Fluga*," she whispered.

With a mighty flap, the abbadax soared into the darkness, heading west toward Solis.

𝕏 II 𝕏

DÉJÀ VU ALL OVER AGAIN

Culach hurried through the keep, calling Mina's name. She wasn't in her chambers and she wasn't in his either. He bit back an oath. He'd never begrudged her restlessness before. Trapped within the ice, everyone was claustrophobic, the Danai most of all. Added to her preoccupation with Galen, he knew Mina needed to walk the corridors. It kept her from falling apart.

But the ice was gone. Culach could hear the wind again, as well as distant shouts in the stables. So why hadn't she come looking for him?

He was starting to panic when he remembered the last time he'd sought her out with dry mouth and racing pulse. His father Eirik had announced that he intended to kill her if Victor and his Danai overran the keep.

That is the ultimate point of a hostage, Culach.

He shook off the memory of his father's rasping voice and hastened down to the vast hollowed-out caverns where Val Moraine's supply of grain, fruits and vegetables grew under special lumen crystals that mimicked sunlight. They sat on the level above the crypts, life and death nestled side by side.

"Mina," he cried, wandering through the rows, branches slapping his face and hands. "Are you down here?"

The air was much warmer and sweat trickled down his back. He tripped over a root, arms flailing, and then a hand steadied his arm.

"You big oaf," she muttered. "I'm right here. Are you blind?"

Culach barked a breathless laugh, so relieved to hear her voice he could have danced a jig. He swept her up and kissed her hair.

"What are you doing down here?"

"I wanted to find the cistern that unholy bitch from Delphi used to escape. I thought there might be some sign." She sighed.

He set her on her feet and began pulling her back to the staircase. "It's over, Mina. Nazafareen came and took the diamond from Victor. She gave it to the holdfasts. The ice is gone!"

"Oh, thank the gods. Who's Nazafareen? Is she the one Eirik wanted to kill?"

"I'll tell you everything once we're gone. But we have to hurry. She said she'd make sure we were permitted to leave, but I don't trust them."

They reached the stairs. Culach forced himself to slow his pace to match hers. He wanted to throw her over one shoulder and take them three at a time, but he doubted Mina would go along with that.

"How do we get out?" she demanded.

"I'll take Ragnhildur."

"Where's Victor and Mithre?"

"No idea." He drew a deep breath as they reached the concealed door leading into the keep proper. "Just pray Nazafareen remembered to put in a word."

He pressed the hidden stone and the wall swung wide. The corridor beyond was silent. Culach was about to step through when Mina seized his hand.

"Shouldn't we wait until the stables are empty? Sneak out?"

He shook his head. "Better to do it while they're still flush with victory. And the memory of their oath is fresh. They'll leave guards anyway." He squared his shoulders. "By all rights, I should be the master of Val Moraine now. I have no interest in pressing the matter, but it ought to count for something."

"It ought to, but it won't," she objected. "I don't wish to stay here another moment, but it seems rash to go marching in there."

Culach thought of Ragnhildur, waiting for him. "My abbadax is dying, Mina. She's half-starved. I don't know how much longer she can hold out."

Another woman might have berated him for placing an animal's welfare over their own.

"You're an oaf," she said. "But you have a big heart. Let's go."

Culach smiled. They hurried to the stables. He heard hostile mutters as he strode to Ragnhildur's pen, but no one approached them.

"Do you see a saddle?" he asked Mina quietly. "And harness? They should be hanging on the wall."

Without a word, she slipped away, returning with both items. Culach was buckling the saddle to Ragnhildur's back when he heard three sets of boots crackling on the ice.

"Look who's joined us."

Culach sighed and turned around. He knew that deep, gravelly voice. "Runar."

"Who's the Danai wench?"

"Don't." Mina moved to his side. "It's not worth it, Culach."

His fists unclenched. She was right. He turned back and continued buckling the leather straps.

A new voice, softer but equally deadly—more so, perhaps. "Where's Victor?"

"I don't know, Stefán," he replied wearily. "But he's your problem now."

"Is he?" The boots moved closer. "I'm afraid he's yours as well."

"And why is that?"

"We had a deal. Victor Dessarian would vacate the Maiden Keep. In exchange, he and his Danai wouldn't face retaliation. Most of them are gone, yet Victor is nowhere to be found."

"I'm sure he's in there somewhere," Culach snapped, losing patience.

"And when we find him, we'll uphold our end of the bargain."

Culach knew it was pointless to argue. He dropped the straps. "Fine. We'll rout him out for you." He started to move to the door and found himself frozen mid-step in bonds of air.

"Runar, do you think it's advisable to have a traitor running around the keep?"

"Not just a traitor, but Eirik's whelp. No, Stefán, I can't see my way to allowing that."

"Better to keep him in the cold cells, don't you think?"

Culach couldn't help it. He laughed. It was all so familiar. If *he* ever infested someone's dreams, they'd be bored to death. "Fuck you." Hardly original, but they'd expect it. And now the usual refrain: "If any harm comes to Mina—"

"I'll see to her." A woman. That must be the third set of boots, though her voice didn't sound familiar.

"Like hell you will," Mina spat.

Cue the stone trembling. Cue her shouts of fury as they bundled her off.

Cue the mournful cries of Ragnhildur. Poor darling, she'd almost had the saddle on.

Flurries of snow pattered against his face. Nazafareen will murder them when she returns, he thought.

If she returns.

"Would somebody please feed my abbadax?" Culach shouted as they dragged him back inside.

12

ASHES TO ASHES

The harsh light of a hundred pitch-soaked torches banished any scrap of shadow from the chamber at the heart of the Rock. Perched like a faithful hound at the foot of the throne, Javid wished for the gentler candlelight that had illuminated the bier of old King Cambyses. True, it smelled better since his body had been whisked away to its tomb. But Javid had come to dread the daily ritual that was about to unfold, and there would be no looking away.

A discreet snuffling behind him indicated the presence of King Shahak. He slouched in the throne, red eyes fixed on the terrified courtiers assembled before him. The sound had become so familiar, Javid barely registered it. The King was either snorting spell dust or stanching a nosebleed with his handkerchief. He'd grown alarmingly emaciated and the purple robes hung on his bones like a deflated air sack.

Or like the horrors decorating the far wall.

"Where are our pets?" he asked.

Shahak's voice was the only thing that hadn't changed. It was pleasant, mellifluous. If you didn't look at him, you might think he was still sane.

A whey-faced chamberlain bowed low and scampered to the door, gesticulating frantically at the guards there. The King did not like to be kept waiting. It was a fine line between disobedience and disloyalty, and finer still between disloyalty and treason.

Shortly after his ascension, there had been the usual slew of assassination attempts orchestrated by factions loyal to the Queen. The skins of these traitors had been nailed up for display, which, while perhaps stretching the bounds of good taste, wouldn't be unheard of except for the fact that they were whole, without a single mark.

Corporeal division was the technical term for it, Shahak had confided to him later.

All Javid remembered were the screams as the unfortunate assassin found himself standing there with his skin in a pile next to the platter of poisoned dates.

After the last one, three days prior, things grew quiet. Subdued, one might say.

The chamberlain hurried back inside the throne room and made the prostration.

"They are here, your Royal Highness," he informed the floor. "A small matter with the leashes caused the delay."

Snuffling. "We understand. But see it doesn't happen again."

The courtiers shrank against the walls as three handlers entered, each wearing leather gloves and holding a thin gold chain. Creeping along next to them were creatures unique in the annals of natural science. Feathers mingled with scales and fur. Two had beaks, one a hairy snout. The smallest licked its chops and Javid felt a stab of pity.

It was feeding time at Shahak's private zoo.

Two cooks trailed the handlers, bearing platters of raw meat, minced and bloody.

Javid rose to his feet as the King descended the throne and selected a morsel.

"Come." He patted his leg and the little one waddled over,

sniffing at the treat. "Yes, this is for you, Dadash." Shahak fed the creature, patting its head fondly. Dadash, which meant little brother, was his favorite, being the most compliant.

But the handlers had to yank on the leashes to get the others to come. The biggest emitted a low growl, its gaze fixed on the king. Shahak gave a rattling laugh that sounded like pebbles tossed into a well.

"Now, now. You will eat from my hand or not at all."

With a temperamental lash of its tail, the thing opened its beak and snapped the scrap of meat from Shahak's palm, swallowing it whole. She—Javid still thought of it as *she*—had fierce yellow eyes and he feared she might peck the king, but she thought better of it and gobbled the rest.

The middle one still hung back, as far away as its lead would permit. Shahak strode over and seized the leash, dragging the thing to heel. Javid could never tell if it was fear or defiance that made the middle son recalcitrant, but Shahak was having none of it. He whispered a few words, too low to hear, and gave it back to the handler.

"Return them to their cages."

The nobles watched silently as the royal family trotted to the door, the smallest one waddling a bit from its repast.

Shahak stood frozen for a moment as if he'd forgotten where he was. Then he made a brusque gesture and the audience withdrew, velvet slippers whispering against stone. Javid sensed their relief at being dismissed and tried not to feel envious.

After all, he'd gotten what he wanted. He was a wealthy man in his own right now. Asabana had paid him a handsome bonus for that first delivery of spell dust, enough to settle Javid's debt. And the King had grown so insatiable, he was making the runs to Pompeii with Leila and her father twice a week, with a bonus each time.

Javid didn't mind crossing the Gale so much, although it was still stomach-churning, but he hated desecrating the burned bodies of the Vatras. Such an act went against everything he'd been taught by the magi and by his own father. He still asked for forgiveness each time, but he'd stopped making the sign of the flame. It felt heretical.

Now Shahak turned to him with hollow eyes. A tiny smear of blood darkened his upper lip.

"Let us have a cup of wine in my chambers. I wish to show you something."

Javid bowed and fell into step behind the King and six of his guards as they strode to the enormous double doors leading to the corridor. The Hazara-patis, Master of a Thousand, waited just outside. His calculating gaze flicked to Javid as they passed. King Shahak might make the nobles tremble, but the Hazara-patis was still the eminence-gris, running things in Samarqand and Susa while their monarch dabbled in dust. He had sealed the gates to the city that morning, which Javid thought entirely prudent.

A thousand rumors circulated about the Pythia of Delphi, but they all had a common thread. Her army was marching and it was only a matter of time before she showed up *here*.

Once inside his personal chamber, Shahak gave a tremulous sigh and collapsed in his favorite chair. Javid poured him some wine. The King waved it away and Javid set the cup on the table. Shahak often grew melancholy after the feedings.

"Fetch me the box," he said, an edge of hunger in his voice.

Javid did so, averting his eyes as the King scooped out a heaping spoonful of dust. Shahak coughed—a violent, clotted hacking—and inhaled sharply, then coughed again, spitting into a silver bucket at the foot of the chair.

"Do you see that blue pot? The one with a bit of earth in the bottom? Bring it here."

Shahak sniffled into his handkerchief as Javid located the clay pot. It had a beautiful indigo glaze. The King's eyes shone like polished coins as he reached into the pocket of his robe and took out a seed, then poked it into the soil. With his left hand, he tossed a pinch of spell dust into the air.

"*Annitu*," he whispered, too-dark blood tracing a slow path to his upper lip.

A green sprout poked through the soil. Two tiny leaves unfurled, then four, then eight.

"*Shi*," Shahak urged in a reverent, gentle tone. "*Gishtil.*"

Breath of life. Vehicle of life.

The seedling twined upwards, thickening and putting out secondary branches, and with the first spiky yellow blossom, Javid realized it was a tomato plant. Seconds later, the roots cracked the pot, scattering dirt over Shahak's silk slippers. Fuzzy stems hung heavy with fruit that turned from green to red before Javid's eyes. The King laughed in delight. In that moment, he seemed happy and guileless as a child.

"Try one." Shahak plucked a tomato and offered it to Javid with a hand that trembled only slightly.

Javid swallowed. "I had a late breakfast, Your Highness." Shahak's eyes hardened and Javid hastily accepted the tomato. "But this looks too delicious to resist, O King of Kings."

He took a cautious bite and found it every bit as good as the ones from his mother's own garden.

"Imagine the drylands beyond the river turned to productive farms," Shahak said, staring at the opposite wall as if he saw straight through the labyrinth of stone to his kingdom beyond. "The potential of dust to benefit my people is limitless. My mother used to call me selfish. She never understood. But you do, Javid. Only you."

He succumbed to another coughing fit, this one worse than the last. Javid sank down and held the wine cup at his knee until he gathered the breath to take a sip. It seemed to calm him.

"I understand the price. Of course I do, I'm not a fool. But I must carry on. There is great work to be done and none with the courage to see it through but you and I, eh?"

At times like these, Javid found it advisable to say as little as possible.

"Yes, Your Highness."

Shahak studied him for a long moment. The warmth leached from his eyes and they became coins again, flat and blank.

"Tell me again what you know about the source of the dust."

Javid met the King's gaze with perfect steadiness. If he'd been a poor liar, he would have been dead a hundred times over already.

"It's to the northwest, Your Highness. Near Delphi."

"But where does it *come* from? What is it?"

Shahak set the plant aside and picked up the lacquered box, running his hands over the lid like a man caressing his lover. Javid kept his face smooth. Asabana had forbidden him to reveal anything of importance. The dust was his single lever of power and if Shahak discovered how to obtain it himself, the jig would be up. Asabana didn't seem to grasp the fact that Shahak wouldn't take no for an answer. The merchant rarely appeared at court, sending Javid in his stead.

"The alchemist Marzban Khorram-Din always makes me wait at the wind ship, Your Highness. It is somewhere in the desert—"

"Yes, yes, you've told me that before." Shahak sounded irritated and Javid blotted a patina of sweat from his brow. "I fear your employer is avoiding me. Perhaps it is time I summoned him."

"I would be delighted to convey that message, Your Highness," Javid replied with sincerity.

Shahak opened the lid and held up a pinch of dust, rubbing it thoughtfully between his fingers.

"It glitters," he observed. "Yet it has a chalky consistency. Almost like ash."

"I have wondered about it myself, Your Highness," Javid murmured, praying he would be dismissed.

Shahak's tongue darted out and tasted the dust smudged on his thumb. He grimaced.

"Bitter," he muttered. "Some essence of a plant, perhaps. Yet there is a metallic aftertaste." His reddened eyes grew distant again. "I have blood in my bowels, you know. And strange dreams. Yet I cannot give up the dust. No, no. But to discover what it is. Well...." He gave Javid a look that was remarkably self-aware. "It might explain what I'm *becoming*."

13

MIRRORS

The mountains sped past, their peaks shrouded in chill mist that dampened Nazafareen's cloak. Every now and then the clouds parted and she saw Artemis through the ragged gap, an unearthly blue against the star-studded sky. The giant moon the daēvas called the Wanderer seemed to be sailing alongside them as they flew west toward the Umbra.

Riding an abbadax was nearly as good as having wings herself. They were swift as a storm and agile as hunting hawks. This one was named Brynjar. She responded to the lightest touch of rein or knee, like a war stallion. And her great wings steadily devoured the leagues with no sign of tiring. Altogether, Nazafareen thought there was no finer way to travel.

Darius sat behind her, arms wrapped around her waist. He'd been quiet for the last hour. She twisted her head and caught a glimpse of his profile, the sharp nose and glacial eyes.

"You're taut as an arrow quivering against a bowstring," she said. "Yet you didn't seem bothered when they dangled you over that ravine."

He looked at her askance.

"Or are you worried about Delilah and the others?" When he

didn't reply, she added, "They're still crossing the Umbra. We'll catch them before they reach Delphi."

"That's not it." He paused and cleared his throat. "If you must know, I had an unpleasant encounter with some abbadax in the Dominion. Hatchlings."

Nazafareen laughed. She couldn't help it. "Hatchlings? Come now, how bad could they be?"

"Worse than you think. It didn't help that I was tied up and naked."

Nazafareen pondered this image for a moment. "I'm sorry I missed that," she said at last, keeping her tone neutral.

He snorted. "Even the infants are formidable. Their wing feathers cut like knives. The mothers leave them to fend for themselves and these were hungry."

"How did you manage to escape?"

"Luckily, I wasn't alone." He didn't elaborate and Nazafareen sensed a hint of bitterness. Darius disliked talking about what had happened in the Dominion, when he'd been captured by Culach's sister, Neblis.

He still keeps secrets, she thought, though I suppose I can't begrudge him that.

She never spoke of what she'd done to Nicodemus at the gate. For the first time, she'd felt a complete mastery over all four elements. The weaves had come to her without conscious thought, air and earth mostly. She'd wrapped them around his heart, felt it beating in the palm of her hand. And she'd squeezed —but not enough to kill. She'd intended to take her time about it.

A monster to face a monster. Her lips thinned. *So be it. I never asked for this power, but I won't run from it anymore.*

She felt Darius's warm breath in her ear.

"Look. The Cimmerian Sea."

Brynjar broke through the clouds enveloping the easternmost mountains of the Valkirin range and Nazafareen felt the bond begin to stir as they passed into the twilight of the Umbra. It was still a faint thing, like distant music on the wind. She rubbed her own jaw, sensing a ghostly ache there. Not her pain. *His*.

And what would he feel from her? Did he know how much she longed for the sun? Not the heat or light, but the power it bestowed? Did he know about the anger that never went away?

He must, but he never commented on it. He simply accepted her for who she was. For the thousandth time, she wished she knew what she had done to inspire such loyalty. Not the dry words, not the story itself, but what she had felt at the time, what it had meant to her. She'd traded those memories to defeat Neblis. Would she do the same again if she'd known what would happen?

Nazafareen didn't know the answer to that. But she still had the bond. And where once it had seemed a manacle, now she treasured it above all other things.

Daniel of Val Tourmaline and his nine riders had insisted on taking the vanguard. They spread out in a ragged formation ahead like a flock of overlarge, savage-looking geese, the Maenads and Herodotus following behind. Nazafareen saw a quick flash of the Great Forest and then they were skimming the shore of a vast sea, its waters wine-dark and calm. Somewhere along the low bluffs lay the Temple of the Moria Tree, where the Maenads' mothers kept watch for the return of the Vatras. But before she could look for it, the company turned southwest toward the plain between Nocturne and Solis.

The flat, featureless landscape made Nazafareen think of Javid and the astonished look on his face when he found her hiding beneath a canvas tarp on the ill-fated *Kyrenia*. She'd been afraid he'd throw her overboard. Nazafareen smiled, suddenly missing his snaggle-toothed grin.

I wonder what you're up to at this very moment, she thought. Probably drinking wine with rich lords and scheming to part them from their gold. Knowing Javid, he had his own wind ship by now—maybe a fleet of them. He was clever enough and had devilish luck, considering he managed to survive their acquaintance.

Brynjar hit one of the powerful currents flowing from east to west and dove sharply, her wings rigid with strain. The heat of Solis met the cold of Nocturne in the Umbra, making the plain treacherous for anything airborne. The *Kyrenia* had been dashed to bits here. But Brynjar was accustomed to harsh weather and soon found calmer air. Nazafareen relaxed her grip on the reins, squinting into the distance.

The twilight made it hard to see more than a few leagues ahead, but she could see a hint of light on the horizon, a band of lighter grey against the darkness. Her pulse picked up a notch. They would reach Solis in another few hours.

She thought of Delilah and Tethys, of the Danai marching across the plain unaware of what awaited them. They *had* to be turned back. The Pythia already held Galen hostage. If she had hundreds more, collared and forced to fight.... It didn't bear thinking about.

She twisted to look at Darius. "There's something I haven't told you yet." She paused. "Thena was at Val Moraine."

The bond was still a fragile thing, but she sensed his shock, like a bucket of icy water in the face.

"How?" he asked hoarsely.

"She came with Daniel. They used some kind of talisman to get inside." Nazafareen kept any hint of pity from her voice. Darius wouldn't welcome it. "Haven't you wondered about his collar?"

"Of course I have," he snapped. "But that's behind me now. I've no wish to revisit it. Should I have asked him who his mistress was? Compared notes on their techniques?"

Nazafareen held her tongue. Unlike her, Darius kept his temper on a tight leash. That it had slipped his grasp revealed the strain he was under. She decided not to tell him that Daniel had allowed Thena to leave the keep.

"She's the one who took Galen. I don't know how she managed it, but she'll be with the Pythia."

His laugh chilled Nazafareen to the marrow. "I should have killed her when I had the chance. It was stubborn pride. She asked me to, so I refused."

"I imagine you thought the Pythia would mete out a worse punishment," Nazafareen said carefully.

She took his silence as confirmation.

"I have no love for Galen," Darius said finally. "But I wouldn't wish Thena on anyone."

"Not even Nicodemus?"

He didn't smile. "Not even Nicodemus."

"Well, I have no problem cutting her head off," Nazafareen said. "Or perhaps something slower and vastly more painful. I'll have to think on that."

She leaned back against his chest, felt it rise and fall. The emotions coming through the bond were subdued again, barely decipherable. He'd thrown up a wall against her.

"How long was Thena at Val Moraine?" he asked.

"I don't know. I should have asked. A while, I gather."

"I wonder if she spoke with Victor?" He paused. "She must have."

"Why does it matter?"

"It doesn't really."

But she knew he was lying.

"Tell me, Darius."

"Tell you what?" He didn't raise his voice, but it had an edge. A note of warning. Nazafareen ignored it.

"What could Victor have told her?"

His whole body tensed and she prepared for another angry outburst. Then Darius took a deep breath and she felt his shoulders relax.

"My name," he said finally.

The weariness contained in those two words told her all she needed to know.

"You never gave it to Thena," she said gently.

"I never did. Sometimes I forgot everything except for that. Where I came from and how I ended up there. Lack of sleep does strange things to a person." He sighed. "But I always kept my name locked away. I would have died before telling her. I fully expected to."

Images of what Thena might have done to extract this information from Darius crowded her head. Nazafareen felt nauseous.

"Why did she let you go? I've never understood that."

He was silent for a long time. Nazafareen sensed he knew, but was reluctant to put it into words.

"She told me a story once. About lovers named Psyche and Eros. She said we were like them. That I had been sent to test her faith. She was mad, Nazafareen." He pulled her closer, resting his chin on the top of her head. "There's an emptiness in Thena. She tries to fill it with devotion—to her god, to the Pythia—but it's a bottomless hole."

"That doesn't answer my question."

He swallowed. "I think.... As revolting as it sounds, she came to care for me. In her own twisted way." His voice grew wintry again. "I encouraged it. I used the bond to try to understand her. To crawl into the cesspool of her head. I could have blocked her out to some degree, but I didn't. I wanted her to *know* me too. To make it harder for her." He shifted back so they were no longer touching. "I must sicken you."

Nazafareen's heart lurched. "How could you say such a thing? Don't ever think that. I would have done the same. You were very clever. And if you hadn't...." She trailed off, the sentence unfinished.

If he hadn't, Darius would be dead.

She understood now what survival had cost him. She said she would have done the same, but in truth, Nazafareen wondered if she would have had his strength. She knew how to sharpen her hatred to a fine point. She knew how to kill without regret. But it was another matter to have your mind chained to a sadistic monster. To hold the broken pieces of yourself together, not knowing if each hour would be the last.

It wasn't simply a matter of courage. Darius had the ability to distance himself from pain and suffering to an extreme degree. It was almost as if part of him welcomed it.

But nor would it be honest to say Thena's warped affections meant nothing to Nazafareen. She remembered a woman standing next to the Pythia, with long black hair and olive skin. She had been very beautiful. Nazafareen suddenly wondered if Thena had seen him naked. This led to fury and inevitably, shame at her own petty jealousy. Darius seemed to sense an echo of it. She felt him tense up again.

"Let's not speak of it anymore," she said. "Unless you wish to?"

"I don't," he replied fervently.

"If it helps to ease the burden—"

"There's no burden."

Nazafareen doubted the truth of this, but she decided to change the subject.

"I forgot to tell you," she said. "Culach and Galen's mother, Mina."

Darius lifted an eyebrow.

She lowered her voice in an approximation of Culach's. "They're very fond of each other."

He laughed and the sound—not cold or despairing anymore, but warm and amused—gladdened her heart. "Mina was at Val Moraine?"

"I didn't meet her, but yes." Her brow wrinkled. "I told Culach to tell Mina that I forgave Galen. I didn't mean it though. He's a git."

Galen's betrayal still stung. She hadn't known him well, but he never gave any sign that he wished her dead.

Darius snorted. "I haven't forgiven him either and he's my brother."

"Why did he do it? What did he have to gain?"

"You'll have to ask him yourself."

She tossed her head. "I can't think of two people less suited to the power than Galen and Katrin. Especially Katrin. She'll probably use it on me the moment I break her ward."

"If she has one. We don't know for certain yet."

"Oh, it's her, all right," Nazafareen said darkly. "The gods are perverse."

They flew on without talking for a while. Darius produced some bruised apples and they made a quick meal in the saddle. Nazafareen must have drifted off, her back nestled against Darius's chest, for when she opened her eyes the horizon was distinctly brighter.

"Any sign of the Danai?" she asked, rubbing her eyes.

He gave his head a slight shake. "Nothing's moving on the plain."

"Are we on the right course to intercept them?"

"Should be. I can check the globe again."

Nazafareen felt him lean forward.

"Wait.... I do see something. But it's not on the ground."

At the same instant, Daníel raised a fist. The other riders slowed and he circled back around to fly alongside Nazafareen and Darius. She peered into the gloom, but saw nothing.

"Wind ships ahead," Daníel called. "About five leagues off."

"The Pythia's?" Nazafareen called back.

Daníel's hood lay across his broad shoulders. His unbound silver hair streamed out as he leaned carelessly from the saddle. "Must be."

"What are they doing?"

"Nothing. Just sitting there." Daníel's eyes burned like green coals. "They can't maneuver like the abbadax. We'll knock them out of the sky."

Nazafareen frowned. The Pythia had set a trap before at the Ecclesia and sprung it with ruthless efficiency. She'd waited for precisely the right moment. Like a hunter stalking prey.

"We have to stop thinking of her as the Oracle," Nazafareen muttered. "She's a creature of the Kiln. So the question is, what's she got up her sleeve this time?"

"Something nasty," Darius ventured.

"No doubt. Let me send the Maenads to scout," she called to Daníel. "We need to know if there are Vatras on those ships before we do anything."

Daníel gave a sharp nod and banked away to tell the other daēvas.

"Megaera!" Nazafareen bellowed.

She flew over, her cheeks flushed. Rhea clung to her back, looking slender as a birch sapling next to Megaera's solid bulk. Their long braids streamed out behind them.

"There are wind ships ahead. Go take a look. Just a look!"

Megaera signaled that she understood. Their abbadax sped into the gloom.

"Find the Danai," Nazafareen said to Darius, passing him the globe. He took it and blew on the runes.

"They're already past the ships," he said a moment later. "But only by a few leagues."

The temptation to race forward was overwhelming, but she was no longer a rash girl. The last months had taught her some hard lessons.

Brynjar flew in circles while they waited, the monotonous landscape passing beneath her wings. A few minutes later, Megaera and Rhea returned with Herodotus and Kallisto. Daníel flew over with Katrin. The abbadax slowed and hovered over the plain.

"Each has two pilots," Megaera reported. "They look like mortals. We counted twenty ships, strung in a line across the Umbra. We came close but they did nothing."

"A blockade," Katrin said, her eyes narrowing.

"Yet they allowed the Danai to pass," Darius said.

Daníel frowned. "We have to get through them."

Nazafareen's unease grew. The Pythia had demanded her presence at the Gale. Why would she attack now?

"We stick together," she said. "Only use the power if you have to. If they attack, go for the air sacks. It's the most vulnerable part of the ship. And I don't have to tell you to retreat at the first sign of fire."

Daníel shouted commands and his riders formed up. They sped forward and Nazafareen spotted a line of dark specks on the horizon, sitting motionless over the plain. Power gathered as the Valkirins and their Danai passengers raced ahead. Brynjar lowered her head and screeched, wings beating hard. They closed the distance. She could see the ships clearly now, each tethered to a black air sack blazoned with a dancing red flame.

Nazafareen reached for her breaking power in case they tried to use magic, but came up empty. She was still too deep in the Umbra.

A league, then half a league. The abbadax flew in a tight cluster, aiming for the wide gap between the ships and the ground. Two hundred paces. A hundred. Still the ships made no move to intercept. Perhaps they were placed there to scout for the Danai and report back.

She gripped the reins with sweaty fingers. Wind gusted in her ears. Exhaustion fell away and everything snapped into sharp focus—the upward-curving prows of glossy dark wood with lit braziers hanging below the air sacks. The pilots, wearing tunics with loose, billowing sleeves and flat caps, peering intently at the oncoming abbadax.

At fifty paces, she saw movement on the decks of the nearest ships. Canvas coverings were flung aside and men in the breastplates and crested horsehair helmets of the Shields of Apollo rose up. An instant later, the arms of concealed catapults swung back and a hail of rocks hurtled toward the abbadax. Several struck home, causing the mounts to spiral away, screaming.

"Tricky bastards," Darius swore.

The hair on Nazafareen's arms lifted as he sought the Nexus and drew deeply on earth. Fear gripped her. If the ships unleashed fire, she couldn't sever him. He'd reach for it and—

Elemental power burst from the vanguard of Daníel's abbadax, whipping curtains of loose dirt up from the plain and engulfing the ships in a yellow cloud. Brynjar flew straight into it. Nazafareen blinked against the grit. The mounts were trained for war. Brynjar didn't need her guidance.

Nazafareen dropped the reins and drew Nemesis from the baldric on her right shoulder.

No battle's won in bed.

Her lips parted in a wolfish smile.

"For Ygraine Grimsdottir!" she cried, leaning forward.

A ship loomed ahead. Brynjar dove at the air sack, talons extended. They were only a few paces away when the abbadax slammed into an invisible barrier. They plunged toward the earth, harnesses yanking tight, but then with an angry screech, Brynjar righted herself, climbing steeply.

Nazafareen thought they'd been hit by the backwash of power unleashed by Daníel's Valkirins until she noticed that a bubble of clear air enveloped the ship below. She scanned the men crowded on deck. Nearly hidden amid the soldiers were two bearded men in the long white robes of philosophers. During her time as a servant at the Great Library, Nazafareen would often see the philosophers walking to and from their Guild. Javid had said some of them were sympathizers of the Pythia.

She peered at the pair, both frail and stooped. Their eyes were closed and their lips moved. One of them raised a hand and tossed something into the air. Even at a distance, she saw it glitter.

Nazafareen twisted in the saddle to look at Darius.

"They're using spell dust!"

He raised an eyebrow, assessing the chaos erupting around them with his usual calm.

"Some kind of shields," he said. "But earth is stronger than air. I think I can...."

He winced in pain as three boulders from the catapults reversed course in midair and hurtled back toward the ship. They struck with catastrophic force, smashing through the hull. In an instant, Darius snapped the ropes tethering the ship to its sack. The soldiers screamed as it plummeted to the ground.

"That's one down," he muttered, pressing a hand to his side.

Brynjar dove back into the dust cloud. Nazafareen heard the creak of ropes, the harsh cries of the abbadax and bellowed commands. Suddenly, the outlines of another ship appeared in the murk just ahead. Nazafareen locked eyes with a philosopher, whose own widened in surprise. He opened his mouth, lips forming the words to cast a protective spell. Before he could complete it, she leaned from the saddle and plunged the blade into his chest. Brynjar's long tail lashed across the deck, sweeping a dozen soldiers over the edge. An instant later, her talons ripped a gash in the sack. The ship fell.

They used this sneak attack twice more with success, darting in and out of the dust cloud. Brynjar was cunning, navigating by sound and using her sharp feathers like daggers. Nazafareen hunched over the mount's neck, her gut tightening every time she heard one of Darius's bones crack. He was drawing too much earth, but it would be useless to order him to stop. She struck out with Nemesis whenever they neared a ship, slashing at the ropes and the sacks—and the men when she could reach them.

Confusion reigned, the battle glimpsed only in flashes, but she got the sense they were winning. The dust had begun to settle and only half the ships remained. Nazafareen saw with relief that the Maenads and most of the daēvas, including Daniel and Katrin, were still airborne, though a few of his riders seemed to be missing.

Then the philosophers tried something new.

From one moment to the next, the horizon vanished. There was no sky or ground. In every direction, up and down, left and right, forward and back, she saw only the line of wind ships, identical in every respect. It was like standing in a box of mirrors. Vertigo made her stomach lurch.

"What the bloody hell?" Darius growled.

Brynjar gave a low moan, eyes rolling in distress. Nazafareen sheathed her sword and laid her hand on the abbadax's neck, stroking the softer feathers around the ear. She'd seen Daníel soothe his own mount that way.

"It's an illusion," she said. "But a convincing one."

Darius leaned over and spat to the side.

"That's still down," he said. "They can't alter the natural laws. We just have to—"

A jarring collision snapped her head back. They'd hit another abbadax. Both mounts plunged toward the earth, though it looked like they were rushing *toward* the wind ships.

"Brynjar!" she screamed, grabbing the reins. "Pull up! *Fluga!*"

Bone thrust through the mount's crumpled left wing. The right flapped frantically, but it wasn't enough to arrest their fall. The illusion concealed the ground, but she knew it must be close. Panic welled in her chest. Then a blade slashed through her harness and strong arms threw her free of the saddle. Nazafareen landed hard, biting her tongue, and Brynjar slammed down next to her a moment later.

Darius was already on his feet, running to the abbadax they'd collided with. The illusion was gone, the world righting itself again. Katrin groaned in the dirt, her nose bloodied. She looked more angry than anything else. Her abbadax hissed at Darius, its neck feathers rising.

"Peace, Berglaug," Katrin muttered, sitting up.

Nazafareen turned at a terrible cry. Brynjar lay on her side, flanks heaving. Spatters of blue blood covered the ground.

"Help her!" Nazafareen cried. "She's badly hurt."

Katrin ignored Darius's outstretched hand and pushed to her feet. She limped over and examined the abbadax, her face grim.

"She has to be put down," Katrin said softly.

Tears sprang to Nazafareen's eyes. She scrubbed them away. "We can set the bone. We can—"

"It's not just her wing. She's broken inside. It would be a mercy." Katrin drew her sword.

"No." Nazafareen pulled Nemesis from its baldric. "She was my mount. I'll do it."

"Just below the beak. A swift upward stroke. It's the quickest way."

Nazafareen pressed her forehead to Brynjar's bloody beak. The abbadax blinked.

"You fought bravely," she whispered, placing the blade where Katrin had directed. "Be at peace."

Brynjar gave a single convulsive jerk. Her yellow eyes dimmed.

Nazafareen knelt, sword in her hand, and wept silently. Katrin's footsteps receded. A hand touched her shoulder.

"We must see to the others," Darius said quietly.

She wiped her eyes and stood. Eight of the twelve abbadax lay broken and scattered across the plain. Katrin and Daníel had already reached the nearest riders, who slumped in their harnesses. All the Valkirins were volunteers. Daníel had asked the soldiers of Val Tourmaline who among them was willing to fight the Pythia and five had stepped forward. They'd agreed to ride with the Danai who had occupied Val Moraine. Good men and women, the bravest and least bigoted of their holdfasts.

She and Darius hurried over, offering help where they could. All the abbadax were dead or so badly hurt they had to be put down like Brynjar. It was grim work and her heart lifted when she saw the three Maenads and Herodotus approach, all appearing unharmed. The wind ships had been hovering over the plain, watching them. Now the fleet sped away to the west.

"Why didn't they try to finish us?" Megaera wondered.

"It was a delaying tactic," Darius replied, cold fury on his face. "Those ships weren't for the Danai. They were for us."

"Give me a mount," Nazafareen said. "I'm going after them."

He shook his head. "It's too late."

"It's not! Give me the globe."

Wearily, he took it from his pocket and handed it to her. Nazafareen activated the runes. Since the exchange with Nicodemus, she'd learned how to make the device convey sound as well as sight.

"Show me the Danai," she whispered, dread filling her heart.

And there they were at the far western edge of the Umbra, near the Cimmerian Sea. She could hear the low moan of the wind as it swept across the plain. The walls of Delphi and the white pillars of the Acropolis loomed in the distance.

Sunlight gleamed on the quivers of arrows they wore on their backs. Delilah walked next to Tethys, though neither woman spoke.

Their gazes were fixed on the army waiting ahead.

❧ 14 ❧

THE BATTLE OF DELPHI

Nicodemus pushed the flaps of his tent aside and strode through the camp, searching for the Archon Basileus. Armored infantrymen carrying spears and shields stood in a phalanx facing the Umbra. The light cavalry occupied the western side of the camp, bristling with javelins and bows. There was none of the usual joking and boasting of men on the eve of a battle. Their faces were grim. They expected to die today.

None of them knew they were just for show.

A dust plume hovered on the eastern horizon. He wondered if it was the Danai, though it seemed too large and high. The sight made him uneasy.

He scanned the camp and caught a flash of red cloak beyond the edge of the infantry. The Archon stood alone, peering at the same disturbance.

"What is it?" Nico asked.

"I don't know, my lord."

"Could the Breaker have brought her own army from the darklands?"

Basileus glanced around. No one else was within hearing. "The

Pyth— Domitia deployed wind ships in that direction several hours ago."

"What for?"

"She didn't say, though I imagine she wished to scout the position of the Danai."

Nicodemus cursed under his breath. She'd told him nothing since they marched for the Umbra the day before. And he was starting to realize this plan of hers had more holes than the infamous Sinking Sands of the Kiln. Even if Nazafareen could be induced to break Galen's ward, could the collar even control that much power? And what if she broke the ward and the collar at the same time? Of course she would.

He thought of the wave Meb had summoned and imagined a similar catastrophe unfolding, but this time with earth. Or the ground might just swallow them. There were any number of unpleasant possibilities.

That's if the Breaker didn't just kill everyone first.

"What about Thena?" he asked. "What have you learned?"

They both glanced at the acolyte, who stood with Galen inside a semicircle of Shields, the bracelet on her wrist.

"She's nineteen and comes from a farm outside Delphi. She's served the temple for six years. She has four sisters, all older. I was unable to make extensive inquiries for lack of time, but by all accounts she hasn't seen them since she entered service to the god. The cook reported that she heard the call at a young age after hearing the legend of the three moon goddesses—"

"Skip to the dirt, Basileus," Nico growled.

He cleared his throat. "Yes, there are a few things. She's a sullen girl. I had to threaten her with dire punishment, but she finally admitted that she freed one of the wit— collared daëvas. One of the Shields told me the story, but I wished to hear it from her own lips."

Nico arched an eyebrow. "She freed a daëva?"

"Galen's half-brother, in fact," the Archon replied dryly. "She wasn't very coherent about what happened. Stammered some nonsense about Apollo's will. But she seems obsessed with getting him back."

Nico frowned. "Domitia said the daēva escaped."

"Escape is impossible," Basileus said flatly. "No, she unlocked his collar herself. Rumor has it Domitia burned her for her transgression and she still has the scars on her legs."

"So the girl betrayed her once before," Nico mused. "I'm surprised Domitia gave her a second chance. That's...unusual."

To say the least.

"Well, she redeemed herself with Galen. Now she seems to believe that if she pleases the Pythia, she'll be permitted to take a contingent of Shields and hunt this daēva down. I got the impression she blames him for her own weakness of character."

Thena glanced over at them, her face expressionless. She was pretty, but her features had a wooden, immobile quality, as if her mind were far away. A strange woman, Nico thought.

"Does she hold a grudge for her punishment?" Nico asked.

"She denies it, but I think so, yes." Basileus stiffened, his thin lips pursing. "Movement on the plain," he said hoarsely.

Nico turned from his scrutiny of Thena and gazed into the twilight. Something was stirring there. Hints of green and brown against the grey landscape.

The camp roiled like a kicked anthill. Orders were shouted and the infantry's shields locked together to form a defensive wall. The cavalry wheeled around and took the left flank on the banks of the river. A runner disappeared into Domitia's tent. Moments later she emerged, her long white gown whipping in the wind. As always, the serpent brooch adorned one pale shoulder. She had no shoes.

In the Kiln, Domitia wore thick-soled boots that laced to above the knee. She rarely took them off and taught Nico to do the same. If you had to run, the difference between boots and barefoot could decide whether you lived or died. The only time he'd seen her feet was that day she saved him from the crab. She told him later she'd been wading in the sea when she heard him scream.

Somehow, seeing her feet now felt bizarrely intimate. They were small and delicate, with high arches. She saw him staring and her lips twisted in a smile. A flush crept up his neck.

Of all the fucking things to be thinking about, he thought savagely.

Domitia ambled over to Nico and Basileus. Her gaze swept across the Danai.

"Look at them," she said mildly. "So full of piss and vinegar."

Nico could see the host clearly now, at least five hundred daēvas. They jogged toward the camp in a loose formation, bows at the ready, though when the attack came it would be with the power. Nico sensed their alert readiness. The dust beneath his feet seemed to shiver with anticipation.

"I hope you explain matters before things get out of hand," he said.

Domitia's eyes glittered. "Oh, I will." She turned to Basileus. "Are you ready for them, Archon?"

The Archon shifted nervously. He was resplendent in his crimson cloak and gold chain of office, but his eyes had the look of a deer who's just caught the scent of a predator. Whether it was directed at the Danai horde, Domitia herself or both, Nico couldn't tell.

"The Shields of Apollo await your orders, Oracle," he said. "May the gods watch over us."

Fifty paces away, the daēvas stopped. They wore coats and trousers that would blend perfectly into the forest but looked out of place on the barren plain. Seven in the front—all women—conferred briefly and then walked forward.

Domitia snapped her fingers at Thena, who hurried to her side, Galen trailing her like a whipped dog. A leather gag covered his mouth and shackles bound his feet, with just enough length between them to take short steps. He cast desperate glances at the Danai.

The women halted a short distance away, ignoring the legion of Greek soldiers as if they were rocks in the landscape. Their attention focused on Domitia, who strode forward to meet them until the two sides stood a mere twenty paces apart. Brittle silence descended, broken only by the restless movement of the horses.

"Oracle of Delphi," the tallest called out, her voice ringing across the plain. It was deep for a woman and resonant with authority. "You stand guilty of kidnapping and murder. You have shattered the peace between mortals and daēvas."

"Shattered the peace? That's a curious expression." Domitia inclined her head. "I'm sorry, who are you again?"

"My name is Tethys Dessarian," she said with contempt.

"Raisa Baradel," said a stout woman to her left.

"Jann Fiala," shouted one with a thick streak of white in her hair.

"Sorcha Martinec." Hawk-nosed and fierce.

"Rhedyn Kaland." Her round, motherly face stood in sharp contrast to the acid tone.

"And I am Sauvanne Suchy," said the last, a willowy woman with cords of slender muscle on her bare arms and eagle feathers dangling from pierced lobes. "We are the Danai Matrium and your reign of terror is over." She surveyed the soldiers, who watched the exchange with palpable tension. "Surrender your prisoners and throw down your arms, and we will give you a life of exile."

"Exile?" Domitia called back. "That sounds severe." She turned to cast an amused look at Nicodemus.

"If you do not, the Acropolis and the Temple of Apollo will be razed to the ground. You will die, along with all who follow you. The walls of Delphi will be broken and the Archons cast down."

Basileus made a small unhappy noise in his throat.

"I see. Your position is clear then." Domitia paused. "And what of *your* crimes?"

"She's playing for time," Jann Fiala snapped.

Tethys Dessarian glowered. "We have always treated you with respect and courtesy. We ceded you the sunlit lands—"

"You sentenced women and children to a life of brutality and want. You betrayed the ancient covenant and made a pact with diabolical forces to harness obscene power." Domitia's voice grew harder with each word. "*You lusted for what was not yours.*"

The Danai women exchanged glances. Nico saw they had no idea what Domitia was talking about.

Then a younger woman strode forward from the ranks. Wild black hair framed a long, mournful face. Her body appeared painfully thin, but Nico sensed deep currents of earth swirling about her. She stabbed a finger at Domitia.

"Enough of this. My name is Delilah Dessarian and you stole my son." Her eyes flicked to Galen. It was only an instant, but Nico had the distinct impression of animosity. "Now you flaunt his half-brother, chained like an animal." She shook with rage. "You *dare*."

A slender thread of power lashed out. Nico heard the faint but distinct snap of bone. Domitia winced, clutching her hand. Her face grew very still. Nico knew that look. The calm before the storm.

"Gaius Julius Caesar Augustus," Domitia said softly. "Do any among you remember that name?"

Tethys stiffened. She looked suddenly ashen, as did Raisa Baradel. The others merely frowned, glancing at each other with questioning looks.

"He is my father. And he taught me about *you*. There will be no bargains and no mercy." Domitia drew herself up. "The heir is mine. He will atone for your sins."

Heat built in Nico's veins, weakening his knees. He felt the situation spinning out of control.

"Stop," he shouted, striding toward the Matrium. "You must listen to her. Submit and you will be spared!"

Domitia looked at him, her pale eyes empty. She turned to Delilah, who stared back defiantly. Tethys laid a hand on Delilah's arm, whispering to her, but the Danai woman shook it off.

"Crawl to me, Danai lizards," Domitia said. "Crawl to me and I will give you the Kiln for your new homeland. Perhaps I will hunt you as *we* were hunted. That might make for interesting sport."

The earth began to tremble. A crack opened at Domitia's feet and she staggered back. Rage pinched her face. She raised a hand and Delilah was engulfed in flame. Long black hair blazed as she fell to one side, limbs drawing into charred sticks.

Galen made a strangled sound through the gag. Shock rippled through the ranks of the Danai, but they did not run. Instead, five hundred arrows knocked to bows.

"The Lost Clan," Tethys gasped, staring at Delilah's remains with an expression of horror. "They have returned."

The other women seemed stunned, still trying to grasp what had just happened.

Nico reached Domitia and grabbed her arm, spinning her around. "Don't do this," he rasped. "It's enough. You've had your fun."

"Fun?" Domitia echoed, her brow wrinkled in a slight frown. "No, this is justice."

She wrenched free of his grip, shoving him away. "Do you hear me?" she screamed. "This is the justice of Gaius Julius Caesar Augustus. King of the Vatras, survivor of the Kiln, and the new master of Solis and Nocturne!"

Tethys brought her arm down and the arrows loosed from their bows, flying in a deadly rain toward the camp. The Greeks raised their shields, hiding beneath as the missiles clattered down. One whistled past Nico's face and he threw himself to the side, landing hard on his left shoulder. He caught a glimpse of

KAT ROSS

Basileus's crimson cloak streaming out like a banner as he scuttled
for cover behind the wagons.

But the arrows were only a distraction. Screams erupted as the
Danai sent wave after wave of bone-shattering power at Domitia'a
army. Horses reared, throwing their riders. A hail of rocks
smashed into the ground and the earth itself cracked and shifted
as though an enraged giant strode among them.

All this lasted perhaps eight seconds.

Then Domitia raised her hand and the Danai burned.

It started with a line of flame racing across the ground toward
Tethys Dessarian. She saw it coming but didn't flinch. Nico saw
she'd known how this would end, yet she chose to fight anyway.
To die on her feet.

It took only an instant for the blaze to spread through the
Matrium, and to the first ranks of the archers, and the second,
and the third, as they reached haplessly for the flames. The
Fourth Element that no daēva could resist but only the Vatras
could work.

Nico fell to hands and knees, his gorge rising. The stench of
burning flesh filled the air.

The Greeks who weren't injured from the Danai's initial
assault did try to flee then, but Domitia's voice froze them in
their tracks.

"Run and you share their fate!" she shouted. "Stay and you will
get rich and fat from the plunder of the darklands!" She walked
toward the cowering ranks of soldiers, kicking Tethys's burned
body aside as she passed. "You claim to follow the Sun God. Does
he fear fire? Of course not. It is his birthright." She pointed to the
Danai. "They are witches, born of night, but the children of fire
are the children of the god. Pure of heart and beloved of Apollo.
And our task is not yet done. We march for the Gale!"

No cheers greeted this statement, nor did anyone try to
escape. They simply watched her with wide, terrified eyes.

And then two women ran forward through the carnage, the

only ones untouched by the flames. They looked young and carried staffs.

Domitia frowned. "What is this?" she murmured. "Mortals?"

The pair made straight for Galen and had covered half the distance before Thena shouted at the nearest soldiers. "Do something!" she screamed, seizing Galen's hair and dragging him back. The Danai looked dazed, his eyes red and unfocused. He fell to his knees, retching through the gag, and Thena gave his head an impatient yank.

One of the commanders had the presence of mind to confirm the order and two dozen burly soldiers surged forward. *This* was a fight they could win at least.

Or perhaps not.

The two staffs whirled in blurring arcs and within seconds, half lay groaning on the ground. The women moved with almost inhuman grace and speed, using the length of their staffs to deadly advantage. Domitia watched with an unreadable expression, though Nico thought he saw a hint of admiration in the set of her mouth.

The pair fought with a brutal efficiency that reminded Nico of the warrior priests of Tjanjin. For a minute, he thought they might actually break through to the heir. But for every soldier that went down, two more joined the fray. Finally, a Hoplite used his shield to batter a path inside the smallest one's defenses, sinking his sword deep in her side. With no one guarding her companion's back, the other fell quickly.

Nico shoved his way through the swarm of panting, bloodied men.

The second was already dead, staring glassily at the pewter sky. The first still breathed, though he could tell from the bubbling hitch that she wouldn't for long. Nico sank to his knees and touched her hand. Brown eyes fluttered open.

She looked like a child, hardly older than Atticus.

"You're not Danai," he said gently.

"I am parthenoi." Her eyes lost focus. "He comes... the Father." She smiled through red teeth.

"Parthenoi?" he echoed. "What is parthenoi?"

But no answer came.

Nico raised a shaking hand to his forehead. When he took it away, his palm was coated with a fine layer of white dust. Ash, he realized. It drifted through the air like snowflakes, carried on the wind. He scrubbed the hand on his coat sleeve. He felt soiled. The smell of death had sunk into his clothes, his skin. The girl's insane courage suddenly made him want to weep.

He sensed Domitia standing over him.

"You're angry with me," she said. The storm had broken and she was composed again. "You want to pretend you didn't know. But you did, Nicodemus. You knew."

Her words cut like a razor. "Yes, of course," he replied numbly. "None are to be spared. We will cleanse this land and make it our own."

"Yes." She seemed pleased. "That's right."

"And Nazafareen?"

"Let her find the bodies." Domitia smiled. "I'll make sure she can't miss them."

Nicodemus watched her walk over to one of her captains. The man visibly cringed at her approach, his head bobbing as she issued new orders. Half the horses had thrown their riders and galloped off. Wounded men lay everywhere. But discipline was slowly being restored, lines of command firming up. Those who could still walk were helping their injured comrades to the wagons. The rest moved to break camp and begin the march to the Gale.

Nico forced himself to look at what remained of the Danai army. Burnt husks heaped on top of each other, so many of them, limbs drawn into tight fetal positions. In the smoky twilight, it was a scene from nightmare.

He remembered how the young ones would gather in Gaius's

burrow, hanging on his every word. He told them stories about the Vatras' glorious past and how the other clans' jealousy had led to the long banishment. They thought he was a god—or as close to one as you could find in the Kiln. Gaius was disfigured in the fire that destroyed Pompeii and had swathes of bare skull where no hair grew. But it hadn't touched his face, which was deceptively mild. Nico had learned to avoid looking into Gaius's eyes for too long. The man could cast a spell on you.

The captain assembled a group of soldiers. They wrapped cloths around their noses and mouths and started dragging the Danai bodies into lines. It was a grisly task and more than one of them doubled over to spew up their breakfast.

Maybe she's right, he thought dully. Maybe I did know. And if I didn't, I should have. She is her father's daughter.

Nico followed her into the tent. Rugs covered the ground, but the only furniture was a simple cot. Iron gleamed from the mouth of a half-open sack in the corner. Collars. He flicked his gaze away before she saw him looking.

Domitia bent over the cot, rummaging through a small chest. She straightened as he entered and glanced at him over one shoulder. When he saw what she held in her hands, Nico froze.

"You kept it," he said. "After all this time."

She shook out the long lizard skin cloak. It was the exact color of sand, with darker blotches of pointed scales like a miniature mountain range. A matching shirt and trousers sat folded on the bed. Domitia gazed at the cloak with fondness.

"When I face Nazafareen, it will be as myself. I will walk into the Kiln as Domitia."

She unwrapped a length of linen from a narrow object about three hands long. Nico guessed what it was even before he saw the sharp flint lashed to the tip. Her thigh bone spear. There was no wood in the Kiln, so Domitia had scavenged the leg from a desiccated corpse and turned it into a weapon. She always said it was better than his shitty knife, which Nico couldn't really argue with. It was such things that set Domitia apart. She held the spear gently, reverently.

"And what of you?" she asked. "I remember when you stitched your first cloak together. You were clumsy with a needle. The hem was too long, always dragging in the dirt. But you were so proud of it." She eyed him teasingly. "When you put it on, you became a man. Or thought you did."

Nico remembered that day well. It wasn't long after his mother died. He was determined to be Atticus's protector. To show Gaius he could take care of them both. And to hunt, he needed a cloak. That meant catching at least a dozen of the poisonous lizards that lived in cracks in the ground. Domitia didn't help him do it—if you couldn't make a shadowtongue cloak on your own, you didn't deserve one—but she gave him his first weapon. The jagged tooth of a wyvern. And she taught him how to skin them in one piece and safely remove the venom sacks without contaminating the meat.

"Where's yours?" she asked, running a hand along the horny scales.

"I burned it."

"Well, to each his own." Her gaze raked his embroidered coat. "But the Kiln still lives inside you, Nicodemus. It always will." She turned her back. "Since you're such a fine gentleman now, perhaps you'd prefer to leave while I change."

Nico frowned. "You're putting it on now?"

"Why shouldn't I?"

Because I need to get you alone. Because this must be done at the Gale.

"I don't know," he said, pretending to think. "But the army hangs by a thread. They're terrified, but they still believe in the Oracle. She is a symbol. The voice of the god." He shrugged casually. "Do as you wish, but they might need that symbol for a while yet. Until the final moment comes."

Domitia was silent for a moment. "Perhaps you're right. I don't have time for a rebellion."

He let out a breath as she balled up the cloak and thrust it back into the chest, along with the shirt and pants. A hesitant voice trickled through the tent flaps.

"Oracle?"

"Enter," Domitia said, closing the lid.

A young man in the garb of a wind ship pilot sidled inside. He kept his gaze firmly on the carpet.

"Did you find the Breaker?" she asked.

"We did, Oracle. She was with a small party of witches. We used the spell dust as you commanded."

"Where is she?"

His Adam's apple bobbed. "Her mount went down—"

Instant rage flared. The temperature in the tent rose a few degrees. "I told you not to harm her, only delay her!"

The man looked green with fear. "It was an accident. She collided with another abbadax. But she took only minor injuries, we made sure of it."

"How many others survived?"

"The Danai who rode with her. Four mortals and two Valkirins." He paused. "One wore a collar."

"Demetrios." She smiled. "Good. Let him return to my tender care. Who was the other?"

"A female."

Domitia looked at Nicodemus with a frown. "Could they have found the heir?"

"She gave no sign of that, but it's possible."

"That would complicate things." She thought for a moment. "Even if she is the Valkirin talisman, we no longer need her. We'll burn her on sight." She turned back to the pilot. "Where are they now?"

"Licking their wounds, Oracle, but at least three of the mounts are uninjured. They will come."

"Prepare the ships to leave," Domitia told the pilot. "A second unit of Shields awaits us west of the river. Captain Leonidas will give you the exact location. How fast can you get us to their camp?"

"Less than an hour."

She nodded in approval. "That should be ample time. Nicodemus, you will travel with me. There are things to discuss. You have ten minutes to be ready. We cannot delay."

He inclined his head in assent.

She pointed to the chest. "Load that into one of the ships," she told the pilot.

Domitia strode outside and conferred with a clutch of her commanders, who waited near the wind ships floating at anchor above the Umbra.

"That too," Nico told the man, indicating the sack of collars in the corner. "And the rugs. She might want it later and you wouldn't want to explain that you'd left it behind, would you?"

"No, my lord," the pilot said fervently.

Nico slipped out of the tent. A line of wagons was carrying the injured back to Delphi. Most of the cavalry had already departed, riding hard for the Gale.

After making sure that Domitia wasn't watching, Nico set out to find the Archon Basileus. He'd last seen the man running for the wagons and hoped he hadn't decided to sneak away on one. For all that Basileus had twined his fate with Nico's, the man was still a snake.

Nico needed him. He still carried some degree of authority. And Nico couldn't be seen pulling Thena aside. Domitia would surely notice that.

Then he saw him standing next to one of the wind ships. He had a blank-eyed look, but it cleared a bit when Nicodemus clapped him hard on the shoulder, raising a puff of dust from his red cloak.

"We need to talk," Nico said. "Come to my tent."

Four soldiers were about to take it down, but Nico waved them off and ducked inside. He'd brought few possessions. The clothes on his back, a skin of wine (still full), the pair of knives—and the bag of talismans he'd taken from the collection of the emperor of Tjanjin. He rummaged through it and took out a small gold chalice.

"This induces a deathlike slumber if one takes liquid from it. Even the tiniest sip."

Basileus eyed the chalice. "I presume you mean this for Domitia."

"The massacre of the Danai is just the prelude. When Gaius comes through, this land will burn, Basileus. From the White Sea to the Austral Ocean."

The Archon licked his lips. "Yes, I see that."

"But there is one person who might be able to stop him."

"The Breaker?"

"That's why I like you, Basileus. You're quick. Yes, the Breaker. We need to offer her something. An olive branch."

Basileus arched an eyebrow. "An olive branch, my lord? After what just occurred?"

"I know. But there might be a way." Nico cocked his head. "Have you ever wondered why only certain mortals can wear the bracelets?"

"I have. It seems an innate talent. But the girls have nothing in common otherwise."

"Are you certain of that?" he paused. "What if they have daēva blood?"

Basileus looked shocked and Nico laughed.

"Come now, Archon. You're a man of the world. The races might live apart, but that doesn't mean there haven't been...secret liaisons. These things happen. The powers of the resulting offspring would likely be weak. They might be unaware of them. And no one would know, except that Domitia came and started testing for the ability to wear the bracelets."

"I suppose it could be possible," Basileus said thoughtfully.

"More than possible. And if they can use one talisman, they can use another."

"You're speaking of Thena."

Nico nodded. "Promise her anything you want. She can be disposed of later." In fact, Nicodemus would make sure of it. If Basileus was a snake, Thena was a rabid dog. "Don't tell her *why* she can use the talismans. I don't think that would go over very well."

"No, my lord. I'm certain it wouldn't."

"Tell her Apollo has granted her special power. She'll like that. Here's what she must do."

He paced up and down, laying out his plan. Basileus listened in silence.

"I will be Tyrant of Delphi?"

"You will be Tyrant. That I swear."

"And if it goes wrong?"

Nico laughed mirthlessly. "There are a hundred ways it could go wrong. But if it works, we'll be rid of Domitia. And Nazafareen will have no choice but to kill Gaius."

"I suppose it would be fitting," Basileus conceded. "But why don't you just—"

"I have my reasons," Nico interrupted coldly. "The main question is whether the girl will go for it."

"If she doesn't, we will be exposed."

"Yes."

They stared at each other for a long moment.

"I think she will," Basileus said finally. "Though with all due respect, I'm not sure if you're a genius or an imbecile."

Nico gave a thin smile. "Nor am I, Archon. Nor am I."

15

CALIGULA

When Cyrene died, Nazafareen was unable to watch anymore. She let the scene in the globe vanish. No one objected.

Megaera and Rhea embraced each other, crying silently. Herodotus seemed to have aged ten years. His hands, usually tugging at his beard or scribbling on a piece of vellum, hung limp at his sides, his gaze blank. Kallisto leaned on her staff, whispering to herself. Perhaps she was praying. Nazafareen stifled a nasty laugh.

Let Kallisto have her imaginary god. Nazafareen had no use for him anymore.

Her gaze followed Darius as he strode off into the twilight. He stopped about a hundred paces away and put his hands to his face. Then he straightened and stood there, staring at the darkness to the east.

She looked at the stiff lines of his back, the dark hair curling against the collar of his coat, and wondered what he was thinking. If he blamed her.

He had every right to. If she hadn't pushed to go to Val Moraine, they would have been marching with the Danai.

Or maybe he was angry at himself. The last time he saw his mother, he hadn't treated her kindly.

Nazafareen returned the globe to her pocket. She felt an eerie calm, though it masked a rage so catastrophic she held it in a tight vise, to be unleashed at the proper time.

Once, he would have slammed his walls down and built a protective shell. Once, she would have let him brood. But now he needed her.

Nazafareen walked over and put her arms around him. He pressed his cheek against her forehead—it was scratchy, she noticed distantly, he needed to shave—and though he didn't make a sound, her own face grew wet with his tears.

After some time, he gently unwound her arms.

"Give me a minute alone," he said, his voice rough but steady.

She nodded, still not quite trusting herself to speak, and walked over to Daníel and Katrin, who waited with the wounded. Only three of the company had survived, two Valkirins and the Danai who'd joked about it being hot in Delphi. She nursed a broken arm and was sharing a water skin with one of the Valkirins. The other was barely alive and Nazafareen doubted he'd last another hour.

She saw her own hatred reflected in Daníel's eyes. If he was afraid, he covered it well. But Katrin looked shaken. For the first time, she didn't sneer as Nazafareen approached.

"The mounts have to rest," Katrin said. "They can't make the Gale in this condition. It's another fifty leagues."

"How long?"

"A few hours."

"Fine."

The delay chafed, but what did a few hours matter? Every beat of the Pythia's heart marked the countdown to her death.

Katrin jerked her chin toward Darius. "They were his close kin?"

"His mother and grandmother. Cousins."

Nazafareen thought of Tethys's garden and the centuries she must have spent tending it. Would anyone care enough to save it? Or would it slowly be devoured by the forest?

Katrin nodded slowly. It was strange to see sympathy on the woman's face. Her primary emotions seemed to be fury and condescension, but she had her own ghosts.

"He'll manage," Nazafareen said. "I wouldn't go near him for a while though."

Her voice sounded so cold. Daniel frowned and Nazafareen turned away before he could see the truth. That she was on the verge of a precipice so deep and dark it might swallow her whole if she took a wrong step.

"When it's over, we'll return our dead to the crypts," Daniel said in a tight voice. "And the Danai to their forest. But for now we should protect them from carrion. I can make a shield of air."

Nazafareen cast a glance at Darius, who remained where he was, apart and unmoving. She left him there and went to Rhea and Megaera.

"Will you help us gather the dead?" she asked.

Megaera was red and puffy, Rhea pale and hollow-eyed.

"Of course," Megaera mumbled.

"Charis and Cyrene," Nazafareen began. Saying their names nearly punctured her self-control and she paused, feeling the weight of Nemesis against her shoulder, the dry air in her lungs. She imagined the Pythia pleading for mercy she would never receive. "They fought well."

"Yes," Rhea replied, her throat convulsing once. "They fought well."

"When the mounts have rested, we'll ride for the Gale. We will avenge them. Completely and utterly."

"It will be done," Megaera growled, something of her old self surfacing though the tide of grief.

"I still don't understand," Rhea muttered. "Why did the Vatra do it? They would have been far more useful as hostages."

Nazafareen gave a hollow laugh. "Why else? Because she could."

"It is more than that, I think," Kallisto said, coming over with Herodotus. They'd been standing close enough to overhear the exchange. "She's a calculating creature. Perhaps her aim is to anger you beyond reason. Goad you into making a mistake."

Nazafareen said nothing.

"Don't blame yourself," Kallisto said sternly. "Any blood shed today is on *her* hands."

Nazafareen waited. There was obviously more. Some lecture to be delivered.

"Say what you came to say," she snapped. "We have work to do."

Kallisto stared at her. "I know you want revenge. All I ask is that you proceed with caution. Don't let your fury blind you."

Kallisto meant well, but she didn't seem to grasp the central fact of Nazafareen's power. The angrier she was, the greater its destructive power. No magic would stand before her—not spell dust, not talismans, not any of the elements—and the daēvas could easily decimate whatever mortal army the Vatras had brought.

"I won't," she said.

Nazafareen felt Kallisto's dark eyes studying her as she strode off toward Daníel and Katrin.

She forced herself to look at the shattered limbs and ghastly impact wounds as they gathered the bodies and laid them out, Valkirin and Danai side by side. Eventually Darius noticed what they were doing and came to help, though he spoke not a word. Daníel laid a shield of air over the bodies to preserve them until they could be seen to properly. Within minutes, the wind covered it with a fine layer of dust.

The abbadax were too heavy to move, but the Valkirins paid respects to each of them: Alsvinder and Fenrir, Dain and Heidrun, Glaor and Gullfaxi, which meant golden feathers.

When it was done, Darius sat down next to Brynjar. He opened one of the saddlebags and took out a water skin, offering it to Nazafareen. His eyes were red but dry.

"Thank you." As the water touched her cracked lips, Nazafareen realized how thirsty she was. Darius had already found another skin, so she drained it. She sat down next to him, their shoulders touching.

"At least Victor wasn't here to see it," he said.

"Darius—" she began.

"It's all right. I'm all right."

"No, you're not."

"Must you argue with everything?" he asked wearily.

"Only when I'm right."

He was silent for a moment, tilting his head back to look at Artemis. Tattered clouds made the moon seem to leer down at them like the grey, bloated face of a corpse. "They didn't stand a chance. Not a chance."

"No," she agreed.

"What if we lose?" His lips thinned. "What if we've already lost?"

She knew he'd just suffered an unimaginable loss. His despair was understandable. Yet for an instant, she hated him for it.

"Don't say that. It's not true."

"No?" His gaze searched hers. "Then tell me what winning looks like."

She had no answer—not that she would speak aloud. But Sauvanne Suchy had made a good start.

The Acropolis and the Temple of Apollo will be razed to the ground. You will die, along with all who follow you. The walls of Delphi will be broken and the Archons cast down.

And the Oracle....

What you did to the Danai is child's play compared to what I will do to you.

"Whatever advantage the Vatra thinks she has, it won't be enough. I will destroy her, Darius. I swear it."

"That won't bring Delilah back."

"No, but it will stop the spread of this evil so no others share her fate."

"I hate this world we've come to," Darius spat, his reserve cracking. "It's worse than the Empire."

Nazafareen couldn't remember the Empire, but she wondered if this were true. From Darius's description, it was a hellish place to be a daēva. Yet his kind were no better, were they? Danai hating Valkirins, Valkirins hating Danai, Vatras hating *everyone*. Only the Marakai seemed to have any sense, holding themselves aloof from the other clans except to trade.

How like us they are, she thought darkly. Driven by fear and greed.

"We're here for a reason," she said. "To do our duty."

He closed his eyes, his voice barely a whisper. "I'm tired of duty."

"All the more reason to finish it quickly." Nazafareen watched Kallisto and Herodotus make their way over. "Here they come. She probably has another lecture planned about keeping a cool head."

"Can we talk?" Kallisto asked. Herodotus hovered at her side. They both looked at Darius with wary sympathy.

Nazafareen stowed the water skin, every movement deliberate. "Go ahead."

"You see now what the Vatras are capable of. And if the Pythia is truly Gaius's daughter, it's no surprise she's so ruthless." She paused. "The other one? That was Nicodemus?"

Nazafareen nodded.

"He didn't know what she planned, I think. He seemed sickened by it."

Nazafareen had barely registered the Vatra's reaction amid her own horror.

"Does it matter?"

"It might." Kallisto looked at Herodotus. "Tell them what you know about Gaius."

He nodded. "While the Viper led a force to the Great Forest and the Valkirin holdfasts, Gaius marched on the mortal cities with his own legion. They burned the Marakai ships in the harbor of Delphi, which was then only a large village, and set out for Samarqand. At the time, it was a port city on the Austral Ocean. General Jamadin sealed the gates. Unfortunately, they were made of wood. The Vatras burned them and entered the city, rounding up those who hadn't already fled in a field now known as the Abicari."

The name sounded familiar, although Nazafareen couldn't place where she'd heard it. She thought of all those terrified people. Suddenly, she despised Herodotus.

"I don't want to hear the end of this story," she said roughly.

He eyed her with a level gaze. "Nor do I wish to tell it. But I think you should know who your enemies are."

Nazafareen gave him a cold stare. "Very well."

"Gaius chose two dozen women for his harem, tearing children from their mothers' breasts, and slaughtered the rest. He scorched the Rock of Ariamazes and tried to pull it down, but failed. It was Danai work, you see. Built to last for millennia." Herodotus blinked. "I suppose he would have gotten inside eventually, but then word came that the surviving Danai and Valkirins were marching on Pompeii so he put the city to the torch and left. That was the last they saw of him. He never offered any explanation for why he turned on the mortals.

"Most historians think him mad. One dubbed him Caligula, which means tiny boots in the language of the Vatras. Apparently his feet were quite small." Herodotus cleared his throat. "The implication being that he might be, ah, diminutive in other anatomical aspects as well."

Nazafareen snorted. "They could be right. Culach told me the war started because Gaius was rejected by a Danai woman." She rubbed her stump, thumb caressing the smooth flesh where it met bone. "The Pythia seemed to blame the other clans, but she didn't mention Farrumohr. If he were loose in the world, I think we'd know it by now."

"Unless he's hidden himself," Darius said. "Taken her body."

"Then he will die with her." Her face darkened. "I'll make certain of it this time."

They turned at the sound of footsteps. It was Katrin. She stopped a short distance away, one hand resting on the hilt of her broadsword.

"It's time." She glanced toward Daniel and the abbadax, which were saddled up and ready to fly. "The wounded will wait until we return for them. Jormun cannot be moved, and there aren't enough mounts anyway. As it is, we'll have to ride double."

Nazafareen stood, a jolt of adrenaline singing through her limbs.

"Who will you take?" she asked, assuming Katrin would prefer Darius at her back.

"You can both have Berglaug. I'll ride with Daniel."

Her flat eyes signaled that she didn't wish to explain this sudden generosity.

Darius nodded. "Thank you."

Katrin whistled for Berglaug and whispered something to the mount. "There's no need to cut your palms. She'll take you without the blood scent."

"We'll land the moment we reach Solis," Nazafareen said. "I'll be able to break your ward then."

Katrin gave a brief nod of acknowledgement and vaulted into the saddle behind Daniel. Kallisto and Herodotus, Rhea and Megaera climbed aboard their own abbadax and buckled the harnesses.

As promised, Berglaug accepted Nazafareen and Darius without complaint, though her yellow eyes watched Katrin closely. The Valkirin woman gave a hand signal and the four abbadax climbed into the sky, speeding west across the Umbra. Nazafareen saw no sign of the Pythia's wind ships, but it wasn't long before they reached the site of the battle. Darius's breath hitched as he stared down at the scorched plain.

The bodies of the Danai had been arranged to form an arrow pointing toward the Gale.

He said nothing and she didn't either. They flew on. Nazafareen kept her eyes fixed on the western sky, now tinted a pale rose. When they reached the outskirts of Delphi, a molten sliver of sun crested the horizon, its light striking her face. The bond with Darius burst to life—sudden pain in his left arm, followed by a tidal flow of other emotions and sensations—and so did her huo mofa. A dark euphoria swelled in her heart. She'd craved both like a balm.

Rich farmland rolled past below, green-gold fields of wheat, stands of olives and dates. People labored in the fields. When they saw the abbadax, they threw down their hoes and ran.

Nazafareen signaled the others to land in an open pasture near a farmhouse. It was similar to the one that had once belonged to the Maenads, a long, low-slung building of stone and mudbrick. A family spilled out the door as the mounts alit, hurrying for the road that led toward the city. The children were crying. Nazafareen considered calling out and telling them not to be afraid, but they were gone before she had a chance.

And perhaps they were right to be afraid.

She dismounted and walked up to Katrin, who stood a full pace taller. The Valkirin woman squared her shoulders. Her breath came in short, shallow bursts.

"It will hurt," Nazafareen warned.

Katrin looked disdainful. "I don't fear pain, mortal."

"Then what do you fear?" Nazafareen said in an acid tone. "That you are not the chosen one after all? That you are simply *weak*?"

The anger was trickling through cracks in her walls now, the pressure building.

Katrin gave a tight laugh. "I guess we'll find out in a minute." She squinted against the sunlight peeking through the low hills and stripped off her leather coat, tossing it aside. "Fucking hot."

She wore a sleeveless shirt beneath and her arms were corded with lean muscle that rippled as she moved. Her physique made brawny Megaera look like a ten-year-old girl. Rhea eyed her with frank appreciation.

Katrin thumped her chest, eyes like chips of green ice. "Do it."

Nazafareen tried to think through the red mist. Her own cuff was a talisman. It hadn't broken last time with Meb, but she didn't want to take a chance. She yanked it off the stump and tossed it to Megaera.

"Move away," she snarled, hardly recognizing her own voice. "All of you."

Kallisto lingered and Nazafareen cast a pointed look at her staff.

"Stay if you want, but don't blame me when you lose that."

Kallisto's brows drew down but she retreated toward the farmhouse with the others, leaving Nazafareen and Katrin alone in the field. A breeze rippled the wheat. In the grove, she heard the warbling notes of a wren.

Sweat rolled down her brow. She stared at Katrin, waiting for the familiar tug of magic to draw the baleful eye of her power. It didn't come. The huo mofa just roiled in her belly. Saliva filled her mouth. She spat on the ground and it sizzled for a moment before sputtering out.

She couldn't feel the ward.

Had she felt Meb's? Nazafareen didn't think so. She'd only broken it because the girl stood in the path of a talisman. This magic was different somehow. Wards upon wards, to hide them even from a Breaker's sight.

Nazafareen took the globe from her pocket. She hated to lose it, but she already knew where the Pythia was.

"Hold this," she said, walking up to Katrin.

The Valkirin shrugged and took the glass orb.

When her magic returned, Nazafareen had forced the talisman from her mind, just as she'd learned to ignore her own cuff.

Not those, she'd whispered to her power. *Those are not for you.*

But now she let herself see the fine threads of air and water that bound the globe together, just as she had with the chimera and the gates. Her magic leapt in its traces and she barely managed to raise her hand before black lightning shot from her palm. The globe exploded in a cloud of pulverized glass that glittered in the sunlight. And then the huo mofa passed straight through into the woman beyond.

Katrin went rigid. Her head lolled back, fingers splaying wide as every muscle seized. Even having seen it before with Meb and knowing Katrin was not truly injured, Nazafareen winced. She hurried forward, catching Katrin in her arms just as she collapsed to the ground.

Daniel ran over, his face stricken. "What's happened? Is she dead?"

Nazafareen shook her head, easing Katrin down into the soft wheat. "Just wait."

Long minutes ticked past. The others gathered close, holding a silent vigil. Katrin did not stir. In truth, she *looked* dead. But when Herodotus laid an ear to her lips, he reported faint breathing. Nazafareen was just starting to worry when Katrin rolled to her side with a groan.

"The Drowned Lady," she murmured. "She kissed me."

Katrin looked up at the sky and began to laugh. It was a sound full of wonder and joy, the carefree laughter of a child. After the unrelenting horrors of the last day, Nazafareen barely recognized it.

"The Drowned Lady," Herodotus exclaimed. "She is real then. Nabu-bal-idinna spoke of her, but I never thought…" He cut off abruptly as Katrin floated a few feet off the ground and hovered there, little whirlwinds making the wheat around her dance and sway.

"She kissed me!"

"Come down," Nazafareen snapped, in no mood for games. "This instant."

"Yes, I will," Katrin said dreamily. Her face darkened. "But first, the mortals will know my presence."

Nazafareen shared an uneasy look with Darius. Kallisto hurried forward, leaping up to catch the edge of Katrin's shirt, but she'd already floated out of reach. Rhea was grinning foolishly, but Megaera, who'd seen the wave Meb summoned, wore a deep scowl.

The clouds began to thicken and roil, racing west from the darklands. Within moments, the sun had vanished. Megaera shook her head in disgust.

"Must they all show off?" she muttered.

"Katrin!" Kallisto yelled.

The Valkirin paid her no attention. She had a faraway look on her face and her short silver hair whipped in the wind. The temperature dropped until Nazafareen's breath plumed white. Herodotus let out a surprised laugh. Fat flakes dusted his beard.

"Do you know, this is the first time in a thousand years it's snowed in Solis," he said.

Katrin grinned down at him. The abbadax, which had been drooping in the heat, made burbling sounds that Nazafareen interpreted as happiness. It never became a full-blown blizzard, but by the time they persuaded Katrin to come down and behave herself, two inches of snow covered the field.

"I could have summoned more," Katrin said happily, her feet planted on the ground again, as the rest of them shivered. "*Much* more."

"Well, your restraint is appreciated, Katrin Aigirsdottir," Kallisto said dryly.

"Tell us about this Lady," Herodotus said. "Did you speak with her?"

Katrin frowned. "It's like a half-remembered dream now. But she came to me, fearsome and pale." Her gaze turned to Nazafareen. "I asked what I should do. She said it was my decision." Katrin's face hardened. "So I will go with you to fight the Pythia. She and her army will be swept away like pebbles in an avalanche." She touched her sword in an oddly formal gesture. "This I swear."

Something loosened in Nazafareen's chest. She nodded.

"Thank you."

Katrin flushed and turned away. But some of the old bitterness seemed to have left her. Nazafareen watched her walk over to Rhea, their heads together, one dark, one light, laughing over something, and thought she understood Katrin a little better now. The Valkirin woman was a warrior above all things, and the burden of shame she'd carried her whole life was lifted.

Nazafareen turned to Darius. "The Pythia doesn't know we have Katrin," she said quietly. "Unless she's been spying on us with the globe this whole time. But I don't think she has. I sensed it, when I was in Culach's chambers and Nico found me. A feeling of being watched." She took his right hand. The left was a withered husk again. "We have her now. She won't escape."

He nodded. The thought seemed to cheer him a little.

"How far to the Gale?" she asked.

"An hour, perhaps."

"Then let us waste no more time." She glanced at the snow-covered saddle. "I'll be going into battle with a frozen bum, but you can't have everything."

❧ 16 ❧

CAT AND MOUSE

Thena propped her elbows on the gunwale of the wind ship, the world rolling itself out like a carpet beneath her feet. They were well past Delphi and entering the last of the fertile lands irrigated by the river. To the north lay the barren, uninhabited peninsula that sheltered the western shore of the Cimmerian Sea.

Korinna used to claim it was infested with bandits—dangerous, cruel men who had fled the Polemarch's justice. She said they ambushed travelers and sold them to the witches for meat. Thena had always doubted this since no one ever went that way in the first place, and the southern roads were well guarded.

Poor, foolish Korinna. She had a vivid imagination. The other girls lapped up her tales of star-crossed lovers and hair-raising rescues, of monsters and heroes and babies switched at birth. Thena sighed. If only her constitution hadn't been so frail. But the girl had succumbed to a terrible fever at Val Moraine. She vaguely remembered the rattling cough that came from her throat. The thrashing and gasping at the end.

It wasn't a pleasant memory and Thena decided not to dwell on it.

The wind ship entered the final reaches where the sunbaked mudflats west of the river gave way to sand—and there it was, just as she'd left it all those years ago. Her father's farm.

The thatched roof of the main house was now tiled, but otherwise it looked the same. There were the goats, grazing in their fenced enclosure, and the shed where she and her sisters did the milking. The old gnarled oak she climbed as a girl. Thena would hide in its spreading limbs and dream of Apollo, chained in his chariot, his beautiful face tight with suffering. Sometimes she imagined finding a magical talisman that would shatter his chains. He would place her above other mortals, perhaps even make her one of his brides....

On the morning of her thirteenth birthday, she'd set out for the Temple to pledge herself as an initiate. Her father drove her through the gates of Delphi in his wagon, up the long winding road to the Acropolis. When she saw the temple, tears of joy ran down her face, though in the months to come, she suffered bouts of homesickness so severe she could hardly leave her bed. The old Pythia said she suffered from melancholia. A darkness of the soul. She was not unkind, but Thena could tell the Pythia thought she was unfit to be an acolyte. There were many girls waiting to take her place and if she could not perform her duties, perhaps it was best if she returned to the farm.

Thena begged not to be sent away. She only missed her mother's cooking and her sisters' good-natured ribbing, that was all. Everything seemed new and strange. So she learned to hide the strange, disconnected feeling that stole over her sometimes, to fix a smile on her face and pretend she was perfectly content even when her limbs were heavy with torpor and queer things capered at the edges of her vision.

Then one day, while she was pulling weeds in the kitchen garden, Apollo spoke to her. A sudden voice in her head that froze her with terror. But his words filled her with exhilaration.

He told her how special she was. That one day, she would be the salvation of humanity.

After that, Thena adjusted quickly to her new life. The melancholia retreated. She never told anyone of her visions. Only the Pythia was supposed to commune directly with the god. Her talents would be called blasphemous or worse. But she always knew the call would come one day, and she would be ready when it did.

Now she looked down at her father's farm and felt nothing. It was as if a stranger had lived there. The girl she had once been was long dead and a new Thena had risen in her place, like a phoenix from the ashes. The Archon confirmed this. He too was an instrument of the god. Thena knew it was not Basileus who had quietly spoken to her minutes before the wind ships departed. It was Apollo.

His plan was clear to her now. Such a complex weaving, but her thread had found its proper place in the loom again. And men would fall to their knees in wonder when they saw the final tapestry.

She glanced at the witch, huddled in the stern. His shock and grief saturated the leash between them. So much hatred in his heart! But Thena understood it. She looked at him with something approximating sympathy.

"You despise her for what she did. And you were right when you called her a witch. I shouldn't have punished you for it. Violence is her nature."

He was gagged and thus didn't answer, but his black eyes stared murder. Thena sighed. They were like wild animals.

"That is why we must civilize you. It is our burden. One day I will find your brother again and civilize him properly. I was too gentle last time. It did neither of us credit."

She glanced at Galen. No, Calix. That was his new name.

"If you don't survive the next hour or so, please know I bear you no personal malice. It would be like hating the rats that infest the granaries." She flashed her dimples. "They are a plague, yes, but that is why we have cats to catch and eat them." Fingers curled into mock paws. "I am like a cat, little witch. I earn my keep."

Calix was still staring defiantly at her and Thena administered a jolt of pain, like a needle in the soft part of his armpit. He flinched and looked down. She laughed.

"I have claws too, don't forget."

The farm fell away behind them. It was the very last. And then the sands began. She gazed down at the dunes. "I grew up out here, you know. On the edge of the world. But I was never afraid. We had the Gale to protect us. The Pythia means to destroy it, but we shall see, little witch. We shall see."

She ran her hands down her braid, tucking the loose wisps of hair back into place. The talisman Basileus gave her burned in her pocket. Magic was wicked, but it could still be used for the greater good.

The sun rose higher...and then vanished like a snuffed candle. The hair rose on her arms as the Gale appeared as a dark line on the horizon. As it grew closer, she could see the clouds stretched right down to the earth, black as a starless night in Nocturne. The wind gained strength, bringing gusts of rain. Thena drew up the hood of her cloak.

The pilot began dumping heavy sacks of ballast over the side. The ship descended toward a stand of scrubby trees, where a small camp had already been set up. Three other ships carried Shields of Apollo, the Pythia, the red-haired witch named Nicodemus and the Archon Basileus. The rest of the army was following on foot and by horse, but it would be some time before they caught up.

When the ship landed, Thena descended a rope ladder, followed by Galen. Soldiers scrambled to erect the Pythia's tent, blazoned with a dancing red flame. Thena went to her side.

"The time is upon us, daughter," the Pythia said, her eyes fixed on the Gale. "We must take courage. The Breaker is coming, but we stand in Apollo's light. It is his will that guides my hand."

Thena absorbed this blasphemy with a bland smile. Blasphemy because it was spoken by a lying, treacherous witch, but the words were true enough.

"I am ready, Mother," Thena said.

The Pythia gave her a hard look and Thena wondered if she suspected something. "Are you? If you harbor doubts, you would do well to remember the last time you stood before the god in judgment. He granted you a second chance, but I would not count on a third."

Rage simmered at this reminder of her torture in the brazen bull, and Thena cast her eyes down before the Pythia saw it.

"I know that, Mother. I wish only to serve the light."

"See that you do. There can be no mistakes." The Pythia seized Thena's chin in a rough grip, forcing her to meet her cold eyes. "We must take the heir closer to the Gale. As close as we can get without being devoured by the storms. You will hold his leash."

Thena's heart pounded. As much as she hated the witch, she feared her, too.

She could burn me up in an instant.

"And what will happen then, Mother?"

The Pythia released her grip, a faint smile touching the corners of her lips.

"A new age will dawn, Sun Daughter."

Thena felt a prickling sensation and turned her head. Nicodemus was looking at her. Their eyes met for an instant and he dropped his gaze, striding over. A muscle flickered in his jaw, but his voice was relaxed.

"Do you have the globe?" he asked. "We should find the Breaker."

The Pythia signaled to the soldiers who were unloading the wind ships. Two of them brought over a small chest. She opened it and took out the glass orb. Black storm clouds boiled in its depths, as though it contained a tiny version of the Gale. She blew gently and the carved runes on its base glowed blue. Three abbadax appeared, each carrying two riders. A river unfurled below them.

"She's still an hour away," the Pythia said briskly. "I need a few minutes to prepare. Then we ride for the Gale."

She strode toward her tent. Basileus nodded at Thena, who slipped inside after her.

NICODEMUS WATCHED THEM GO, HIS HEART THUDDING AGAINST his ribs. A dozen Shields of Apollo formed an honor guard around the tent. Others ringed Galen, who looked half-dead with exhaustion. A league distant, the Gale ground its teeth, chewing up the landscape and spitting it skyward.

Basileus stood very still beside him. Neither man spoke. They were past the point of words. But a thousand thoughts raced through Nico's mind. A thousand ways this day could end in disaster. Suddenly, it all seemed like madness, but it was too late to stop Thena now.

A single piercing shriek came from inside the tent. The Shields drew their swords just as the flap twitched aside.

His breath caught as Domitia emerged, still in the white gown with its serpent brooch. Basileus made a strangled noise. Her face twisted with fury as she pointed at Nicodemus.

"That little chit Thena attacked me," she growled. "She would never have had the courage to do it on her own. Your hand is behind this!"

The Shields surged forward, but Domitia made a sharp gesture and they halted.

"No," she said. "He's mine."

She strode forward, her pale gaze fixed on Nicodemus. Ice

trickled down his spine. He didn't dare look away from her, but he heard the soft scrape of Basileus's boots retreating.

An opportunist to the last.

Domitia regarded him without speaking for a long moment. The camp was so quiet, he could hear

"You sought to betray me," she said at last, a touch sadly. "Why?"

Nico shook his head, the hilt of Sakhet's knife sliding toward his palm from where he'd concealed within his coat sleeve. "Whatever the girl did, I had nothing to do with it—"

"I burned her to ash. A waste, but you left me no choice." Rage flared. "I needed her! You've ruined everything. And now you will burn too." Her eyes flared with a mad light. "The god has proclaimed it!"

She raised a hand. His fingers closed around the sweat-slicked knife.

"Abbadax!" Basileus cried in a high, cracked voice, sharp with terror.

She turned, just for an instant, and he brought the knife down with the speed of a striking serpent. Domitia screamed as red spurted from her chest, splattering his face. The flames building inside him erupted outward, surrounding them in a fiercely blazing circle. He yanked the blade free and she tumbled into the mud. A crimson pool spread beneath her as she stared at him, her mouth opening and closing, back arching. The Shields of Apollo ringing the tent took a few uncertain steps forward, but the circle of fire kept them at bay.

She bared her teeth at him and gave a twitch. Her eyes fixed on a point over his shoulder.

Nico drew a sharp breath, waves of heat sweeping across his skin, followed by the fatigue that always accompanied working fire.

"Raise a hand against me and you all die!" he shouted.

The Shields froze. They were an elite unit, trained to capture daēvas, but they'd seen what happened to the Danai. One of the men turned away and quietly vomited.

Nicodemus dropped to his knees and placed a finger to her neck, then bowed his head, shaking with relief.

It was done.

He rose and looked at the tent, at the flame blazoned on the side.

I'm sorry, but you left me no choice, he thought. Or none that I could live with.

"Bring her back to Delphi," he said to Basileus. "She will be buried with all the honor afforded to the Oracles." The Archon stared at the body. "Move! She can't harm you now. Put her in the wagon."

Basileus lifted Domitia in his arms, staggering to the wagon bed. Nicodemus wiped his face on his coat sleeve and turned back to the Shields. They were built like battering rams yet now they looked more akin to frightened children, flinching beneath his gaze. One made the sign to ward off evil.

"You there!" He pointed to the commander, a hatchet-faced man with a short beard named Leonidas, who was the only one to meet Nico's eyes. He hurried over, his expression wary.

"I don't doubt that you are a man of honor with only the best interests of the people of Delphi at heart," Nicodemus said gravely. "The Pythia did not share your loyalty. In the end, she would have seen the city burn." He paused. "You're not stupid. You know what I am now. She was the same."

Leonidas said nothing, though the blood drained from his face.

"I am a Vatra, but I have no hatred for mortals. If you follow my orders, Delphi will remain a free city—with a few changes." He turned to Basileus. "The Archon acts for me, and you will obey him as you would myself. If you do not...." He gave a chilly smile. "I will know when I return with more of my kin. Is that clear?"

Leonidas drew a slow breath and nodded. "Aye, it's clear enough."

"All the men will return to barracks. This campaign is concluded. You will instruct the Shields accordingly. Intercept the infantry and horse and bring them back with you."

"Yes, my lord."

"You're dismissed, general."

The man gave a brisk salute and went off to relay the orders to his men. Domitia had chosen her leaders well, Nico reflected. Leonidas might be appalled at the turn of events, but he'd mastered his fear and carried on. It was possible to adapt to almost anything with sufficient motivation.

He watched as the soldiers broke the camp down in record time. They seemed eager to be gone. Few spared Domitia a second glance, though he noticed they gave the wagon a wide berth. She would not be mourned.

Nico strode over to Galen and unwrapped the gag from his mouth. The Danai stared at him with wide eyes.

"There's a good lad," Nico muttered. "It will all be over soon."

Basileus emerged from Domitia's tent, looking pale.

"Thena is dead," he said.

Nico glanced at Galen. "I can't imagine you're sorry to hear that."

"I...I felt it happen," he mumbled, stunned relief on his face. "The connection broke."

"You will personally escort both bodies back to Delphi," Nico told Basileus. He eyed Galen's collar with distaste. "But first I need the keys to unlock that thing."

"It will be done, my lord," Basileus said. His lips pursed. "Thena was badly charred. I rolled her up in one of the rugs."

"Good. You can remove the body. Put it in the wagon with Domitia." He glanced at Galen. "Come with me."

The Danai shuffled along next to him as they entered the tent. It was in disarray, the table toppled over. A pair of bare feet stuck out from the end of a rolled-up carpet. Basileus dragged it to the opening, where he bade two of the Shields to carry it to the wagon.

"I took her keys, my lord," Basileus said, panting a little. He handed Nicodemus a heavy ring.

"Good." Nico found the globe of seeking in one of the boxes, along with Domitia's shadowtongue cloak. The feel of the rough, papery hide in his hands brought back a wave of memories, most of them ones he preferred to forget. It even smelled like the Kiln —dry and barren. But he might need it.

Nico shook it open and draped it across his shoulders. She was slightly shorter so it only reached his shins, but the fit wasn't bad. Basileus looked away, discomfited by this reminder of his master's past.

"I'm counting on you to keep Delphi under control until other matters are sorted out," Nico said. "You have the army now. The nobles you must convince yourself."

The Archon licked his lips. "I will handle them, my lord. Most of them feared the Pythia's growing influence. They will not be sorry she is gone."

Nico looked at him sharply. "If you turn the people against you with cruelty, I will not save you from the mob."

Basileus gave him an offended look. "I am not Domitia, my lord. I never approved of the brazen bull in the first place. Do not fear, I will hold the reins of power with a just but firm hand."

"Will you?" Nico murmured.

"What, my lord?"

"Nothing. You have my thanks for that bit of diversion, but do not cross me. I *will* return."

Basileus gave a quick bow and swept off in a swirl of his crimson cloak. Nicodemus sighed and led Galen outside, watching as the wagons and horses disappeared into the rain. The solution was far from perfect, but the Archon could hardly be worse than Domitia.

He jangled the ring of keys.

"I'm willing to unlock that collar, but if you attempt to run, or to strike at me in any way, I will not hesitate to use fire. Is that understood?"

Galen stared at the keys. "Perfectly."

"Turn around."

Nico slipped the key into the lock and twisted. He lifted the hasp and the collar fell to the ground. Galen kicked it away and rubbed his throat.

"Thank you," he said hoarsely.

Nico shrugged. "Save your thanks. I have my own reasons and they're nothing to do with you."

"Well, I don't care what they are. I'm still grateful." He paused. "What now?"

"We wait for a woman named Nazafareen. She's a breaker of magic."

"Nazafareen?" Galen swallowed. He looked ill.

Nico shot him a sidelong glance. "You know her."

"She hates me. And she has every right to."

He laughed feebly. "That's two of us then."

❧ 17 ❦

DEATH BECOMES HER

The whitewashed buildings of Delphi flashed by beneath Berglaug's wings. From high above, flattened and shrunk to miniature, the Temple of Delphi no longer looked so impressive. Like the Pythia, Nazafareen thought. She was no mystical seer. No mouthpiece of a god. Strip away her false authority and she was just a vengeful creature with a bone to pick.

Berglaug swooped lower as they followed the beaten trail of horses, boots and wagons from the edge of the Umbra to a wide, shallow place where the Pythia's men had forded the river and continued toward the Gale. The sky grew darker and a light rain began to fall. Within minutes, the line of storms came into view. Grey anvil-shaped clouds stretched from north to south, lightning forking in their depths. A construct of magic so vast and awe-inspiring even her huo mofa shrank back from it.

The gates to the Vatras' prison.

Nazafareen leaned into Berglaug's neck, blinking water from her eyes, and then she saw two figures. They both wore cloaks with the hoods raised.

Some sixth sense made the taller one turn and look up. The face was a pale smudge, but she recognized Nicodemus.

Darius did too.

One moment he was tightly controlled calm. In the next, an explosion swept through their bond as the grief and anger he'd held in check burst its dam. Before Nazafareen could react, Darius tore free from his harness and dropped twenty paces to the ground, landing with feline grace. Nicodemus raised empty hands in surrender and was bowled over as Darius landed on top of him, his right fist lashing out in a blind rage.

Berglaug skidded to a stop. Nazafareen heard the harsh screams of the other abbadax as Katrin and Daníel alit on either side, leaping from their saddles with bared swords. Herodotus and the three Maenads circled around as she fumbled with her own buckles, clamping down on Darius's elemental power. Breaking magic crackled at her fingertips, ready to quench any flames the Vatra might summon.

But he didn't even try to fight back. He'd curled into a ball, trying to protect himself from the hail of blows. She had never seen Darius so utterly out of control. Mud splattered his face as he straddled Nicodemus, slamming him against the ground again and again.

The second figure stood frozen, its back to her. Nazafareen grabbed the dark cloak, spinning it to face her. She expected the Pythia, but to her surprise it was Galen, looking eerily like a younger version of Victor. He was pale and sodden, much thinner than she remembered. A scraggly beard failed to conceal the hollowness of his cheeks. Overall, he looked as terrible as one would expect. Yet something struck her as off. Then his hood fell back, exposing his throat, and she realized what it was. No iron collar encircled his neck.

Galen shook her off and took a half step toward Darius, who pinned the limp, bloodied Vatra with his bad arm. The other hand fumbled for his belt knife, but the scabbard had twisted around.

"Stop!" Galen screamed. "He freed me!"

Nazafareen scanned the empty landscape. The flat plain offered no cover for leagues in any direction. They were alone.

"Where's the Pythia?" Nazafareen shouted through a gust of rain.

"Dead. She's dead." Galen pointed to Nicodemus. "*He killed her.*"

Nazafareen shared an uncertain look with the others. She walked up to Darius and seized his wrist just as he found the knife. The look in his eyes could have frozen the sun.

"Let go," he grated.

"We might need the Vatra alive," she said firmly. "You've beaten him badly. It's enough."

"He was there—"

"And he tried to stop it. You saw that." She paused. It was a strange reversal of their usual roles. Darius was usually the sane one. The ice to her fire. "Galen says he killed the Pythia. If it's true, I want to know why."

Darius's jaw clenched. He stood and turned his back on Nicodemus, who stirred weakly.

Nazafareen looked at Galen. She had a few choice things to say to him, but not just yet.

"What exactly happened here?"

He drew a deep breath. "The Pythia planned to take me to the Gale, but then she accused Nicodemus of betraying her. They had words and he stabbed her with that knife." He pointed to the Vatra's boot. The hilt of a dagger protruded from his trouser leg.

Nazafareen yanked it free and examined it. Traces of red caked the eel coiled around the hilt. Sakhet-ra-katme's knife.

"He threatened to burn the soldiers if they did anything." Galen's mouth twisted. "I don't think they cared. They were probably glad she was dead. Gods know I am."

"Where's the body?" she demanded.

"They took it back to Delphi."

A sickening feeling stole over her. This was all wrong. The Pythia belonged to *her*.

"Search the Vatra," she snapped at the Maenads.

The two women rolled Nicodemus over, turning out his pockets. He had a second knife in his belt, with a hilt of finely wrought silver. A few paces away lay a mud-spattered bundle. Rhea retrieved it, unfurling a cloak made of some kind of pale reptilian skin.

"There something inside," she muttered, unwrapping the folds. "Looks like another one of those globes."

Nazafareen took the glass orb, weaving the flows without thought.

"Show me the Oracle of Delphi."

The runes ignited and men on horseback appeared, Shields of Apollo by their crested helmets. Her gaze narrowed as she saw the Archon Basileus riding next to a wagon. His dark hair swept back from patrician features, crimson cloak pooling around him. The walls of Delphi loomed in the distance. The view arrowed in on the wagon and Nazafareen's breath hitched. A woman in a blood-soaked white gown lay atop a pile of carpets, her sternly handsome features softened in death. It was the Pythia.

"What about Thena?" she demanded.

"Dead as well," Galen said with satisfaction. "Killed by the Pythia. I felt her die through the collar." He winced. "They don't simply let the mortals control us. I sensed her emotions as well. The woman was mad."

Nazafareen glanced at Darius, who listened with a grim face.

"Thena went into the Pythia's tent," Galen continued. "A few minutes later, the connection between us broke. They say she was burned up. After Nicodemus stabbed the Pythia, he sent the soldiers away. Then he unlocked the collar. He said we were to wait for you to come." Galen still seemed astounded at this piece of good fortune.

Kallisto smiled. "It's a great relief to know you are free, Galen

Dessarian. I fear the Pythia hoped you would break the Gale for her, but that won't happen now."

Nazafareen knew she should be rejoicing—and yet she felt a deep bitterness.

"What do we do with him?" she muttered, glancing at Nicodemus. His face was a bloody pulp.

Katrin put the point of her sword to his neck. "I say we cut him into pieces and feed him to the abbadax."

Megeara gave a grim nod. "The Valkirin speaks sense. You saw what he did in Tjanjin. He's a snake."

"And our only source of information on the Vatras," Kallisto reminded them. "What if others are loose in the world?"

"He did kill the Pythia," Galen muttered. "He doesn't deserve—"

"Shut up," Darius snapped. He stared at Nicodemus with loathing. "Kallisto is right. We need to question him first."

Katrin seemed to interpret that *"first"* as a minor delay to the inevitable bloodletting and sheathed her sword.

The rain pelted down, soaking them to the bone. It showed no sign of letting up.

"We passed a farmhouse a few minutes ago," Daníel ventured. "I say we take shelter there. The mounts need rest, and so do we."

No one objected to this plan. The ferocity that had filled Nazafareen was seeping away, leaving exhaustion in its wake.

Rhea and Megaera took charge of the Vatra without being asked. If he did wake up, his fire magic would do little good against either of them. They trussed Nicodemus in a rope from Rhea's pack and tossed him in front of their saddle.

"I expected a little more," Katrin sniffed, eyeing his limp body. "The Vatras aren't so fearsome after all."

"He chose not to fight," Nazafareen replied. "But don't under-estimate him. He's still dangerous."

Kallisto led Galen to her own mount. He didn't seem afraid of it and Nazafareen realized he must have seen abbadax at Val Moraine. *The little rat.*

"You've broken your harness," she said to Darius as they reached Berglaug.

His blue eyes caught hers. Most of that wild, savage rage had ebbed, though she still sensed echoes of it in the bond. Perhaps it was callous, but she was glad he took it out on the Vatra. His pain needed an outlet and it might have turned inwards if left too long to simmer. Pain like that could eat you alive.

"I'll hold onto you," he said. "We won't be going far."

"I don't blame you for wanting to kill him. I still might myself. But we'll see what he knows first."

Darius swung himself into the saddle and offered her a hand.

"This isn't over," he said softly.

~

THE FARMHOUSE HAD A STONE FOUNDATION AND WALLS OF sundried brick painted white with blue shutters. Sheep grazed in a pasture enclosed by a rock wall. They bleated in alarm when the abbadax swooped down, huddling together in a far corner of the pen. The five mounts studied them with hungry yellow eyes as Daníel and Katrin led them to a second fallow pasture, tossing strips of dried meat that they snapped out of the air with curved beaks.

The others approached the front portico, Rhea and Megaera carrying a limp Nicodemus. Kallisto called out, but no one seemed to be home.

"Those wagon tracks are fresh," Darius observed, pointing to a parallel set of ruts in the muddy road leading toward Delphi.

"The family must have fled when they saw the Pythia's army coming," Kallisto said. "The Shields of Apollo used to be viewed as protectors of the people, but that was a long time ago. Now they only inspire fear."

Nazafareen saw sadness in her eyes and wondered if she was thinking of the vineyards she'd left behind. Back on the *Chione*, Megaera said the temples to Dionysus had been razed to the ground. Most likely the Maenads' farm had suffered a similar fate.

"Will they mind if we take shelter inside?" Nazafareen asked.

"I have coin to leave for whatever we take," Kallisto said briskly, pushing the door open. "Come. I am weary of this rain."

The house formed a hollow square around an interior courtyard. Potted plants and herbs provided a kitchen garden, and a long wooden table sat beneath overhanging eaves that offered shade on hot days. The floor was hard-packed dirt except for a sitting room, which had patterned tiles. It was all very tidy and domestic, although whoever lived there had left in a hurry. Plates of half-eaten food sat on the table, too fresh to have attracted flies.

A basket of sewing was positioned between three chairs and Nazafareen imagined the women of the house sitting together, sharing idle gossip as they mended clothing. For a moment, she envied their simple life. Had she ever known such a peaceful existence? Perhaps as a child, but she had no recollection of it. A part of her had given up hope of restoring those holes in her memory. It was easier that way. Wishing for the impossible only brought bitterness.

Kallisto found the larder and dug out some bread and olives and smooth white cheese. They passed a quick meal in the courtyard, the rain dripping from eaves and hissing on the roof. Galen ate silently, apart from the others, his shoulders hunched. Afterwards, they each drifted away to separate rooms. One side seemed to be the men's quarters, the other the women's. Nazafareen and Darius chose a corner room, depositing their saddlebags inside.

"I'm taking a bath," Nazafareen declared. "I saw a copper tub. Will you help me drag it in here?"

Darius smiled, a real smile, and her heart lightened. "Of course. I wasn't going to say anything, but you smell...."

She narrowed her eyes.

"Very much like yourself," he finished hastily.

She laughed. "That I do."

She pointed out the tub and he lifted it with ease, carrying it to their chamber and filling it from the well. There was a brazier in the courtyard, but it would be in poor taste to light a fire with the daēvas present so she didn't bother heating the water. It was a bit chilly, but the air was warm.

She stripped off her dirty clothes and sank into the tub with a sigh. Darius sat on a stool behind her and soaped her hair, then began teasing out the tangles with a comb he'd found on the vanity table.

"Do you think it's safe to leave the Vatra with Rhea and Megaera?" she asked.

Darius considered this. "He can't harm them with fire. They'd raise the alarm if he tried anything else."

"Why did he wait for us? He could have fled."

Darius didn't reply. She sensed he felt a twinge of regret for his behavior. Or perhaps it was simply for losing control.

"I suppose we should be thankful. Meb is safe, and so are Katrin and Galen. The Pythia is dead. Thena is dead."

"And yet?"

She sighed. "You were right. It's not over, Darius. I can feel it in my bones."

"I feel the same," he said quietly.

"I keep thinking about Farrumohr. It can't be a coincidence that he's haunted Culach's dreams. There's a connection some-where and I think it lies in the Kiln."

"With Gaius?"

"Perhaps."

Darius's fingers tensed in her hair. He stopped combing. "You want to hunt him down."

"What if that's why I have this breaking power?"

"Herodotus says you were meant to shatter the wards of the talismans."

"But what if there's more to it?"

"Are you certain it's not simple revenge you seek?"

"No," she admitted. "I'm not. But perfectly pure motives are a rare thing. I'm not sure they even exist."

Darius gave a low laugh. "That's true enough." He laid the comb aside and began to massage her shoulder. Nazafareen sighed.

"Do you think the old me would have done the same?" she asked, her eyes slipping closed. "Or was I more sensible?"

Darius laughed. "That's not the word I would choose." His thumb pressed into the hollow beneath her skull. "But you were always truthful, even if it cost you dearly. You were unfailingly brave. And you hated bullies more than anything in the world."

Nazafareen grinned. "I'm ashamed to admit I became a skilled liar during my time with Javid. As for brave, I only do what I must to survive." Her expression darkened. "But I do hate bullies, and Gaius is exactly that."

Darius worked on her sore muscles, eliciting small sounds of delight. She could hear the Maenads singing faintly through the walls.

I'd wager my sword they've gotten into the wine, Nazafareen thought fondly.

"The only way into the Kiln is through the Gale," Darius said at last. "You don't intend to bring it down, I hope?" The words were spoken lightly, but she heard an edge to them.

"No. Of course not." She twisted around to look at him. "But Nicodemus came through another way."

"And you wish to discover what it is?"

She nodded. "What do you think?"

His blue eyes grew cold. "If there is indeed a way, I say we go. If we don't bring the fight to the Kiln, finish it there, we might end up facing the Vatras in the human cities and the darklands. Just like last time."

Darius took risks, but he was never reckless. She knew how badly he wanted to avenge his mother. She did too, but it was more than that. The breaking power was a gift she'd never asked for. But how she chose to use it—that was her purpose. Gaius was a malignancy. Perhaps he did have some secret communion with the Viper, but she'd defeated Farrumohr once before. This time she'd make sure he stayed dead.

But she didn't wish to think of those things right now. Nazafareen touched Darius's jaw, which was still swollen.

"This may be the last time we have alone together," she murmured, sliding the cuff off and setting it on the floor. Their bond remained, but metal would hurt him if he touched it.

He gave a small smile. "Are you asking me to join you?"

"I'll wash your hair. I might even give you a shave if you're nice."

He looked at her for a long moment, lazy but calculating. Then he pulled the shirt over his head, kicked his pants off and slid into the tub, sloshing water over the sides. Besides the infirmity caused by the bond, bruises and scrapes stood out lividly against his night-pale skin. Being thrown from the back of an abbadax had left Nazafareen in similar shape. She moved gingerly to lie against his chest, slipping her fingers into his damp hair as he kissed her neck, his own hands moving under the water.

"Oh yes...Ow....No, it's all right....Yes...."

They were forced to go slowly, gasps of pleasure alternating with gasps of pain and breathless laughter, and when Darius finally cried out, muffling it against her shoulder, she no longer knew where one ended and the other began. She felt his release through the bond and it pushed her over the edge. Her teeth sank into the salt sweat of his neck, not quite breaking the skin, and she clamped tight around him.

As the euphoria wore off, though, Nazafareen's practical side felt a twinge of anxiety. It was a topic she should have raised before.

"I could get pregnant, you know," she said, sitting up to face him.

"I've been told where babies come from," Darius replied dryly.

"You know what I mean."

He shrugged. "If it's a girl, we can name her Delilah."

"But what would I do with a baby?" She frowned. "And what if it's a Breaker?"

"Then you can teach her to harness her power."

Nazafareen fell silent. The idea of Darius's children made her happy and afraid at the same time. What if she was a terrible mother? She had no patience and spent half her time daydreaming about killing people.

"I'm going to ask Rhea and Megaera what *they* do," she said diplomatically. "I have a feeling they would know how to...."

"Prevent pregnancy?" He traced his lips along the edge of her ear. "We will have children when you wish, Nazafareen. And I won't leave all the burden to you, I promise." He grinned. "Just don't refuse to touch me again out of caution. That I could not bear."

She looked at his intelligent, teasing blue eyes, his mouth made for kisses and laughter.

"I couldn't if I tried." Nazafareen reached over the edge of the tub and found a wickedly sharp knife in his boot. "My toes are getting puckered. What do you say I give you that shave and then—"

A fist pounded on the door. Her hand tightened around the knife.

"What?" she called.

"The Vatra," Megaera growled. "He's awake."

18

AN UNEASY ALLIANCE

Nicodemus sat trussed hand and foot in the corner of the kitchen. One eye was swollen shut and dried blood streaked his face. He looked up as Darius and Nazafareen entered, more wary than fearful. She'd have to do something about that.

Kallisto was already there with Herodotus and Katrin, who watched him with a stony face.

"You should have waited for me before getting so close to him," Nazafareen admonished Katrin. "What if he'd worked fire against you?" She glanced at Megaera and Rhea. "It might not harm them, but you'd be ash in a matter of seconds."

"I said the same," Kallisto muttered. "She wouldn't listen, though Daniel had the sense to go tend to his abbadax."

Katrin arched a pale eyebrow. "I am the talisman."

"That doesn't make you immortal," Nazafareen snapped. "You would still reach for the flames like any other daēva and they would consume you."

"If I wanted to burn you all, I would have," Nicodemus murmured from his corner.

Nazafareen rounded on him, ice in her tone. "Try it, Vatra. Try it and see what happens to you. I would be happy to finish what I started in Tjanjin." She was gratified to detect a flash of worry. "Now. I want to know how you escaped the Kiln and why the other Vatras haven't done the same."

He shifted, drawing his knees to his chest. "Can I have some water?"

She nodded at Rhea, who brought a cup and put it to his lips. He drank deeply and sighed.

"I came through a gate. Domitia and I managed to revive one with our own blood, but it wasn't stable. It closed again after a few seconds. Our companions were killed."

Nazafareen remembered the gate to the Kiln she'd stumbled on with Javid. It had nearly trapped them like flies in amber.

She gave him a hard stare.

"Are there any other gates leading into the Kiln?"

"There were, once. Now they're lost to the sands."

"You spoke of Domitia. Is that the Pythia's name?"

He nodded. "She saved my life more than once, and my brother's. I couldn't let her unleash Gaius on the world, but I allowed Basileus to take her body to be buried with the other Oracles. I felt duty-bound to allow her a final honor."

"Honor?" Nazafareen spat. "The woman had no honor."

"Not according to your standards. Domitia lived by the code of the Kiln. All she knew came from her father, Gaius." Dark blue eyes regarded her with a trace of contempt. "Go to Delphi if you want to abuse her corpse."

Darius took a step forward and Nicodemus flinched.

"What about Thena?" he demanded. "Tell me how she died."

"She was not the loyal servant she pretended to be. After what happened with the Danai.... I had to do something. Basileus and I made a plan, and Thena agreed to help us. I gave her a talisman to use against Domitia, but she failed. Domitia burned her. So I took matters into my own hands." His voice grew low and urgent.

"You must believe me, I tried to stop her. I didn't know what she planned."

Nazafareen tried to reconcile this new Nicodemus with the one who'd kidnapped Meb. It didn't add up. "What do you want?" she asked coldly.

He held her gaze. "Basileus told me there are reliable reports of wind ships crossing the Gale south of here. It must be the Persians."

She frowned. "Why would they do that?"

"I don't know. But since the new king took the throne in Samarqand, the sightings have multiplied. He's said to have strange powers. It won't be long before Gaius learns about it, if he hasn't already."

Nazafareen turned to Herodotus. "Could such a thing be possible?"

The scholar considered her question. "The Persian alchemists are adept at using spell dust. I suppose it might be accomplished, but it would require a great deal of skill and nerves of steel."

"It's the sort of thing I could almost see Javid trying, that great oaf," she muttered. "Though even he can't be that stupid." She studied the Vatra with quiet anger. "A week ago, you were trying to drag Meb through a gate to force her to break the Gale." She held up the eel knife. The Vatra eyed it warily. "And what about this? You stole it from Sakhet-ra-Katme after you burned her."

He bristled. "I didn't kill her! She drank poisoned chai."

Nazafareen crouched down, the knife in her hand. Nicodemus leaned back.

"We both know you're a murderer, so don't bandy words with me. Why did you unlock Galen's collar? After all the other foul deeds you've committed? Why let him go?"

This was the part that made no sense, no matter how she chewed on it. What could he gain by freeing one of the talismans?

Nicodemus looked away, raw emotion in his voice. "I never

wanted Gaius to escape. I only wanted my brother. I had to leave him behind when Domitia and I left the Kiln."

"He's a fucking liar," Katrin said in a low voice. Her green eyes grew cold as the night-shrouded mountains of Nocturne. "Let me have him alone for a while. I'll get the truth out of him."

Nicodemus looked back at her with a challenge in his gaze.

"I'm not afraid of you, Valkirin. You have no idea what true pain is."

Katrin gave an evil laugh. "Perhaps not, but I'm willing to learn. Shall we find out together?"

He opened his mouth to reply when Herodotus stepped between them, a scowl on his face.

"I will not condone torture," he said sternly. "Not even of a Vatra. Fortunately, there are other methods." He glowered down at Nicodemus. "You will answer these questions again, this time while you're holding Kallisto's staff. It compels truth."

Nazafareen felt a fool. *The staff.* She really did need to get some sleep.

The Maenad nodded her approval, gesturing to Megaera to loosen his bonds, though her sharp black eyes watched the prisoner like a bird of prey. Nicodemus took the staff without hesitation. When his hand closed around the haft, he closed his eyes, brows quirking in concentration.

"Yes," he murmured. "I see how it was done. Fascinating."

Herodotus tugged at his beard. He looked on the verge of peppering the Vatra with questions.

"Get on with it," Nazafareen snapped, before they embarked on a long exploration of the staff and how it worked.

Nicodemus opened his eyes. His gaze was steady.

"I despise Gaius with every fiber of my being. I wish him dead and painfully so. He is an evil man. Everything I have done, the crimes I have committed, are for the sake of my brother, Atticus. So that he has the chance to live without fear and want. To grow old and have children. It's all I've ever wanted."

Rain pattered on the roof. The staff lay quiet.

"I will tell you about Gaius Julius Caesar Augustus. The things I have seen with my own eyes. The things I know to be true." His knuckles whitened around the staff. "He has many wives. Any girl over the age of eleven is fair game. When he has used them up, when they have borne his children, he discards them. Some survive, most don't. When he hunts, it's not for food but for sport, to inflict pain on weaker things. He teaches that survival is the only worthwhile pursuit. Compassion, mercy, these are weaknesses. Anyone who defies him in any way, no matter how small, is driven out into the wilds, naked and without weapons. That's if he doesn't kill them himself."

Kallisto studied him, her face grave.

"Do you truly believe Gaius will escape the Kiln?" she asked.

Nicodemus held her gaze. "Yes. I do."

Again, the staff lay quiet. Whether it was true or not, he believed it. And that sent a stab of dread through Nazafareen's gut.

"It might not be for many years. Or it might be quite soon, if his scouts discover the wind ships. But he will, someday." Nicodemus stared at Nazafareen. "I did."

Thunder clapped in the distance. Nazafareen felt the others watching her, though no one spoke.

"You speak only of Gaius. What about the rest of the Vatras? Do they stand behind him?"

"We're a broken people. None of us even remember the war."

"That's not an answer."

"There's a cadre who call themselves the Praetorians, Gaius's enforcers," Nicodemus admitted. "But the rest of the Vatras are terrified of him. They aren't bad people, just desperate to survive."

"And what of the Viper? What of Farrumohr?"

She watched his hands, gripping the haft of Kallisto's staff.

"I've never heard that name."

"He cannot lie," Kallisto murmured.

"Who's the Viper?" Nicodemus asked, glancing between them.

"That's what your own people called him. He was Gaius's advisor. He's supposed to be dead, but I have serious doubts."

Nicodemus considered this. "I know everyone. There aren't many of us. Gaius is the only one still living who survived the exile. No one else is remotely as old."

"Would you know where to find him?"

He nodded. "And I know the Kiln. I've ranged across most of it with...." He trailed off and she wondered if he was about to say *with Domitia*. "I'd willingly guide you through it."

"Why?" She stared at him. "Why would you go back to such a place?"

A spark of fury lit his eyes. "Because I want Gaius dead. Because he's the reason for my people's suffering."

Nazafareen rubbed her stump. "We still have to find a way in. I won't break the Gale. That's out of the question."

"I'm relieved to hear it," Kallisto said dryly.

"I suppose we could try a wind ship. That means traveling to Samarqand and convincing this new king to give us one, assuming he's the one behind it."

Katrin pushed off the wall and walked forward, her green eyes inscrutable.

"You're going into the Kiln?" She jerked a thumb at Nicodemus. "With *him*?"

Nazafareen held her gaze. "Maybe."

"You're crazy." Her face suddenly split into a grin.

Nazafareen didn't smile back. "It's not a joke."

"I guess it's not." Katrin grew sober again. "What if we could pass through the Gale without disturbing the spell?"

"Leave it intact, you mean?"

"Yeah."

"How?"

"Air shield. I can make a wedge. Pry it open long enough to get to the other side."

Kallisto laid a hand on Nazafareen's arm. "May we speak in private?"

She hesitated and Kallisto sighed. She seemed to be trying to rein in her temper. "Please."

So the two of them went to the courtyard and sat at one end of the long wooden table, leaving the others to watch Nicodemus. Nazafareen remembered the first time she had talked to Kallisto, at a kitchen table much like this one, the Maenads sparring in the yard outside. How long ago it seemed.

"So you intend to hunt Gaius in the Kiln," Kallisto said tartly. "You are a rash child—"

Nazafareen opened her mouth with an angry retort, but Kallisto held up a hand.

"A rash child, yet I am not here to speak against it. Not yet. It may be that you are right. But I have questions before you go haring off. I think this Vatra has told us the truth, but not all of it. How has Gaius survived so long when the others die like flies?"

"Sakhet-ra-katme did."

"Not in the Kiln."

Nazafareen returned her level gaze. "We must pull this evil out by the roots or it will simply grow back. Gaius is a bane to the world. He warped his own daughter into a monster. And I'm certain the Viper has a hand in this somehow. He lingers in the Dominion. There is a place...." She remembered a house and a stone well, black as night. "I don't pretend to understand it, but his soul never passed on. It clings to some kind of half-life."

Kallisto forked her fingers against evil.

"Perhaps such a creature should be left alone," she said mildly. "Not poked with a sharp stick."

"And what would you do?" Nazafareen asked tightly.

"We have two of the talismans safe in our hands. The third is with her people and no longer defenseless." Kallisto's gaze softened. "We've done what we set out to do. The Pythia is dead. The Gale will stand another thousand years."

"And what about Nicodemus?"

"He is not innocent, but his crimes are less. I could take him to the Temple of the Moria Tree. The Maenads would keep him out of trouble." Her lips curled in the barest hint of a smile. "I think they would not object to the duty."

"No."

Kallisto leaned back. "Do you make decisions for all of us now?"

"I'm not asking for your blessing or aid."

"How about my advice?"

"You've already given it." Nazafareen met her onyx eyes with subdued defiance. "The girl I used to be is dead. I'll never get my memories back and I'm done mourning them. Perhaps I have this negatory magic for a reason. Or perhaps it's just a random accident. But I'm going to use it as I see fit."

"To punish your enemies."

"For the greater good. Darius will come with me. I can protect him from fire with the bond."

"And if Nicodemus has managed to conceal something from us? He's a clever one."

"I will deal with him as I must. But we know he spoke truth about Gaius."

Kallisto nodded wearily, as if she'd expected no less. "I would seek guidance from the god before you make a final decision. Will you grant me this?"

"Can you do it tonight?"

She nodded.

"Then, yes."

A cask was found in the cellar. The wine was rough and Nazafareen stopped after a few sips, but the three Maenads drank it down to the last drop with relish, toasting Dionysus and singing a paean to the god. Then they went outside beneath the open sky, the Gale looming on the western horizon, and began to spin in giddy circles. Nazafareen didn't join in this time, only watched from the sidelines, sober as a judge, and part of her regretted calling their god false (even if she hadn't said it aloud) because she sensed an eerie power gathering.

The rain lashed down. The Maenads whirled and leapt in a frenzy, arms flung wide, mud streaking their faces. Kallisto suddenly stopped, her eyes rolling back in her head. When she spoke, the words came so fast they ran together.

"I see three towers standing in opposition, one grey, two black. I see a great fleet sailing north. I see a king with fire in his veins." Spittle ran down her chin and Megaera ran forward to keep her from falling. "I see a shadow and a burning crown. I see a snake with jeweled eyes." Her face grew taut with fear. "It sees me...." She collapsed in a faint.

They carried her inside and lay her on a sleeping pallet in one of the bedrooms. Rhea patted her forehead with a cool cloth and Kallisto's eyes fluttered open. Nazafareen was relieved to see they were no longer that ghastly white.

"If you do not go to the Kiln, the world will burn," she whispered hoarsely. "That is certain. If you do go...." She looked away with a haunted gaze. "The path is shadowed, with too many branchings to see the outcome for certain. But there is a chance." She squeezed Nazafareen's hand. "You will make the right choices. You *must*."

Nazafareen nodded uncertainly. If only Kallisto weren't so bloody *cryptic*. None of it seemed of much use. And she had the distinct feeling the woman knew more than she was telling.

"What are these towers?"

"I don't know. I have never seen them before."

"And the crown. Could it be the same the Viper forged for Gaius?"

Kallisto didn't answer. Her eyes were already closing again.

Nazafareen sighed and turned to Darius.

"Let's ask the Vatra."

They returned to Nicodemus, who'd had a clear view of the yard out the kitchen window. He looked up lazily as they came in.

"Was that the Dance of the Maenads? I've heard about it, but never saw it before. Quite a spectacle."

"Shut up. Does Gaius wear a crown?" she asked.

"I'm confused." He frowned. "Am I still supposed to shut up?"

Nazafareen gritted her teeth and pushed Kallisto's staff into his hand. "Just answer the question."

Nicodemus sighed. "A crown? Not that I've ever seen."

"Do you know anything about three towers?"

He shook his head. "There are no buildings in the Kiln. Not a one." He gave her a grim smile. "Nothing to build with."

Nazafareen thought about the cask of wine the Maenads had consumed. Perhaps it was better to focus on practical matters.

"How far would the journey be?" she asked. "Where do the Vatras live?"

"Our homes are spread out, but roughly two days' walk. South and west, near the coast. Gaius has a camp there with his wives." Lines of revulsion creased his mouth. "I know it well."

"Why do you think I can kill him when others have failed?"

"He rules by fear and intimidation, but he has never faced a Breaker before. I doubt he has any idea you even exist." A small, cold smile touched his lips. "It will come as quite a surprise."

"That doesn't answer my question. How is it he's never succumbed to sickness or wounds in such a harsh place?"

Dark blue eyes stared at her. "I don't know."

Nazafareen crouched down. Something in her face made him shrink away.

"You're holding back on me."

"I don't know, I swear it! He just...recovers somehow. Lucky, I guess."

"Lucky," she repeated. "Does he carry any talismans?"

The Vatra slowly shook his head. "They don't work in the

Kiln. Domitia had a Talisman of Folding. She used it to send Thena to Val Moraine. But it couldn't penetrate the wards of the Kiln. Trust me, she tried. If it had, she wouldn't have needed to bring down the Gale."

"There's another possibility," Nazafareen said to the others. "That Farrumohr is protecting him." She turned to the Vatra. "Did Gaius's eyes ever seem strange?"

Nicodemus barked a harsh laugh. "Yeah. He's insane."

"I mean really *strange*." She paused. "Have you ever seen flames in the iris?"

He frowned. "No. Nothing like that."

"Perhaps you can seek out Gaius using the Vatra's globe," said Rhea, cool and logical as always. "See where he is."

"Won't work," Nicodemus grumbled. "But test it if you doubt me."

Nazafareen took the globe from her pocket and blew on the runes.

"Show me Gaius Julius Caesar Augustus," she whispered.

At first, it seemed the Vatra was wrong. The view sped toward the Gale, lances of lightning spearing down from the black clouds. But half a league away, it struck an invisible barrier. The globe went dark, just as it had when Darius tried to find Nicodemus in the Dominion. She fed more power to the runes but it made no difference. Nazafareen's lips tightened as she released the weaving.

"I told you," Nicodemus said patiently. "Magic can't penetrate the wards."

"It confirms that Gaius is in the Kiln and he's alive," Darius said coldly. And in a softer tone to Nazafareen, "Perhaps we can discover more once we're through."

She eyed the Vatra. He wasn't a pretty sight, but nothing looked broken. "Are you fit to travel?"

"I can make it."

"You won't carry any weapons, let's be clear on that right now."

He shrugged and gave her an impudent grin. "I'll have you to protect me, won't I?"

Nazafareen scowled. "How long have you been gone?"

"Two years."

"Was Gaius waiting for your return?"

The Vatra shook his head. "It was Domitia's idea. In truth, I think she wanted to get away from him. Gaius never thought we'd make it. By now, he must assume we died in the attempt."

His head turned and Nazafareen followed his gaze to Kallisto, who stood in the kitchen doorway. Her face was wan and she propped one hand on the frame. Herodotus hurried over and ushered her to a stool.

"You shouldn't be up, my dear," he chastised.

Kallisto gave him a fond look. "You worry too much. I'm fine now." She looked at Nazafareen. "We will go to the Temple of the Moria Tree. The other Maenads must know what has happened. We must prepare for the worst."

"Take the talismans with you," Nazafareen replied. "We cannot risk them. If I fail—"

"I speak for myself," Katrin interrupted hotly. "You will not have all the glory of killing Gaius. I will come with you into the Kiln."

Nazafareen gave her a hard look. "Are you not afraid of fire?"

"I can smother it with air."

Nazafareen sighed, though she didn't mind having Katrin. The woman was formidable. But Kallisto shook her head.

"Katrin Aigirsdottir. I'd hoped you might have a modicum of sense."

The scolding tone was the wrong approach. Katrin's green eyes went cold.

"I do. And I say we kill the fucker."

Kallisto rolled her eyes heavenward. "If the Valkirin talisman goes, then one of you must go with her," she said to her Maenads.

"I will," Rhea said quickly.

Megaera seemed to be suppressing a smile. "Don't you think I should—"

"No," Kallisto said firmly. "One of you is adequate."

Megaera frowned and crossed her arms.

"Then it's settled," Darius said. "We'll leave tomorrow."

"There is one yet to decide," Kallisto reminded him. "Galen."

"He's all yours," Nazafareen said tartly.

"You may not like him, but he is a talisman. We will do the courtesy of asking him."

GALEN STOOD OUTSIDE, WATCHING THE RAIN DRIP FROM THE eaves. He turned as they approached.

"Come with me," Kallisto said gently. "You'll be safe at the Temple of the Moria Tree."

He gazed at her with haunted eyes.

"Safe?"

"We are Maenads. Followers of Dionysus. For a thousand years, we have waited for the talismans to return. To protect them until they are needed."

Galen scowled. "How do you know I'm one of these talismans?" he burst out. "That's what the Pythia said. She wanted to use me." His mouth twisted. "But I have no power."

"You have a block," Kallisto said. "It must be broken."

Nazafareen stared at Galen. When he'd been collared, she'd managed to dredge up some pity for him. But now.... The thought of him wielding that much power was almost worse than Katrin.

"I'm not doing it unless I have no other choice," she said.

"Do what?" Galen demanded.

Nazafareen ignored him. "You don't know him like I do. He

can't be trusted," she said to Kallisto. "He betrayed me to the Valkirins. He told them where I was and they sent an assassin to kill me. So forgive me if I won't hand him an unimaginable amount of power."

"And what if you don't return from the Kiln?" the Maenad demanded.

Nazafareen's jaw set. She wouldn't be bullied. "It's *my* decision. You'll still have Meb."

Kallisto muttered something under her breath.

"It's true. Everything she said is true. I'm a selfish bastard," he said dully, avoiding Nazafareen's gaze. "I tried to trade her for my mother, Mina. Eirik was holding her hostage. It wasn't personal."

Wasn't personal? She nearly laughed.

"Why did you save Darius?"

He looked into her eyes then. "I could say it was out of brotherly love, but that would be a lie. I did it so the assassin wouldn't betray me to Tethys. But I regret everything. I can't tell you how much."

"That's nice. I'm still not breaking your block."

"I'm not asking you to." He paused, his voice strained with emotion. "But if you're going after the man who ordered the killing of the Danai, I beg you to let me come. I don't have my bow, but I can still fight. I was *there*. I saw it happen. You can't...." Galen trailed off, his throat working.

Nazafareen looked at Darius. He gave a slight, reluctant nod.

"You'll do as I say," she told Galen. "No questions or arguments."

"You have my word." His cheeks flamed. "For what it's worth."

Kallisto closed her eyes and turned away. Herodotus looked troubled, but kept his own counsel.

Nazafareen pointed to the abbadax, which sheltered beneath an elm tree.

"Can we take the mounts? They would shorten the journey."

"Absolutely not," Daníel snapped. "They would die. If you go, you go on foot."

"You're not coming?" Katrin asked in surprise.

"I came to kill the Pythia. She's dead. My place is at Val Tourmaline." He shook his head. "Why are *you* doing this? Talisman or not, Valkirins are not made for the Kiln."

Katrin rested a hand on her sword, her expression fierce and proud. "Our ancestors fought the Vatras once. The time has come to face them again." She lifted her chin. "I will not run away and hide."

Daníel looked angry. "I'm not running, nor do I have a death wish. And we left our wounded on the twilight plain. I will not abandon them."

They stared at each other for a long moment.

"You are sworn to Val Tourmaline, are you not?" he asked.

Katrin nodded tersely.

"And if I ordered you to return with me?"

Her cheeks flamed. "I... I would go. I swore on my honor to Halldóra."

Daníel looked at Nazafareen. "Would you still attempt this without her?"

"We need her to get us through the Gale. But, yes. If she escorted us and then returned to you, I would still go."

He looked away. "Runar will call me a fool. But I leave the choice to you, Katrin. I will not compel you."

She squared her broad shoulders. "You know my mind."

Daníel gave a rueful nod. "The clans will sing of you, but whether it will be a dirge or a heroic ballad, I cannot say." He turned to Kallisto. "I'll take you to this temple on the Cimmerian Sea on my way back to the mountains."

Kallisto tilted her head in grateful assent.

Daníel strode over to the abbadax he called Wind from the North and reached up to pat her flank. As his coat fell open,

Nazafareen saw the dull glint of metal around his neck. She'd forgotten, and he had never asked.

Wind from the North watched her approach with slitted yellow eyes.

"I should have done this before," Nazafareen said quietly.

Daníel tensed as she reached for the collar, his eyes searching hers. The iron was warm from his skin. Anger flared and it crumbled to dust that was snatched away by the wind and rain.

"Thank you," he said hoarsely.

"Thank *you* for coming this far. It gives me hope that the clans will set aside their differences. You have a kind heart." She smiled. "For a Valkirin."

"And you have courage," Daníel replied. "For a mortal."

His face was perfectly straight, but when he walked away, it was with a new lightness in his step.

THEY SNATCHED A FEW HOURS SLEEP, WATCHING NICODEMUS IN turns. After a hasty meal, the six who planned to enter the Gale got busy preparing for the journey ahead. They packed hard bread and cheese wrapped in oilcloth, and as many waterskins as they could carry. With the rain sweeping down and lakes of mud outside, thirst seemed an abstract problem. But Nicodemus assured them that the heavy rucksacks would lighten quickly once they reached the Kiln.

Kallisto stood apart while they carried out these tasks, her back stiff and demeanor distant. Nazafareen felt sure she knew more than she was admitting. It hurt that Kallisto didn't seem to trust her. *You must make the right choices.* What did that mean? The choice to enter the Kiln had already been made. Would she face another choice? And if so, why couldn't Kallisto give her guidance about it?

Herodotus spoke to his wife in a soft voice, though it seemed to have little effect. But Megaera readily helped them pack, sneaking glances at Nazafareen. At last she sighed and dragged Nazafareen into a crushing embrace.

"You understand, don't you? Someone must remain behind. To continue the fight, if...." Megaera looked desolate.

"If we fail. I know. And you are right." She took Megaera's hand, holding it tight. "Find out what's happening in Samarqand. The wind ships. It could be important."

Megaera nodded. "I will. And we will gather the Maenads. We will stand ready, Nazafareen."

The others waited in a line—Galen and Nicodemus, Katrin, Rhea and Darius. Other than the first two, and possibly the third, Nazafareen thought she could not wish for better company.

Daníel stood with the abbadax as they gathered one last time, the rain sweeping down from heavy grey skies.

"Be well," Kallisto said to Nazafareen, her gaze painfully intent. "You must be more than the huo mofa, or it will not serve you at the end. Do you understand?"

"I'm trying to," Nazafareen replied tartly. "But you're about as clear as mud."

"Your magic will be strong in the Kiln. Don't forget who the true enemy is." She turned to Darius. "Keep the Fourth Talisman safe. Don't let her do anything colossally stupid."

"I would die for her," he said, heat in his eyes.

"That's what I'm afraid of." She climbed onto an abbadax and sat there in stony silence as Herodotus made his farewells. Nazafareen felt the weight of Kallisto's doubts and wished it could be otherwise. But she could not order Katrin to stay, and Galen had earned the right to come, even if she had scant trust in him.

Daníel and Katrin gripped hands, and then the mounts soared away, dwindling to specks in the east. Those remaining set out for the Gale. When they got within a quarter league, forward progress became impossible due to the winds and swirling debris.

"Gather close," Katrin shouted, beckoning the others forward.

They clustered around her, Nicodemus and Rhea to either side, then Nazafareen and Darius, and finally Galen, hanging back in the rear.

"Closer," Katrin growled at him. Galen pressed forward until he was practically breathing down Nazafareen's neck. She suppressed an urge to elbow him in the ribs.

"We move together," Katrin said, her voice just audible over the tumult of the storm. "Match my pace. The shield will block the worst of it, but the ground is uneven so there might be some leakage around your feet."

Leakage? Nazafareen mouthed at Darius. She didn't care for the sound of that.

He arched an eyebrow.

Power built around them, lifting the hair on her arms. Her own breaking magic reacted immediately and she felt an overwhelming urge to oppose Katrin, to smash her weaving. Her control nearly slipped, and then Darius's calloused hands closed around her face and he pulled her close, so close their lips almost touched, and calm flowed through their bond.

"Control it," he whispered. "You can."

The initial shock faded. She drew a shaky breath. The desire passed.

Nazafareen heard a steady drumming sound and realized it was rain pattering on a dome of air two paces above her head. She reached out and felt a diamond-hard shell on all sides. Instantly, the air inside grew clammy and humid. She fought down a twinge of claustrophobia as Katrin started walking toward the Gale in her cage of air, the others close behind.

The wind outside grew stronger, howling and battering at the walls. Bits of debris shattered unnervingly against the barrier mere paces away. Gusts snatched at their feet where it imperfectly met the ground, stirring up clouds of dust inside the dome. She pressed her sleeve to her face, slitting her eyes. Darkness descended, tinged with yellow and red.

Darius gripped her hand as they entered the heart of the Gale. The storm on the *Chione* was child's play compared to the monstrosity that raged around them now. She could hardly imagine the strength it would take to hold the shield intact against the forces trying to tear it apart. And if it slipped, even for a single instant....

"Just a little further," Katrin screamed.

And then the walls started to bow inward. A hot wind rushed inside, tearing at Nazafareen's clothes and hair. Her breaking magic surged as Katrin unleashed a blast of power that pushed the storm back and the shields stabilized. She glanced quickly at Darius and the others. No one else seemed to notice anything, but the matrix of wards trembled like a spiderweb flexing in a strong wind.

Don't let it tear. And don't let the shield break either.

They shuffled along, heads bowed, and bit by bit, the blackness lightened to grey, and then to white as the sun broke through a dense cloud of dust. Wind still swirled around her, but Nazafareen could see again. Blank sands stretching to the horizon.

They were in the Kiln.

❦ 19 ❦

THIEF OF HEARTS

The chickens scratched in the dirt at his feet as Javid picked six plump tomatoes from the leafy tangle of plants in his mother's garden. He eyed them ruefully. He'd lost his appetite for tomatoes since King Shahak forced him to eat one grown with spell dust. There'd been no ill effects, but now the taste conjured images of black blood oozing from the king's nose, the tremor in his fingers and that awful wracking cough.

Javid wrapped them in a cloth and returned to the kitchen, where his ma stood at the scarred wooden table, peeling and chopping eggplants for a stew.

"You look thin, Yasmin," she said, her dark brows drawing together. "Don't they feed you at the palace?"

"You spoiled me with your cooking, ma," he said lightly. "Even the king's table doesn't compare."

She sniffed but looked pleased. "Rinse the tomatoes and put them in that bowl." She pointed to a cracked earthenware vessel. "I'm making your favorite. You'll stay for supper?"

He nodded. "I told Lord Asabana I needed the night off."

Javid had pretended to be ill and even then Asabana only dismissed him with obvious reluctance.

207

"He works you too hard, Yasmin."

"Maybe. But he pays well."

Javid slept at home, but he barely saw his family. He rose at dawn and returned late in the evening. If Asabana wasn't sending him on runs to Pompeii, Prince Shahak was demanding his presence at the palace. Once, Javid would have been thrilled. Moving in such circles was something he'd dreamt of for years. Yet the reality was turning out to be not remotely as pleasant as he'd expected.

"That was a sweet thing you did for Golpari," she said, dropping the cubes of eggplant into a pot of boiling water and turning to the tomatoes.

Javid shrugged. Golpari was getting married in a little over a week and he'd used Asabana's blood money to pay his sister's dowry. But that was entirely selfish. It eased his guilty conscience to spend it making someone else happy.

"I told da I'd bring a magus to look at his hands, but he's too stubborn. Says it's a waste of money."

"He's proud. But I know he's grateful for your help. It's hard for him to accept that he can't work anymore." She sighed. "Holy Father, having that man underfoot all day isn't easy on anyone."

He watched her stir the pot with a wooden spoon, her hands strong and weathered from digging in the garden and washing clothes and scrubbing floors. She was a petite woman, still slim as a willow despite being well into middle-age, with dark hair wrapped in a scarf. Javid had her thick, expressive eyebrows, which she used to great effect for glowering when her brood was unruly—or to lift into mischievous peaks when she cracked a joke.

"It's good you decided to be a boy, Yasmin," she said matter-of-factly. "Else we'd be living on the streets."

"My name is Javid now," he reminded her gently.

She flapped a hand. "I know. But to me you are still Yasmin. Come, taste this."

Javid took the spoon. "More cumin."

"That's what I thought too." She took an onion and sliced it in half. "You chop the garlic."

After Savah Sayuzdri first took him on as an errand boy at the Merchants' Guild at the age of twelve, Javid had spent every waking hour watching the agents of the greatest noble houses. He studied how they dressed and ate, the subtle way their hands moved when they spoke. He memorized the endless rules of etiquette, the titles and proper forms of address. Savah recognized his ambition and intelligence, promoting him steadily through the ranks.

Javid had always wanted to be a wind ship captain, but not for the Guild. For himself. To save enough that he could own his own ship one day and get so rich he'd be untouchable. Even before he finagled his way into Savah's favor, he'd earned money on the side by befriending the neighborhood bullies and convincing them to stage boxing matches. The bullies got a cut of the admission price, but the real money was in the betting, which was where Javid made his biggest profit. He'd give half the money to his ma, who would tuck it into her dress and tell him she knew he'd go places in life.

The irony was that for all those years, he dreamed of making enough so he could finally move out. And now that he had the money, he didn't want to leave. Home was the only place that seemed sane to him. So he spent what little time he got off in the kitchen helping ma chop vegetables or with Bibi, collecting eggs and feeding the chickens. In truth, he disliked the man he'd become—not the money, but how he was earning it. More to the point, he worried that each day might be his last.

"I've been thinking about Bibi," he said, lowering his voice. "Maybe I can convince Savah to give her some jobs running errands at the Guild."

His ma arched one of her famous eyebrows. "A girl?"

"Things are changing, ma. Lord Asabana's alchemist is training his daughter in the Art. She's brilliant and her brothers are idiots.

Her father intends to make her the first woman alchemist in Samarqand."

He didn't mention that some of the other pilots made crude jokes behind Leila's back. Javid had nearly come to blows over it with the loudest and most obnoxious of the bunch. They shut up when they saw him now, but Javid knew he'd made himself an enemy. He didn't care. He doubted he'd live long enough for the man to carry out his grudge.

Now his ma frowned. "I don't want Bibi anywhere near that Asabana character. He might be a lord, but I remember when he was just a criminal from Bildaar." Her lips thinned and she smacked the cleaver down on the diced onion with extra force. "It's bad enough you're in his clutches."

"I'd never send Bibi to Asabana." Just the thought sent a shiver down his spine. "But Savah is our cousin. He might do it if I ask. She doesn't want to get married, ma. She wants to make something of herself."

"I know." She dumped the onion in the pot and added the garlic Javid had chopped to her ultrafine specifications. "We'll wait one more year, until she's eleven. The child is a handful, but I won't have her hanging around a bunch of dirty men."

"They're not dirty."

She gave him a dark look. "You know what I mean." She peered toward the front of the house, where giggling had erupted. "What are those girls doing? They'll wake your da. Go tell them to quiet down."

Javid leaned over the pot and took a long, happy sniff. The stew was bubbling merrily now and would be done soon. He noticed she hadn't added any lamb. She was being frugal. He resolved to force her to take some more money, not telling da of, course.

Only four of his sisters still lived at home—Golpari, Farima, Bibi and Mahmonir, the baby of the family whose name meant *shining moon*. She was only five, but already showed signs of being more like rebellious Bibi than demure Farima.

"Little monsters," he called, heading out of the kitchen. "You're annoying the big monster, and if you don't be quiet I'll have to eat you up...."

He trailed off. Bibi and Farima stood by the front door, gazing at their visitor with open admiration. He was tall and lean, with dusky skin and curly hair. A well-coat cut in the long, high-collared style of Tjanjin covered a rather wrinkled white shirt and tight breeches that ended in a pair of soft knee-high boots.

Javid gave a low, sardonic whistle, though his heart was pounding fit to burst his chest.

"Sure you have the right house? The palace is a league or two down the street."

The thief broke into his trademark white smile. "Are these enchanting creatures your sisters?"

Bibi, who resolutely refused to mind her manners, reached out and stroked the sleeve of his coat.

"This is almost as nice as Javid's," she said, fingering the cloth. "You must be rich."

Katsu laughed as Farima thrust her aside, sticking out her bony chest.

"Don't mind *her*. She's a savage. I'm Farima. Please, come in."

Bibi's face darkened and Javid stepped in before the two started brawling on the carpet.

"Go fetch da," he said quickly. "This is Katsu, a friend."

The pair scampered up the stairs, pigtails flying.

Javid looked into the clear grey eyes he'd thought of so often and, to his horror, found himself tongue-tied. Katsu studied him and Javid saw a glint of approval. He was still wearing the clothes he'd had on at the Rock of Ariamazes to attend the King that morning—a scarlet coat with embroidery on the sleeves and loose silk trousers. His hair was neatly cut to chin length, parted in the middle and tamed with a pricy aromatic oil. He probably reeked of garlic, but you couldn't have everything.

They both opened their mouths to speak at the same time.

"Sorry," Javid said.

"No, I...."

And then his father was coming down the stairs and his mother bustling from the kitchen, her eyebrows lifting when she saw Katsu, and the moment slipped away. They piled into the kitchen. His ma ladled out bowls of stew while Javid made up a story about meeting Katsu in Delphi. He glanced at the thief and saw with relief that he approved of the deception. Javid's family knew what had happened to him, but he'd never mentioned his savior in the Polemarch's dungeons. And the topic would open a can of worms he didn't want to deal with in front of his little sisters, particularly.

Bibi peppered Katsu with questions all through supper, while Farima mooned over him with cow eyes. Golpari picked at her food, clearly preoccupied with her upcoming wedding. Mahmonir kept trying to steal sips of Javid's wine, most likely at Bibi's direction.

"It's so nice Yasmin has a friend," his ma pronounced, causing Javid to wince. "She needs more friends." His da must have kicked her under the table because she switched pronouns awkwardly. "He works too hard. He has no social life."

Katsu shot Javid an amused look. "I was hoping he might take a walk with me after supper so we can catch up."

"That's a fantastic idea." Javid nearly knocked his bowl over he stood up so fast. "I'm stuffed. Unless you want dessert?"

In fact, Javid was so nervous he'd hardly touched his food. It was too surreal having Katsu sitting in his kitchen.

"Date and walnut pie," his ma said enticingly.

Javid knew she'd intended it for the wedding and was touched.

"It sounds delicious," Katsu said regretfully, stretching his long legs. "But the stew was so good I'm afraid I have no room left."

He stood and gave her a low bow. "Thank you for your hospitality."

His ma beamed. "I'm just glad he has a friend. I think he's lonely."

"Zhala," his da said warningly.

"Not that he isn't pretty. I mean *handsome*," she went on, flustered. "He just keeps to himself too much.... Enjoy your walk!"

The last words were hollered since Javid had already given her a stiff nod and stalked for the front door. He could clearly hear his father admonishing her for "embarrassing the poor boy" and his ma's indignant rattling of crockery as she cleared the plates.

"Please ignore my parents," Javid said when they reached the garden gate. "They're a little overprotective."

"Really?" Katsu said with a grin. "I hadn't noticed."

Javid shook his head. "I never thought I'd see you again." He snuck a sideways glance. "I hoped to, but it's certainly a surprise. How did you find me?"

"I asked around at the Abicari." Katsu looked Javid up and down. "You've come up in the world since last we met."

"So have you."

"I got in two days ago, just before the city gates were sealed. Lucky, I suppose."

They meandered down the dirt street. The low sun lit rows of mudbrick houses with children and dogs playing out front.

"Are you still hunting for that talisman?"

Javid thought this the most likely explanation. Katsu had picked up the trail again and it led to Samarqand. He probably hoped Javid could give him information.

Katsu shook his head, his face grave. "I found it in Tjanjin, but you'll never believe the tale."

"Try me."

"I went to the Isles and caught a ship to Chang-un. It turned out two of the passengers had the globe. They took it from a fire daēva. I helped them and they gave me the globe in exchange."

Javid stumbled and Katsu's hand shot out to steady him. "Did you just say they took it from a *fire daēva?*"

The Stygian nodded. "His name is Nicodemus. He was an advisor to the emperor. No one at court knew what he was, of course. But I saw him work fire myself."

"Holy Father. Where is he now?"

"He escaped through a gate to the Dominion, so I suppose he could be anywhere."

Javid made the sign of the flame, fingers brushing forehead, lips and heart.

"How did these people manage to take a talisman from a Vatra?"

"They were the oddest group I've ever encountered. A Maenad, a Greek scholar, a Danai and a mortal girl."

Javid froze. "Did this girl have one hand?"

Katsu gave him a sharp look. "How did you know?"

"That's Ashraf! The girl who got me arrested. Though her name isn't really Ashraf. It's—"

"Nazafareen." His grey eyes held Javid's as they halted in front of a potter's shop. "Life is strange, wind pilot." Katsu paused. "I would ask you something."

"Go ahead."

"When you saw me, you looked surprised. Yet you haven't once asked how I got out of the Polemarch's dungeons."

Javid shrugged, warmth creeping up his neck. He made his tone light. "It was you or a new pair of boots, and I have a closetful already."

The Stygian eyed him with skepticism. "It must have cost a fortune. Do they pay wind pilots so much in Samarqand?"

"Not exactly." He lowered his voice. "There's a noble named Izad Asabana. He's the source of the spell dust. He hired me and I finally got a big run a couple of weeks ago. He paid me a huge bonus."

Katsu frowned. "But I've been free for more than a month."

Javid silently cursed his loose tongue.

"You took out a debt for me."

"It's paid off now," Javid said hastily.

"Then I must repay you. I have more gold than I need from the bounty." Katsu reached for his purse and Javid impulsively laid his hand over the thief's.

"Please, it's not necessary."

Katsu'd frown deepened. "Then I am in your debt."

"No, you're not. I'm tired of debts. Is an act of kindness so rare?"

Katsu gave a small smile. "Yes, it is. But I will accept. On one condition."

"And what's that?"

"You leave this noble and work with me. I'm thinking of investing in a wind ship and I need an experienced pilot. Someone I can trust."

Javid's spirits soared—then plummeted to earth again. "Thank you, Katsu. I would love that, truly. But it's complicated." He took the thief's arm and led him deeper into the trees, looking around to be sure no one was listening. "I was there when Prince Shahak took the throne. Holy Father forgive me, I helped him do it. Now he barely lets me out of his sight. And Asabana is ruthless. I know his secrets. In truth, I think my days are numbered."

Katsu scratched his short beard. "There has to be a way out."

"Trust me, that's all I think about. It's no use." He smiled, trying hard not to show his bitter disappointment. "But I will help you choose the best, most honest shipbuilder. I'll see if I can get away tomorrow. Meet me at the Abicari in Hecate's ninth hour?"

"I will, Javid. Thank you." Katsu flashed a white smile. "But I have not given up on you yet. If you were content, I would walk away without regret. But I sense that you are not happy serving this Lord Asabana."

"I wouldn't drag you into this," Javid protested. "Asabana is nothing compared to King Shahak. The man's a lunatic. But Asabana is blinded by how much money he's making." Javid closed his eyes. "And now you tell me Nazafareen had a run-in with a fire daēva." An unpleasant thought struck him. "Did this Vatra come from the Kiln?"

"Where else? Though I've no idea how he managed to escape." He saw Javid's tense expression and assumed it was simple fear. "Don't worry, he's the only one I know of. Nazafareen nearly killed him, though he managed to get away." He shook his head. "She has some fey power I'd never heard of. Huo mofa, she called it."

"I know." Javid missed her despite the fact that she attracted trouble like flies to a midden. Nazafareen always meant well, even if her plans tended to go horribly awry. "Was she well when you left her?"

"Quite well, and her Danai lover too. When we parted, they were planning to go to the darklands." He eyed Javid. "Come back to Tjanjin with me. Samarqand is too dangerous."

Javid glanced back at the house. "I can't leave, Katsu. I'm in too deep."

Katsu nodded. "I understand. Let me think on this some more. Tomorrow at the Abicari?"

"Tomorrow."

They clasped hands. Javid watched Katsu walk away, his smile fading.

❧ 20 ❧

WEDDINGS AND WIND SHIPS

The falcon glided in wide circles over the ancient olive trees growing along the riverbank, its pale breast flashing in the sunlight. Suddenly it dove, a dark missile streaking for the earth. At the last second, the bird banked and climbed, some small creature dangling from its talons.

Javid leaned his elbows on the marble balustrade, Leila at his side. Their employer stood a few paces off. He raised a gloved hand and the falcon sped toward its master, alighting on his wrist. Asabana took the mouse by its tail and dropped it into the bird's open beak.

"Why does she always return to her jailers?" Javid murmured. "She could just fly away and never look back."

"Because she has been trained to do so," Leila replied with a darkly amused look. "Her masters feed her well."

Asabana gave the bird to its handlers and strolled over, pulling the thick leather glove off. He seemed to be in a good mood. Javid steadied himself.

"My lord, I was hoping to request some time off. My father's health is declining. He cannot use his hands. And my sister is getting married—"

"I pay you enough to take care of them," Asabana said gruffly.

"Indeed, you are very generous, my lord. But—"

"No."

Javid had expected this, but it still rankled.

"A few days only...."

"It's a sensitive time. Ask me again in a few weeks."

In a few weeks, we'll all be dead. Or worse.

Javid bowed his head. It was pointless to argue. But he could try again to make his boss see reason.

"King Shahak is growing impatient, my lord. He's demanding to know the source of the dust. I don't think I can put him off much longer."

Asabana scowled. "If we tell him where the source is, he'll cut us out."

"Not necessarily," Leila ventured. "He'll still need your ships to get it."

"Perhaps. Or he might hire someone cheaper. There's always some hungry newcomer looking for a piece of the action."

"My lord," Javid said, "he threatened to summon you to court."

Asabana chewed thoughtfully, then flashed his gold teeth. "Don't worry, lad, I can manage him."

Javid doubted this. Asabana had attended the coronation along with the other nobles, but he hadn't spent time in Shahak's company. He didn't seem to grasp what the prince was capable of.

"You'd best get back to the palace. Tell our King, the Holy Father bless his name, that the next shipment is on me. That should keep him happy for a while."

Asabana must have seen the skepticism in Javid's face because his gaze hardened a fraction.

"Unless you have a better idea, in which case, do share it."

Javid stifled a sigh. "No, my lord."

Gold teeth flashed, though the smile didn't reach his eyes. "Glad I can count on you, son." His stare lingered for a few moments longer as though he saw into Javid's secret heart, but he said nothing, signaling to a servant who hurried forward with a cup of iced wine.

Asabana rarely issued outright threats. He didn't have to. Everyone knew his reputation and unlike other crime bosses, it wasn't inflated. If anything, the truth was worse.

Once Javid would have quailed. But he'd grown accustomed to weathering the volatile moods of King Shahak, who was far more frightening in his way. Asabana might be a thug, but his motives were simple. The classics: money and power. Shahak, on the other hand, was not entirely sane. He had moments of genius, even kindness and generosity, but the dust was eating holes in his brain. One could never be sure where one stood with the king—or what he might do at any given moment.

So Javid simply brushed off his coatsleeves and bowed to his employer.

"I beg your leave then," he said, shooting Leila a look. "I'll bring your warmest regards to the king."

"And I have work to finish," Leila said quickly. "Father will be wanting me."

Asabana waved a hand. He was already digging into the array of savory dishes laid out on the canopied table.

"How is your father?" Javid asked politely as they walked away, conscious of Asabana's eyes following them. The man had hearing like a bat.

"Quite well. He will raise me up to a full alchemist soon."

"A great accomplishment for one so young."

"How kind of you to say," she murmured.

The moment they'd passed through the door to the manor, Javid dropped his formal tone.

"Full alchemist, eh? And what will you do then?"

"Remain in his lordship's service, of course. I'm his hawk too. Besides which, no one else would hire a woman even if I did find the courage to leave." She paused in front of the splashing fountain in the manor's grand entrance hall. It was loud enough to drown out their words if any servants were listening. "What's happened? It's obvious you're bursting to tell me something."

Javid leaned closer. "The Vatras aren't all dead. I know someone who saw one in Tjanjin."

Leila's eyes narrowed. "What? Who?"

"I can't say."

"It's that thief of yours, isn't it? I can tell by the flush creeping up your neck." She grinned. "How sweet. He came looking for you."

"Didn't you hear what I just said?" Javid hissed. "A Vatra! He must have come from the Kiln."

She sighed. "Don't get your knickers in a twist. Just slow down and tell me the whole thing."

"I don't have all the details yet, but I'm sure he's telling the truth. When Katsu got out of the Pythia's dungeons, he went to Tjanjin, seeking a talisman that had been stolen from the emperor. He met a woman I know, a breaker of magic. Her name is Nazafareen."

"I've heard of that," Leila said thoughtfully. "Rare creatures. My father says they are like white stags. Every so often, one turns up."

"Well, they ended up crossing paths with a Vatra. He fled through a gate." Javid saw her dubious expression. "Katsu said he witnessed the man working fire directly. I don't think he would exaggerate such a thing."

"Yet you didn't tell Asabana any of this."

Javid shuddered. "He has enough leverage on me already. If I told him, I'd have to explain how I knew. No way is he getting anywhere near Katsu. The poor bastard finally got a break. I'm not about to ruin his life." He stared at her. "You mustn't tell anyone, not even your father."

"I won't. But whether it's true or not, it doesn't change anything."

It changes everything, he wanted to shout. But Leila was right.

He supposed he could feign sickness the next time they made a run for the Kiln, but that wouldn't work forever.

"I want out," he declared. "I don't care about the money anymore. Katsu offered me a job. A partnership."

"So take it."

"You know I can't."

He saw sympathy in her eyes. "If there's any way I can help, just ask. As long as it doesn't put myself or my father at risk."

"Thanks." He gave her an awkward pat on the shoulder. "You're a good friend, Leila."

"Did you kiss him yet?"

"None of your business." Javid stalked out the door and down the wide steps, heading for the *Ash Vareca*. Leila followed.

"I'll take that for a no. You really must conquer your shyness. Katsu clearly likes you or he wouldn't have come all the way to Samarqand."

"It's complicated," he snapped, hauling himself up the ladder and lighting the burners.

"All love is complicated."

"You know what I mean."

"You're scared. I suppose that's understandable. But there are many types of intercourse between men and women, men and men, women and women. You can teach each other—"

Javid's flush deepened. "I get it. Untie that mooring line, would you?"

Leila tossed the line to the deck and the ship drifted upward. She smiled at him indulgently.

"You are simply in want of an education, Javid," she called. "I'd be happy to—"

He gave her a wave and set a course back to the city. The wind cooled his burning cheeks and he laughed. Leila Khorram-Din was certainly one of a kind. He wondered what his ma would make of her. Bibi, he knew, would fall in love with her.

The thought of his family sobered him quickly. He had a

sudden image of Bibi screaming as faceless men dragged her from the house.

You'll get out of this with your skin somehow, he thought grimly. *You always do. Just keep your head down and your eyes open. Once you have enough gold, you can get them to safety.*

From the air, Samarqand resembled a spiral shell, with its streets running in concentric circles from the Rock of Ariamazes. Smoke from the forge fires hung in a thick haze over the blacksmith's quarter, but Javid could see the smudged outlines of the adjacent slum known as Bildaar. Izad Asabana had been born there. He'd started off as a small-time smuggler and slowly built up a black market empire. Then he'd discovered spell dust, thanks to Leila and Marzban Khorram-Din, and made his fortune, with a noble title from old King Cambyses to boot.

Shahak's father had indulged his pleasures and left the affairs of state to the Queen and his advisory council. Asabana didn't comprehend that the son was a very different sort of man. He seemed to think he was still the boy's puppet master, but Shahak would not dance for him much longer.

Javid landed at the western edge of the Abicari. It was a hive of activity, though less than usual. Most of the ships sat at anchor and Javid recalled the rumors he'd heard about the Marakai. As he strode across the field, the other pilots nodded at him with new respect and a touch of envy. Everyone knew he worked for Asabana now. They figured he'd hit the big time. Javid almost laughed, though it wasn't funny. He'd trade places with them in a heartbeat—even if it meant being a bucket boy again. Savah Sayuzhdri might be a perfectionist, but he wouldn't have you killed if you screwed up.

Katsu waited outside a large hangar filled with ships in various stages of construction and repair. He broke into a warm smile when he saw Javid.

"I watched you land," he said. "It must take great skill."

"Nothing that can't be learned," Javid replied with uncharacteristic modesty.

Katsu laughed. "So says an experienced pilot. I imagine it took you many years."

"I suppose I do have a knack for flying."

"What does a new ship cost?"

"It depends what you're looking for. Come, I'll introduce you to the boss."

They found Savah in his cluttered office, going over invoices for the Merchants' Guild. He held a magnifying lens in one huge paw, which he quickly hid under the table as they walked in.

He's getting old, Javid thought with a touch of surprise. It was hard to fathom. Savah was a force of nature—he'd been the master of the Abicari when Javid was in swaddling clothes. He knew his ships down to the last peg and could probably build one single-handedly. Javid couldn't imagine anyone taking his place.

"Well, well." Savah slid the glass into a drawer and shifted his right leg, which stuck out stiffly. "Haven't seen you around here in a while. I hear you're the man of the house now."

"Just helping out a little."

"That's not what your mother says." He studied Javid. "You look good, kid. Who's your friend?"

Katsu gave a low bow. He looked elegant in a pearl grey coat that set off his dark skin and tilted eyes. "My name is Katsu."

"You're not from Samarqand."

"Tjanjin."

Savah eyed him skeptically. "Well, Katsu from Tjanjin, it's nice to meet you, but I've got a bloody mountain of work to do, so—"

"Katsu wishes to commission a wind ship," Javid said.

Savah leaned back. "Who do you represent?"

"Myself."

The master of the Abicari drummed his index finger on the table. Only the wealthiest nobles commissioned personal wind ships and despite Katsu's fine coat (which was a bit tattered at the cuffs), he was obviously no lord. Besides the scars on his hands, his face was a bit too hard, his beard too scruffy.

"What do you want it for?"

"Just to travel, make a little money on the side."

"A little money on the side." Savah shook his grizzled head. "You *do* know the Marakai have vanished. Not a single ship has come into the harbor at Susa for the last week. Nothing's moving. The docks are clogged with fresh meat and produce bound for the Isles. It's all going to rot. And that's just the perishable goods. The prices for silks and spices are skyrocketing, but no one has any to sell." His mournful gaze landed on Javid. "You're lucky you work for Asabana. He's the only one whose bottom line isn't getting erased."

"I saw the Marakai fleet sail away myself," Katsu ventured carefully. "The Five is meeting. What will happen after, I cannot say. But I do know the Marakai captains personally. If they return to Susa, I might be able to secure a contract or two."

"And cut the Guild out?" Savah growled.

Katsu looked alarmed. "That's not my intention. I'll follow the proper channels, of course. I assume there are...licensing fees to be paid."

"You assume right."

"Come on, uncle." Javid flashed a grin. "He's an honest man. I'll vouch for him. Perhaps his contacts with the Marakai can be of use."

Savah stared hard at them both, then heaved a sigh. He pulled a small, dusty cask from underneath a stack of papers and poured three cups of wine.

"Remember when I told you we'd be reduced to the swill they brew in Susa?" he asked Javid. "Well, this is even worse. Vinegar from the cellars of the magi, the Holy Father bless them. But it's all we've got, so bottoms up." He raised his cup. "To the health of King Shahak. May he save us from the bloody Pythia and whatever else is headed our way."

"To the health of King Shahak," Javid murmured.

He took a bracing sip. From the corner of his eye, he watched Katsu swallow with an admirably blank expression.

Savah slammed the cup down and let out a discreet belch. "I'll need a down payment before we can start work."

Katsu placed a heavy bag on the desk. It made a clinking sound that warmed Javid's heart.

"Will this cover it?"

Savah peered inside, then nodded. "More than enough." He rubbed his hands together. "Now, what did you have in mind?"

"I'm not sure. Can any of the wind ships cross the sea?"

Savah laughed. "It's never been tried, so I won't say no. But you'd be crazy to make the attempt. First storm you hit.... Well, the air sacks aren't made for storms and smashers."

Katsu nodded as if he'd expected this answer. "I'd like something that can carry cargo but also with sleeping quarters below decks."

They spent half an hour discussing the various options. Katsu finally settled on one of the newest styles, a swift cutter thirty paces long—modest by the standards of the Guild's cargo ships but more than adequate for Katsu's needs.

"It'll take a couple of weeks," Savah said.

"Can you finish it faster?" Katsu asked, glancing at Javid.

"Sure, but that'll cost extra. Say five thousand darics."

"I have the money."

"We'll start today then."

Savah drew up the contract and Katsu placed his mark on it. Then they toasted Golpari and her upcoming wedding and Katsu and his new ship. Javid was pleased, but he also felt a bit depressed that the Stygian would be leaving so soon.

"I hope you'll reconsider my offer," Katsu said as he walked Javid to the *Ash Vareca*.

"I have," Javid replied firmly. "It's impossible. But I'll make sure you hire the best pilot."

Katsu seemed to accept this. "If I may ask one last favor then. Perhaps you can direct me to a good tailor? I had no time before I left Tjanjin and I've been wearing these clothes for days."

"Of course. I'll take you to Bahruz. But you have to let me do the haggling. I know his tricks."

Katsu laughed. "I heard you Persians like to argue over price. In Tjanjin, it would be considered unforgivably rude."

"You mean you pay whatever they ask for?" Javid asked with disbelief. "Where's the fun in that?" He nearly told Katsu to come to the house again, then thought of his parents. "Where are you staying?"

"An inn called the Four Dervishes."

"I know it. I'll meet you there tomorrow morning if I can. If not, I'll send a message."

Their step slowed as they reached the *Ash Vareca*. Katsu gave him one of those dazzling smiles.

"Clear skies and steady winds, captain," he said with a small salute.

It was the ritual greeting and farewell between pilots at the Abicari.

Javid arched an eyebrow. "How did you know—"

"I listen," Katsu laughed, tugging his ear. "You see? I am a quick study."

He strolled away, loose and wolfish, drawing curious looks from the other pilots. Javid imagined Leila's approving grin.

Have you kissed him yet?

He swore under his breath. Somehow he'd gotten the mooring line tangled around his foot.

Head down and eyes open, he reminded himself sternly. *Katsu doesn't need your troubles. If you're a true friend, you'll watch him sail away in a week. You'll wave and you'll smile. And if there are any scraps left when the lion and the hyena are done with you, well, you can stitch them together and go down to Susa.*

~

He'd anticipated a tedious afternoon in the throne room watching the nobility try to curry favor with the new King with gifts and flattery. These audiences were a bore, enlivened only by the occasional assassination attempt. But when Javid arrived at the palace, he was told Shahak had holed up in his chambers and couldn't be disturbed.

"*Experiments,*" whispered the chamberlain, who knew Javid well by this point and couldn't resist gossiping. "He won't open the door for anyone, not even his own steward. I don't think he's eaten in days." He glanced around. "The guards hear strange noises inside. Like the growls of wild beasts."

Javid arched an eyebrow. "Has the King of Kings requested any deliveries?"

"No." The chamberlain wrung his hands. "We dare not knock. He flew into a terrible rage when the Hazara-patis tried to enter."

If the Master of a Thousand, the powerful official who administered the entire palace staff, was being refused entry, Javid had no intention of trying it himself. The Holy Father only knew what Shahak was getting up to now.

"I shall return tomorrow," he said. "Send a messenger if he calls for me in the meantime."

The chamberlain bobbed his head and Javid walked away, feeling lighter than he had in weeks. Perhaps this was the end. The King's final self-destruction. Javid just hoped he was far from the Rock when it happened.

The next morning, he went to the Four Dervishes and found Katsu having breakfast in the common room. With the city withering under the Pythia's trade embargo and now the disappearance of the Marakai, Bahruz was delighted to see them, though he pretended to be awash in orders from other clients. Javid haggled over the last sock, and despite Bahruz's protestations that his family would starve, he thought the tailor was secretly pleased to have *someone* to argue with.

Over the following days, he became Katsu's guide to Samarqand. They visited the public gardens and the royal zoo, and watched a game of chaugan, the players thundering across the field on horseback to chase a little wooden ball with long mallets. They wandered through the bazaar, admiring carpets and incense and perfumes of rosewater.

Each morning, Javid dutifully went to the palace. Shahak remained indisposed, although the chamberlain said he'd accepted a tray of food left outside his door. Izad Asabana had gone off to Susa, supposedly to negotiate a new contract with some minor noble but more likely to avoid the King, so Javid found he'd gotten his leave after all.

At the end of each day, he and Katsu would buy skewers of roasted meat from the colorful stalls at the edge of the Abicari and check on the progress of the new ship. Javid watched Katsu's delight as it took shape. True to his word, Savah was pushing the carpenters at a relentless pace. The hull had already been completed and they were laying down the deck and fixtures. It had two snug berths with storage compartments and brass-trimmed portholes. At Katsu's request, the seamstresses embroidered a silver oyster on the air sack—some obscure Stygian deity called Babana.

All progressed satisfactorily. But whenever Javid suggested they meet some of the other pilots for hire, Katsu found a way to put him off. He would change the subject or pretend to be tired and beg his leave. Javid knew what he was doing but found the Stygian slippery as an eel.

Indeed, beneath his easy manner lurked a shrewd and determined man. During their wanderings around the city, Katsu asked intelligent questions about which goods turned the highest profit and who could be trusted to honor a contract. Javid told him all he'd learned during his long years of service to the Guild, and also about Asabana and how he'd made his fortune.

The only thing he omitted was where the dust came from—and Katsu never asked. It wasn't a matter of trust. Javid felt ashamed. He was, in simple terms, a grave robber. Yes, the Vatras had done terrible things. But some of those bones belonged to children. Javid himself only used spell dust now when he absolutely had to, and it made his skin crawl.

Still, he was happy to take Katsu for short trips in the *Ash Vareca* so he could learn the basics of piloting a wind ship. During one of these jaunts, Katsu told him the full story of what had happened in Tjanjin. Javid found it hard to believe the naïve girl he'd known as Ashraf had gotten embroiled in such a wild adventure. It seemed more like a story than anything real. The thought of the Vatras' return troubled him, but he took comfort in the fact that it had transpired far away, on the other side of the White Sea. Nothing to do with him—as long as he didn't run into any fire daēvas in the Kiln.

They were drifting southward over the hills between Samarqand and Susa when Katsu brought up the dungeons again.

"Do you remember promising me a ride in a wind ship?" he asked with a grin. "Bet you never expected me to collect."

"That was right before I got hauled before the Pythia." He glanced at Katsu. "We're lucky bastards to have gotten out."

"Luck had nothing to do with it. I'd still be there if not for you."

Javid opened the valve beneath the air sack. The ship began to rise. "And I would likely be dead if you hadn't taken the side of a stranger from Samarqand."

Katsu gave him a sidelong glance. "My old master used to say a thousand years cannot repair a single moment's loss of honor."

"An admirable sentiment," Javid replied seriously. "*My* master says, when in doubt, take the money."

Katsu laughed. "You're even more mercenary than I am."

"I don't think you're mercenary at all." Javid studied him. "Why did you really come here?"

"I was looking for you."

"But why?"

Katsu considered for a moment. "True courage is rare. Nazafareen showed it when she walked up to that Marakai girl and talked her into releasing the wave. And you did in the dungeons."

"Me?" Javid laughed. "Holy Father, all I did was get myself arrested."

"You could have told your jailers you were born a woman. They might have mocked you, but they wouldn't have put you in with rough men like Aknos. The Greeks are not barbarians. They have cells for women. You would have been safer."

Javid gripped the rail. Wagons crawled along the road between Samarqand and Susa, tiny as ants.

"But that's not who I am."

"So you risked everything. It is a choice, one you make every day." Katsu looked away. "I've drifted around for most of my life. My parents are dead. I have no brothers or sisters. If I'm careful, I have enough money to live comfortably. But I'm tired of solitude. I wish to take on a partner and you're the most interesting person I've met in a long time."

He ran a hand through his curly hair. Javid had a sudden urge to take his fingers and tenderly kiss the half-moon scars.

"I want to," Javid said. "More than anything. But...."

"I know. You have four sisters still living at home?"

"Yes. Soon to be three, after Golpari gets married."

Katsu held his gaze. "What if we could get your family to safety? Would they go?"

Javid had thought about this many times. "I'm not sure. But even if my parents agreed, where could we run to?"

"What about Susa?"

"It's part of the King's writ."

"Yes, but surely they could hide there until the Marakai

return. Then we could leave for Tjanjin. Chang'an is a beautiful city. I know the emperor personally. I can promise your family would be safe."

For the first time, Javid felt a surge of hope.

"But what about the wind ship? It can't cross the White Sea."

"Perhaps not. But with Marakai help, who knows? We would be the first in Tjanjin to own a wind ship." Katsu rubbed his hands together. "The nobility would pay a fortune for a ride in the clouds."

Javid felt a lump in his throat. "You would do this for me?"

"I would not be standing here if not for you, Javid. Let us say we owe each other only friendship from now on. Agreed?"

"Agreed. But we must wait until after Golpari's wedding." He sighed. "There's nothing I can do about my sisters who are already married with families of their own. We'd need a fleet of ten wind ships to carry them."

"Would the King punish them in your stead?"

"I don't think so. If they were male, yes. But women are treated like much children. They have fewer rights, but it would be dishonorable to hold them responsible for my actions. And Asabana.... Well, once I'm gone, he'll have to face the King himself."

They spent the rest of the trip planning their escape. The soldiers at the wall kept a close eye on travelers entering and leaving Samarqand, but windships were still permitted to fly directly out of the Abicari. And Javid knew plenty of seedy taverns down by the docks in Susa. His mother wouldn't like it, but he felt sure they could disappear there for a week or two until the Marakai returned.

When the deep blue waves of the Austral Ocean came into view, he used a pinch of spell dust to change course and head north back to Samarqand. His heart was lighter than it had been in ages.

And so the days passed and Javid found himself in a state of severe infatuation. He laughed too loud and daydreamed at inappropriate times. Katsu treated him like a man, but there was an undercurrent in glances that lingered a fraction of a second too long. In the way the Stygian might sit so that his thigh brushed Javid's and neither moved away. In the occasional awkward silences that descended.

But despite his famous courage, Javid found he was a shameless coward when it came to making the first move. And Katsu seemed to be waiting for a clear sign—perhaps for fear of causing offense.

In desperation, Javid finally sought Leila out and asked her advice. She told him sensibly that Katsu already knew his deepest secret. Javid was simply afraid of the unknown, so the best thing to do was to face it. Then she gave him a slender volume called a pillow book and told him to go peruse it in private. He'd glanced at the cover and replied that he couldn't read Tjanjinese and Leila had laughed and said it was mostly pictures anyway.

When he opened it, his eyes popped and he'd shoved it hastily under his coat. Javid snuck the book into his room, poring over it in the wee hours while his sisters slept. It was fascinating and disturbing at the same time. He had a healthy imagination, but truly, he'd only scratched the surface.

Even if he was misreading Katsu completely, the information would prove useful *someday*. Javid didn't plan to stay a virgin for the rest of his life. Of course, that might not be long if one of his patrons decided to snuff him out—all the more reason to leave as soon as possible.

He still hadn't worked up the nerve to talk to his father. Javid knew his da wouldn't be happy about it. Everything and everyone he knew was in Samarqand. His ma wouldn't want to go, either. Her grandchildren were here. Her garden. Bibi would see it as an adventure and Mahmonir was too young to know better, but Farima might kick up a fuss. She was thirteen and he'd seen her eyeing one of the neighbor boys like a dealer appraising horseflesh. She probably had her wedding dress picked out already.

Javid rubbed his forehead. Asabana would be back from Susa any day now. His reprieve was almost over.

He threw the pillow book aside. Girlish laughter erupted in the hall, followed by an outraged yell from Farima.

Love stinks, he thought.

On the day of Golpari's wedding, controlled chaos reigned at the house. His ma barked orders from the kitchen, where she'd been bunkered like a general on the eve of battle, while Golpari dressed with the help of her sisters. The wedding would be witnessed by an assembly called the Shahjan, and both the house and garden were bursting at the seams with friends, neighbors and relations dressed in their finest.

Javid had already greeted the pair of officiating magi and seated them on a couch in the front room. Katsu chatted with his father about the new wind ship. Javid's da had been a rope maker at the Abicari before his hands grew too gnarled. He knew the fleet almost as well as Savah and clearly relished having company. Katsu listened attentively, soaking up each bit of unsolicited advice with good humor. Every few minutes, one of Javid's sisters would creep down the stairs and peek at them with cow eyes, then run back up giggling.

"Javid!" his ma called from the kitchen.

Not Yasmin. He felt pleased, even though it sounded a trifle strange. Javid had a feeling his da had talked to her about it. Now his ma stood red-faced over a gigantic vat of lamb stew. Tantalizing smells drifted from the many pots bubbling on the fire.

"Have you seen Bibi?" his mother demanded. "The girl is supposed to be peeling carrots." She gestured to a mound of vegetables on the counter.

"She's not in Golpari's room?" Javid asked.

His mother lifted an eyebrow. Bibi had made herself scarce all week, as if Golpari was contagious with some dread disease.

"Don't worry, I know her hidey-holes," Javid said.

He checked the dark recesses of the chicken coop and the highest branches of the walnut tree at the edge of the garden. He looked behind rain barrels and under furniture. Finally, he ran upstairs to ask if his sisters had seen her. They hadn't.

He was heading back downstairs when he heard a furtive rustle from his room.

"Bibi?"

Javid opened the door. Bibi lay on his bed with the pillow book open on her knees and a faint tinge of pink in her round cheeks. A normal girl would have been mortified. But Bibi was not a normal girl.

"Have you done all those things?" she asked with a frown.

"Holy Father, no!" He grabbed the book and shoved it under his bed. "You must forget you ever saw any of that."

Her brown eyes glinted. "You mean the part where—"

"All of it." He crossed his arms and prayed she hadn't gotten to page twenty-seven.

"What do I get for keeping my mouth shut?" Bibi eyed him with a ruthless expression that would have made Asabana proud. "I'm still waiting for that spell dust you promised."

She squealed as he grabbed her arm. "You get to go downstairs and behave and not get a thrashing."

Bibi laughed in his face.

"A thrashing, eh? By who?"

Javid hauled her back down to the kitchen, past the magi and Katsu and his da, and gave her a firm shove toward the carrots. He didn't trust the look she shot over her shoulder, so he thought it prudent to lead Katsu outside before Bibi decided to disgrace them both.

"Where was your sister?" Katsu asked.

"Praying," Javid said quickly. "She's very religious."

Katsu looked doubtful—he'd seen enough of Bibi at that disastrous dinner.

"You're joking."

"No, it's true. She takes after my da's sister over there," Javid added, looking at a stout woman in a black headscarf. "Total fanatic. She's got about a hundred figurines of the Prophet Zarathustra in her house. The eyes follow you everywhere." He jerked his chin at the slight, bearded man next to her. "That's Uncle Ervin. He'll get very drunk later. He always does at these things."

Javid pointed out the groom and his family, and the two branches of cousins who despised each other.

"They only cross paths at weddings and funerals," he said, sipping a cup of wine as he watched for Bibi. "The feud goes so far back, no one even remembers how it started."

"One of my masters used to say, *Before you embark on a journey of revenge, dig two graves*," Katsu observed.

"Yeah, well, tell that to cousin Hafuz. He nurses a grudge like it's his firstborn son."

Golpari finally came out in a blue dress trimmed in lace. She blushed and smiled at the handsome young groom, Farhad, who laid a hand on his heart. Two chairs waited in the garden, with a curtain separating them that was held up by the official witnesses —Javid's older sister Razma and one of the groom's brothers. The magi emerged, the crowd hushed, and the betrothed sat down on either side of the curtain. Smudges of red paint marked their foreheads and garlands of flowers hung about their necks.

Javid leaned over and pointed to Farhad, who wore a loose, flowing garment.

"That's called the Jama-pichori," he whispered. "It's always white. But the bride is free to wear color if she wishes to."

The magi wound the pair in a bolt of cloth, creating a circle to symbolize unity. Lengthy prayers were intoned. The couple's right hands were joined and bound seven times with another twist of cloth while the magi uttered the sacred Ahunwar formula. After yet more binding and more prayers, one of the magi burned frankincense in a brazier. The happy couple were each given some rice in their left hands—the right still being bound together—which they tossed at each other. Everybody clapped, and the celebration began.

Javid watched Katsu dance with Farima, spinning her around breathless and bright-eyed. Savah Sayuzhdri held Mahmonir on his broad shoulders. She patted his head as he bounced her up and down, while his da told some funny story that had Savah wheezing with laughter. On the other side of the garden, Bibi chased a fugitive chicken back into the coop. She seemed to sense his gaze for she turned and gave him a little smile over her shoulder. Not an evil smile—Javid knew that one well. No, this was friendly enough and meant she had no plan to embarrass him before their friends and neighbors—not today, at least. Javid held out a hand and she came running over, already a bit sticky-looking despite ma's vigorous scrubbing that morning.

"Let's dance," he said.

Bibi grinned, showing off a newly lost tooth. The other dancers had formed a circle and they hurried to close the gap, stomping to the drums and snapping their fingers. Several times, as the lines swept forward and back, he passed Katsu, though they never quite ended up next to each other. Finally, Javid fell onto a bench in the shade, wiping sweat from his brow.

He felt flushed and happy, but also wistful. This would be the last time he'd see most of them. Even cousin Hafuz, for all his grumbling, had made Javid his first pair of men's boots, a gift for his fourteenth birthday. He'd worn them until they literally fell to pieces.

"What's troubling you, son?" his da asked.

Javid looked up. "Nothing. Everything's fine."

His da gave him a shrewd look. "I know you. You've been walking around with a cloud over your head for weeks."

Javid nearly told him everything then, but he didn't want to ruin the wedding. More importantly, Asabana still owed him a month's pay. One he collected his money and added it to the stash of gold beneath his bed, they'd have enough to start fresh someplace far from Samarqand.

"Can we talk later?" he asked.

His da laid a shriveled hand on Javid's shoulder. "Of course."

They ate and drank and danced late into the evening, and by the time he thought of speaking to his da, everyone had stumbled off to bed.

Tomorrow, he thought, yawning into his blankets. I'll do it first thing tomorrow.

21

A GILDED CAGE

P*ounding.*

At first it was part of his dream, the heavy tread of a giant chasing him through a blasted landscape. But the sound grew louder, more insistent, and Javid's eyes flew open. The low sun slanted through his window, pooling on the wood floor. Someone was at the front door.

He hurried downstairs. His ma stood in the hall, a blanket wrapped around her shoulders and her hair unbound, so it must be early morning still. She looked frightened.

"Who is it?" he mouthed.

"A soldier," she whispered. "Go hide. I'll tell him you're not home."

Javid shook his head, the last remnants of sleep fleeing. He slipped to the window and glanced through the crack in the shutters. A man in a red tunic with a roaring griffin on the breast had his fist raised to pound on the door again. He caught Javid's eye and made an impatient gesture.

"It's okay, ma. Just a royal messenger. I know him. Go back to sleep."

She shot her son a skeptical look, but retreated up the stairs.

Javid threw open the door.

"You're summoned to the Rock," the messenger said. He had greying hair and a bluff, world-weary face.

"Has something happened?"

The man shrugged. "The King of Kings commands you to attend him without delay. It is not for us to ask why."

Javid dashed upstairs and changed into a high-collared blue coat and loose trousers. He grabbed the small box of emergency spell dust he kept hidden beneath his dirty laundry. When he came out, the messenger was waiting at the garden gate with his horse. Javid awkwardly clambered up—he'd ridden only a handful of times—and they galloped for the palace.

The streets were still quiet, a few early risers staring in curiosity as they raced past. They reached the Rock of Ariamazes in short order and the messenger handed him off to the chamberlain, who said little beyond a formally polite greeting. Javid assumed Shahak had emerged from his rooms in dire need of fresh supplies. Asabana's stores were running low, which meant he'd want Javid to make another run soon—to Pompeii.

Holy Father save me, but I won't go back to the Kiln, he thought as the chamberlain led him to the Inner Court. *Not with Vatras in there*. He imagined filling the sack with bone-dust and turning to see one standing behind him. Javid couldn't suppress a shudder and the chamberlain gave him a strange look.

As soon as Katsu's ship is ready, we'll make a run for it, even if I have to shove my ma into a sack with the chickens.

They reached the King's chambers. The pair of royal guards stepped aside, stone-faced and inscrutable, and threw open the double doors.

Shahak sprawled in his ornately carved chair, eyes hooded. To his left stood Izad Asabana. Javid was glad to make the prostration because it gave him time to think. He snuck a quick glance at his employer. Asabana looked perfectly at ease. Perhaps they had already resolved things.

"You may rise," the King said. "Allow me to offer my congratulations on your sister's wedding. Golpari, is it?"

Javid masked his surprise. "Yes, Your Majesty, thank you."

So the King knew all about him. Of course he did.

"I was just telling Lord Asabana how pleased I am with you. My father used to say loyal servants were as rare and precious as jewels."

Was that a jab at Asabana? The King hadn't looked at him, but there seemed to be a drop of venom in his tone.

"I am overcome with delight, Your Majesty." Javid bowed his head.

"These are troubled times," Shahak went on. "The Pythia of Delphi has marched into the Umbra to prosecute some grievance against the Danai. Trade has halted to both the south and north. My tax collectors say the royal treasury is suffering as a result." His gaze turned to Asabana. "It is imperative that we reclaim the drylands west of the river. It would be the greatest capital project Samarqand has seen since the Rock." The vein at his temple throbbed. "I can accomplish this, but I will need a great deal of spell dust. Far more than the dribs and drabs you dole out."

For the first time, Javid heard open anger in his voice. Asabana looked untroubled.

"Thank the Holy Father we have a strong leader," he said cheerfully. "Your father was a great man, but I think the son will overshadow him."

"Do you?" Shahak asked, his voice deceptively mild.

Javid knew the tone. It often preceded swift, brutal retribution. His gut tightened a notch.

"Indeed." Asabana waved an arm expansively. "There is nothing we cannot accomplish. I will provide all the dust you need."

"You fail to understand. I intend to exercise my royal prerogative to procure the dust myself from now on. There can be no delays." He stared coldly at Asabana. "Where is the source?"

Asabana didn't hesitate, Javid had to give him that.

"Of course, you have every right, Majesty. You are the King of Kings." The old smuggler leaned forward, lowering his voice to a conspiratorial murmur. "There is a secret cave in the Kiln with magic crystals. It is guarded by a ferocious beast, but my alchemists know how to put the creature to sleep. It is terribly dangerous, Your Highness. Savage teeth and claws. I can lead you there if you wish, but perhaps it might be simpler to maintain our current arrangement."

Shahak studied him for a long moment, dark eyes glittering.

"A secret cave."

"Yes, Your Highness. It lies deep in the Kiln."

Brittle silence descended. A flash of uncertainty crossed Asabana's face. Shahak snuffled, raising a mottled scrap of red silk to his nose. When he lowered it, his mouth had curved into a tight, crooked smile, like a fishhook.

"Before my father found you, you were a crow, were you not? One of those soot-stained unfortunates who pick through the slag heaps?"

"I rose from humble beginnings," Asabana replied, a bit stiffly.

"Crow is an apt name. You squawk and squawk."

"Your Majesty—"

Shahak's smile faded. "I think you've mistaken me for a stupid child," he said quietly.

Asabana fell to his knees. He realized his mistake and thought he could still worm his way out of it. Javid almost pitied him.

"A jest, Your Highness," Asabana babbled. "It was in poor taste. A thousand apologies! Please, allow me to make amends. My servant Javid will escort you personally—"

"*Nungarra usemi salamu essuru.*"

Which, roughly translated, meant *pompous fool turned into a black bird.*

Asabana's eyes bulged as ebony feathers sprouted from his neck. Fingers curled into claws, sending a shower of rings to the floor. They bounced and rolled in all directions. Embroidered robes fell away as his body shrank and his nose sharpened to a hook. Black wings fluttered. Asabana emitted a harsh, surprised *caw*. Shahak laughed and clapped his hands.

"My pet crow," he said. "Oh, fetch him back, Javid, do not let him get away!"

And so Javid had the lamentable task of catching his former employer and clutching him to his coat while the King bade the guards to fetch a cage. Asabana tried to peck his wrist, but Javid had experience wrangling chickens and held him firmly, wings pinioned to his sides. He could feel the bird's heart thrumming in its breast.

When Asabana was safely ensconced in his new home, hanging from a hook near the door, Shahak turned to Javid.

"Let us speak frankly now. What is the source of the dust?"

"It's the bones of dead daēvas," Javid blurted, the words tumbling out in a rush. "There's a place called Pompeii. A half-built city. It was the capital of the Vatras. It lies on the other side of the Gale. The Vatras were burned in a great fire, but their bodies were preserved." He swallowed. "The ash is spell dust."

Javid wasn't sure what reaction he expected, but the King merely frowned.

"Dead daēvas, you say?"

"Yes, Your Highness." He collapsed in a full prostration, nose pressed deep into the carpet. "I am a pitiful worm unworthy of life, but I throw myself on your mercy, Majesty. Do what you will with me, I only beg that you spare my family. They had nothing to do with any of it. Oh, Holy Father—"

"Enough. I am not some heartless monster. I imagine Asabana coerced you."

Javid didn't dare reply, or even look up, though he felt a spark of hope. He heard the lacquered box open and a short, sharp inhalation. It was only then he realized Shahak had not used a pinch of spell dust to transform Asabana. Apparently, he hadn't needed to. The words alone sufficed.

"Yes," he said thoughtfully. "It makes perfect sense. I have long been fascinated with the fire daēvas. Felt a certain...kinship." He chuckled, then sneezed violently. From the corner of his eye, Javid saw crimson droplets spray across the carpet. Where the blood touched the weave, the fibers *twitched*, rearranging themselves from roses to lilies. The King didn't appear to notice.

"I forgive you this time, Javid. Asabana is to blame. He was a vile, greedy man. But do not lie to me again."

"I swear it, Majesty," Javid lied, kissing the hem of his robes.

"You will collect the spell dust directly for me now."

"Of course, Your Highness."

"Can it be accomplished alone?"

Javid shook his head. "Crossing the Gale is tricky, Your Majesty. I require the assistance of Lord Asabana's alchemists."

Shahak regarded the crow hunched on its perch, eyes bright with malice.

"Go then. Inform them that they belong to the King now. All of Asabana's lands, titles and material property are forfeit to the crown. I will send soldiers to collect the wind ships and other necessary equipment." He drew a deep, satisfied breath. "I look forward to speaking with other accomplished adepts. I hope they are not fools like their old master."

Javid thought of Leila. "They are not fools, Majesty."

"Good." Shahak flicked a finger in dismissal. He'd gone pale and looked on the verge of a coughing fit.

Javid made the prostration and left the palace with a blend of relief and terror. He knew he was next. It was only a matter of time. Perhaps he would end up as a yappy dog, earning pats on the head when he was good and kicks to the ribs when he displeased. Or a nightingale, so he might spend the rest of his days singing for Shahak from a gilded cage. Or a beetle, to be crushed beneath the King's silk slipper. Truly, the possibilities were endless!

He thought of Izad Asabana, once the most powerful noble in the entire Persian court, now hunched in a cage pecking at birdseed, and felt the last of his illusions pop like a soap bubble. All of Javid's life, he'd wanted desperately to be rich. It seemed the answer to every problem. An impenetrable shield against the world.

But in the end, Asabana's gold had not saved him.

When Javid emerged into the sunshine, he brusquely ordered the chamberlain to fetch him a horse. Then he rode for Asabana's estate as fast as he could.

MARZBAN KHORRAM-DIN LAY IN A DARKENED ROOM, BLANKETS pulled up to his white beard. His skin looked thin as old parchment. Javid paused in the doorway. He hadn't even realized the alchemist was ill, but he'd barely seen him in weeks. Leila always said he was busy in their workroom. Now Javid wondered if she'd been covering something more serious.

"I'm sorry," he said softly. "May I come in?"

Leila sat at her father's bedside. She beckoned Javid forward.

"How long has he been like this?" he whispered.

"I'm not dead yet," the alchemist croaked, his eyes flying open. "I can hear you."

Javid muttered hasty apologies.

"A touch of consumption," Leila said. "I will nurse him back to health." She patted her father's hand. "He's stronger than he looks."

Marzban Khorram-Din grumbled something under his breath.

"I can't stay long," Javid said, glancing at the door. "The King's men are on the way."

He quickly related what happened to Asabana. Leila shook her head.

"A reasonably clever six-year-old wouldn't have fallen for that," she said.

"I know." Javid paused. "I had no choice. I told Shahak everything. It didn't put him off. The opposite—he said he felt a kinship with the Vatras." He glanced at Marzban Khorram-Din, who had closed his eyes again. "I'm leaving. This very night, if possible. What will you do?"

"Serve the King," Leila said without hesitation. "Don't take this the wrong way, but there are plenty of other pilots with your skill."

Javid frowned. "But—"

"Shahak will tolerate the loss of you as long as he gets his dust. But if we're all gone, he will hunt us to the ends of the earth."

Javid looked at Leila. Besides Katsu, she was his only true friend. "Then I will stay too. I cannot ask you—"

"You aren't asking." She sighed. "I would stay regardless. My father is too ill to flee. And I can manage King Shahak."

"That's exactly what Asabana said."

"Asabana got greedy. I'll manage Shahak because I have no intention of lying to him." A flicker of amusement crossed her face. "You probably think me mad, but I've been curious to meet him. We are both seekers of knowledge. I cannot approve of what he does, but it intrigues me." She gave Javid a sharp look. "You'd better go now. Don't tell me where. But give my regards to your Stygian."

Javid nodded and embraced her. She smelled of myrrh and rosemary and other more bitter things. Marzban Khorram-Din merely watched him with slitted eyes, enigmatic to the last.

"Thank you, Leila," he said, voice choked with emotion.

She smiled. "Go be happy. We'll see each other again someday."

Javid ran down the manor steps and called for Asabana's groom. The boy helped Javid clamber onto his horse. Javid kicked his heels into the animal's sides and galloped back to Samarqand.

"I'm looking for the Stygian," he breathlessly informed the

innkeeper of the Four Dervishes, who had just pulled a tray of fragrant loaves from the oven.

The man wiped his hands on a dishrag. "He's not here."

"Do you know where he went?"

The innkeeper shrugged. "He comes and goes. I'm not his mother."

So Javid set out for the Abicari. He hurried into the hangar and felt weak with relief. Katsu stood there with Savah, admiring the new ship. It was one of the finest vessels of its class Javid had ever seen. Clean, elegant lines and a jaunty prow that would make her swift as a falcon.

"I've decided on a name," Katsu said, as Javid approached. "The *Shenfeng*. It means *Divine Wind*. She will be the first Tjanjinese wind ship." He grinned. "I was thinking, it's possible we might be able to fly alongside a Marakai ship. We could tie down to the deck in a storm. If I could transport the *Shenfeng* to Tjanjin and present her to the emperor, he might grant me trade concessions. Perhaps even a piece of land on the twilight side of the island."

Javid's smile felt three sizes too tight. "That's a brilliant idea. May I speak with you for a moment?"

Savah was paying them no attention, his eagle eye trained on the carpenters who swarmed over the ship putting on the finishing touches. Javid took Katsu's arm and drew him out of earshot.

"The King turned Asabana into a crow," he said without preamble. "He knows everything. If we're going to leave, we need to do it today."

Katsu's brows creased in alarm. "Thank Babana he spared you."

"Yeah, well, I got lucky. He likes me. Problem is, I'm not even sure he's human anymore." Javid looked the ship over, bouncing on his toes. The rigging was in place and she looked ready to fly. "Where's the air sack?"

"They're supposed to finish it today."

"Good." He looked into Katsu's grey eyes. "Are you sure you want to go through with this? The King will send men here looking for me. It won't take long to learn I helped you commission a wind ship. You could lose everything. You could end up back in the dungeons—"

Katsu seized his coat and gently pulled him closer. They stood in the shadow of another wind ship scheduled for repairs, a large cargo vessel. Just beyond the stern, Javid could hear Savah cursing at the carpenters over some tiny detail.

"I don't care," Katsu said.

"You don't?" he asked stupidly.

Katsu leaned forward. "No. I want to kiss you." A rough whisper in his ear. "Can I?"

Javid nodded, not trusting himself to speak. He felt Katsu's warm breath on his lips and laid a hand on his shoulder, which felt pleasantly firm. He'd kissed a girl once when he was sixteen, but this was even better. The Stygian's tongue tasted of dates; he always kept a few in his pocket. Javid curled fingers into Katsu's springy hair. His heart pounded wildly in his chest and he could feel Katsu's doing the same. Several intriguing pages from the pillow book flashed through his head. After a long minute, Javid broke away before he lost himself completely. Katsu heaved a sigh, but he was smiling.

"Thank you," he said softly. "I've wanted to do that since the Polemarch's dungeons."

Javid knew he was grinning like a fool, but he couldn't help himself.

"I'm glad you waited. We both smell better." He straightened his coat. "Get the *Shenfeng* ready to sail. I'll be back within the hour."

Katsu reached for his hand, their fingertips brushing.

"I'll come with you."

"No, we need supplies. Forget Susa. It's too close. We'll fly into the Umbra, hide there for a while. Savah can send some boys to the market to buy food. Just tell him you got a hot lead on a commission."

Katsu nodded and squeezed his hand. "Hurry back."

~

JAVID TIED UP HIS HORSE IN THE SAME PLACE THE ROYAL messenger had done hours earlier. The chickens weren't in the yard. He ran inside.

"Ma?" he called. "Da?"

The house was quiet with no signs of violence. He checked each room, praying his gut feeling was wrong. They could be visiting with Golpari. It was customary to see the bride settled into her new home. Yet Javid noticed that Bibi's favorite doll was missing, along with his mother's prized hairbrush and the little wooden horse on wheels Mahmonir was always dragging around the house. Shaken, he went outside and found a gang of dirty kids petting his horse.

"Arash, have you seen Bibi?" he asked the oldest.

"Oh yeah, a fancy carriage came," Arash replied. "Everyone got in."

"How long ago?"

The boy shrugged. "Dunno. A while."

Javid cursed himself. He should have come home first.

"Was there any sign on the carriage?"

The children looked at each other.

"I saw it too," a smaller boy chimed in. "It had a griffin painted on the door."

The sign of the king.

Javid nodded calmly, though he was screaming curses inside. He tossed the boys a coin. Then he rode back to the Rock. The chamberlain who took his horse was not one he knew well so Javid kept his mouth shut as he was escorted through the corridors to the audience chamber. He waited there in a state of nervous anxiety until King Shahak finally called for him.

He made the prostration with a dry mouth and racing pulse.

"You look unwell," Shahak said.

"I am fine, Your Highness, please don't concern yourself."

"Did you tell Asabana's alchemists to come to me?"

"I did, Your Highness. Leila Khorram-Din is looking forward to meeting you. Her father is ill, but I'm sure he will attend you as soon as he is able."

"Very good." Shahak studied him. "I hope I didn't frighten you. But I realized after we spoke that if you are to be my personal wind pilot, it would be shameful for you to live in poverty outside the palace." His hands twisted the scrap of stained silk. "I know how close you are to your family. I could hardly bring you here and leave them behind."

"Your Highness is too generous," Javid murmured.

"I've placed them in the east wing. They will be my honored guests. I can assign a tutor to the girls." He smiled, though it didn't touch his eyes. "They can learn to read and write, as well as the womanly arts of sewing and music."

Honored guests. Until Javid did something Shahak took offense to—then they'd all join the menagerie. But for now, he would play the game. What choice did he have?

"You are too kind, Highness. Would it be possible to see them?"

"Of course. But return to me afterwards. We must discuss the next trip across the Gale."

He thought of Katsu waiting for him at the Abicari. If he was smart, when he learned what happened, he'd get in his ship, hire a pilot to set a course for Susa, and never look back.

Javid made the prostration and backed out of the room.

"Take me to the east wing," he told the servant who waited outside.

∼

THE ROOMS GIVEN TO HIS FAMILY WERE LARGE AND comfortable—the gilded cage Javid had imagined. It wasn't the Inner Court, but it was deep enough within the Rock that there were no windows to the outside. Tapestries depicted pastoral gardens and thick rugs covered the floor that were probably worth more than his whole house.

His parents sat next to each other on a silk couch. Cups of iced punch sweated on the ivory-inlaid table. They looked unharmed but a bit dazed. The moment Javid stepped through the door, Bibi jumped up. She'd had a chicken in her lap and it squawked indignantly. She ran to him, throwing her arms around his waist.

"I'm to be the king's new pilot," he said cheerfully, tugging her braid. "Isn't that wonderful?"

Everyone knew you had to watch what you said in the Rock. The Hazara-patis had a thousand ears pressed to the walls. Javid glanced pointedly at the door, hoping they'd get the picture.

I'm sorry, he mouthed to his parents.

His mother glared at him. His father gave a weak smile.

"How come you didn't tell us we'd be moving here?" Bibi demanded. "They tried to make us leave the chickens. I said I wouldn't go if we couldn't bring them and the men got mad, but they finally let me." She threw herself into a chair and slouched down, crossing her arms with a mutinous expression. "There's nowhere to play outside. I want to go home."

"They ought to throw you in the dungeons," Farima told Bibi. "You'd fit right in since you never take a bath."

"Farima," his ma said sharply.

"It won't be forever, I promise," Javid said. "But we must do as the King of Kings commands." He bent down to kiss Mahmonir, who sat cross-legged on the carpet, playing with her horse. "He says he will send a tutor for the girls."

"How kind," his ma said in a neutral tone.

"I don't know why everyone's so glum," Farima declared. "I think it's the best thing that's ever happened!"

Bibi cast her a disdainful look, but said nothing. She might be two years younger, but she clearly grasped the situation more clearly than her sister.

"Leila Khorram-Din will be coming to the palace too," he said to her. "I can introduce you. She's an alchemist."

Bibi's frown faded. She looked intrigued.

"Is there anything you need?" he asked his parents.

His ma sniffed. "After Bibi's tantrum over the chickens, I was afraid to waste any more time. The guards who came said we had to hurry. They promised the palace seamstresses would make new clothes for us." She smoothed her apron self-consciously.

"And that the King's magus will have a look at my hands," his da said.

Javid nodded and forced a smile. He held out his hand to Bibi.

"Why don't you give me a tour?" he said.

She jumped up and they walked through a connecting door to a hall with three bedrooms. They were small but well-appointed, with oil lamps casting a warm glow.

"Farima says I have to share with Mahmonir," she muttered. "She's a baby, but I still like her best so I guess I don't mind too much."

Javid knelt down and lowered his voice. "Be careful about what you say. People could be listening."

Bibi nodded solemnly. "What's King Shahak like?"

"He's wise and kind."

She gave him a searching look and didn't seem to like what she found. His sister had always been too clever for her own good.

"I'm scared," she whispered.

Javid's heart cracked a bit.

"Everything will be fine," he lied. "I promise."

22

THE HORN OF HELHEIM

Deep in the belly of Val Moraine, a river of blue ice flowed down the walls of a tiny cell. It faced the winds of the Cold Sea and they assaulted the keep with gale force, a howling symphony its sole occupant found oddly soothing. The wind was the first sound he'd heard as a newborn infant and it had rarely ceased over the nearly two hundred years since he arrived in the world slippery with blood, his mother dying even as she held him in her arms.

Culach sat with his chin on his chest and his blind eyes moving beneath the lids. He was dreaming of the Viper again. But for the first time, the sense of dread, of violence and death and treachery, was absent. He felt safe. Loved.

A smile tickled the corners of his mouth.

HE STANDS NEAR A SMALL HOMESTEAD IN THE DESERT. RED AND yellow flowers riot in pots on the windowsills. His father is turning the winch to haul a bucket of clear, cold water from the well. The day is cloudless, the shadows clear and sharp. His mother is cooking in the kitchen and he hears her humming to herself. He dips a cup into the bucket and drinks from it. His father sweeps him up in a hug and kisses the top of his head.

"I want to go to school with Julia," he says. "When can I, father?"

His father ruffles his hair. "Next year, Farrumohr. You must be five years old."

He pouts, but then Julia skips over and takes his chubby hand.

"Come, I will show you my lessons, if you promise to pay attention and listen."

His face lights up. "Yes, please!"

She smiles at his enthusiasm. They go to the shade tree and she starts to tell him about talismans, and he has so many questions, but Julia is patient with him. That evening, when the cool breezes come, they sit outside together and watch the moons rise and he thinks he must be the luckiest boy in the whole world.

In the cold cell, Culach shifted restlessly against the ice. Some half-buried part of him knew there would be no more dreams, that he had finally reached both the beginning and the end.

The rest of Farrumohr's life unfurled in the blink of an eye, but this time it didn't stop at the suffocating sands. Culach saw him pass through a gate into the Dominion. He felt the grinding weight of centuries and saw Farrumohr change, ever so slowly, into something else, like metal refined down to its purest essence. A creature of shadow and flame, of hate and fear.

Culach saw himself the day at the lake and the great blow Nazafareen struck the Viper, or what remained of him. He watched Farrumohr slink off to lick his wounds, down and down into velvety darkness. Culach watched him dream, a ghostly crown of gold flickering above his head.

THE CLANG OF METAL DRAGGED HIM FROM SLUMBER. CULACH

tried to hold onto it, his chest tight with inexplicable loss, but it quickly faded as he remembered where he was. The cold cells.

Valkirins—three, four?—hauled him out, stumbling and shivering.

"Where are we going?" he demanded. "Did you find Victor?"

The only reply was a cuff to the head that left him seeing star-bursts in the blackness.

But he knew the keep well enough to figure it out for himself after a few minutes. The Great Hall.

The doors must have been open because he heard it from a distance. The raucous buzz of a large gathering. The Valkirins fell silent as he entered, though he could hear a few whispered taunts. *Traitor. Coward.*

His captors led him to the center of the Hall. Five hundred pairs of hostile eyes bored into him.

"Culach Kafsnjór."

He turned toward Runar's voice.

"Where's Mina?"

"The punishment for treason is death, as you well know," Runar continued in a maddeningly calm tone. "By law and custom, you'd be thrown over the edge of the battlements. But that death is too honorable for you."

"*Where is she?*"

"The cells." A woman's voice. Frida of Val Tourmaline. "We asked her if she wanted to witness your execution and she grew... difficult. So you will face your sentence alone."

Real fear gripped him then. Mina in the cold cells? She'd never survive, not for more than a few days.

"You bastards! You swore to let her go."

"Only if we found Victor," Runar said smugly. "He must have crawled into a hole and died somewhere. I suppose we'll find him by the smell eventually."

Laughter rolled though the hall. Culach kept his face blank.

"Go ahead, then. Murder a blind man."

A drier voice came now. Stefán of Val Altair. "Yes, the Dessarians had a soft spot for you, didn't they? I'm afraid you won't find the same pity from the holdfasts."

Culach was dragged forward. Mailed hands drove him to his knees.

"Nothing fancy," Runar said in a bored tone. "Just chop his head off."

Culach drew a shallow breath. He had no witty last words. Not even a good curse. All he could think of was the Viper and the random, pointless nature of evil.

VICTOR CREPT THROUGH THE CATACOMBS, HIS HAIR MATTED with cobwebs, a scraggly beard climbing like ivy down his chin. They'd come looking for him, but they didn't know about the secret chamber. He'd used earth power to rebuild the wall and hidden there as they searched the catacombs. It wasn't a perfect job, he could see fine cracks where he'd torn it down when he first discovered it, but the Valkirins didn't look too closely.

He'd wandered through the tunnels after that, moving by touch through the darkness. The cold flesh of the dead no longer troubled him. It was the living he feared.

When Nazafareen took the diamond away, Victor had been so sick with longing it was like a fever, wracking his bones and soaking him in waves of cold sweat. His stomach emptied itself again and again until he felt hollow as a rotten log. Afterwards he had slept, the first time in days, weeks perhaps. When he awoke, his head was clearer.

The talisman was deadly, he could see that now. He was glad to be rid of it and eager to rejoin his wife, Delilah. Yet if he tried to leave Val Moraine, Runar and Stefán would surely kill him. And they had Mithre. He'd heard the Valkirins talking. So now he stumbled along, a faint light guiding him forward. It came from the hidden chamber.

The wall lay in ruins again. And there was the old Valkirin, with the black horn in his hands.

Victor had come to look at it several times, but always his nerve gave out at the last moment. Now, starving and weak and out of options, he reached out and prised the horn from the Valkirin's frozen fingers. Runes circled the mouth of it, jagged and dire-looking.

Victor couldn't stifle a giggle.

Good thoughts, good words, good deeds.

No. Not that. They said something else, he felt sure. Something not as congenial.

He giggled again and it sounded too loud in the crypt. He stroked the curling horn with a frown. *You're not mad. Not yet.*

But what's a man to do when they've taken everything from him?

What's a man to do?

The metal felt like oiled silk beneath his fingers. It gave off the faint glow he'd seen from the corridor, just enough to make out the old Valkirin's features. He fancied the fellow's thin, bloodless lips curved in an encouraging smile.

Moving as if in a dream, Victor placed the horn to his mouth and blew.

No sound came from the fluted bell, but a wind rushed though the catacombs, dragging chill fingers through his hair. He heard something like a sigh on the very edge of hearing. Suddenly afraid, Victor retreated into the tunnels. He ran blindly through the oldest part of the catacombs.

Behind him, shadows began to rise.

Footsteps.

They grew closer, stopping a pace away. The echoes fled to the far corners of the Great Hall and died, leaving perfect silence. Culach didn't know which one of them was his executioner and found he didn't care, as long as they had a strong arm. In his mind's eye, he saw the broadsword as it lifted for a two-handed stroke. He tipped his head forward, exposing the back of his neck.

"Make it clean," he muttered.

Culach tensed for the final blow. And then a wavering scream broke the silence. It was high and raw and full of wild terror. He heard a *crunch* from the far side of the chamber—very much like a sword slicing through muscle and bone. This was followed by the rasp of iron on stone—very much like a blade scraping the ground on the followthrough.

Culach jerked his head up. Had Nazafareen returned? It seemed unlikely, but he couldn't think of a single other person who cared about his fate besides Mina, and she was in the cold cells.

Or could it be Victor? Had he gone so mad he'd try to take on five hundred Valkirins at once?

More screams and shouts erupted from every side. And then he heard something that made his blood turn to icewater in his veins.

A cackling laugh that sounded like his great-great-grand-mother Gerda.

A heavy weight crashed into him and Culach rolled to the side, slamming a shoulder into the stone floor. Manacles bound his hands but they'd unchained his legs to walk to the Great Hall. He started crawling away, swords ringing around him, chairs scraping against the floor. Bodies stumbled into his path, boots stomped down on his fingers, and still he kept crawling until he found shelter beneath one of the long stone tables.

Chaos reigned. He heard Runar bellowing, trying to regroup, an edge of fear in his voice that Culach never thought to hear from the master of Val Petros. Something slammed down on the table above his head. He heard a wet squelch and horrid gurgle.

I don't want to go out there again, he thought. *Bloody hell, I don't.*

But if he stayed much longer, they would find him—whoever *they* were.

He cursed his own blindness and crept out from under the table toward what he hoped was one of the exits. The smell of blood filled his nose. It slicked the floor beneath his palms, warm and sticky.

No one tried to stop him. They were too busy getting killed.

Culach fully expected to join their ranks. To feel the bite of iron as an invisible foe finished what his executioner failed to accomplish. He remembered striding across the Great Hall a thousand times. It took perhaps a minute to get from one side to the other. Yet the journey on hands and knees, amid the moans of the fallen and other sounds he didn't wish to examine too closely, seemed to take years.

And then his fingertips brushed the far wall. Culach followed it until he reached an opening to the corridor beyond. Bodies clogged the doorway where they'd been trapped trying to escape. He clambered over them, gaining his feet and running for the staircase that led down to the cold cells. Whatever had come to Val Moraine, he had to find Mina.

The sounds of battle faded as he descended, keeping a map of the keep fixed in his mind. The staircase wound around on itself in a tight spiral, the steps worn smooth from centuries of use. His thundering heartbeat began to slow. Not far now.

Culach thought of that harsh laughter. It couldn't have been Gerda. He'd felt her body stiffening when he laid it in the crypts with Halldóra. Shock, that was all. He'd been seconds from death and his mind had conjured things out of whole cloth. But what, then, *had* come to the Great Hall? What had frightened Runar, who once held the pass to Val Petros alone for three days with a gut wound you could fit a fist into?

Mina. Just find Mina.

Culach wasn't sure how he'd get them both out of the keep, but he'd find a way. He descended six more turnings until he was nearly at the level of the cold cells. He paused to listen.

And heard a soft rustle from the stairway above, just beyond the next curve.

He licked dry lips, straining in the darkness.

Long seconds ticked by. It came again, closer now. A sibilant whisper, like the scales of a snake. Or leather skirts dragging on the floor.

He smelled a trace of sour wine. The hair on his arms tingled.

"Culach No-Name."

The voice was familiar, yet not. It sounded like it came from the depths of a pit.

"Your father wants to see you, boy. He says you've been naughty again."

The breath froze in his lungs. "Grandmother?" he croaked.

A sucking sound. It took little imagination to picture a black tongue running over teeth.

"You stole Ygraine's sword. Gave it to a mortal, wicked boy."

Feet shuffled forward. Culach edged down the stairs, his manacled hands trailing the wall.

"But you're dead," he objected, part of him wondering if his mind hadn't finally snapped.

Gerda laughed, gristle falling into a meat grinder. He heard sudden movement, a rush of air against his skin, and feinted to the side, slamming into the wall.

"I was called back." The voice took on a wheedling tone. "I'm cold, boy. Come warm these old bones."

Culach shrank away. A foot kicked out and knocked him off-balance. He tumbled down the steps, landing hard on his back. The dragging sounds came closer. He smelled Gerda standing over him. Dried blood and a whiff of decay.

"I laid you to rest in the crypts—"

Bony hands closed around his throat, squeezing with inhuman strength. He remembered carrying her down to the catacombs. She'd been frail and light as a child. He was easily three times her size. Yet when Culach tried to break her grip, he found he couldn't. Her fingers were like iron bands. He bucked in desperation and she squeezed harder, dragging him toward a well of blackness.

"There's a place waiting for you, boy," Gerda whispered.

He fought for breath.

"In the deep and the dark...."

Culach heard a thump and Gerda collapsed across his chest. He shoved her away, choking in revulsion as his fingers brushed frozen flesh and the stump of a neck.

"*Revenants*. They won't admit they're dead until you cut their heads off."

Culach scrabbled backwards. He could still feel those claws around his throat.

"What the bloody hell is going on, Dessarian?" he growled.

"There was a horn. A talisman. I found it down in the crypts." Victor paused. "I didn't know what it did, I swear. I just wanted to get out of here."

A strong hand gripped Culach's arm, pulling him to his feet. The manacles around his wrists tumbled open and clattered to the floor. *Earth power*. Culach had always disdained it, but now he felt a new appreciation.

"I blew it. And the dead answered." Victor's voice sounded distant, a mystic pondering some existential riddle. "I always wondered where they came from. The revenants. Neblis learned how to call them too, but she used necromancer chains." He sighed. "I saw empty shelves in the crypts. Now I understand why."

"Revenants," Culach said flatly. "My dead kin, you mean." He steadied himself against the wall. "I can't believe it really exists.

And that it fell into *your* grubby hands." He laughed mirthlessly. "Of all people."

"You know of this talisman?"

"It was just another crazy legend. One of my distant ancestors, Magnus the Merciless, supposedly had a number of dangerous talismans. He hid them in various parts of the keep."

Like countless other Valkirin children, Culach had spent many idle afternoons with his friend Petur hunting for Magnus's treasure trove. They never found anything but dust and spiderwebs.

"It's called the Horn of Helheim," he said. "You found it in the crypts?"

"A secret chamber. It was in the hands of a frozen corpse. One brown eye, one blue eye."

"That's Magnus. My father stumbled over some of the talismans, including that diamond you were so fond of, but he never did find the body—"

A distant sound jerked Culach's head toward the stairs spiraling down. Victor had saved his life, had killed Gerda *twice*, yet he couldn't quite thank him for it. "How many revenants are out there?"

"I don't know. A lot."

Culach swore softly. "We have to get to the cells."

Victor didn't reply. Culach groped around until he found the man's coat and gave him a shake.

"Are you listening? I need your help!"

"What? Yes. The cells. I was on my way there when I found you."

They hurried down the stairs until they reached the level just above the catacombs, where the dungeons began. Culach smelled the revenant before it lurched around the corner. He called out a warning and Victor dispatched it. Culach imagined Mina trapped in her cell, those *things* getting in.

"Hurry," he snapped.

The temperature dropped as they reached the first row of iron doors. Victor's footsteps slowed. Culach imagined him peering through each of the small grills set at eye level.

"Do you see her?"

"Not yet. I have to find Mithre too, if he's down here."

They moved on, turning a corner. Despite the aching cold, sweat trickled down Culach's spine. He smelled nothing but stone. Heard only the wind. Then Victor stopped. When he spoke, his voice was a groan.

"The cell door's been torn from its hinges."

Culach couldn't breathe.

"What do you see?"

"No blood. No bodies." Victor's voice moved inside the cell. "I think it was blown *outward*."

A muffled cry came from somewhere up ahead. Culach ran toward it and smelled her familiar scent, wool and a flowery soap.

"Mina!"

Victor's broad-shouldered bulk pushed past and air sang against the edge of a blade, followed by the now familiar thump of a head tumbling across the ground. Fingers twined with Culach's. He pulled Mina to his chest, burying his face in her hair. She was shivering through a fur-lined coat.

"What *is* that?" she demanded. "It looks like...." Mina swallowed hard. "It looks *dead*."

"That's because it is dead," Culach replied.

"What dark magic did this?"

He gave her a grim smile. "Ask Victor."

"Gods, never mind. I don't want to know. Is the keep overrun?"

"Pretty much." Culach winced. "I ran into Gerda. Death did not improve her temperament."

"Oh no." Mina's thumb stroked the stubble on his jaw. "Runar said they were going to kill you. I managed to break the door down just before that thing came around the corner."

"We're getting out of here," Culach said. "I have to find Nazafareen. There's something she needs to know—"

Metal groaned as a cell door scraped open.

"Victor," Mithre rasped from inside. "Kind of you to show up."

"Forgive me, old friend. You were right. About everything."

Mithre grunted. "Where the hell did the revenants come from?" A pause. "You didn't." Another, longer pause. "Did you?"

"I'll explain later," Victor snapped, some of his old arrogance returning. "But right now we need to get moving. Revenants are drawn to living flesh. Most will have gone to the upper levels, but there could be a few more stragglers."

Mithre barked a harsh laugh. "I don't believe this. The hero who defeated Neblis's undead armies actually summoned—"

"We'll make for the stables," Victor interrupted. "Fight our way out. You can take that revenant's blade."

Mithre snorted. "My arm's broken. The Valkirins weren't gentle when they threw me down here."

"I've got it." Mina dropped Culach's hand. He heard her grunt as she hefted the broadsword.

"Have you ever fought with one of those?" Mithre asked.

Mina sniffed. "How hard can it be?"

"Cut their heads off," Victor advised. "Otherwise they'll just keep coming."

"Understood. Stand behind me, Culach."

He swallowed his pride and did as ordered. They crept from floor to floor, Victor and Mina in the lead, carving a path through knots of revenants on the stairs. Culach's acute sense of smell alerted them to the dead before they drew close. He was almost glad he couldn't see their faces. No doubt he'd recognize many of them.

"Where will you go from here?" he asked Victor as they strode down one of the keep's endless corridors, circling the sounds of skirmishes with the undead.

"To Delilah." Victor's voice was taut with regret. "I should have done it a long time ago."

That was Victor's wife, Culach remembered. The one who'd been there when he stormed Val Moraine.

"Nazafareen went after her," he said. "The Oracle of Delphi is a Vatra. The Danai meant to free the daēvas she captured, but they didn't know what they were facing."

Victor grabbed him. "And Delilah was with them?"

"She was leading the force with Tethys. We were supposed to leave with Nazafareen," Mithre said in acid tones. "But *you* disappeared."

"When was this?"

"Couple of days ago."

"I'll find her," Victor said stubbornly. "It's not too late."

"Let's pray you're right," Mithre muttered.

"I would go with them," Culach said quietly to Mina. "I had a dream about the Viper just before the Valkirins came for me, but this one was different. I fear Nazafareen is right. He does live on somehow. And there's a connection to Gaius. She needs to know about it." He hesitated. "Will you come too?"

"I'm not abandoning you now, foolish man. Of course I will. And you say the Pythia is one of these Vatras. I'm not sure how to fight her, but I won't let her have my son."

"Then we'll head into the Umbra," Mithre said. "With any luck, Nazafareen and Darius will be with Delilah and the others." His voice softened. "They may have already rescued Galen. If not, we'll find a way."

Icy wind struck Culach's face. It carried the pungent smell of dung. They'd made it to the stables. He heard movement ahead, and the rasp of a sword being drawn.

"Get out of the way," Victor growled.

"*You did this.*" Rage choked Stefán's normally smooth voice. "I don't know how, but you'll pay, Dessarian."

Iron blades rang together like the tolling of a great bell.

"Go," Victor grated. "I'll hold them here."

Mithre spoke at Culach's shoulder. "But—"

"Just go! I'll follow."

Mina sighed heavily. She pressed the cold hilt of the broadsword into Culach's palm. He felt her tense, then give a soft moan as her bones flexed to the edge of breaking. She was using earth power, the heaviest and most painful element to work.

An instant later, Valkirin voices cried out in alarm. The ice shelf supporting the stables shifted and cracked. Culach heard running feet and the scream of an abbadax.

"Ragnhildur!"

He stepped forward and met empty air. Culach flailed, overbalanced by the heavy broadsword. He dropped it into the chasm below, teetering on the edge, when a hand jerked him backwards.

"Idiot," Mina muttered. "Oh gods, here it comes."

Hot breath blasted his face. Culach reached out, his finger brushing a hooked beak. It nuzzled his hand.

"I assume you know this beast," Mina said warily.

"She's mine." Tears froze to his lashes. "Does she have a saddle?"

"No."

"Do you see any spares?"

Mina hesitated. "Hanging against the wall. But the revenants are at the door. Stefán and a few others are trying to hold them, but there's too many. They'll break through any moment."

He could hear the harsh shouts from Stefán's men, the crunch of bone and crash of metal. Culach climbed onto Ragnhildur's back, hauling Mina up behind him. He slipped his fingers into the barbs of her neck feathers, gripping them tight. He'd only ridden once without a saddle and harness, on a dare from Petur. It was dangerous and stupid but it could be done.

"Dessarian!" he bellowed.

"Over here," Victor answered from somewhere off to the left. "I found Njala."

Mina's arms clamped around Culach's waist. She uttered a string of curses. Now that Ragnhildur had her beloved master on her back, there was no stopping her. She lumbered for the edge of the stables and dove into the abyss. The shouts at the door turned to screams and Culach pitied his clansmen, even if they *had* tried to murder him. But there was nothing he could do to help them now.

He leaned forward, whispering a brief command into Ragnhildur's ear. *Vestr. Mot Sol.*

Fly west. Toward the sun.

The sounds of fighting faded, replaced by the low shriek of the wind. If other abbadax had escaped with riders, Culach heard no sign of them. He wondered what the revenants would do when they'd slaughtered the last of the living. Would they return to their crypts, or would they seek out fresh prey?

Either way, Val Moraine belonged to the dead and Culach knew he would never return there.

The hours passed and the air grew warmer, carrying briny hints of the sea. Then Victor called out to them that he saw something ahead.

"*Elda*," Culach murmured, asking Ragnhildur to land. She gave a breathy snort that sounded grateful. He knew she must be exhausted from the long flight.

"What's down there?" he asked Mina.

"Looks like bodies," she said tightly. "Hundreds of them."

Culach fell silent. He could smell it now, a smoky, charnel house stench, but not fresh. No, he guessed this battle had happened a day or two before.

Mina leaned against his chest. "Oh gods," she whispered. "I see part of a green cloak."

She said nothing more until Ragnhildur alit on the plain and Culach helped her dismount, then slid down himself, his fingers stiff from holding on for so many hours.

"Any survivors?" he asked.

"They're all gone," Mina said in a shocked voice. "The Matrium...."

"What about Nazafareen? Darius? They were going after the Danai."

"I don't know. It's impossible to tell, the bodies are too charred." Mina's voice rose, cracked and harsh. "What if Galen's here? I've got to find him!"

Culach despised his own helplessness. He should be sparing her the task of searching through the bodies for her only son.

"I'm so sorry," he said softly.

He heard her sniffle and wipe her face. When she spoke again, there was steel in her voice.

"I'll see if any of them wear a collar," she said. "It would have survived the fire." She touched his cheek and moved away, skirts swishing.

That was the Mina who had survived years of captivity among her enemies, who had shamed him into getting out of bed when he wanted only to die.

He waited as she walked among the bodies. Victor ranted in the distance, something about a small silver ring his wife used to wear. Someone retched, Culach wasn't certain who. Then a terrible scream pierced the air. He could hear Victor sobbing and Mithre trying vainly to calm him down.

"They found Delilah," Mina said in a voice that trembled with rage. "And Victor's mother Tethys. But Galen isn't here. The Pythia must have taken him."

Once, Culach wouldn't have given a damn about the Danai. They'd been a thorn in the holdfasts' side for centuries. But the thought of the slaughter made him sick. The burn scars on his chest tingled as he tried to focus his thoughts, to piece together what had happened here.

"If Nazafareen had caught up with the Danai, she would have stopped it," he said slowly. "So I think she must live too."

"Perhaps." Mina didn't sound convinced. "What do we do now?"

"We go to Delphi," Victor roared. "We hunt the Pythia down and kill her."

"How?" Mina demanded. "She's a fireworker, Victor. A Vatra. There is no defense against her."

Heavy footsteps approached and Culach tensed. Victor no longer smelled like his mad father, but now he had a different stench. The madness of despair.

"Do what you will," he spat. "I'm going to Delphi."

"Then you'll die too," Mithre said wearily. "Culach is right. We must find Nazafareen."

"Get out of my way!"

"Don't be a bloody fool."

They began shouting at each other. It occurred to Culach that whether or not Victor was consciously aware of it, he wished to die. Culach had felt the same when he'd lost his ability to touch the elements. Yet here he stood and it was partly thanks to Victor Dessarian.

I should just let him go and be grateful to be rid of him. He screwed my sister, killed my great-great-grandmother, threw me in the cold cells of my own fucking keep. He's my worst enemy and an arrogant prick to boot.

"Victor?" he called.

"What?"

"Can you come over here for a moment? I have something I meant to give you. It's from your son."

Victor stomped over. "Make it quick," he snarled. "I'm leaving in—"

Culach's fist shot out and clipped Victor on the jaw. He dropped like a stone.

"Find something to tie him onto Njala. He might try to jump when he wakes up."

"Nice shot," Mithre murmured.

Culach smiled. "I might be blind, but I can still hit things if they're close enough and talking."

The three of them hauled Victor over to Njala and wrangled him across her back. A gentle rain pattered down and Culach tipped his face to the sky. How long since he'd tasted rain on his lips? A hundred years?

"I'd follow Nazafareen," he said, "if I had any idea where she went."

"We could return to the forest. Some of the Danai must have stayed behind," Mithre said. "They might have news."

"*You* can," Culach replied. "But I doubt they'll welcome Eirik Kafsnjór's son on their lands."

He thought of his own humiliating weakness—blind and unable to touch the power that was his birthright—and not for the first time wondered what was left.

I am still a Kafsnjór. Still a rock-stubborn bastard who doesn't know when to roll over and die.

He thought of what Nazafareen said to him in the catacombs about a young girl named Meb. He thought she should know about Farrumohr—about all of it.

I'm not completely useless. A sardonic smile twisted his lips. *I have a dead man's memories from a thousand years gone, which doesn't sound like much except that he might not be dead after all—or at least about as dead as Gerda.*

"We need strong allies," Culach said. "Somewhere safe, until Victor comes to his senses. I'm all for revenge, but I'd prefer to live to enjoy it."

"Makes sense," Mithre grumbled.

"So where then?" Mina asked.

Culach's sightless eyes turned east, back toward the darklands.

"To the Isles of the Marakai," he said. "To the Five."

23

A DROP TO DRINK

T he sun floated a few hands above the horizon, trailing long, slender shadows from the six figures who trudged across the sands. They walked southwest in single file. The sky was a cloudless blue. A smudge of low hills rose in the distance, or perhaps it was simply a trick of the heat.

Nazafareen lifted the water skin and shook it over her mouth.

Bone dry.

Her rucksack had started out as a heavy burden, most of the weight consisting of water. She'd done her best to ration, but that was the last of it. Nicodemus said he knew where to find more though it was still a half day's journey.

She wiped a bead of sweat away. *Soon I'll stop sweating altogether and shrivel up like an apple left in the sun*, Nazafareen thought darkly. With each league, the heat grew more blistering. The few scraggly plants that grew at the eastern edge of the Kiln were long gone. Out here, there was nothing but dunes of fine, broiling sand.

Nicodemus said that when the sun reached its zenith over-head, they would be in the lands of the Vatras. When she asked why his people chose to live in the hottest part of the Kiln, he gave her a flat stare.

"We didn't *choose*," he said. "This region is too unstable for digging."

She looked at him blankly and he sighed.

"We live in burrows." He pointed at the sand. "You need hardpan or the walls collapse."

"Like caverns?"

Nicodemus gave her a mirthless smile, made even more ghastly by the spectacular bruises on his face.

"No, like holes in the ground."

"Does Gaius live in a burrow?"

"Yep."

She had a sudden image of a blind creature with sharp teeth digging in the darkness.

"What are the defenses?"

"Pairs of Praetorians guard the entrances."

"Armed with?"

"Spears, mostly. A few tooth knives."

"How many Vatras are there in the whole Kiln?"

He thought for a moment. "About a hundred, give or take."

Nazafareen was surprised. "That's all?"

"Kiln won't support more than that." Another hollow laugh. "It has its own methods of population control."

"What do you mean?"

"The magic binding this place warped the native desert creatures. They evolved—rapidly. Almost without exception, every species became deadly in one way or another. There's not a single snake or reptile or insect that isn't poisonous. Just pray we don't meet some of the bigger ones."

She frowned. "You make it sound like the other clans did that on purpose."

He shook his head and walked a little faster.

"They wouldn't have," she insisted, hurrying to catch up. "They only wanted to wall your people away so you could do no more harm."

Nico rounded on her, his face cold. "How do you know? Were you there? Have you spoken to the ones who sundered the world?"

"Well, no. But—"

"This place." He flung an arm out. "It's not just a prison. It's *hell*. And I find it hard to believe that was done by accident."

Nazafareen fell silent, letting him walk away. Part of her wondered if he was right.

The list of potential dangers in the Kiln was not short. He'd already warned them about rock spiders (small, brown, seemingly harmless) and something called a shadowtongue. Disturbing one was a bad idea, so you had to watch for the spines on its back, which were the only warning as the rest of the lizard was usually submerged in sand. At first, she'd placed each step with care, scanning the ground ahead, but it made her head ache. Now she simply tried to follow in the Vatra's footsteps.

His cloak was made from the skin of shadowtongues. Sometimes he left them to scout ahead and after a few steps, he practically disappeared.

Darius watched her curse softly and give the empty water skin a last futile shake.

"Here," he said, rooting through his pack. "I have one left."

"Sure?" she croaked.

"You look ready to keel over."

She suspected he'd gone without on purpose, knowing she'd drink hers faster. The water was the same temperature as tea, but it was wet. Her terrible thirst receded a little.

"I saved some," she said, handing it back.

"Finish it. I'm fine."

From the cracked state of his lips, this was a blatant lie. But Darius would just dig in if she insisted. Nazafareen glanced longingly at the last of the water, then trudged over to Katrin.

"There's a little left," she said.

Katrin took it without a word, draining it in three gulps. Her fair skin was red and peeling. The Valkirin suffered the most, stumbling along with slumped shoulders and glassy eyes.

"Thank you," she whispered.

"Thank him," Nazafareen replied, looking at Darius.

Katrin caught his eye and gave a brief nod. The fact that he was Victor's son did not endear him to Katrin and she'd largely ignored his presence. But water was a precious commodity.

Galen took up the rear, walking with the hood of his cloak raised against the sunlight. He held himself apart from the others, which was fine with Nazafareen. She was starting to regret letting him come, but it was too late now.

Only Nicodemus seemed unaffected. He constantly scanned their surroundings, quick flicks of his dark blue eyes. There was something of both predator and prey in him, the alert stillness of the hunter and the wariness of the hunted. They were still far from the lands of the Vatras, and Nazafareen wondered uneasily what he watched for.

The low hills turned out not to be hills at all, merely undulations in the desert, like a rumpled blanket. In places, she saw scattered piles of white stones. Closer inspection revealed that they were bones, bleached from the sun, but the shapes looked strange as if they belonged to creatures whose bodies moved in alien ways.

The horizon stretched out before them, flat and blurry. It was hard to believe anything survived out here. The Valkirin range had a stark beauty and Nazafareen supposed the Kiln did too, with its sea of golden sand against an azure sky. But she found it hard to appreciate, plagued by thirst that grew more maddening with each hour.

As she walked, Nazafareen slipped into fantasies of the sweet, chilled concoction distilled from cherries called *vissinada* they sold in the agora at Delphi. Of bathing in the cool ponds of the

Danai forest. Who cared if there were snakes? She'd happily wrestle a python for five minutes of blessed darkness and the taste of fresh water.

"Almost there," Nicodemus called over his shoulder, shaking her out of her reverie.

She squinted ahead, seeing nothing but a jumble of rocks. As they got closer, Nazafareen saw they were too regular in shape to be natural. They'd reached the foundations of a rectangular stone building. Only the bottom half remained and it was filled with sand.

"What was it?" she asked.

Nicodemus shrugged. "No idea. It dates back to before the sundering. The walls and roof were likely made of wood."

He walked through a gap that must have been the doorway and led them to the rear, where a hole yawned, stairs winding down into darkness. Sand covered the steps in drifts, the surface smooth and undisturbed. Still, Nicodemus paused at the entrance, head cocked to one side.

"Domitia and I found this place on our way to the gate," he said finally. "Doesn't look like anyone's been here since."

"What's down there?" Nazafareen asked.

"Water."

She started forward and he held out a hand.

"Wait here. Let me check it out first."

He disappeared down the stairs, his cloak trailing behind him. Katrin sank down and leaned against the foundation wall, dropping her pack with a sigh. Rhea stood beside her, peering into the hole. Nazafareen studied the Maenad's dewy, unblemished skin with irritation.

"You don't burn like the rest of us, do you?"

Rhea smiled. "It's warm for my taste, but Apollo holds no sway over me."

Katrin barked a dry laugh. "That's a nice trick. Perhaps you can move a little to the left. I might just take a nap in your shade."

Rhea did so with a gracious smile, and Nazafareen bit her lip to keep from laughing. If anyone could thaw Katrin Aigirsdottir, she'd put her money on Rhea. The Maenad was striking to look at and nearly of a height with Katrin, but she also had a generous heart that might soften the Valkirin's hard edges.

Nazafareen turned away, leaving them to their banter.

"What do you think this place was?" she asked Darius.

"A house, perhaps. If it's as old as the Vatra says, these lands must have been different then."

Before the sundering, the sun moved across the sky. From what Nazafareen understood, the Kiln had always been desert, but there were also oases here and there. Perhaps this place had been green once.

She felt a twinge of anger. Culach said the clans had coexisted in peace until Gaius and the Viper came along.

"Do you think the three talismans could reverse the sundering?" she wondered aloud.

Darius frowned. "Who knows? Perhaps. Or perhaps in trying to fix it, they might make it worse."

"Of course, I'd have to break Galen's ward. Two of them could never manage it alone."

They glanced at Galen. As usual, he hung back from the others, appearing lost in gloomy thoughts. He'd barely spoken a word since they entered the Kiln and Nazafareen was glad he hadn't tried to seek her forgiveness. Easing his guilt was the last thing she was in the mood for.

Nicodemus returned a few minutes later and beckoned them down the stairs. Sunlight trickled in from above, illuminating a series of stone chambers connected by wide archways. The ceiling seemed too low for living quarters and Nazafareen guessed it had been a root cellar. She imagined twine sacks of onions and garlic hanging from the ceiling, casks of wine stacked neatly in a corner. Perhaps it had been a grand manor with servants in livery and gay parties. She scanned the naked stone, searching for some sign of life, but of the former occupants no trace remained.

She followed Nicodemus to the second chamber, wrinkling her nose. The air was cooler underground, though it had an odd, musty smell. Tiny holes honeycombed the walls as though something had been burrowing there.

"Get out your skins," he said, rooting through his rucksack. "That bucket is rusty but serviceable."

The chamber had a well with a winch and chain. Darius hooked the bucket and dropped it down into darkness, hauling it back up brimming with tepid water. They crowded around, even Galen, dipping their hands in and using cupped palms to drink. Nazafareen splashed some on her face, rinsing off a day's worth of sand and sweat. When it was gone, Darius filled a second bucket. Nicodemus moved with brisk efficiency, filling each skin and stacking them to the side.

"If there's water, why hasn't anyone reclaimed this place?" Darius asked.

Nicodemus slapped at his neck, leaving a smear of red. He held up the offending insect between thumb and forefinger.

"Blood fly. They're a nuisance, but the main thing you need to know is that they only hatch in the dung of wyrms."

Nicodemus flicked it into the shadows. Something pale was wriggling out of one of the holes in the wall. It wasn't large, about the length of his little finger. He strode over and stomped on it.

"Doesn't look like much, does it?" He nudged the remains with his boot. "No teeth. No bones. But they can squeeze through pinprick holes. Once they latch on, they excrete a digestive acid." He pulled up his pant leg and braced his boot against the wall. The calf was puckered with tiny circular scars. He lifted his shirt. More scars pocked his stomach. "I ran into a nest when I was thirteen."

He let his shirt fall. "Wyrms are only dangerous in swarms. The one to fear is the queen. She's big and she can birth a thousand wyrms a week. Queens are blind, but they have vestigial eyes. Maybe they used to be something else, I don't know. It's rare that one will leave its nest. The offspring do the hunting. When they return, bloated from whatever prey they found, the queen devours them. Then she births more."

"Have you ever seen a queen?" Nazafareen asked, horrified.

Nicodemus turned away. "One killed my mother," he said quietly, gathering the full skins of water and handing them out. "That's why we won't be spending the night here. This isn't the nest, but it can't be far off. They'll sense the vibrations in the earth. Trust me, you don't want to be here when hundreds of those things come out of the walls."

Rhea shared a look with Katrin. They were both hard women, but his tale—and the scars—had its intended effect. Everyone hoisted their packs and climbed the stairs. The heat felt worse after the cooler cellar, but Nazafareen had no desire to linger. Once the house was far behind them, Nicodemus called a halt.

"We can rest here for a few hours," he said. "I'll keep watch."

He climbed to the top of a dune and sat with his back turned, the shadowtongue cloak merging seamlessly with the sands. To Nazafareen's surprise, Galen joined him, sitting a few paces away. Nicodemus glanced over but didn't object.

"He's your brother?" Katrin asked Darius.

"Half-brother," Darius replied. "We share the same father."

Katrin scowled. "Victor Dessarian."

Don't start up now, Nazafareen thought wearily.

"I know you don't believe it, but Victor didn't kill Halldóra," she said. "Gerda did. She wanted the Valkirins to ally with the Vatras. Halldóra wasn't having it."

Katrin looked ready to argue, then subsided. She took a long drink from her water skin.

"I didn't see what happened," she conceded. "Halldóra and Gerda were already dead when I entered the room. I heard them arguing through the door."

Nazafareen tipped her chin toward Nicodemus. "Just ask the Vatra. He spoke to Gerda through the globe."

Now Katrin's jaw dropped. "How do you know this?"

"He told me himself."

"I can't believe it." Katrin sighed. "Actually, I can. She would have done anything to restore Val Moraine to its former glory." She glanced at the baldric slung over Nazafareen's shoulder and barked an amazed laugh. "So Culach gave you Ygraine's sword. What the hell did you say to him?"

"The truth. That I never meant to burn his army."

Nazafareen told her what she'd seen that day at the lake and about the creature called Farrumohr who whispered in Neblis's ear. How Culach had been possessed by it.

"I was only trying to save myself. The flames got away from me." Nazafareen paused. "I'm so sorry about your sister."

Katrin gave her a long look, then nodded. "I sensed it too," she admitted. "Culach seemed strange after he came through the gate."

"Farrumohr was driven out, but some part of him remained. Since that day, Culach has been plagued by dreams."

"Nightmares, you mean. I had to listen to them," Katrin replied ruefully. "His cell was next to mine."

"He said he dreamed of Gaius when he was young. Before the Sundering."

"Does it mean anything?"

"It might." Nazafareen rubbed her stump. "Just don't ask me what."

Katrin took her sword out and began to sharpen it with a whetstone. "I don't trust the Vatra."

"I think he told the truth. He wants Gaius dead. But no, I don't trust him either." She stared at Nicodemus, his hair bright against the shadowtongue cloak. "He's lying about something, I can feel it."

"Want me to make him talk?" Katrin sounded eager.

"Not yet. I don't think he's an immediate danger." She yawned. "I suppose we'd better get some rest."

Rhea and Katrin rigged up a shelter with their blankets and sat cross-legged, talking quietly. Nazafareen lay down with her head on Darius's shoulder, face turned away from the endless sun.

"I keep thinking about Victor," he said. "He loved Delilah more than anything in the world."

Nazafareen wondered if it was easier for Darius to focus on Victor's anguish rather than his own. "I know."

"When he finds out, he'll lose his mind."

"I'll bring him Gaius's heart."

His voice was sad. "That won't help. It won't matter."

"It does to me."

Darius didn't reply, but she sensed fear in him and knew it wasn't only for his father. She wanted to reassure him, to tell him there was nothing to worry about, that Gaius couldn't harm her, but the words felt empty.

So she rested her cheek on the cuff around her stump, making sure it was far from Darius's bare skin, and fell into an uneasy slumber.

NICODEMUS SCANNED THE HORIZON, ALERT FOR ANY HINT OF movement. He didn't expect to encounter any of his people so far east—the hunting was poor in the middle of the Kiln—but there were other things to be wary of.

Nazafareen wasn't what he had expected. He'd sensed genuine sympathy when he showed his scars, yet he couldn't shake the memory of her at the Gate. The look on her face—as pitiless and cruel as Gaius. He glanced over to where she slept curled in her cloak. Only the Danai remained awake. His cold blue eyes meet Nico's.

He doesn't trust me. Well, I wouldn't either.

Nico had spoken the truth when he held the staff. Its magic bound him as surely as anyone else. But he did manage to omit a few things.

Like the fact that he'd seen Gaius take mortal injuries and survive—more than once.

If he'd told Nazafareen, she might have had second thoughts. And she was his only chance.

When he judged four hours had passed, Nicodemus stood, signaling to Darius with a nod that he should wake the others. They continued the trek south. Before long, Nazafareen caught up and slowed her pace to walk beside him.

"How much farther?"

"About thirty leagues."

She was quiet for a minute. "What's your brother's name?"

He glanced at her. His right eye still stung like hell and probably looked a horror.

"Atticus."

"How old is he?"

"Sixteen now."

If he lives.

"Why didn't you take him with you?"

Nico's mouth set. "Atticus was always frail, prone to illness. When he was ten, he caught a fever. It left him with a twisted leg." He touched his face. "And it did something to his muscles. They droop on the right side. He's a smart kid, but he never would have made it across the Kiln."

"Where is he now?"

Nico drew a breath. "With Gaius."

He saw Nazafareen's shocked look. "No one else would take him in. They could barely feed themselves." His mouth twisted. "Of course, Gaius didn't want him either. Said he was useless. Domitia wheedled and begged. She's the only one he ever had a soft spot for. He finally relented."

In truth, they'd only survived at all because Domitia brought them food until Nico grew old enough to provide for himself. She'd dump a carcass outside the burrow and slip away, though he knew it was her.

"It was leave him with a monster or leave him to certain death. I chose the first."

Atticus had begged Nico not to go. He was terrified of being left behind with Gaius. But they both knew he wouldn't survive the harsh journey across the Kiln. And finding a way out was his only chance. Nico had nearly died a hundred times searching for food and water. One day, he wouldn't return to their burrow. It was only a matter of time. When Domitia proposed they seek out the gates and try to revive one, he'd grasped at the chance.

But he still remembered his last glimpse of Atticus, standing beside the hole into Gaius's burrow, his eyes swimming with unshed tears.

The guilt ate at him every single day.

Nazafareen nodded to herself. "That's the real reason you want me to kill Gaius." She gave him a shrewd look. "So you can get your brother back."

Nico said nothing.

"It's been two years and even if he's alive, Gaius might not let him go. He could have poisoned his mind—"

"Don't."

She fell silent, then said quietly, "He could be like Domitia now. That's what you're afraid of."

Nico felt a surge of irritation that she'd read him so well. He should have kept his mouth shut.

"I know what you think of her. That she's pure fucking evil." His lips curved in a sardonic smile. "I've thought the same more than once. But she saw herself as a force for right."

Nazafareen snorted.

"Gaius says the other clans tried to enslave us," Nico persisted. He knew now it was all bullshit, but some perverse part of him wanted to needle her. "To force us to make talismans—"

"That's a lie! The war started over a woman. A Danai. Gaius wanted her and she didn't want him. So he burned her lands and then he turned on the others."

Nicodemus blinked. "Who told you that?"

"A Valkirin at Val Moraine. He had visions. He *saw* the war, through the eyes of Gaius's chief advisor."

"The Viper?"

"Yes."

Nicodemus thought of the mortal accounts he'd read at the Temple of Apollo. They didn't mention a woman, but they did say the Vatras had invaded without provocation.

"We may never know what really happened," he said wearily. "I'm not sure it even matters anymore."

Nazafareen scowled. "Of course it matters."

"My point is that Domitia didn't know any of that." He looked at Nazafareen. "If you were her, you might have done the same."

She looked outraged. "I'd never kill innocent people."

"They weren't innocent to Domitia." He shrugged. "Believe what you wish. But she told me once that she thought you were alike, and I think she was right."

"She burned people alive in the brazen bull! People she accused of *witchcraft*. She only did it to spread fear. To stoke their hatred of the other clans so they wouldn't object when she enslaved and killed them."

He gave her a cockeyed grin. "I never said she was perfect."

Nazafareen snorted in disgust. "You're despicable."

"And what about you? I know what you're capable of. Maybe better than you do yourself."

She stiffened and strode ahead. Nico watched her go, wondering why he'd provoked her. It was a foolish impulse. She could crush him like an insect. And he needed her on his side. Needed her to trust him.

He scanned the horizon. Talking with Nazafareen had

distracted him, but now he realized they'd reached the edge of a faint bowl-shaped depression.

"Stop!" he shouted.

She turned back with a questioning look, but it was too late. With a yelp, Nazafareen sank to her waist in the sands.

❧ 24 ❧

THE RED HILLS

One instant, the ground beneath her feet was solid. The next, it collapsed like a trapdoor springing open. Nazafareen spread her arms and her descent was arrested, but she could feel how unstable the surrounding sand was. Little trickles ran toward her on all sides. Darius started to rush forward, but the Vatra flung out a hand.

"Stay back. You'll be swallowed too."

Nazafareen shifted and slid a few inches deeper.

"Don't struggle," Nicodemus barked. "Don't move a muscle."

Darius spun toward Katrin. "Can you lift her up with air?"

Katrin studied the sky with a faraway expression. "I'll try."

The Vatra's shadowtongue cloak stirred as a breeze rose, blowing sand into Nazafareen's face. It had little effect on her predicament except to make it worse.

"I'm sorry," Katrin said after a minute. "My power isn't what it was beyond the Gale." She frowned. "I can still touch the clouds, they would answer me if I called, but I cannot forge bonds of air to lift her."

Darius cursed. "I can't either."

Nicodemus pulled a rope from his pack and started to tie it around his waist.

"I'll go," Darius snarled.

"I've done this before," Nicodemus said evenly. "You haven't. I'll just end up having to rescue both of you."

Darius hesitated, then gave a brusque nod.

Nicodemus secured the rope and tossed the other end to Darius. He took a step forward, sinking to his knees. The sands shifted and she slipped lower. The sands nearly reached her chin now. The heat of them was like an oven. Their bond was muffled, but she could feel a hint of Darius's fear.

"Hurry," he said, his voice tight.

Nicodemus tested each step, his hand extended toward her. He was up to his waist now, four paces away.

"Very slowly," he said in a calm voice. "Try to move one arm."

She did. The sands gave way a little more.

She suddenly remembered what Culach had told her about the Viper, that he was swallowed up by the desert. She wondered if it had been at this very spot.

"How deep is the hole?" she whispered.

"Deep. But don't worry, I've—"

The last layer collapsed. She squeezed her mouth shut, sinking down into suffocating heat. She fought the urge to breathe, but her lungs screamed for air. And then something gripped her tunic, hauling her up inch by inch until she emerged, gasping. It was Nicodemus, plastered with sand.

"Got her," he called.

Darius and Rhea had the other end of the rope, and quickly hauled them both to safety. When Nazafareen's feet touched firm ground, Darius gave a shaky smile and made the sign of the flame —a pious gesture she hadn't seen in a long time. Nicodemus spat and wiped his mouth with the back of his hand.

"You've been here before," Katrin snapped. "Why didn't you bloody warn us?"

"I only passed through it once, farther west." His face darkened. "We lost two people." His finger traced a line around them. "If you look closely, you'll see the edge."

Nazafareen could just make out a slight subsidence, though she wouldn't have known what it meant.

"This area is riddled with holes. They're covered by the wind, but the slightest pressure causes the top layer of sand to collapse."

"What now?" Rhea asked.

"We go around. Follow in my footsteps."

Nicodemus moved cautiously, leading them west towards the blazing sun. Several times he tested the ground ahead with a rock from his pocket.

"The wards on the Kiln dampen elemental power," Nico said. "I expect the clans did so we couldn't forge talismans to escape."

"Wise of them," Katrin murmured. She scratched her head. "I think I could make it rain, though I'd have to call the clouds from a long way away."

"Don't," Nico said sternly. "Unless you wish to light a signal fire for Gaius that we're coming."

She scowled. "I didn't say I would, Vatra. Only that I could."

He raised an eyebrow. "Well, we might need your power yet."

They skirted the Sinking Sands, turning due south again. The ground grew firmer and they made faster progress. Nazafareen plodded along behind Nicodemus, her thoughts turning to Herodotus. She missed his company. He was always interesting to talk to and their conversations had made the time on the *Chione* pass quickly. If he were here, he would be cheerfully grilling the Vatra about his clan's customs—what they ate and what they wore, how they made their burrows and what they used for weapons.

With the Marakai, the questions had seemed innocuous. But out here, in the middle of this unforgiving land, the answers could be important. What if something happened to Nicodemus? She sensed he regretted telling her about his brother, but perhaps he would consent to tell her more about the Kiln.

Nazafareen fell into step beside him.

I must do it the way Herodotus does, she thought. With a light touch.

"Easier walking," she remarked.

Nicodemus grunted.

"I haven't seen anything besides those wyrms. What do you hunt for food?"

He glanced at her. "Bush rats."

"Oh. Where do they live?"

"Not out here."

She waited for more, but his gaze had returned to the horizon.

"Are they tasty?"

"What?"

"Bush rats. How do you cook them?"

He stared straight ahead. "Oh, we make a lovely stew with peaches and wine. And honeyed cakes for dessert."

"You needn't mock," she growled. "I was only asking."

His mouth twitched. Nazafareen cursed her temper.

"The Marakai eat raw fish," she said. "And black kelp."

"I know." He looked down at her. "What about your people?"

"Mine? I....I'm not sure."

He looked puzzled. "How can you not know?"

"I lost my memories," she muttered. "All of them beyond a few months ago."

"How?"

"I did it to myself."

"On purpose?"

"No, by accident." She frowned. "Why are we talking about me? I meant to—" She caught herself and fell silent.

"Meant to what?" He seemed decidedly amused now. "Interrogate me?"

"No." She made a show of pulling out a water skin and taking a drink, then examining the skin. "What about water? Where do you find it?"

Nicodemus laughed. "You're terrible at this."

"This?"

"Being subtle."

Nazafareen sighed. "A friend of mine is writing a book about the different cultures. More than one book, actually. A set of histories. I'd like to be able to tell him about the Vatras when I return." She gave a small smile. "If he was here, he'd pry every last scrap out of you."

Nicodemus was silent for so long she thought he wouldn't answer. Then he said, "There are dunes by the sea. The Sand Hills. It's the only place we get rain. If you dig down, the fresh water sits on top of the salt water."

"What's the coast like?"

"The waters are infested with sharks. No ship can come near because of the reefs offshore. Most of the hunting parties stay near the coast. They catch crabs and a few other things that live in the dunes." He paused. "Gulls were the only birds I'd ever seen before I left the Kiln."

He answered her questions readily after that. As he spoke, Nicodemus seemed to relax a little and even enjoy himself. He carefully avoided anything personal, but it occurred to her that the last two years must have been lonely, pretending to be other than what he was. He told her where to find the handful of healing herbs that grew in the Kiln and how to track a bush rat to its hole. He told her about the nine types of sand in the Kiln and how to treat the bite from a rock spider. He explained how to use thorns to sew a shadowtongue cloak. He said the reason the Vatras lived apart from each other was that too many together attracted predators.

Nazafareen filed away the answers, but she soon ran out of things to ask. Beyond day-to-day survival, the Vatras had no true culture. No music or art. None of them seemed to live long

except for Gaius, and their knowledge of the past came from him
—all of it lies.

Finally, she thanked him and fell back to walk beside Darius
again, relating her conversation with the Vatra.

"I want to hate them all," she said. "I really do."

He looked at her shrewdly. "But you think they got a worse
punishment than they deserved?"

"I don't know. Yes." She sighed. "The ones who were born to
this. They never had a chance."

"We're not here for them," Darius pointed out. "We're here
for Gaius. You'll be doing his people a service, Nazafareen."

"That's true. But is it enough?"

He cast her a narrowed glance and she let it drop.

As they moved south, the hardpan began to crack and rise up.
Buttes of rock thrust from the earth like islands in a dry sea. The
gullies winding between them lay in deep shadow. Nicodemus
held up a hand and the party halted.

"The Red Hills," he said. "They were shaped by ancient rivers.
Gaius's burrow is on the other side."

"I don't like it," Darius said, studying the terrain. There were a
hundred places to hide. "Why can't we go around?"

Nicodemus shrugged. "We can, if you're willing to walk an
extra sixty leagues or more." He paused. "Without stopping for
water. Because there isn't any."

"Are the Red Hills inhabited?" Nazafareen asked warily.

He shook his head. "No, but we must watch the skies. Drakes
hunt here."

"You mentioned them before. What are they?"

"The smartest thing in the Kiln." He gave a hollow laugh.
"You'll know one when you see it. With any luck, we won't."

"And if we do?" Darius demanded.

Nico's cobalt eyes glittered. "Run like hell."

"Fucking great," Rhea muttered.

Nazafareen raised an eyebrow. Her language had grown saltier since she'd been spending time with Katrin.

"What about Vatra scouts?" she asked.

"They avoid the Red Hills. But I'll range ahead to make sure."

"No, you won't." Darius took a step forward, blue eyes chips of ice. "You're not leaving us alone. Anything could be waiting in there."

Nicodemus's face darkened. He still wore the faded bruises from his beating.

"If I wanted you dead, you would be. I could have left you in that cellar, let the wyrms come for you. I could have let you both drown in the sands—"

"It's not a matter of trust," Nazafareen interrupted, before they ended up fighting again. "But he's right. No more ranging ahead. We go together or not at all."

Nicodemus scowled and stalked away. He stopped on a rise, scanning the badlands. Darius watched him go, a muscle in his jaw working.

"I want to know what a bloody drake is," he muttered, heading after Nicodemus. Nazafareen considered following him, then decided not to. Let them hash it out on their own.

She turned to Galen. He sat on a flat rock, pulling his boots off and shaking the sand out. Tattered cloth rags bound his feet. He unwound them and she winced. Half the toes were gone. The skin looked healed, but she knew what it was to lose a piece of yourself.

She wondered what had transpired at Val Moraine after Victor took the keep. He wouldn't have been gentle, but she hoped this wasn't his doing.

"What happened?" she asked, sitting down next to him.

Galen glanced over. "Frostbite."

"Oh."

He kneaded the stumps, then started rewrapping his feet. More scraps of cloth filled the toes of his boots.

"Does it hurt?"

"Sometimes. But the pain is in my mind." His gaze slid across her stump. "Do you ever feel your hand?"

"I don't know. Maybe I did once." She felt a familiar surge of frustration. "I can't remember having a right hand at all."

Rhea and Katrin had wandered over to the others and they were alone for the first time. Galen seemed to gird himself. He looked angry and ashamed. "Listen, I didn't know about the chimera. I wouldn't have helped Eirik if I had. Never." A shadow crossed his face. "I've lost more than you know, Nazafareen. I'm not asking you to forgive me, but—"

She was spared from answering by Darius, who called them over. Galen yanked his boots on, his face pink. She thought of the superior grin he used to wear. The sly mockery in his tone when he spoke to Darius. Recent events had taken him down several notches, but she wondered if that person still lurked inside.

When she reached Darius and Nicodemus, they were conferring together without rancor, studying the maze of canyons ahead. And therein lay the difference between Victor's sons, she thought. One was a boy, and the other a man.

"We'll make for the gullies," Nicodemus said, shouldering his pack. "I know a route through. It's only half a day's walk to the other side."

He set a brisk pace, the sun a blazing forge overhead. When they reached the shade of the first gorge, Nazafareen heaved a sigh of relief. It was about twenty paces wide and wound through high, jagged escarpments on either side. The walls had been worn smooth and had a reddish cast, layered with strata of blue and grey.

Nicodemus set a course through the canyon, the sky a white ribbon far overhead. It narrowed and then widened again, branching into three other canyons. He hesitated for a moment, then chose the middle one. They walked for a time in silence. The only thing they encountered was a large web with a small brown spider in the center.

"Don't break it," Nicodemus said, ducking under one side.

"Is it poisonous?" Nazafareen asked, following his lead.

"Very. But she won't mess with you if you don't mess with her."

The deeper they went into the Red Hills, the longer he paused when they encountered places where secondary ravines cut through. Twice, he chose one way and then changed his mind, backtracking with an irritated expression. Nazafareen felt sure they were lost when the ravine widened and he turned to her with a grin.

Nicodemus pointed. "Do you see the rock formation that looks like a spire?" Nazafareen nodded. "This is the halfway mark. I passed it with Domitia."

"And when we get to the other side?"

"It flattens out. Gaius's burrow is a few leagues off."

"What about scouts?"

Raised voices made them turn. Katrin and Galen were staring at each other. Galen's face had gone white.

"You're just like your father. A murderer with no honor." Katrin spat on the ground. "You blow with the wind."

"And you helped make the chimera to hunt Darius and Nazafareen," Galen grated. "Don't pretend you're better than me."

Katrin's gaze narrowed. "I pretend nothing," she said stiffly. "But do not think we are alike in any way. I'd sooner trust the Vatra."

"You Valkirins are all the same. Think the bloody moons shine out of your ass. Well, I'll tell you something—"

Their angry voices echoed through the canyon.

"He tried to befriend her," Rhea whispered. "Asked if she'd been weak in air power. I guess it's a sore spot."

Nazafareen looked at Galen, bemused and annoyed at the same time. He seemed destined to always do precisely the wrong thing.

"I'm glad I didn't break his block," she said. "Imagine if the two of them decided to settle it with the power."

Darius shook his head wearily. "I'd rather not."

An instant later, Nicodemus strode between Galen and Katrin, his face white with fury.

"Shut the hell up," he growled. "You'll get us all killed. It might look empty out here, but it's not, you got me?"

Katrin opened her mouth, then snapped it shut. She glared at Galen, who looked ready to chew rocks.

"You two, come with me." Nicodemus stabbed a finger at Katrin and Rhea. "We'll take a look ahead." He muttered something that sounded like *fucking children* and stomped away.

"Go on," Nazafareen told Rhea. "We'll wait here. It won't hurt to scout the terrain."

Rhea gave a quick nod and laid her hand on Katrin's arm. The Valkirin blew out a breath.

"The Vatra's right," she said. "Eirik would have knocked our heads together and sent us out for a nice long run in the snow. Naked."

Rhea grinned. "Would he really?"

"I should tell you about the time he caught Culach and Petur scaling the battlements. They were stinking drunk, of course, and Culach thought it would be funny to sneak into Gerda's chambers...." Her voice dwindled as they followed Nicodemus around the next bend.

Nazafareen looked for Galen but he'd taken off too, standing with his back turned at the other end of the canyon.

"Let him stand guard," she said, dropping her pack with a sigh. "I'm happy to rest for a spell."

"We should have come alone," Darius said. "Forget Gaius. I might kill the two of them first."

She couldn't argue with that sentiment.

"Got any food left?" she asked hopefully.

"Some bread. It's hard."

"I don't care."

He broke it in half and handed her a piece. Nazafareen bit down and grimaced. She studied the lump of bread.

"Do you see my tooth? I think it's in there somewhere."

Darius gave a half smile. "The dried meat is worse. Better suited for a saddle than supper."

She set the bread aside and rested her head on her pack. "If you happen to see a bush rat wander by, let me know." Her stomach rumbled. "Or anything that looks the least bit edible. I'm not picky."

Darius leaned back next to her, propping his head on a bent elbow. He'd pushed his shirtsleeves up and his left arm lay dead against his side—the price he paid for the bond. How Nazafareen wished it maimed her instead.

"I've been thinking," he said. "When this is over, there's little to keep us here. My clan is gone. And Victor.... He's made his own choice. Would you be willing to leave?"

"Return to the Empire?"

"It's not the Empire anymore."

She considered this. "I would like to see the mountains I grew up in."

"The Khusk Range is a beautiful place."

"I wish I could remember it," she said with sudden bitterness.

"Maybe going back would help."

"I doubt it."

"You told me you had a brother named Kian. We could look for him."

Kian. She tried to picture his face, but all she saw was a shadow. A shadow with flames for eyes.

"Darius?"

"Hmmm?"

"What if the Viper *is* waiting for us? What if he wears Gaius's body?"

"You're wondering if he can be killed."

She nodded.

"I don't know. You drove him back once."

The memory of that day threatened to sweep over her and Nazafareen pushed it away.

"My breaking power is strong here. I think I could shatter the flows of twenty Vatras." She paused, considering. "If I do find him, I'll throw it all at him."

He gave her a sharp look. "Be careful, Nazafareen. There's no gate to the moonlands here. Don't draw too much."

"I think I'm past that point now." She sighed. "But I'll do my best."

He looked stricken and she changed the subject.

"Something should be done for the Vatras. It isn't right to make the ones who knew nothing of the war suffer so. Especially the children."

Darius rubbed his forehead. "Domitia killed five hundred Danai alone. All it takes is one of them."

"I know. But maybe the talismans can do something about the Kiln. Bring water and shade. Hunt down the monsters who terrorize the Vatras."

"It's a kind thought. But that would require Katrin and Galen to work together, and you to break his block." He studied the narrow band of sky above, white against the dark rim of the canyon. "What did Galen say to you?"

"That he was sorry. I think he is." She looked at Darius. "He's been punished. More than I would have wished for."

"Galen is a troubled man."

He stiffened an instant before a shadow passed across the sun. Darius leapt to his feet. There wasn't a cloud in sight.

Then they heard Galen yelling.

❧ 25 ❧

SPAWN OF THE KILN

Galen stood with a hand cupped over his eyes, the strong muscles of his neck cording as he scanned the ribbon of sky overhead.

"Something's up there," he said as Nazafareen and Darius approached.

"Did you see it?" Darius asked.

Galen shook his head, pushing back a lock of dark hair. "Not clearly. But it's big. At least five times the size of an abbadax, I'd reckon."

"A drake," Darius said grimly.

Nazafareen looked down the canyon, hoping to see their companions, but Nicodemus, Rhea and Katrin were nowhere in sight.

"How do you kill it?" she asked.

"You don't. The Vatra said they have an armored carapace. If there's a vulnerability, he doesn't know what it is."

"We have to find the others." Nazafareen grabbed her rucksack and slung it over one shoulder. "Stay close to the walls."

They moved in single file through the canyon, which began to gradually widen. The ground was made up of hard-packed dirt and rocks, with occasional tumbles of boulders that they had to scramble to cross. Nazafareen was picking her way across one when the light flickered. She looked up quickly, but whatever it was had already passed.

"It's stalking us," Darius said softly. "Hurry."

They broke into a trot, pressing against the walls when the creature passed over. It was too fast to make out, but she could sense its watchful presence.

"Where the hell is the Vatra?" Darius growled.

"He won't abandon us," Galen said, stubbornly loyal to the man who'd freed him.

But Nazafareen wondered. She should never have let them go on ahead. Would Nicodemus lead them into a trap? He was a Vatra, after all. She tried to imagine him overpowering Katrin and Rhea, but it didn't seem likely. Rhea fought like a demon with her staff and Katrin was famous even among the Valkirins for her skill with a sword. Plus she had a greater measure of power than any of them.

Nazafareen set her doubts aside as they reached a place where the ravine broadened and then branched into two passages barely wider than crevices. The ground ahead was open but the walls rose steeply on all sides. They paused under the shelter of a deep overhang.

"Which way did Nicodemus go?" she asked Darius.

"To the left," he replied, keen eyes scanning the canyon. "I can see scuffmarks in the dirt."

Nazafareen hunched lower, her pack dragging against her back, a rabbit wondering if it dared make a run for its hole. And then she felt a sudden tug, deep inside where the breaking power lived.

She peered into the shadowy recess. The walls sloped sharply inward. At the very back lay a rectangle of pure darkness, solid and unmoving. Her huo mofa stirred again. Just the faintest twinge—but she sensed something. The echoes of old magic. She tugged at Darius's sleeve and pointed.

"Look. I think it's a gate," she whispered. "Or was."

If they hadn't stopped, she might have walked right past it.

Darius and Galen turned from their study of the canyons and leaned into the darkness. She suddenly saw the resemblance between them, in the identical way they moved, the set of their broad shoulders. The intent, wary expressions.

"Gates need water to stay open," Darius murmured. "I'd guess it's been dry for centuries."

"Don't get too close," Galen warned as Nazafareen took a step forward. "I don't like the look of it."

She stopped a few feet away. The fractured magic set her teeth on edge. It was like listening to the endless drone of a fly. She tore her gaze away and returned to the entrance.

"I vote we keep going," she said. "Find the others. They can't be far ahead. We need to warn them about the drake and we're better off fighting together, if it comes to that."

"Agreed," Darius said.

They both looked at Galen.

"Nicodemus said drakes were cunning. What if it's waiting for us to come into the open?" he grumbled. "I think we should wait here, where it's safe."

"We don't know it's safe," Darius pointed out with a touch of impatience. "And we have a broken gate at our backs. I don't particularly want to be driven toward it."

"Fine." Galen glanced at the left-branching crevice, which lay about a hundred paces away. "I'll go first then."

They studied the skies above. Nothing moved. The silence was absolute.

Galen shouldered his pack, drew a deep breath, and darted across the canyon. He moved with liquid speed and gained the other side in a matter of seconds.

"You next, Nazafareen," Darius said. "I'll watch your back."

She gave a firm nod. "Give me a kiss for good luck."

Darius pulled her close, his mouth warm against hers. "Go," he whispered.

She ran forward, keeping her gaze on Galen, who beckoned encouragingly. The terrain was strewn with boulders piled helter-skelter atop each other. She wove around them, boots pounding against the dry earth. Light hit her face as the sun peeked over the rim of the canyon. Halfway across, she encountered a scree of loose pebbles and slid but managed to recover without falling. The last fifty paces looked easier. Relatively flat and open.

Almost there.

When the drake came, it was with shocking speed—a streak of movement erupting from the far edge of the canyon. It alit with a flap of leathery wings that raised a cloud of dust. She skidded to a stop too fast, one leg twisting beneath her. Fire swept through her knee. She reached for Nemesis but the baldric had gotten tangled up with straps of her rucksack.

The drake had a golden mane but its body resembled a scaled green serpent—thrice the size of a draft horse. It slithered forward, wings folded against its sides. Huge silver eyes flecked with copper regarded her, full of ancient intelligence. Clear liquid dripped from its fangs. Where it struck the ground, the rock melted with a hiss.

Behind her, Darius shouted a warning. She spared a glance over her shoulder. A second drake wriggled through the canyon they'd come from, its massive body filling the space nearly from edge to edge. It must have entered at one of the wider points farther down. Darius had his knife out, but it was scarcely larger than one of the drake's teeth.

Nazafareen muttered a curse. She turned back and scanned the opposite ravine for Galen but didn't see him. He must have run to find the others.

Or to save his own skin.

She backed away as the drake advanced. From the corner of

her eye, she could see Darius dodge snapping strikes by the second drake, his speed and agility the only things keeping him alive. She gripped Nemesis in her sweaty hand, searching for some weakness, something to stab. The silver eyes might be vulnerable, but she couldn't imagine getting close enough to find out.

So she retreated and the drake advanced, its gaze never leaving her for an instant. Another shuffling step and the rock wall dug into her back. She searched desperately on either side for a crack she might wiggle into but the overhang they'd stopped at was at least twenty paces away and the rest of the cliff face stretched unbroken.

No battle's won in bed.

Nazafareen snarled and raised her sword. The sky grew suddenly dark.

For fuck's sake, not a *third* one, she thought wearily.

A drop of rain hit her face. Then two more. She risked a quick glance upwards. Dark clouds boiled over the ravine. With a great clap of thunder, the skies opened. Heavy rain began to fall, dashing on the arid ground and cascading down the walls of the canyon. The drake paused, chuffing uncertainly. She wondered how long it had been since the beast saw rain. By the looks of that gate, a very long time indeed.

She seized the chance to make a run for Darius, but the drake was not so easily distracted. Muscles bunched beneath its scaled hide and it slithered to cut her off, rearing up on its coils like a cobra. The drake's mouth yawned open as it prepared to lunge forward. Its barbed tail whipped around behind her.

And then a rock arced through the curtains of rain, bouncing off the drake's snout. The creature ignored it, but a second rock— even larger—provoked an angry hiss.

Nazafareen squinted through the downpour. It was Galen, pale and drenched.

"Over here!" he shouted at the drake, another rock in his hand. "Come on, you great dumb lizard!"

The drake gave a contemptuous flick of its tail that sent Nazafareen sprawling. Then its head shot forward and a jet of clear liquid streamed from its throat. The rain sizzled and steamed. Galen screamed as it splattered against his chest. He dropped to one knee, six inches of brown water coursing around him.

Nazafareen grabbed Galen's coat and hauled him toward the overhang, which had been transformed into a waterfall by the sheets of rain pouring from the canyon rim above. She ducked through into the hollow behind, the sound of rushing water echoing in her ears. Galen's teeth clenched as she propped him against one wall. She smelled burnt flesh. On the other side of the waterfall, the blurry shape of the drake swung its head from side to side, hunting them.

She tore off Galen's smoking coat and threw it aside. Her breath hissed when she saw the wounds beneath. The venom had eaten through layers of clothing and skin, exposing white bone. There was blood, so much of it.

"Galen." She hooked an arm around his back, holding him upright. His head lolled away, his eyes unfocused. Her throat tightened with sudden emotion. Nothing he'd done in the past mattered anymore.

He's better than I gave him credit for. Better than anyone did. He doesn't deserve this.

The gate lurked a few feet away. Floodwater lapped at its base. It was still dark, but she fancied she saw little ripples on the surface. The gate's magic throbbed in her head like a rotten tooth. Weak, but enough for what needed to be done.

She gently moved Galen so that he lay a few paces ahead of the gate and stoked her breaking magic to a boil. It wasn't hard. She was already livid at the thought of yet another pointless death.

"I'm sending you to the Lady," she whispered furiously. "Don't you dare bloody die until you see her."

Would it make any difference? Nazafareen couldn't be sure.

But perhaps the surge of earth magic when his ward broke would help him survive.

If he had a ward. If he even *was* the last talisman.

"Only one way to find out," she muttered, unleashing her magic straight at Galen.

He stiffened with a scream, dark eyes flying wide. Behind her, she sensed sudden movement.

The drake.

Nazafareen lifted her sword with numb fingers as the drake exploded in a blur toward the overhang. *The eyes. Aim for the eyes,* she thought, even as part of her knew it was hopeless, she'd never get close enough....

A shattering explosion and flash of white light knocked her back. The world fell silent except for the insistent buzz of the gate. Nazafareen clung blindly to the rock wall, her head ringing, every hair on end. Floodwater swirled around her. When she opened her eyes, she saw two humps like boulders beyond the waterfall. They slowly slid together and she realized that it was in fact a single hump, and that it had been the drake.

She checked Galen. His pulse still beat weakly. Nazafareen crawled out from the overhang. The drake was charred to a crisp. More lightning forked across the sky. A miracle. She gave a weak laugh.

"Nazafareen!"

She dragged herself up and saw Rhea on the opposite side of the canyon. Katrin stood next to her, swaying on her feet as Rhea held her up. Katrin must have summoned the storm, though it had clearly cost her to work so much power in the Kiln. Nicodemus was with them. He ran towards Darius, fearless despite his lack of a weapon, and Nazafareen felt ashamed that she'd ever doubted him. The second drake gazed at the body of its companion, spat a jet of venom that Nicodemus easily eluded, and spread its wings, flapping off into the storm.

She sheathed her sword and waded over to Darius, who seized her in a one-armed hug.

"Thank the gods you're unharmed," he murmured in her ear. "I thought it had you."

"It almost did."

She pulled back as Nicodemus joined them. "We came as fast as we could," he shouted over the rain. "I saw the drakes heading this way." He shook his head in wonder. "It was Katrin's idea to call a storm. I didn't think she'd manage it, not in time."

"We found a gate," Nazafareen shouted back. "I think it might be reviving. Galen is hurt badly. Maybe we should—"

Her words were cut off by a rumble from the canyon they'd come from. A wall of water raced toward them, at least eight paces high. She took a step toward the overhang where she'd left Galen, but it was too late. Darius clasped her hand. They turned and ran toward the left fork, Nicodemus sprinting behind. She saw Katrin and Rhea disappear into the opposite canyon, their heads bobbing above the whitewater. There was no sign of Galen.

And then the flood hit, a torrent of churning brown water. The world spun upside down as the current swept them into oblivion.

✤ 26 ✤

THERE WILL BE BLOOD

Coarse sand scoured her cheek. Nazafareen pushed up to sit, Ygraine's sword digging into her back. The rain had stopped. Sunlight poured down, relentless and brutal. She heard running water and above it, a rhythmic sound, like a bellows pumping.

A few paces off, Nicodemus knelt on the ground, copper hair plastered across his forehead. He was pounding on Darius's chest. Nazafareen hurried over. Her body felt like one big bruise, but nothing seemed broken thanks to Darius. When the wave hit them, he'd held her tight and shielded her from the rough canyon walls. Now he lay limp, skin white as birch bark. He wasn't dead, she could feel him through the bond, but he looked close to it.

"What are you doing?" she demanded.

Nicodemus glanced up. "He took in too much water. I saw fishermen in Tjanjin revive a man this way. Pinch his nose closed and breathe into his mouth."

She obeyed immediately. Four quick breaths, then Nicodemus resumed his pumping.

"Come on," she whispered. Darius's lips looked blue. Like a corpse.

304

"Again," Nicodemus said.

Desperate, she cupped Darius's face in her hand and filled his lungs with air. Something stirred in the bond. He gave a weak cough. Muddy water trickled from the corner of his mouth. Together, she and Nicodemus rolled him to one side and let him spew it out. His misery made her own stomach roll in sympathy. At last, Darius rolled to face the sky again, swiping his mouth with a sleeve.

"Where are we?" he croaked.

"Back end of nowhere," Nicodemus replied with a half smile.

"I knew *that*," Darius muttered.

"About six leagues from where we started. The flood carried us more or less the right way, at least."

Nazafareen looked around. The Red Hills lay behind them. The flood had washed them out to the plain and then dissipated, flowing into broad slow-moving channels that shimmered like mirrors. But the sun's heat was already evaporating the shallow rivers and Nazafareen could see they'd soon be gone. She didn't know how they'd cross the Kiln again without water skins.

"Have you seen any sign of the others?" she asked Nicodemus.

He shook his head. "The canyons are a maze. Assuming they survived, they could have come out leagues away." He glanced around. "We can't stay in the open long. We're too close to Gaius's burrow."

"Will he suspect the rainstorm was unnatural?" Darius asked.

"How could he not? I've seen rain out here perhaps twice in my entire life."

Nicodemus tugged his shirt off and wrung it out. Scars covered his torso and chest—not only the round puckers from wyrms he'd shown her before, but others too. Some looked like tooth marks.

"How old *are* you, Nicodemus?" Nazafareen asked.

He pulled his shirt back on and threw the shadowtongue cloak across his shoulders. "Thirty, or thereabouts. I don't know my exact birthday."

She couldn't hide her surprise. He raised an eyebrow.

"You thought I was older."

"By at least a decade," she admitted.

"The ravages of the Kiln," he said lightly. "Wreaks havoc on one's delicate complexion."

She smiled. Fine lines creased the corners of his eyes, but that wasn't the only reason. He had a self-possessed, competent air that was unusual for one so young. Darius had it too, the result of his harsh upbringing among the magi. She wondered how old Nicodemus had been when his mother died.

"Yes, I can't say I've grown fond of this place," Darius said, pushing up to sit and making a quick inventory of his knives. "So where's this burrow?"

"A few leagues west," Nicodemus replied. His face set into stubborn lines. "I plan to find Atticus even if I have to continue alone. But I understand if you want to seek out your friends. I leave the choice to you."

Nazafareen thought of Galen, of Rhea and Katrin. She hated to abandon them, but searching the Red Hills could take days and they had no food. Their packs had been washed away in the flood, along with the globe of seeking. And without Nicodemus, they'd likely never find Gaius—or he'd find them first.

"That wasn't the deal, Vatra," Darius growled. "You promised to follow orders."

Two pairs of blue eyes locked. "And I did. I could have abandoned you a hundred times. Gone my own way."

Darius's tone was icy. "Don't play the hero. You stayed because you need Nazafareen to kill Gaius."

"Ah, but your motives are pure, is that it? Saving the world from evil. Or is it simple revenge you seek?"

Darius scowled. The hair on her arms rose as power flowed

through the cuff. Little cracks appeared in the earth at Nicodemus's feet. His own expression darkened, then shifted to surprise.

"You're working earth power," he said softly.

Darius blinked. The ground settled itself. "So I am."

And then, like becoming suddenly aware of music that's been playing faintly in the background, Nazafareen realized that the full bond had returned. She could read Darius's emotions and physical sensations—lingering frustration, a blister on his left heel—and had been for some time now, at least since they'd washed up at the riverbank but possibly even before. It had been gradual and she'd been too focused on the drakes to notice.

"What does it mean?" she asked, fearing the answer.

"Only one thing," Nicodemus said grimly. "The barriers around the Kiln must be failing."

Darius muttered a curse. Nazafareen remembered the surge of power from Katrin when the shield almost failed. The way the wards of the Gale had shivered and flexed.

"It's our fault," she said. "We shouldn't have tampered with it."

Darius closed his eyes. "How long until they're gone completely?"

Nicodemus shrugged. "Another day? Perhaps a week or a month, if we're lucky. But if the wards are no longer dampening elemental power, I expect the storms are failing too." He paused. "Gaius and his followers will sense it. They'll realize what's happened and they won't hesitate to take advantage of it."

Darius cursed again, more bitterly.

"So if we go after Katrin and Galen, if we wait to have the brute force of the talismans on our side, he could be gone by the time we return," Nazafareen said.

Nicodemus didn't reply.

"Then I say we dig him out of his burrow," she said. "Finish this while we still can. If he gets out of the Kiln, countless more will die before we stop him."

Darius blew out a slow breath. "Is your power returning too?" he asked Nicodemus.

The Vatra gave a thin smile. "Yes. I would demonstrate, but...."

"No need," Darius said quickly. He looked at Nazafareen. "If we go in, can you break their flows?"

She nodded. Her breaking magic drew on the sun, which now hung directly overhead. It sizzled in her veins and marrow. "I can obliterate them."

He fingered a knife, then slid it back into the sheath and turned to Nicodemus.

"Any second thoughts?"

"None," Nicodemus said with a level gaze. "And you?"

"I just want to kill the bastard." Darius's tone softened. "Look, I'm sorry for what I said before. I was being a prick."

Nicodemus inclined his head. "No apology necessary."

"Let's do it then. Which way?"

"Across the plain."

They walked for an hour, slaking their thirst from the rapidly shrinking pools of water. The ground rose and became rougher, with sheer pinnacles of sandstone rising up like sentinels. Nicodemus stopped in the shade of a large boulder and pointed west.

"Do you see that rock about three leagues off? Gaius's burrow lies beneath it."

Nazafareen stared at the dark mass. It thrust straight up from the earth, unbroken and flat on top, a thousand paces high. The stone was the color of tarnished silver. She thought of Kallisto's words.

Three towers in opposition, one grey, two black.

It did look a bit like a tower, though one forged by the geological forces of the Kiln. But she didn't see how that knowledge helped them, nor where the other two towers might be found.

"How do we get in without being seen?"

"Leave it to me." Nicodemus squinted at the valley. "I have a good idea where to find Gaius's sentries. Will you give me a knife?"

Darius stared at him. Then he reached into his boot and took out the eel knife Nicodemus had been carrying when they found him near the Gale.

"You swear you didn't kill Sakhet-ra-katme?"

"I swear I didn't. Though Nazafareen was right. I'm to blame for her death." Nicodemus paused. "I'd rather have the other one, if you don't mind. Silver-chased handle?"

Darius chewed the corner of his mouth, then produced the second blade. Nicodemus eyed it with a funny expression, half amused, half abashed.

"I stole this too," he admitted. "It belonged to Meb. If I ever run into her, I'll give it back." He slid the blade into his coat pocket. "I meant to ask, what happened to her?"

"She went with the Marakai," Nazafareen said.

The Vatra smiled and for a moment, his face didn't look so hungry. He held out Sakhet's knife, hilt first, but Darius pushed it back.

"Take them both. Always better to have a spare."

Nicodemus accepted with a slight dip of his chin.

"I have to scout alone. Do you trust me?"

"Yes," Nazafareen said without hesitation.

After a fraction of a second, Darius nodded.

Nicodemus turned and loped off, his cloak vanishing against the landscape. Nazafareen's head throbbed like a rotten tooth. She couldn't imagine how the Vatras lived out here. It was two degrees short of hell.

She stared at the pinnacle of rock and felt an instant of vertigo. Yes, there was a darkness lurking beneath it, a malignancy. She could sense it in her bones.

"What's wrong?" Darius asked, concern in his eyes.

"Nothing. I'm fine."

"You're not. You can't conceal it from me, Nazafareen."

She looked at him. "The breaking magic. Does it leak through our bond?" She'd never asked him this question outright before, though she'd wondered.

He seemed to frame his response carefully. "Not the magic itself, but its effect on you."

"The anger, you mean."

"Partly." He studied her. "Right now, I can feel you responding to something. Is it a talisman?"

"I...I don't know." Her head pounded. The blackness of the void rose in her throat like acid. "I don't think so. This is something different." She gave a weak laugh. "The only way I can describe it is pure evil, Darius."

He didn't smile. "I believe you."

She looked away. "I hope I can find the source of it."

What she didn't tell him was that it stirred up her own streak of cruelty. Not evil. Even on her worst days, she didn't believe that. She was a force for right, a champion of the weak.

I am not like Domitia, she thought. Whatever Nicodemus thinks.

But part of her was also no longer bound by traditional morality. Part of her would balance the scales no matter the cost.

Part of her would enjoy it.

She tore her gaze from the jagged tooth of rock and met Darius's eyes. He knew. How he still loved her was one of life's great mysteries. The pain in her head eased a fraction.

"My mother was a hard woman too," he said softly. "Fearsome, even. I wish I'd known her better."

"She tried to stop me when I left," Nazafareen said. "To talk me out of it."

She sensed his surprise. They both knew Delilah had never liked her much.

"She said my hatred would only poison me and I should let it go."

Darius gave a sad laugh. "That doesn't sound like my mother."

"It's true."

"She gave me my set of woodworking tools. Victor kept offering me a sword."

Grief tightened her chest and Nazafareen realized it was not simply her own, but his as well.

They shared memories of Delilah and Tethys until Nicodemus materialized like a wraith out of the desert and dropped a pair of shadowtongue cloaks at their feet. One had a splash of fresh blood on the hood. Darius arched an eyebrow, but she sensed he was impressed.

Nazafareen threw the cloak across her shoulders. It was made for a taller person and the hem dragged on the ground. She expected it to be suffocating, but the cloak felt light as air and shielded her from the worst of the sun. Nicodemus handed her a water skin and she drank gratefully. Then they crept through folds of earth toward the towering rock pinnacle. Half a league away, Nicodemus stopped. He pulled aside a patch of bramble to reveal a dark hole leading into the earth.

"This is where I found the sentries," he said. "The bodies are over there."

Nazafareen glanced at another patch of bushes a few paces away. Two pairs of soft boots stuck out.

Nicodemus crouched down and used his finger to draw a diagram in the dust.

"This tunnel runs to the burrow. It has several chambers. I can't be sure which one he'll be in. But he's home. The Praetorians wouldn't have been guarding this exit if he wasn't." He sketched a series of interconnecting circles. Two had similar passages leading north and south. "If we get separated, these are the ways out."

Darius glanced at the diagram, memorizing it in an instant. "Understood."

"Who else is inside besides your brother?" Nazafareen asked.

"Gaius's wives and kids. At least a dozen."

Children. Her heart sank. No matter what, she wouldn't harm a child. And it didn't sound like his wives had any choice in the matter, either.

"Will they resist?"

"I doubt it. They hate him. Once I've found Atticus, I'll try to get them to safety."

"What about the Praetorians?" Darius asked.

"There are usually four or five at most. You'll know them by the ritual burns on their faces. It's a requirement to enlist. Gaius says it's so they never forget what the other clans did to us. But he has no reason to expect an attack. If anything, he might think Domitia and I succeeded in bringing down the Gale." Nicodemus moved toward the tunnel, then turned back to Darius. "Be careful if you use earth. I don't fancy being buried alive."

"Nor do I," Darius agreed. "I'll stick with my knives."

"Good."

Nicodemus seemed about to say something more. For a brief moment, he hesitated. But then he dropped down and crawled into the passageway. Nazafareen went next, Darius behind her. Darkness closed in after just a few paces. She crept blindly, following the soft scuffles ahead. The shaft had a downward slant and the air was suffocating. Sweat ran down her face, soaking her tunic. She could feel the breaking power gathering inside her, seeking an outlet, and the rage rising with it.

They crawled until her stump bled from the sharp stones lining the floor of the tunnel. At last, a faint light appeared ahead —enough to see that Nicodemus had stopped. He waited in silence for a long moment, then eased himself out into a larger chamber. Nazafareen slid forward and stepped out of the way as Darius emerged behind her.

They stood in a hard-packed dirt chamber a dozen paces wide with three other tunnels branching off in different directions. A tight rock chimney pierced the ceiling, admitting a shaft of anemic sunlight. Dust motes drifted in the stuffy air. Nicodemus crept to one of the adjoining passages, then beckoned. Nazafareen and Darius followed, passing more empty chambers with interlinked tunnels just high enough to walk at a crouch. The shafts of light were few and far between, leaving the rest of the burrow in gloom.

There wasn't a stick of anything that could be considered furniture or art or tools. If these were sleeping areas, the occupants must curl up on the bare ground. Nazafareen figured they'd started at the periphery of the rock tower and were circling inward. She tried to remember the map Nicodemus had drawn, but she'd lost her bearings in the maze of rooms. This didn't trouble her. They would keep moving, keep hunting, until Gaius was cornered.

He was here somewhere. She could sense it.

As they went deeper into the warren, she noticed a foulness to the air. It smelled like the lair of a large carnivore. Bones littered some of the chambers. The stench intensified and Nazafareen pressed a hand to her mouth. The body of a Vatra lay curled in one of the doorways. She stepped around it, her gorge rising. It was impossible to tell if it had been a man or woman. The flesh had mummified in the dry heat, though rich red hair still clung to the scalp.

She looked at Darius. His face was calm, watchful, though he was coiled and ready to explode into violence, just as she was. In a distant chamber, she heard a baby crying, a thin, monotonous wail, though it was impossible to tell which direction it came from.

Nazafareen pointed at the body and raised her eyebrows in a question. Nicodemus stepped close, his voice the barest whisper.

"Someone must have pissed Gaius off. He leaves the bodies where they fall as a reminder."

She felt Darius's disgust. Suddenly, Nicodemus made a sharp gesture, melting into the shadows. Darius followed, but Nazafareen, who was staring at the corpse with morbid fascination, was slower to react.

A face appeared around the corner of the passage. A child. It was thin and ragged. She saw a flash of white skin. A mouth falling open in surprise. Then it was gone.

Her rage ramped up a notch. Not at the child, but at the fact that children were forced to live in this house of horrors.

"Ah well," Darius said softly. "They were bound to notice us sooner or later."

A dagger materialized in his hand. With a rasp that sounded thunderous in the silence, Nazafareen eased Nemesis from the baldric over her shoulder. She felt at ease with the sword now, with its weight and balance. They understood each other.

The baby's cry cut off sharply, as though stifled by a hand.

And the Praetorians came.

Boots padded toward the chamber from four intersecting passages. Without a word, the three of them formed a triangle, backs pressed together. One of Darius's knives flew into the mouth of the tunnel ahead. A Vatra stumbled into the light, the hilt buried in his throat. Half his face was a melted mask of shiny, taut scar tissue. His mouth worked silently, the left side pulling down in a grimace.

Then six others burst through holding crude spears. Fire magic ignited and Nazafareen snuffed it with casual contempt. She hacked at anything that moved, anything beyond their little circle. A stone spearpoint thrust at her face. She sliced the shaft in half, then took the Vatra's head on the backswing. Blades flashed in the darkness. Her link with Darius allowed them to fight as one mind in two bodies—just as they had in another place and time when they served the Empire as Water Dogs. Few things could withstand a bonded pair for long. And Nicodemus was as hard as they came, a ruthless and efficient killer.

One by one, the Praetorians fell. And then it was over, quiet save for the harsh rasp of her own breath. Nazafareen threw off her cloak. She was drenched in sweat. Darius lay on his back, a Vatra sprawled across him. In his death throes, the Praetorian had lashed out with the butt of his spear and landed a lucky blow. Darius was alive, she knew, but unconscious. Nicodemus knelt down and felt his pulse.

"Just a crack to the head," he said with a shaky grin. "I've had worse. Good thing he's got a thick skull."

She'd taken half a step toward them when a soft voice came from the shadows.

"What have you done?"

A man stood in the doorway. He had large, wide-spaced eyes of the palest blue. It took Nazafareen a moment to grasp what was so strange about them. He lacked both eyebrows and lashes, though his face was otherwise unremarkable. If she hadn't known better, Nazafareen would have guessed his age at forty, give or take a decade in either direction. He wore no crown or other adornment, though swaths of bare skull cut through his red hair. He wore a dirty, shapeless tunic and trousers. A girl stood behind him, collarbones jutting from a sunken chest.

Nazafareen's breaking magic sniffed the air. It found nothing. But the sight of him fanned the flames of her hatred. She didn't merely want him dead. She wanted him dead slowly, painfully. The desire was sharp and physical, almost akin to lust.

His gaze swept across the heap of bodies without pausing. In the shadowtongue cloak, with the hood fallen across his face, Darius looked like one of the Praetorians. Then Gaius registered Nazafareen. His eyes narrowed.

"A mortal." Gaius cocked his head. "Or are you?"

"Get away from him," Nicodemus barked at the girl hovering behind Gaius. "Run. Now!"

She stared at them but didn't move.

"Have you truly turned on your own people?" Gaius said softly. "After all I've done for you. Cared for your crippled brother as if he were my own son. Avenged your mother when the Kiln took her." He held out his palms. "All this time, I prayed for your return. The wards are failing, Nicodemus. Our long exile is coming to an end. Why do you wish me harm?"

Nicodemus eyed him with deep hatred. "You're the reason we're stuck in this hellhole. I know the truth now. You started the war. Over nothing!"

"I don't know who told you that, but they lied." Gaius's voice was calm, persuasive. "You weren't there, but I was. The other clans grew jealous of our ability to make talismans. They resented our beautiful new city. I did everything I could to hold the alliance together." Sorrow made his voice quaver. "They united against us. We dared to fight back, so they punished us with the Kiln. You can't imagine the slaughter...."

"You are so full of shit," Nicodemus spat.

"All I have left is my long memory. Memory of the truth. I swore to never forget. To pass the knowledge down to the next generations, so they knew the other clans couldn't be trusted. And now they've poisoned you too."

Nicodemus hesitated, but then he looked at the girl and his resolve seemed to harden.

"I don't care what happened a thousand years ago. I don't care if you were a good king or a tyrant. All I know is that you're a monster now."

Gaius looked stricken, but Nazafareen could see the artifice in his expression. "Don't do this, Nicodemus. We can leave together." He glanced quickly at Nazafareen. "Even the mortal, if she's your new pet."

Enough is enough, she thought.

"Whatever your other crimes, you're responsible for the mass murder of the Danai," Nazafareen snapped. "Your own daughter admitted as much. She said she brought the justice of Gaius Julius Caesar Augustus. Well, you can face *my* justice now and I'm afraid you'll find it is equally harsh."

"Killed the Danai?" He spread his hands. "How could I have done such a thing? I am a prisoner of the Kiln."

"You ordered Domitia to carry out your dirty work," Nicodemus growled. "Just as you always have."

"Domitia is her own woman, we both know that." And now Gaius grinned, the façade slipping away. He had pointy yellow eyeteeth. "But if I *had* given such an order, surely you see the necessity. The Danai are vermin. Better if they're wiped off the face of the earth."

Nazafareen's bloody hand tightened around her sword.

"Guess why I'm here," she said.

Gaius turned to stare at her and she thought she saw a flicker of recognition, just for an instant. Then it was gone. He studied her with eyes like empty holes.

"What's your name, mortal?"

She said nothing.

"I could make do with you, even if you are maimed." He glanced at the girl beside him. "Would you like another sister? A new playmate?"

The girl swallowed, her gaze rooted to the ground.

Gaius smiled at Nazafareen. "Of course, if you produce any whelps, I'll have to smother them in the cradle. It wouldn't do to pollute the bloodlines."

The hatred rose in her, hatred and rage, but beneath it lurked the cold black emptiness of the void.

This is what I was born to do.

She shared a look with Nicodemus.

Now.

She leapt over the body of a Praetorian, Nemesis whistling through the air. Gaius dodged to the side. She let the backswing carry her around and slashed at his throat. He twisted away at the last moment, her blade carving a shallow slice down his arm. She felt savage satisfaction.

He bleeds just like the rest of us.

Nicodemus's arm whipped back to throw Meb's knife. Gaius snatched it midair and lunged, burying the blade in Nicodemus's thigh. Bone cracked. He gave a hoarse scream. With the sound still echoing in Nazafareen's ears, Gaius backhanded him with such force he flew across the chamber and bounced off the far wall.

She'd never seen anyone move so fast, not even Darius.

Gaius grinned at her. She grinned back. In that fleeting moment, they recognized something in each other.

The chamber snapped into sharp focus. She could smell his body, stale and unwashed; see the marbled irises of his pale blue eyes. No flames danced there. He was just a very old daēva.

She raised Nemesis and he moved like a snake, ducking under her sword and dragging her to the ground. She landed on her back, crushed beneath his weight, sword arm pinned over her head. He ripped her tunic down the front. Carrion breath hit her face.

"You'll call me husband," he murmured, a sick light in his eyes. "Or you'll beg for death."

Nazafareen spat in his face.

Gaius slapped her hard. Then he blinked in surprise. A rivulet of blood trickled down his cheek. Over his shoulder, Nazafareen glimpsed the girl. She held a rock in her hand. She started to back away, eyes wide, and Gaius twisted around and caught her by the neck. Bone snapped. The rock fell from limp fingers. With teeth bared, Nazafareen freed her left arm. Fingers scrabbled in the dirt for her sword. They brushed something hard, and then the hilt nestled in her palm.

When Gaius turned back, she slid Nemesis into his gut. He croaked in surprise. She kicked him off, wrenched the sword free, and stabbed him again. For an instant, she saw the flickering outline of a crown over his head, a coiled serpent with jeweled eyes, but it had no substance.

Fire gathered within him and she snapped the flows like threads. His eyes widened.

Nazafareen laid Nemesis against his throat.

"You asked my name."

His lips worked soundlessly.

"I am Breaker."

Nemesis rose and fell. The sword pierced the thick muscle of his heart and the image of the crown winked out. Gaius's mouth hung slack, his eyes glazed with death. Yet still she stabbed him until her arm was slick with blood and it pooled beneath them both, black in the half-light.

Nazafareen rocked back on her heels, her breath coming in harsh gasps. Up close, she could see that his skull was lumpy and misshapen with scar tissue.

She knew now why Nicodemus had chosen her.

Because I'm not a hero. Because I am darkness and death, though of a different sort than Gaius.

Weariness covered her shoulders like a heavy mantle. Nemesis slipped from cramped fingers. On the other side of the chamber, Nicodemus stirred weakly. Nazafareen wondered if she'd have to fight more Praetorians to get them out of there. She crawled over to Darius, touched his cheek.

"Don't make me drag you through that tunnel," she said. "I'm too tired."

He didn't answer, but his heart beat strong and steady. She loved him so much it hurt, and Nazafareen felt the darkness leave her.

There are things worth dying for, but hatred isn't one of them.

Who had said that?

Culach, she suddenly remembered. *When I left him at Val Moraine.*

Perhaps. But I didn't die. I—

A soft sound made her turn. Gaius was on his feet, standing

over her. He held Nemesis in his hand. His face was a mask of blood, but he was very much alive.

Impossible.

The blade slid into her chest between the top ribs, nicking bone as it went. She felt an instant of searing pain, then a deep, numbing cold. A heaviness in her limbs. Nazafareen sat back against the dirt wall, coppery warmth on her lips. Gaius watched her with his pale eyes.

That ghostly crown flickered once, twice, and vanished.

"You shouldn't have come here, Breaker." His lips parted in a red smile. "It's a bad place to die."

He seized Nicodemus by the hair, dragging him through the low doorway. The light dimmed. Darius slept. Nazafareen touched the hilt of the sword in her breast.

"Shit," she whispered.

₰ 27 ₰

COLLAR THEM ALL

F ear blanketed the city of Delphi like one of the pea-soup fogs that crept in from the Cimmerian Sea. People huddled in their homes and only a handful of listless shoppers wandered through the usually bustling agora. Dramatic performances at the amphitheater were cancelled until further notice. The gates to the city remained open, but the usual traffic—farmers, merchants, travelers from the south—had dried to a trickle.

Since the army marched out four days before to fight the witches, no word had come about the fate of fathers and sons, brothers and husbands, though a thousand furtive whispers passed between alleyways and over garden gates. The Danai had destroyed the Greeks to a man. No, the Pythia had led them to victory and now she marched on Samarqand. Strange beasts had been sighted in the Umbra, flying west from the darklands. A few even claimed the Vatras had returned, though these rumors were quickly dismissed as wild imaginings. And so on.

When the first riders appeared, the city heaved a collective exhale of relief. The infantry marched not far behind and were greeted with great cheers and garlands of flowers thrown at their feet. Then came the wagons bearing the injured and dead and the crowds lining the road grew somber, although the casualties were not as severe as most had feared.

They waited for a glimpse of the Pythia, but she was nowhere to be seen.

The infantry and cavalry peeled off toward the barracks, along with most of the wagons, until only one remained. It was escorted up the ring road to the Acropolis by an honor guard of grim-faced Shields of Apollo. Necks craned, but the contents of the wagon were covered. The Archon Basileus rode a charger alongside it, staring straight ahead. He made no announcement and the crowds grew thin, finally wandering back to their homes to speculate on what had occurred. The wagon bumped to a stop in front of the Temple of Apollo and two bodies were carried inside.

THENA THREW OFF THE SHROUD AND DREW A DEEP BREATH. SHE stared down at the red-soaked gown with distaste. The wine fumes had sickened her in the close confines of the wagon. She touched the serpent brooch pinned at her shoulder and the illusion vanished. Blue eyes became brown again. Her face shifted back into its usual proportions.

Basileus watched with hooded, unreadable eyes, though she saw his shoulders relax. The transformation had been so perfect, even he had his doubts.

It had gone off without a hitch. When the Pythia entered her tent, Thena had thrown a cup of wine in her face from the golden chalice. Only a few drops touched her tongue, but it was enough to render her senseless. It had been a simple matter to collar her after that. Thena had stared down at the Pythia for a long moment, imagining the entertainments to come.

Then she'd taken the brooch from the Pythia's gown and

opened her mind to it, just as she'd done with the bracelets. Thena had been most uncertain about that part of the plan, but it turned out to be simple. She'd studied the Pythia's features and imagined them as her own. There was no mirror in the tent so she couldn't be sure it worked, but when she touched her face, it felt different. The nose was longer, the lips wider and thinner.

The true test had come when she walked outside. She could tell from the look of fear in the eyes of the Shields that they were not looking at Thena. They were looking at the Oracle of Delphi.

Nico's knife had plunged into the wineskin held tight under her arm, though the flames had been a surprise. Her scream then had been all too real. But they never touched her, and then it was done. The Pythia had been rolled into a rug and carried out in the guise of Thena's burned body, while Thena played the dead Pythia.

All a show for one person—Galen.

She'd nearly forgotten to remove the bracelet, which would have been fatal. Out of everyone present, Galen was the only one who would have known she still lived. But at the last moment before she left the tent, the god whispered in her ear, reminding her. She'd hidden it away in the same box that held the extra collars. The instant the gold stopped touching her skin, Galen vanished from her mind. It came as a relief. His misery was like an annoying wasp buzzing around her head.

She didn't understand why the witch had to be deceived— surely it would have been simpler to kill the Pythia while she lay sleeping rather than stage a charade of murder—but it must be part of the god's plan. One day, all the witches would be collared, including Darius.

Especially Darius.

Now she walked over to the rolled-up rug, which was rocking back and forth. Muffled cries came from inside. Thena kicked it with a slippered foot, unwinding it across the floor of the adyton.

Domitia lay there, red-faced and sweating. She raised a hand and frustrated rage contorted her face.

"Come now," Thena said in a reasonable tone. "You know you cannot use sorcery against me."

The witch ignored her. "Basileus," she growled, touching the iron around her neck with trembling fingers. "If you do not remove this instantly, you will die the most painful—"

Thena administered a sharp lesson and Domitia subsided, biting her lip until it bled. Rage simmered through the bracelet as Thena stuffed a gag in her mouth.

"Do not make threats you cannot carry out," she said sternly. "The harder you fight, the worse it will go for you. Obedience is the only way to avoid punishment. I shouldn't have to explain this. Now go sit in the corner quietly until I call for you."

A second lesson was required, but Domitia finally complied. She watched with a venomous expression as Thena approached the Archon Basileus. They eyed each other with mutual distrust.

"Leave her to me," Thena said. "She will be properly broken in no time. But for now, we must restore order to the city."

His gaze sharpened at the note of command in her voice. "You do understand the division of authority? Lord Nicodemus was quite explicit in his instructions, and he will be most displeased if they are not carried out to the letter."

Thena nodded with the proper degree of deference this time and Basileus looked appeased.

"We shall do well together." She flashed her dimples. "Apollo has ordained it. I hope your faith is strong, Archon. The god sees into men's hearts."

Basileus gave her a stony look, peering down his long nose. For now, she needed him to control the army and nobles, but he would learn where the true power lay soon enough.

"I will send criers across the city ordering all free citizens to assemble in the plaza," he said. "Under pain of death."

Thena clasped her skirts, gazing up at him through her lashes with just the right degree of uncertainty. "Of course, you have far more experience in such matters than I do, Archon. But the people are afraid and fear can make men unpredictable. They might riot, or even revolt outright."

Basileus considered this. He was not a stupid man, merely corrupt and ambitious.

"Perhaps we should take a lighter touch at first," Thena continued. "Tell the people it is Apollo's will and that the Oracle has important news to share."

He nodded thoughtfully. "A mailed fist in a velvet glove."

"Indeed." Thena beamed. "You are a wise man. I must prepare for the assembly, then. Would you excuse us, Archon?"

He cast a furtive glance at Domitia and seemed eager to be on his way.

"For the Gods' sake, keep her manacled," he muttered. "With a permanent guard. If she ever...." He trailed off and swallowed, looking a bit green.

"Don't worry. I have long experience managing witches."

"And you set one free!" he burst out.

Thena's smile slipped. "That was different. She is in good hands."

Basileus actually laughed at that. Then he strode to the door, his red cloak billowing across the stone floor. A dozen Shields of Apollo waited outside with spell dust should it be needed, but Thena felt her old confidence returning. Everything the god promised her had come to pass.

And she was the best at breaking witches. Everyone said so.

She crouched down before the former Pythia, seizing a hank of flame-red hair and tipping her face back.

"I'll take you to your quarters shortly," she said softly. "We shall get to know each other very well in the coming weeks. Better than you've ever known anyone in your life. I already know your true name. Domitia. If you're good, I might even let you keep it."

Thena cocked her head. The Pythia looked smaller with the collar around her slender white neck. Her blue eyes were no longer intimidating but filled with uncertainty. To think Thena had once scurried to do her bidding!

"I'm glad we have a little time alone together before we must face the multitudes. I've thought often of this moment. But it is not for me to judge you." She gave a slow smile. "No, I am merely Apollo's instrument. Isn't that what you told me once?"

Muffled noises came through the gag. Thena ignored them, dragging Domitia into the corridor by her hair.

"All is well," she assured the Shields outside with a tight smile. "You will stay at your post. This is part of the training."

They exchanged quick looks but obeyed her.

The few initiates who remained in the temple scattered out of the way as Thena hauled Domitia to the storeroom, maintaining a steady flow of muscle-cramping pain through the collar to keep her docile.

The brazen bull waited, mouth agape. Thena could already hear the terrible bellows that would come from the device concealed within its throat. She kicked the panel open and bundled Domitia into the bull's belly, slamming it shut against her frantic struggling. Strands of sweaty hair hung in Thena's face. She brushed them aside and composed herself.

"Do not fear his judgment. If you are truly innocent, the god will spare you," Thena said loudly. "May you be purified, *witch*."

It wasn't quite as satisfying as Thena had imagined. Yes, she could inflict the sensation of fire on Domitia's body, but there was no smoke, no stench of burning skin.

No ugly scars.

But that could be rectified when they had more time together.

After a while, Thena grew bored and opened the panel. Domitia's chest heaved and Thena yanked out the gag. It would be a shame if she suffocated. A Vatra witch could be very useful once she'd been properly trained.

"Oh well," Thena said. "I guess you weren't innocent after all."

"Fuck you," Domitia snarled. "You'll never break me. Never. You have no idea what—"

Thena shook her head and put the gag back on, tighter this time.

"You will address me as Mother from now on," she said. Then she bent over and kissed the gag where Domitia's lips would be. Humiliated outrage rolled through the link between bracelet and collar. And a touch of fear....

The door banged open and Thena quickly straightened. The Archon Basileus stood in the doorway, his brows rising as he took in the bull and the open panel, but he said only, "They are ready for us."

Thena blinked. More time must have passed than she thought. *Hours*.

Basileus gestured and four burly Shields of Apollo trotted inside and seized Domitia by the arms, their gazes fixed straight ahead. She fought like a wildcat until one cuffed her hard on the side of the head.

Domitia had never inspired love among her soldiers, Thena reflected. They were not sorry to see her brought down, and the hatred she'd stoked for the witches was coming back to haunt her.

"Keep her out of sight for now," Basileus said. "But close by."

Captain Leonidas nodded curtly and they dragged Domitia into the corridor.

"Play your part and I will play mine," Basileus said to Thena with quiet menace once they were gone. "But if you think of betraying me, you will find yourself outmatched. I have a vast network of spies and allies, both high and low. That crowd outside could easily be turned into a mob demanding your pretty little head."

Thena smiled sweetly. "My loyalty is first to the god and second to Delphi. If you rule justly, Archon, as I'm certain you will, there is nothing to fear from me. I am merely a simple farm girl."

Basileus looked as if he doubted this, but he gave a gruff nod and straightened his heavy gold chain of office.

"The people grow restless. We should go." He turned to the door and although he tried to conceal it, Thena saw an excited glint in his eye. How long had he schemed for this moment?

Ah well, she thought with amused indulgence. Let him enjoy it while it lasts.

She followed him to the pillared portico facing the plaza. Crowds filled it from edge to edge, spilling down the outer stairways that led to the streets below the Acropolis. She strode halfway down the steps and paused, Basileus at her side.

"Free citizens of Delphi," she shouted in a clear, commanding voice, raising her arms to the sky. A sudden breeze whipped her white gown around her legs. "Heed me now."

The crowd hushed, watching with expectant faces. She pointed to the words inscribed on the lintel of the temple.

"*Know thyself.* That truth is meant to lead us from darkness to light. And yet we have been deceived! A poison has eaten away at the heart of our fair city." She made a sharp gesture and four Shields dragged a bound Domitia from the Temple and threw her down at Thena's feet. Confused murmurs and a few shocked gasps broke the silence.

"This creature was no true Oracle. She did not speak for Apollo. She is a *witch!*"

Thena let this sink in. Jeers and angry shouts erupted. A few stones flew through the air and Thena took a hasty step back. The Shields pushed the crowd back with their spears, bellowing for order.

"Enough," Basileus snapped, flourishing his crimson cloak. "We will not submit to anarchy. The Archon Eponymous is fled. I therefore invoke my authority to name this woman the new Pythia. She speaks for the god!"

Thena raised her arms, expecting to bask in the adulation of the crowd, but they stayed silent.

"Apollo has revealed his will to me," she said, raking the front rows with her gaze. "The Tyrants must return. We must place our faith in the Archon Basileus. Only strength and unity can save us from the witches."

Feet shuffled. People shared doubtful glances. They remembered the Tyrants all too well. This would not do, Thena decided. She strode over to Domitia and seized the manacles binding her hands, dragging her forward. Those closest shrank away, causing a ripple to flow through the densely packed plaza. A child began to cry.

Thena held up the ring of keys. "Shall I unchain her? She works fire. Shall I let her burn you up? Or will you submit to the will of the god?" Stupid, cowlike faces stared back at her. Thena's temper snapped. Spittle flew from her mouth as she turned to one of the Shields. "Tell them what you saw."

The soldier swallowed. "She speaks truth. The Oracle worked fire."

"You see? We are punished for our heresy. We have sunk into sin and dissolution. But we can still be saved. We can still walk in the light!"

For a moment, the crowd hesitated. A few looked ready to riot. But then a half-hearted cheer began toward the back and was taken up through the ranks. It never swelled to the feverish pitch Thena had hoped for, but it would do for now.

Basileus leaned toward her. "Let's quit while we're ahead. Our authority can be shored up later."

Thena gave a brief nod. "I will make a pronouncement shortly," she shouted. "Return to your homes. All will be well, children of Delphi."

The crowds shuffled off under the watchful eyes of the Shields. Thena made her way down the cramped staircase to the adyton, the navel of the world, breathing deeply of the fumes that wafted from cracks in the stone. She perched on the tripod and closed her eyes.

"Come to me, Son of Delos," she whispered. "O Bringer of Light, lift the scales from my eyes. Give me your guidance."

And Apollo did.

🦋 28 🦋

A TEST OF FAITH

Awareness returned to Darius in a sudden rush.

He shoved away the corpse that sprawled across him and sat up, adrenaline lighting his nerves on fire. Dim light filtered into the burrow from one of the chimneys. A mass of flies crawled over seven more bodies on the earthen floor, the blood beneath them already congealed. One was a scrap of a girl with bright auburn hair. Her head was twisted at an unnatural angle.

How long have I been out?

He forced down a wave of nausea. Something was wrong.

An emptiness.

A perfect, devastating quiet.

In this filthy little chamber, but also *inside him*.

It took Darius only a second to realize what it meant. He knew before he saw her.

The bond never lied.

And the bond was gone.

Nazafareen sat against the wall, her eyes half open. The hilt of a sword protruded from her chest. For one endless moment, the world tilted on its axis. Darius felt he might slide right over the edge. He crawled to her, animal sounds tearing from his throat.

Marble flesh met his touch, hard and cold. The emptiness spread like ink in water until it swallowed him whole.

He wrapped arms around her—both of them strong and whole now—rocking wordlessly back and forth.

He was supposed to be her protector. For years they'd ridden into battle together, facing down monsters and emerging bloodied but victorious. They were bonded—an intimate partnership that outsiders could never understand.

And with the bond, she would have lived as long as he did, hundreds of years—maybe more. Even in his darkest moments, Darius never imagined she would be gone before him.

But he had failed her in the worse way imaginable.

She had died alone, while he lay sleeping a few paces away.

Darius carefully drew Nemesis from its sheath in her body and put the tip to his own breast.

What if you cannot find her in the afterlife? What if she's gone on without you?

His hand trembled.

Black despair bubbled up.

It is only what you deserve, witch, Thena murmured in his ear. *You were sent to test my faith, and now yours is being tested.*

What will you do to get her back?

How far will you go?

Darius froze, the tip of the blade digging into his flesh.

A stone chamber, chains binding him and Thena's voice rising and falling as she related the tale of the star-crossed lovers, Eros and Psyche. The lamp and the drop of hot oil. The vows carelessly broken. But no, that wasn't the part that mattered. It's the end I want, he thought with a touch of madness. The very end of the story.

Psyche had performed three impossible tasks to win her husband back—including a journey to the Underworld to beg a favor from the Queen of the Dead.

The Drowned Lady.

Herodotus had spoken of her. So had Meb and Katrin. They'd met her. Talked to her.

She was real.

In that instant, Darius's despair hardened into something else.

He gently closed Nazafareen's eyes and cleaned Nemesis on his coat until the sword was spotless. Then he unbuckled the baldric and slung it over his own shoulder. He kissed her bloody lips. No taint of decay touched her, not yet.

"I'm bringing your sword," he whispered. "Wait for me."

Darius crawled out from the burrow, squinting after so long in darkness. The Vatras had left a clear trail heading east toward the Gale, but he would not follow. Revenge was meaningless. Instead, he made his way back to the Red Hills. The flood had emptied its wrath on the plain, leaving streams of muddy knee-high water in the canyons. He remembered the terrain and waded through them until he found the rocky overhang where they'd fought the drakes.

Darius ducked inside, the hard knot in his chest loosening. He'd been afraid it was still broken. But the surface of the gate was no longer black and still. A gleaming current flowed across it, giving off a green glow.

A doorway to the Dominion.

I'll find you, he thought grimly. You, who style yourself the Drowned Lady.

And I'll trade my soul for hers.

✻ 29 ✻

THE BEAST AT THE DOOR

"Where's my daughter?"

The words sliced through a haze of pain. Nicodemus's leg throbbed with infection. He lay on a flat rock, a crude litter nearby and the endless blue sky of the Kiln overhead. His teeth chattered despite the heat, chills wracking his body.

The last thing he remembered, Gaius was dragging him out of the burrow through the main tunnel and into the scorching sun. More Praetorians ran up and they'd beaten him until he passed out.

He smelled Gaius's breath, like rotten meat.

"You were wearing her cloak. Where the fuck is she?"

Nico's head rocked back as Gaius slapped him.

"Dead," he muttered through cracked, swollen lips. "She's dead."

Gaius's expression didn't change, but a muscle in his neck twitched. He leaned in until his face was inches away. His voice was deadly soft.

"Did you kill her?"

No, but she probably wishes I had.

Somehow he met Gaius's stare without flinching. "Do you really believe Domitia would let me?"

Gaius didn't reply, weighing him with those pale eyes. Suddenly, he reached out and squeezed Nico's shattered knee. The pain nearly made him black out again.

"Where are the talismans?"

"I don't know."

Gaius nodded. Without looking away from Nicodemus, he said, "Cut Aelia's arm off."

Aelia was one of his wives, tall and sturdy with flaming red hair and a nose that looked like it had been broken a few times. Gaius had claimed her when she was fifteen and she must be nearly Nico's age now, which meant she'd survived longer than most. A child clutched her skirts, eyes wide.

Now she screamed as two of the biggest Praetorians grabbed her. They called themselves Romulus and Remus after some old legend. Like Nico, they'd been orphaned at a tender age and lived on their own until Gaius found them. Rumor had it they stumbled on the nest of a queen wyrm, but instead of eating them, she'd nursed them until they could fend for themselves. Nico always thought the story was a load of horseshit, but he'd never say that to the brothers' faces. They were nasty specimens. One had burned the right side of his face, the other the left. It was the only way to tell them apart.

Now Remus pulled out a long, mottled knife.

"Please!" Nico begged, helpless rage and fear making his voice crack. "No, listen, please don't. There was one. The Valkirin. She made the rainstorm. I don't know where she is now, I swear it! You can cut me to pieces, just leave Aelia alone!"

Gaius held up a hand and Remus paused with the dull blade pressed against Aelia's shoulder. She licked her lips, staring straight ahead.

"One of the talismans is in the Kiln?"

"Yes, but she could be dead. I don't know, we were separated in the Red Hills. The flood washed her away."

Some nameless emotion flickered across Gaius's face. Hatred, and perhaps a touch of fear.

"Is it Freydis Sigurdadottir?"

Nico shook his head, sending a lance of pain through his temples. "Freydis died a long time ago. The power passed to one of her descendants. A woman named Katrin."

"What about the other two?"

Nico kept his voice and gaze level. "We never found them. Too much time has passed. The bloodlines are hopelessly tangled. The only one still alive was Sakhet-ra-katme. She killed herself when I found her."

"Sakhet." Gaius spoke the name like a curse. "If you're lying to me—"

"I'm not. I took her knife for a souvenir. It's the one with the eel hilt."

Gaius gestured to Romulus, who produced the eel knife and brought it over. Gaius examined it closely.

"It's Marakai work. Maybe it belonged to Sakhet." He tossed it into the air and caught it, then gave it back to Romulus. "Maybe not." Gaius spat in the sand. "I should kill you slowly, but you're the only one of us who's been beyond the Gale in a thousand years. You might be useful." He glanced at the litter and it erupted in flames, burning to ash in a matter of seconds. Gaius grinned. "But you'll have to walk from here."

Nicodemus leaned forward and gingerly put some weight on his good leg. The world spun around him, a blur of sky and sand. He had a fever, a bad one. And he'd had his ass kicked too many times to count in the span of a few days.

Nico gritted his teeth and forced himself to stand. The Kiln spread out before him, an empty wasteland for hundreds of leagues in all directions. The burrow was far behind and so were the Red Hills. He took a step and nearly pitched onto his face when a hand steadied his shoulder. He looked up and saw dark blue eyes in a thin face that sagged on the right side.

"Atticus," he whispered.

His brother had grown taller in the last two years, more man than boy now. Nico fought back tears. He'd been certain Atticus was dead.

"Keep up or I'll cut both your throats," Gaius said amiably.

He strode to the head of the column with Remus and Romulus. Altogether, Nico counted twenty-seven adults and nine children. The adults were a mixed bag. Nicodemus knew most of Gaius's wives, though not well. Other than Aelia, they were all closer to Atticus's age. The rest were Praetorians with shadowtongue cloaks and scarred faces.

Gaius had abandoned most of the Vatras, the families who struggled to survive each day, to the Kiln. Nico wasn't surprised.

"What happened to your leg?" Atticus asked, putting an arm around Nico to support his weight.

"Stabbed. I think my thighbone's fractured," Nico hissed between his teeth. "It's healing, but not well."

"You're burning up." Atticus frowned. He rooted inside a small bag that hung around his neck and produced a handful of leaves. "Chew this."

They were bitter, but Nico managed to swallow them.

"Are you a healer now?" he asked.

"I do what I can." Atticus lowered his voice. "Gaius only let me live because I saved two of his wives from dying in childbirth." The rest of the party was already moving ahead. "Come on, lean on me."

Atticus had a limp himself, the result of a wasting illness when he was nine. His gait was awkward, but he managed to support Nicodemus over the uneven ground.

I should have brought him with me in the first place, Nico thought, ignoring the bolts of pain shooting through his hip with each step. *He's stronger than I ever realized.* He glanced at his brother's profile, the lines around his mouth and eyes. *Or maybe he's just gotten tougher in the last two years.*

Remus turned to stare at them and Nicodemus waited until he looked away to speak again. "Do you know what happened to the friends I came with?"

And they were friends, as strange as it sounded. Nicodemus prayed they'd escaped somehow.

Atticus gave the barest nod. "The girl is dead. Gaius sent me in to make sure." His voice lowered. "He wouldn't go himself. I think he was a little afraid of her."

Dead. Nico's fingers dug into his brother's arm. The heat haze of the desert made the world look like it was swimming underwater. He struggled not to faint.

"And the other? The Danai?"

Atticus glanced around. Remus had turned away to laugh at some jest of his brother.

"I told them he was dead too," he whispered.

Nico felt a spark of hope. "But?"

"He wasn't."

Nicodemus let out a slow breath. "You did right."

His eyes fixed on Gaius, walking at the head of the column in his bloody tunic. The urge to seize fire and char him to ash was overwhelming. But Nico had gotten a close look at that tunic when Gaius interrogated him. It had more than a dozen holes across the chest and abdomen—all large enough to have come from Nazafareen's sword—yet Gaius had shaken off the wounds like they were insect bites. Now he showed no sign he'd been injured at all.

You should have told her, a voice whispered. *It's your fault she's dead.*

Nico had truly believed Nazafareen could kill him. It's why he *had* to make her believe Domitia was dead—so she'd go to the Kiln to vent her rage on Gaius.

But he'd been wrong about everything.

Once, he'd been driven by righteous anger at the other clans. He'd fantasized about getting revenge on them, making them suffer the way he had suffered. The way his mother had suffered when the queen wyrm got into their burrow.

That turned out to be wrong too, but his hatred remained, a hot coal in the center of his heart. Only this time, it was focused on the man who had lied to him. Who had used him, just as he used the others, for his own gratification.

If Nico attacked and failed, he knew they'd kill Atticus. So he'd bide his time until he discovered Gaius's secret and then he'd kill the motherfucker himself.

The party walked east, the sun at their backs. When Gaius called a stop, Atticus made a poultice from the leaves and bound it to Nico's leg with a scrap of cloth. It brought the swelling down and the bone began to knit itself together again, though he'd have an ugly scar. One more for the collection.

The route they took was farther south than the one he'd trekked with Nazafareen and the others, which had been roughly parallel with Delphi. If he'd been alone, Nico might have simply laid down to die. But he had his brother to think about, so he kept going, fighting the pain and fever and guilt for leading Nazafareen to her death. He lost track of time, walking when he was told to and dropping to the ground when they halted. Sometimes Gaius would come over and ask questions and Nicodemus would try to keep his lies straight. He paid little attention to their surroundings, so it was Atticus who saw it first.

"Look," his brother said, wonder in his voice.

Nico looked up wearily. They'd reached the edge of the Kiln, but only a few tattered rainclouds drifted along the border. The ground was torn up and muddy as a battlefield, with lakes of water in the low places, but there were no night-black funnels, no lances of lightning or screaming winds. Nico stared at it for a moment, uncomprehending.

"Someone did something they shouldn't have," Gaius said with a delighted laugh. "A little mouse gnawed a hole in the Gale. And that hole grew bigger and bigger."

The children stared at the green fields a few leagues beyond with huge, hungry eyes. In the distance, the Rock of Ariamazes rose above the walls of Samarqand. Gaius stared at it for a long moment. Then he chortled.

"Still standing after all this time. Who rules there now?"

Nico was a second too slow to respond, and Gaius casually backhanded him across the face.

"King Shahak," Nico replied, tasting blood. "He just took the throne."

Gaius seemed to find this uproariously funny. He laughed until tears streamed down his face.

"Poor bastard," he said at last. "What rotten luck."

I'll give him some crumbs of truth. Let him think I'm worth keeping alive.

"They say he's an alchemist," Nico said.

"One of those fools who tries to turn iron to gold?"

"No, the mortals discovered something they call spell dust. It works magic of a sort."

Gaius laughed again, but without humor. "Where does it come from?"

"No one knows."

"Someone knows." He peered at the Rock. "I told them I'd be back. I told them that." He turned to the Praetorians. "Our work was left unfinished," he said in a loud voice. "That doesn't seem right. Does it seem right to you?"

Fists pressed to hearts in a salute. Burned and scarred faces cracked into feral grins.

Nicodemus had never been to Samarqand, but he'd read accounts of what Gaius did there. A feeling of hopelessness nearly crushed him.

"I'm tired and thirsty," Gaius declared. "My feet hurt. I want a hot bath." He laughed. "And afterwards, we'll eat their fucking hearts."

His pale eyes turned to an ancient, gnarled oak and it exploded into flames. A singed bird fell to earth, one wing flapping pathetically.

"Let's go introduce ourselves to King Shahak." Gaius gave a happy sigh. "Persian hospitality was always legendary."

EPILOGUE

Nazafareen shuffled along next to an old woman with a kindly face. Dark pines shadowed the path through the woods, following the mossy banks of a stream. The light had no definite source though it was just enough to see by. She smelled the tang of saltwater.

She didn't remember coming here, but she knew one thing. She was not simply a visitor to the Dominion. Not passing through on a quick jaunt between gates.

This time, she was well and truly dead.

She knew because for the first time, she could *see* the other dead. They walked in clumps, not speaking but drawn inexorably toward the Cold Sea. Some were bloody and mangled from violent ends, others wasted from illness. A few paces in front of her, a mother carried an infant in her arms. They all had docile, vacant expressions like the old woman.

Nazafareen, on the other hand, was furious—mostly with herself.

Stabbed with my own damned sword.

She remembered those final moments with perfect clarity. The ghostly crown flickering over Gaius's head. Like a talisman that existed on two planes at once....

Movement in the trees caught her eye. *Shepherds*. The great hounds were keeping pace with their charges, herding them along like cattle. They padded through the dusky woods, triangular heads swiveling, sawtooth mouths panting.

She didn't see Darius or Nicodemus, so perhaps they were still alive. The thought of Darius was a knife to the heart—far worse than the wound she'd suffered from Gaius—and Nazafareen buried it quickly. She couldn't think of him now. If she did, her anger might weaken and it was the only thing she had left.

Then the trees thinned and she saw the Cold Sea ahead. A flat grey expanse, the far horizon obscured by mist. A line of boats waited on the shore.

Had the Viper come to this same place after he drowned in the burning sands? Had he stood and gazed at the shore, just as she did now? He must have. And yet he'd escaped the Shepherds and gone to ground.

Restless dead.

She could feel the tidal pull of the boats. A gentle voice called to her from the other side of the sea. The promise of peace. An end to pain and strife. Perhaps even a new beginning. Another name, in another place.

Bullshit.

She wouldn't try to return to the world of the living. Some part of her knew such a thing was impossible. The gates wouldn't let her pass. But she could do what Farrumohr had done.

And she knew where to find him.

Nazafareen slowed her steps, trying to look blank and biddable like the others. The old woman moved on ahead, a serene smile on her face.

She waited until a group of six newly dead plodded along, momentarily hiding her from the Shepherds. Then she slipped behind a towering spruce tree, pressing herself against the trunk until they'd passed. One of the hounds paused, sniffing the air. Nazafareen froze. After a long minute, it padded on.

Stupid creatures.

Death was a curious thing. She had no pulse to pound. No breath to catch in her throat. Yet she could still feel fear.

And a burning desire for retribution.

She slipped into the gloaming of the forest and ran, boots silent on the carpet of needles. She knew the shape of the mountain she sought and what lay in the valley beyond.

The House Behind the Veil.

When I've put an end to the Viper, I'll cross over, she thought. But not before.

Nazafareen ran and she didn't look back, not even when the Shepherds began to howl.

ABOUT THE AUTHOR

Kat Ross worked as a journalist at the United Nations for ten years before happily falling back into what she likes best: making stuff up. She's the author of the Fourth Element and Fourth Talisman fantasy series, the Gaslamp Gothic mysteries, and the dystopian thriller Some Fine Day. She loves myths, monsters and doomsday scenarios.

ALSO BY KAT ROSS

The Fourth Element Trilogy
The Midnight Sea
Blood of the Prophet
Queen of Chaos

The Fourth Talisman Series
Nocturne
Solis
Monstrum
Nemesis
Inferno

Gaslamp Gothic Series
The Daemoniac
The Thirteenth Gate
A Bad Breed
The Necromancer's Bride
Dead Ringer

Some Fine Day

CHARACTERS IN THE SERIES

Mortals

ARCHON BASILEUS. The head of civic religious arrangements in Delphi.

ARCHON EPONYMOS. The chief magistrate of Delphi.

HERODOTUS. A Greek scholar and former curator of the Great Library of Delphi.

IZAD ASABANA. A wealthy merchant and dealer in spell dust.

JAVID. A wind ship pilot from the Persian city of Samarqand.

KATSU. A Stygian thief-catcher.

KORINNA. An acolyte at the Temple of Delphi.

LEILA KHORRAM-DIN. Marzban's daughter.

MARZBAN KHORRAM-DIN. Asabana's alchemist.

NABU-BAL-IDINNA. An eccentric alchemist of the golden age of Samarqand who claimed to have traveled in the Dominion and met the Drowned Lady.

NAZAFAREEN. A wielder of negatory magic.

THE POLEMARCH. The commander of Delphi's armed forces.

PRINCE SHAHAK. Heir to the crown of Samarqand.

SAVAH SAYUZHDRI. Javid's old boss at the Merchants' Guild.

THENA. An acolyte at the Temple of Delphi.

Daēvas

Avas Danai (Children of Earth)

DARIUS. A daēva of House Dessarian who was born in the Empire on the other side of the gates.

DELILAH. Victor's wife and Darius's mother.

GALEN. Victor's son with Mina. Half-brother to Darius.

MITHRE. Victor's second in command.

MINA. A Danai hostage at Val Moraine.

RAFEL/NIKIAS. A daēva who was kidnapped by the Pythia.

TETHYS. Victor's mother, head of House Dessarian and one of the Matrium.

VICTOR. Darius's father.

Avas Valkirins (Children of Air)

CULACH. Once the heir to Val Moraine, he was blinded and lost his power.

DANÍEL/DEMETRIOS. Halldóra's grandson and heir, he was abducted and brainwashed by the Pythia.

EIRIK. Culach's father and the former lord of Val Moraine.

ELLARD. Galen's friend. Raised as a hostage at House Dessarian in exchange for Mina.

FRIDA: Halldóra's second in command.

GERDA. Culach's great-great-grandmother.

HALLDÓRA. Mistress of Val Tourmaline.

KATRIN. Culach's former lover.

PETUR. Culach's best friend. He tried to kill Nazafareen and was killed by Galen.

RUNAR. Lord of Val Petros.

STEFÁN. Lord of Val Altair.

Sofia: One of Halldóra's riders.

Avas Marakai (Children of Water)

Kasaika. Captain of the *Asperta*. Selk Marakai.
Mafuone. Captain of the *Chione*. Sheut Marakai.
Mebetimmunedjem, a.k.a. Meb the Mouse. A 12-year-old orphan of the Selk who does grunt work on the *Asperta*.
Sakhet-ra-katme. The oldest Marakai and one of the original talismans. A distant ancestor of Meb.

Avas Vatras (Children of Fire)

Atticus. Nicodemus's younger brother.
Domitia, a.k.a. The Pythia, a.k.a. the Oracle of Delphi. Gaius's daughter.
Farrumohr, a.k.a. the Viper. Gaius's advisor. Haunts Culach's dreams.
Gaius Julius Caesar Augustus, a.k.a Caligula. Former king of the Vatras.
Romulus and Remus. Two of Gaius's Praetorians.
Nicodemus. A survivor of the Kiln.

Maenads

Kallisto. Head of the Cult of Dionysus, she seeks to protect the talismans from harm. Her followers are Rhea, Charis, Cyrene and Megaera. Two others, twins named Alcippe and Adeia, were killed by the Pythia's soldiers.

GLOSSARY

Abbadax. Winged creatures used as mounts by the Valkirins. Intelligent and vicious, they have scaled bodies and razor-sharp feathers to slash opponents during aerial combat.

Adyton. Innermost chamber of the Temple of Apollo, where the Pythia issues prophecies and receives supplicants.

Anuketmatma. Worshipped by the Selk Marakai as the spirit of storms, she takes the form of a small grey cat with dark stripes. The Selk carry her on their ships and lull her with milk and honey.

Avas Danai. Children of Earth, known for their dark hair and eyes and strength in earth power. The Avas Danai are divided into seven Houses located in the Great Forest of Nocturne. Their primary trade commodity is wood. Qualities of earth: Grounded, solid, practical, stubborn, literal, loyal.

Avas Marakai. Children of Water. Dark-skinned and curly-haired, they are the seafaring daēvas. They make their home in the Isles of the Marakai and act as middlemen between the mortals and other daēva clans. Their wealth derives from the Hin, equal to one-tenth of the goods they transport. No one else has the skill to navigate the Austral Ocean or the White Sea, so they enjoy a monopoly on sea trade and travel. Qualities of water: Easygoing, free, adventurous, cheerful, cunning, industrious.

Avas Valkirins. Children of Air. Pale-skinned and silver-haired, they live in stone holdfasts in the mountains of Nocturne. The Valkirin Range is the source of all metal and gemstones in the world. Qualities of air: Quick to anger, proud, changeable, passionate, ruthless, rowdy, restless.

Avas Vatras. Children of Fire. Red-haired and light-eyed. No one has seen the Avas Vatras for a thousand years, since they tried to burn the world and were imprisoned in the Kiln. The only clan with the ability to forge talismans. Qualities of fire: Creative, ambitious, generous, destructive, curious, risk-taking.

Bond. The connection between a linked pair of talismans that allows a human to control the power of a daēva. Can take the form of two matching cuffs, or a bracelet and collar. A side effect of the bond is that emotions and sensations are shared between human and daēva. A bond draws on fire and will only work in Solis, not in Nocturne.

Breaker. See *negatory magic*.

Chimera. Elemental hunting packs, they're made from water, earth and air, seasoned with malice, greed, sorrow and fear. Chimera cannot be killed by any traditional means and will track their quarry to the ends of the earth.

Daēva. Similar in appearance to humans with some magical abilities. Most daēvas have a particular affinity for earth, air or water and are strongest in one element. However, they cannot work fire, and will die merely from coming into close proximity with an open flame. Daēvas can live for thousands of years and heal from wounds that would kill or cripple a human. Regarding clan names, *val* means mountain, *dan* means forest, *mar* means sea, *vat* means fire. *Avas* means children of.

Darklands. The slang term for Nocturne.

Diyat. "The Five." The governing body of the five Marakai fleets.

Dominion, also called the gloaming or shadowlands. The land of the dead. Can be traversed using a talisman or via gates, but is a dangerous place for the living.

Druj. Literally translates as *impure souls*. Includes Revenants, wights, liches and other Undead. In the Empire, daēvas were considered Druj by the magi.

Ecclesia. The popular assembly of Delphi. Open to all male citizens over the age of twenty. Elects the Archons and votes on matters of law and justice.

Elemental magic. The direct manipulation of earth, air or water. Fire is the fourth element, but has unstable properties that cannot be worked by most daēvas.

Empire. A land reached through gates in the Dominion, it is a mirror world of Solis and Nocturne in many ways. Nazafareen and Darius come from the Empire. It is the setting of the Fourth Element Trilogy.

Faravahar. The symbol of the Prophet, revered by the Persians. Its form is an eagle with outstretched wings.

Gale. The impassable line of storms created to imprison the Avas Vatras in the Kiln.

Gate. A permanent passage into the Dominion. Temporary gates can also be opened with a talisman.

Gorgon-e Gaz. The prison on the shore of the Salenian Sea where the oldest daēvas were held by the Empire. Victor Dessarian spent two centuries within its walls before escaping.

Great Green. What the Marakai call the collective oceans.

Hammu. A giant carp that causes undersea earthquakes and tsunamis. Worshipped by the Jengu Marakai.

Infirmity. Called the *Druj Curse* in the Empire, it is the physical disability caused to daēvas by the bonding process.

Khaf-hor. Giant fanged eel with slimy, viscous skin. Worshipped by the Nyx Marakai.

Kiln. The vast, trackless desert beyond the Gale where the sun sits at high noon. The prison of the Avas Vatras.

Lacuna. The period of true night that descends when all three of Nocturne's moons are hidden. The timing of the lacuna varies from seconds to an hour or more depending on the lunar cycle.

Magi. Persian priests who follow the Way of the Flame.

Moons. Selene, Hecate and Artemis. Selene is the brightest,

Hecate the smallest, and Artemis has the longest orbit, taking a full year to complete. The passage of time in both Solis and Nocturne is judged by the moons since they're the only large celestial bodies that move through the sky.

Matrium. The seven female heads of the Avas Danai houses.

Nahresi. Skeletal horses that gallop across the waves. Worshipped by the Khepresh Marakai.

Negatory magic. A rare talent that involves the working of all four elements. Those who can wield it are known as Breakers. Negatory magic can obliterate both elemental and talismanic magic. The price of negatory magic is rage and emotional turmoil. It derives from the Breaker's own temperament and is separate from the Nexus, which is the source of all elemental magic.

Nocturne. The dark side of the world.

Parthenoi. Virgin warriors. See *Maenads*.

Rock of Ariamazes. The fortress-palace of the Kings of Samarqand. It was scorched in the Vatra Wars but never destroyed.

Sat-bu. Like the mythological monster Charybdis, she makes a whirlpool in the deep ocean that sucks ships down. Tentacled and faceless, she is worshipped by the Sheut Marakai.

Shadowlands. See *Dominion*.

Shepherds. Hounds of the Dominion, they herd the dead to their final destination at the Cold Sea. Extremely hostile to anything living, and to necromancers in particular.

Shields of Apollo. The elite unit of Greek soldiers that hunts and captures daēvas.

Solis. The sunlit side of the world.

Spell Dust. A sparkling powder; when combined with spoken words, it works like a talisman to accomplish any number of things. Only trained alchemists are fluent in the language of spell dust. Extremely addictive when consumed directly. Source unknown (except to the Persian merchant and dust dealer Izad Asabana).

Stygians. Mortals who dwell in the Isles of the Marakai. They're the only humans to live in the darklands, surviving by fishing and diving for pearls. The Stygians worship a giant oyster named Babana.

Talismanic magic. The use of elemental magic to imbue power in a material object, word or phrase. Generally, the object will perform a single function, i.e. lumen crystals, daēva cuffs or Talismans of Folding.

Talismans (*three daēvas*). They ended the war with the Vatras by creating the Gale and sundering Nocturne into light and dark. Their power passed on through the generations.

Umbra. The twilight realm between Solis and Nocturne.

Water Dogs. Paramilitary force of bonded pairs (human and daēva) that kept order in the distant satrapies of the Empire and hunted Undead Druj along the borders.

Way of the Flame. The official religion of the Empire, and also of Samarqand and Susa. Preaches *good thoughts, good words and good* *deeds*. Embodied by the magi, who view the world as locked in an eternal struggle between good and evil. Fire is considered the holiest element, followed by water.

Wight. A Druj Undead with the ability to take over a human body and mimic the host to a certain degree. Must be beheaded.

Wind Ship. A conveyance similar to a hot air balloon, but with a wooden ship rather than a basket. Powered either by burners or spell magic.

ACKNOWLEDGMENTS

To Deirdre, Christa and Laura for spot-on story advice and editing, I'd be lost without you.

As always, to Jessica Therrien and Holly Kammier at Acorn Publishing (and all my fellow authors there), the seed you planted has grown into something big and wonderful!

Made in the USA
Las Vegas, NV
28 July 2021